D0375020

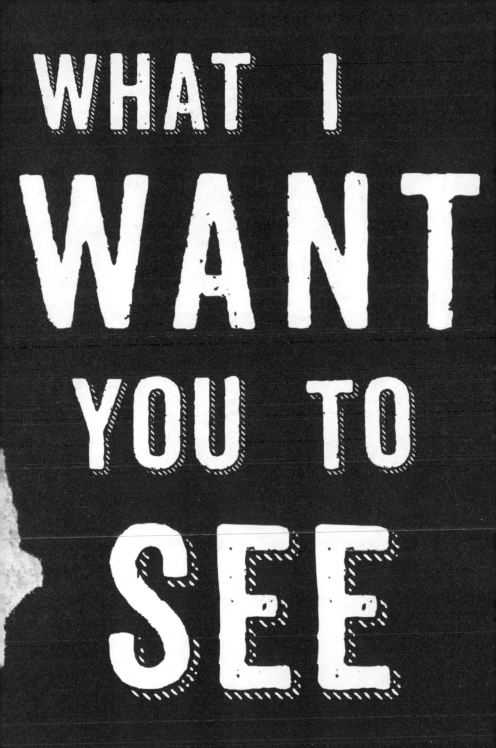

TO SEE

CATHERINE
LINKA

ff **FREEFORM** BOOKS

LOS ANGELES   NEW YORK

Grateful acknowledgment for permission to reprint an excerpt from "One More Down" performed by Mandolin Orange on *Quiet Little Room*, and written by Andrew Marlin (Party Fowl, BMI). © 2010 Andrew Marlin.

First Edition, February 2020
10 9 8 7 6 5 4 3 2 1
FAC-020093-19354
Printed in the United States of America

This book is set in 10.75 Palatino/Monotype
Designed by Jamie Alloy

Library of Congress Cataloging-in-Publication Data
Names: Linka, Catherine, author.
Title: What I want you to see / by Catherine Linka.
Description: Los Angeles ; New York : Freeform, 2020. • Summary: "Sabine's scholarship to a prestigious art school was a dream come true, but one desperate decision might bring her new life crashing down"— Provided by publisher.
Identifiers: LCCN 2018055038 • ISBN 9781368027557 (hardcover)
Subjects: • CYAC: Conduct of life—Fiction. • Art schools—Fiction. • Universities and colleges—Fiction. • Artists—Fiction. • Poverty—Fiction. • Secrets—Fiction.
Classification: LCC PZ7.L662816 Wh 2020 • DDC [Fic]—dc23
LC record available at https://lccn.loc.gov/2018055038

Reinforced binding
Visit www.freeform.com/books

SUSTAINABLE FORESTRY INITIATIVE

Certified Sourcing
www.sfiprogram.org
SFI-00993

Logo Applies to Text Stock Only

To Lauren, Judy, Ed, and Pete

People see what they want to see and what people want to see never has anything to do with the truth.

—Roberto Bolaño

CHAPTER 1

*T*hink of Krell as an angry art god who requires human sacrifice.

Our teaching assistant's warning rings in my ears as I tear into the alley two blocks away from campus. It's five of nine, and I'm cursing myself again for not buying a parking permit. I need to run like hell if I'm going to make it to class before Professor Krell arrives with his chai latte and scathing comments.

The spot behind the abandoned florist shop is empty, so I park the Honda and grab my portfolio case. Then I streak down the alley past the machine shop and out onto the sidewalk, the big black case banging my legs the whole way.

Of course the crosswalk light's red, and a cop's parked outside the homeless shelter across the street. I hammer the button on the light post. I can't jaywalk, not with the cop sitting here. He let me off with a warning a couple days ago, but the fine is a hundred and ninety dollars I don't have.

The light changes and I fly through the crosswalk. Don't stop, don't stop, I tell myself even though my skinny-heeled boots are ridiculous to run in. I can't be late for Krell.

The art institute looms on the next block, four stories of gray cement and glass. I dash past the shelter and the scent of pancakes and warm syrup. I'm halfway down the block and picking up speed when the light turns red, which is good because by the time I get there, it should be green.

My luck's holding out, because as I smack the walk button the light turns, and yes! I might actually beat Krell to class.

I power down the block past the corner of the CALINVA building and the words carved three feet high into its side: **QUESTIONING. PROVOKING. AGITATING.** I slam through the first set of glass doors and up the forty-foot-long ramp to the lobby.

Whoever the sadist was who designed the entry, I'm pretty sure the skateboarders are the only people at CALINVA who like it.

By the time I get to the top of the ramp and through the second set of glass doors into the huge cement lobby, I'm breathing hard, but I still have to get to the third floor. The elevator is notoriously slow, so I sprint for the steel stairs. I'm really moving now, but halfway up, my heel catches in one of the holes in the open weave.

Son of a . . . ! I jerk my foot to get free, and a slip of leather peels off my heel like a piece of tomato skin.

But there are still people scurrying for class, so I charge up the last stairs and down the hall. And no no no. The door of Studio 322 is shut, which tells me that today, for the first time in weeks, Professor Krell's on time for Painting Strategies 101.

CHAPTER 2

I crack open the door. Krell's holding court at the front of the room, where a painting is propped up on a big wooden easel. Bryian Ahring slouches against the wall nearby, gazing humbly at him.

Krell ponders the canvas, his face all angles and points from the widow's peak in his receding hair to the slash of his brows, his sharp nose, and chin.

I duck down, hoping he's too caught up in his critique of Bryian's assignment to notice me winding through the forest of students and easels. It's not easy, because the floor is littered with backpacks, portfolio cases, and plastic toolboxes, and the heels on these stupid boots are so damn skinny I can barely balance.

Finally, I slip onto my stool and set down my portfolio. My fingers refuse to lie still, so I take out a pencil and pocket-size sketch pad and with a few quick strokes capture the line of Krell's stance and the tension in his shoulders as he contemplates Bryian's painting. I glance at the canvas, wondering what Krell's thinking.

Jagged green rivers striated like agate radiate from a blob that looks like a thin section of human cells. It looks a lot like a painting we saw a few weeks ago on our field trip to the

Museum of Contemporary Art, and I wait for Krell to tear into Bryian.

"See how the composition radiates from the center. The viewer is lured in and then . . ." Krell's hands explode outward. "Movement! Electricity! Note the provocative use of color and shape. This is exactly the kind of work I expect in this class."

No, you've got to be kidding me. On my right, Taysha's rolling her eyes. Okay, so I'm not the only one who thinks Bryian ripped off a Kerstin Brätsch.

What is it with Krell and Bryian Ahring? Ever since we arrived at the California Institute for the Visual Arts, Krell has showered Bryian with more praise than any of the other first-years.

Which would be a lot easier to take if Bryian wasn't such a poser with his blue mirror glasses perched on top of his shaved head, and "humbleness" dripping off him.

I unzip my portfolio and slide my canvas onto my lap. I worked my ass off and it turned out even better than I hoped. This time Krell has to admit my work is good.

"I see Ms. Reyes has deigned to grace us with her presence."

Everyone turns to look at me, and I squirm in my seat. "Sorry." I don't bother to offer an excuse or explanation, because if anyone ever tries, Krell silences them with a hand.

"Since you have my attention, Sabine, you may bring your assignment to the front."

I hold my canvas at my side and thread through my classmates. I barely know them, but Taysha nods at me, and Kevin from Kansas gives me a look. *You got this.*

My stomach is a fish flapping on the floor.

4

I am true to myself. I am true to my vision.

I've worked on this painting for over a month, keeping in mind all the ways Krell's faulted my composition, colors, or theme, and a couple of times all three. Since the first class of the semester, he's made it clear my work's not up to his standards. Safe, he's called it. Timid.

I place the canvas on the easel, and I take a position by the wall. At the very back of the room the lights flicker, and I realize there's a maintenance guy on a ladder fiddling with one of the fixtures and he's been in the room the whole time.

"What is the title of your work?" Krell barks.

I snap back to attention and see the smirk on his face. "*Appetite.*"

My painting is a still life, a place setting for a fancy dinner party shot from above. Stargazer lilies artfully arranged. Three wineglasses, silver for four courses, and centered on a platinum-rimmed plate, a dead songbird beside a toasted slice of baguette.

"Is that a photograph?" someone whispers.

"Nope," someone else answers.

I take a deep breath and steel myself. As the artist, I am not allowed to speak, and I'm definitely not allowed to defend what I've done. All I'm permitted to do is answer Krell's questions.

He stalks back and forth in front of the easel, a finger tapping his thin lips. Then he pushes back his wrinkled linen jacket and poses, hands on his narrow hips. "The assignment was to be provocative! To get us to *think*, to respond to your art. And my response is: LAZY!"

Heat surges in my chest. Lazy? I worked for weeks to express the light, to capture the reflective surfaces, to convey the texture of the iridescent feathers, the arched flower petals, the dull look in the dead bird's eye.

Krell jerks his head at the room. "Every. Single. Student in this room can re-create reality. It's nothing more than simple drafting."

My cheeks turn hot and I know they're crimson. Cadmium red #3 if I had to call it.

Krell walks over to the front row and shoves his finger in Bernadette's face. She jerks back, her blue eyes enormous. "What do you think of this painting?" he says.

"Ah, I don't know," she stammers.

He goes down the row. "You, Mr. Walker."

Kevin glances at me, determined to help. "It's intriguing," he says.

"Why? Why is it intriguing?"

"Because a dead bird on an expensive plate is bizarre and unexpected. Like Edgar Allan Poe."

Krell gives me a pitying smile. "Were you thinking about 'The Raven,' Ms. Reyes?"

"No." My leg jiggles, and I hold my head up even higher, hoping it will keep me from sliding down the wall.

"Were you thinking about *anything*?"

I try to swallow. I can hear my artistic statement in my head, every single syllable, but the words are stuck to my tongue like gluey papier-mâché.

Appetite is about the powerful consuming what they want *with no care for who or what they destroy. The ugly dead reality of a bird that was never meant to be eaten served up on the costliest china.*

Krell pounces on my silence. "This painting lacks daring, insight, and soul."

My eyes bore into the wall above everyone's head while my legs turn liquid. I need to get out of here without losing it.

"You may resume your seat, Ms. Reyes."

I lift my painting off the easel and lock my gaze on the floor, because one pity smile as I walk to my seat will send me crashing. I slide back onto my stool and wrap my long crocheted sweater across my body.

Krell starts in on the next critique and I don't look up to see who it is. I dig my nails into my palm, hearing him crow that the abstract is "bold" and "risk-taking."

I don't get it. I thought CALINVA loved my work. You don't give someone a full scholarship if you don't think they're amazing. So why is it that for the last six weeks, Krell has slammed every single piece I've shown him?

Angry tears pool in my eyes, but I blink them away, because I will not, absolutely will not cry in front of these people.

When the bell rings, I'm out the door first and flying for the exit. I've got an hour before Color & Theory, and I'll be damned if I'm going to spend it fending off sympathetic classmates in the student lounge.

CHAPTER 3

CALINVA is five blocks south of the trendy main drag of Old Town Pasadena, so I take off in the other direction. The last thing I want is to run into anyone from the institute or the art supply store where I work.

It's heating up, so I tear off my sweater and stuff it into my messenger bag. Then I head for a taco truck parked a couple blocks away at a construction site.

I'm almost to the truck when "Hey, smile for me, sweetie!" Come-ons and kissing sounds rain down on me.

I swear if any of those guys get down from that roof and come over, I will slam them with my portfolio case. I pull out my wallet and check how much I've got, considering it's got to last until Friday and this is only Monday.

I pay for a can of guava juice, then park myself on a low cement-block wall in front of a battered office building. I roll the icy can over my forehead while Krell's insults burn in my ears. My work *lacks daring, insight,* and *soul.*

What am I going to do? I can't avoid him for the next four years; he's the head of the department.

Oh God, what if I lose my scholarship?

I flash back to Irina Gonzales in the student-aid office. "Do you understand that the Zoich is a *merit* scholarship, Sabine? That it can be revoked if your performance does not meet expectations?"

And what do I do, then? Go back to sleeping in my car, being the girl who scrubs toilets in an office building at midnight, who carries plates of ribs to half-drunk diners, and charges twenty bucks for a pet portrait at the dog park?

My chest starts to tighten, and my lungs feel like they're shrinking. I spread my fingers over the surface of the juice can, telling myself to focus on the sensation of coolness. *Be in the now. Look around you. What do you see?*

I draw my eyes over the truck, taking in the crudely painted combo plates and faded menu on the side, the grease-blurred window, and the beefy arms of the man working the grill. A composition forms in my head with the window as the focal point, and I'm about to reach for my sketch pad when a woman saunters out from behind a building across the street.

Black pants and black tee, she stands out in the bright sunlight like a black line on a white page. A band of fake fur rings her light hair. She walks over to the light post on the corner and leans against it, clutching a handmade cardboard sign that reads GOD BLESS YOU! I'M JULIE. I HAVE CANCER. PLEASE HELP.

She's facing my way and I try not to stare, but I can't take my eyes off her. Her tan cheeks are donut plump around her sunken mouth, and the only word that comes to mind when I look at her closed-lip smile is "beatific."

There is something transcendent about this woman whose skinny pants are almost fashionable, and whose bare feet and hands are black with dirt. Grace and goodwill flow off her like vapor off dry ice.

I fumble with my sketch pad, knowing I can't possibly capture what I'm seeing in pencil, and I put it away. I feel for my phone, then gather up my things and cross the street, sure Julie will walk away before I get there.

9

As I get within ten feet of her, I realize I've been so caught up in her smile I missed how she's stroking a white rat perched on her shoulder.

My phone is right in my pocket, but I hesitate to take it out, because I hated the student at my high school who treated homeless people like props for his AP photography portfolio. Is it using Julie to want to draw her?

I wish I had an extra ten to give her, but I don't. I unbuckle my messenger bag. "Do you like apricot bars?" I say, and hold up a small paper bag.

Her eyes crinkle even deeper. "Apricots? Yes, I love them."

Even up close, I can't quite tell how old she is. Forty? Sixty? I hand her the bag. "My landlady baked them. She's a really good cook." I pause, because I almost hate myself for asking, but, "Would it be okay if I take your picture?"

"Go ahead, dearie. I don't mind. A person takes your picture, it means they see you."

I step back and she tells me to be careful to get Sweetie, her rat, in the picture, so I do. I take five or six shots, and then, feeling awkward, pocket my phone and thank her.

"Have a blessed day," she answers.

I walk away, thinking who am I to take her picture, that I of all people should know better than to do that.

CALINVA's right up ahead, and the last thing I want to do is face everyone who witnessed my critique, but I tell myself: Suck it up and keep going. You've survived a lot worse than this.

And once you figure out what Krell wants, you can get him off your back.

CHAPTER 4

When I get back to CALINVA, the first-years are milling in the hall outside Color & Theory. I hesitate on the edge of the group, because even though I know their faces and names, I haven't really put myself out there to make friends.

After Mom's accident last spring, I couldn't be the artsy, snarky friend that Hayley and her other friends expected. One day, while they complained for the hundredth time about the unfairness of not being allowed to use their phones during school hours, it hit me that my reality wasn't theirs, and if they knew the truth about me, they'd label it, but they'd never understand it. I drifted away, and never drifted back.

But as I look around this hall, I tell myself that these people could be my people; I just need to be sure who to trust.

Bernadette's leaning into Bryian, tilting her head and giving him her full and undivided adoration. She paid me a lot of attention the first couple weeks of the semester, asking what arts-high and intensive art programs I attended (none), who I know in the LA art scene (no one), and is one of the faculty mentoring me (I wish). But I guess I haven't lived up to my hype as the Zoich Scholarship winner, because now she's lost interest. Fine.

Kevin from Kansas huddles by the wall outside class talking to Taysha. Today Taysha's smoky-purple hair is wrapped in a cone of patterned cotton and she's channeling Nefertiti, queen of the Nile, all cheekbones and attitude.

As I head over to them, Bernadette tries to give me a look of sympathy, but I pretend I don't see. Kevin slides his beanie off his head and shakes out his hair so his soft brown curls sproing around his face. "Hey, Sabine," he says, and swivels, opening up the space between him and Taysha so I can join them.

Kevin's friendly to everyone, but I'd like to believe we're actually starting to connect and he's not just taking pity on the classmate who's going under.

"Ten seconds left," he tells Taysha, who's drumming a finger on the strap of her slouchy bag.

She squints and says, *"The Elusive Credence of the Peripatetic."*

I have no idea what I've walked into, but I watch Kevin consider her answer. "It's good," he says. "Unintelligible and therefore profound, but for it to be perfect, it needs one more bullshit noun at the very end."

"Okay, give me a sec." Taysha stares at the pleated concrete wall behind us like it holds the answer.

"You want to join in?" Kevin asks me.

"Depends. What are you doing?"

He glances up and down the hall before leaning in conspiratorially. His eyes are chestnut brown behind his clear, round frames. "We're playing Name That Ahring. You have to come up with the name Bryian Ahring will give his next masterpiece. Here's a hint: bullshit adjective, bullshit noun, the words 'of the' followed by bullshit adjective, bullshit noun."

"Oh, oh, I've got it." Taysha strikes a pose for the cameras. *"The Elusive Credence of the Peripatetic Razor in Homage to Man Ray."*

Kevin nods at me and we clap like fiends. "Genius, pure genius," I tell her.

"Yes, love the 'homage,'" Kevin adds. "And the inspired allusion to French surrealism. You have elevated the art form of Name That Ahring."

"Thank you. Thank you. I accept your accolades, knowing I deserve them."

I catch myself smiling, because for this brief moment I'm one of the cool kids.

Doors open up and down the hall as people change classes, and all of us reach for our portfolios and paint boxes.

"I crave your boots," Taysha says, pointing to my cinnamon-colored booties that now have a shriveled leather worm hanging off the heel. "Zanotti, right?"

Taysha's concentration is fashion design, so I should have known she'd recognize them. Now she'll get the wrong idea that I'm rich. "Yeah, they're Zanotti, but I didn't buy them new."

"You found them at a resale shop?"

"Actually, I snagged them at the Beverly Hills Presbyterian Rummage Sale." The lie comes out so smoothly, even I'm impressed.

"No, you didn't! How much did you pay for them? Because if it was less than five hundred, then you basically stole them."

Guilt prickles down my spine. I keep a smile on my face as we walk into Color & Theory, thinking that even though I never intended to steal Iona Taylor's designer boots, by the time I realized I had, I swore I'd eat dog crap before I ever gave them back.

SKETCH #1

MOM, February 21

Mom is a coiled spring in purple workout gear outside the office at Beverly Hills High. With short quick strokes, I showed how her faded blond ponytail twitched and her feet could barely hold still, she was so eager to run back to the Taylors' house.

I switched partway from a drawing pencil to Prismacolor cloud blue for her eyes, then fringed them with almost invisible lashes. Switched again to Prismacolor black grape for the blurry dragon-claw tattoo creeping out from under her collar, the last remnant of her old life.

Gazing at it now, I remember the feel of the pencil scratching across the paper's rough weave. I chose the texture to suggest Mom's skin was as flawed as her past.

No matter how many times I look at this sketch, I'm never ready for where it takes me. The memories of this day . . . the details spiral in my head.

Mom dropped the keys to the Honda in my hand. "Thank you for picking up Iona's boots. I can't see stilettos working on snow, but Iona says she needs them."

The shoe repair was miles away and I wasn't looking forward to fighting the traffic on Olympic. "Of course Iona Taylor would insist on her boots being professionally waterproofed. She can't use spray-on crap like everyone else?"

The creases around Mom's mouth deepened. "Sabine—"

"I don't understand why you put up with her."

"First, it's my job, and second, I do not have the luxury of disliking the person I work for and whose house we live in." Her gaze held mine, but I refused to give in.

"She's a total narcissist."

Mom pursed her lips and slipped a strand of my hair behind my ear. "People are complicated, honey. If you could look past your feelings, you'd see another side of her."

"You always make excuses for her. You should quit working for the Taylors after I graduate."

"Enough. Right now I need to go back to the house and pack their bags before the limo comes at four."

She drew me into a quick hug. "I know I'm asking a lot, making you stop at both the dry cleaner and the shoe repair when you're trying to get to the gallery early."

"Hayley's coming at five and I need time to get changed in case I meet Collin Krell."

Her eyes pinched, and I knew it was because I invited Hayley to the opening of Krell's show, not her, but then she smoothed on a smile. "My girl's going to study with Collin Krell."

"Mom, don't say that. I haven't gotten in yet."

She gave my arm one last squeeze then she sprinted down the cement steps. Her legs were pumping before she hit the street.

I close my eyes, wanting to hold on to this moment forever.

CHAPTER 5

I'm still licking my wounds from Krell's critique when I'm deep into my shift at Artsy. The after-school rush of moms and kids desperate for art supplies for school assignments died out at 5:30, so the store's quiet except for the alternative rock playing in the background.

The display of Lascaux professional acrylics needs restocking, so I carry several cartons out from the back. I unlock the display case and, one by one, take the silver tubes of paint and slide them into the slots in the case like I'm hanging Christmas ornaments.

Dioxazine Violet Light. Cobalt Blue. Cerulean. Hansa Yellow. Their names are like music the way I hear them in my head and imagine the colors gliding across a canvas.

I'm extra careful not to dent the metal tubes or damage the paper labels. Each tube, even the smallest one, costs way more than what I'm paid to hang them up.

When I get to the Phthalo Turquoise Blue, I rub my finger over the blue-striped label. I can't mix this color from the cheap acrylics my stipend pays for. It's perfect, the way it has depth, but isn't overly bright, so a painting doesn't end up looking like the cheap stuff people hawk on the sidewalk at Venice Beach.

I weigh the tube in my hand, overwhelmed by the feeling

that *I need this*. The taste in my mouth turns to tin and the feeling won't quit. I drop the tube in my apron pocket and reach for the carton of Oxide Black.

What the hell are you doing? Put it back.

"Excuse me."

I jerk and the carton I'm holding goes flying. A dozen tubes hit the polished concrete floor, and I dive to pick them up before Barney, my manager, sees. The customer who surprised me crouches down until we're eye to eye, and as I take in his face, I think I remember him from CALINVA.

"Sorry, I didn't mean to startle you," he says. His eyes are dark and liquid with long, thick lashes, and a thin scar zigzags through his left eyebrow, cutting it in two. He plucks a tube out from under the metal shelving and sets it gently in the carton by my knees.

"I don't normally freak out like that," I say, picking the last tube off the floor. "I was in the zone."

He nods and cracks a smile. "I know the place. I spend a lot of time there."

Current ripples between us. His gaze is about to make me blush, so I stand up and he does, too.

He's holding a ripped piece of sketch paper covered in what looks like scribbled words, and I sense he's about to show it to me when he says, "Your name's Sabine, isn't it?"

My muscles tighten along my spine. He's not one of my classmates, so if he knows who I am, that means people are talking about me. "Yes?"

"You didn't deserve what Krell said to you today. I think your painting is a provocative comment about wealth, power, and privilege."

For a split second, I bask in his compliment, but then I

feel sick, because the only people who've seen my painting were in that classroom. Crap. Tell me no one in class filmed Krell eviscerating me. "How did you—"

"I was on the ladder in the back during your critique? The guy replacing the light?"

"Oh." Great. The maintenance guy's an art critic.

Either he reads my face or he reads my mind, because he gives me an embarrassed grin and thrusts out his hand. "Adam. Master's candidate and work-study grunt who earns his monthly stipend changing lightbulbs, prepping canvases, cleaning studios, and buying supplies for faculty."

So he's a grad student. I smile back as his hand closes around mine. "Nice to meet you, Adam." I nod at his other hand holding the paper, and note the slivers of indigo blue paint that frame his nails and tell me we're the same species: painter. "Looks like you're on a supply run."

His eyes flicker like he wasn't expecting me to get down to business so quickly. "Yeah, but I can't make out half of what Ofelo's written here."

Adam and I walk the aisles together, debating Ofelo's slashes and squiggles as we gather the sculpture instructor's supplies. Adam shares stories about different faculty members' quirks, and as we chat I feel like a CALINVA insider instead of a flailing first-year.

I take in Adam's features, cataloging his curly hair, olive skin, cheekbones, the fullness of his lips, and the slight bump on the bridge of his nose. A tiny silver cross dangles from his ear. If I had to guess, I'd say his family's Greek.

It's only when he stands in front of me at the cash register that I begin to the read the lines of his muscles under his clothes. He's not cut, not like a guy who works out at a gym, but he's solid like someone who's worked construction or a job where he did a lot of lifting.

Adam gives me Ofelo's account info and I ring up the sale. He thanks me for the help and I tell him no problem, and he turns as if he's going to leave, but then changes his mind.

"You don't know why Krell targets you, do you?"

I freeze, because deep inside I'd hoped I was wrong. That Krell wasn't targeting me. That I was being overly sensitive to his comments. But now I know those fears are real and I can barely hear myself answer, "No. No clue."

"Krell never votes for a woman to get the Zoich Scholarship. His pick was Bryian Ahring."

Whoa. I got the prestigious scholarship Krell wanted for his favorite. "So you're telling me no matter how hard I try, Krell will never believe I deserve the Zoich."

He shifts the bag of Ofelo's supplies to his other arm. "I probably shouldn't have said anything, but I believe a person's better off knowing how their opponent thinks."

"No, I appreciate you telling me," I lie.

"No, you don't."

He looks so guilty, I let him off the hook with a smile.

"Listen," he says, "Krell's a dick, but you're only the what—third woman to be awarded the Zoich? If anyone can prove to him that he's wrong, it's you."

I watch Adam stride down the sidewalk, moving in and out of the light of the streetlamps. It isn't until he's out of sight that I go back to hanging up the acrylics.

"Opponent" isn't the word I'd hoped to use for Collin Krell, but I comfort myself with the thought that I could be the girl who shows Krell he's wrong.

CHAPTER 6

It's almost eight by the time I get back to Mrs. Mednikov's house in South Pasadena. The yellow Victorian sits on the corner and there's never a spot out front, so I pull onto the street alongside it and park.

I turn off the engine and let my head fall back against the headrest. My legs ache from standing, and it's almost too much effort to get out of the car so I can go inside and collapse.

Thank God I don't have to waitress tonight. But I do have four hours of work for class tomorrow.

The lights are on in Mrs. Mednikov's living room, and it looks like a scene from a hundred years ago when art collectors hung paintings with the frames touching each other all the way to the ceiling. The canvases in her house are mostly abstracts, and a few landscapes and nudes, all done by scholarship students who lived here before me.

I run my gaze over each painting. All the artists are talented, especially whoever painted the dark blue abstract that looks like a turbulent sea, but I swear I'm as good as any of them.

Lacking in daring, insight, and soul. You just don't say that to people. You don't run a knife through them and expect them to give you great work. Well, apparently you do if you're Collin Krell.

If Adam's right, and Krell's pissed I got the Zoich Scholarship instead of Bryian, he could make my life hell for the rest of the semester, not to mention the next four years, since he's the department chair.

Or, even worse, he could already be dropping hints to the rest of the faculty that my performance is *disappointing*, that I'm *not growing as an artist*, that *as he suspected*, giving me the Zoich Scholarship was not a wise investment.

I don't know how, but I've got to get Krell on my side.

Trees line both sides of the street, but I catch a view of Mrs. Mednikov lowering the shades on the tall windows on the second floor. My landlady comes down the stairs and works her way through the main room until one by one the paintings disappear behind long white shades. Wait for it, I think, and she reaches for the last shade next to the kitchen and pulls it down halfway. Every night, the same thing.

I finally get up the energy to unload my gear from the car. I thump up the wood steps, and when I open the kitchen door the scent of onion and dill envelops me. A pot of magenta-colored soup simmers on a stove decades older than I am.

Mrs. Mednikov stands at the counter, slicing a loaf of dark rye. She's got to be over eighty, but she stands straighter than I do, and draws the knife through the bread so elegantly that if I didn't know she was once a dancer, I'd guess it from watching her slice.

"Long day?" she says, her accent drawing out the word "long."

"Do I look that bad?"

"You look tired. There's soup if you'd like to join me."

"Yes, I'd love some."

It's a play we perform most nights: Mrs. Mednikov

pretending she made too much food and inviting me to join her, and me pretending I'll scrounge around and make my own dinner if she doesn't. I'm not exactly sure what started it, maybe me showing up the first night with nothing but a jar of peanut butter and half a loaf of bread.

I cross the little hall and stow my gear in my room by the kitchen. When I open the door, it barely clears the bed, but after months of sleeping in my backseat, I give thanks every day for this tiny, yellow room with its door and window, and space for all my stuff in the dresser and closet.

I peel off Iona Taylor's boots, vowing never to wear them to CALINVA again, then pad back into the kitchen. It's dark now except for the light over the table set for two.

Mrs. Mednikov sets a large bowl in front of me, and a white dollop of sour cream floats in the purplish-red soup. I swirl it with my spoon so it makes a bright pink comma. "My mom used to make borscht."

"I could not resist the beets at the farmers market this morning," she says. "So fresh."

From where I sit, I have a clear view of the half-closed shade. I point my spoon at the window. "Can I ask why you do that?"

Mrs. Mednikov shrugs and gives me a smile. "An old widow's habit? Many years ago, the FBI suspected my husband and his friends of being Communists. Agents would come to the house looking for Boris, and if he was not home, I would pull the shade closed to warn him."

"And you keep doing it, because . . . it reminds you of him?"

"Yes, it reminds me of a wonderful time in my life."

"When you were harassed by the FBI?"

"When I was young and passionately in love. Now you,"

Mrs. Mednikov says, and leans across the table. "I've waited patiently to hear how your instructor liked your marvelous painting."

"My instructor loathed my marvelous painting."

"No! How is that possible?"

I twist in my seat and can't bring myself to tell Mrs. Mednikov what Krell said, because what if I see a flicker in her eyes telling me she agrees?

"A grad student told me that Professor Krell thinks the Zoich Scholarship should have gone to someone else." I hold my breath and wait for Mrs. Mednikov's reaction.

Her eyes narrow, and she mutters a string of Russian words, none of which I understand. Her lips purse and she switches back to English. "This is not the first time I have heard such talk about him. Learn what you can from this man—and do your art."

I nod so she'll know I heard her, and dip into the sour cream floating on my soup. If only it was that simple.

CHAPTER 7

Krell is still in my head as I scour Mrs. Mednikov's soup pot. How is it that Adam saw what I was trying to say with *Appetite*, but Krell, who's supposed to be such a genius, didn't? I dig the scrubby pad into a black spot of burned-on beet. It makes more sense that Krell did see it, but he's so pissed the faculty gave me the Zoich, he's taking his anger out on me. At least I know now what I'm up against.

The pot's gleaming and spot-free when I leave it in the drying rack and get ready to start in on my homework. Back in my room, I dig through my messenger bag for my pencil case. *I can't let Krell get to me.*

Down deep in the bottom of my bag, my fingers close around a tube of paint. Crap, I think as I pull it out. Now I have to sneak it back on the display.

I stare at the silver tube in my palm, but the *I need this* feeling is gone. *Why the hell did I take this?* I don't need it for the assignments I'm working on. The only things due are some pencil drawings and a pastel study.

But I don't have time to waste wondering. Tomorrow's assignment for drawing class is negative space. I've done this exercise dozens of times before, so I park myself on the bed below Mom's dream catcher. We're supposed to draw the space an object doesn't occupy, and the dream catcher's thin wooden loop, spiderweb weave, and dangling feathers, all its odd and irregular shapes, make it a challenge to get right.

I disappear into my drawing, to a place where nothing and no one exist outside the line, light, and shadows on the paper. When I finally surface, I catch the reflection of an unfinished painting propped up on the dresser. *Oh. That's why.*

Not a painting I'm working on for school, it's a portrait of a young woman with loose blond hair playing a guitar on an outdoor stage. Her head is tilted, she's lost in the music, and her gauzy white dress waterfalls to the floor.

I hold the tube of paint up to the canvas, and it's just as I thought. It's not that Phthalo Turquoise Blue is the perfect blue, but it's perfect for this.

The singer's dress is embellished with two large bluebirds over the breasts, but the blue has never been right. Too bold, too harsh for the gentle singer.

The truth cascades over me. Blue birds. Songbird.

I pull the still life out of my portfolio case and hold it up. Blue bird. Dead bird.

You don't always know *why* you paint something until *after* you paint it.

I collapse on the bed, and my heart squeezes. *Appetite* isn't about greed at all.

SKETCH #2

IONA, February 21

My pencil dug into the paper, almost ripping it. I tried, but I couldn't draw Iona's face, just her words spinning like a hurricane.

```
WHERES YOUR MOM
CANT FIND MY BOOTS
BOYS NOT PACKED
LIMO DUE IN 1 HOUR
WHERES    YOUR MOM
CANT   FIND MY BOOTS
BOYS NOT      PACKED
LIMO DUE          1 HOUR
```

The words flew apart, and the letters shattered into fragments like broken bones.

```
WHERE
                    WHE                        RE
WH          E                    R
                                    MOM
M O
            M

                    O

                        M
```

I rarely look at this page and usually skip past it. Even though it's nearly blank, today when my sketchbook opens to it, I drown in memories.

How Iona's first text interrupted me when I was paying for her boots at the shoe repair. WHERE'S YOUR MOM. BOYS NOT PACKED.

How I texted back NOT SURE and tossed the bag with the boots behind the driver's seat.

How my phone buzzed nonstop, but I refused to indulge Iona by answering as I drove back up Olympic to the elite dry cleaner.

How the owner handed me the dress Iona wore to the Golden Globes and because he'd known Mom forever, shooed me out the door.

How I was so late for Hayley by then I took the box with Iona's beloved Valentino swaddled in layers of acid-free tissue and threw it in my trunk.

How back at the Taylors', I pulled into my spot beside the garage and before I even got out of the car, Iona charged out of the house. "Where the hell's your mom? We're going to miss our flight!"

"Mom's not here?" I remember saying. This was so not like her. "She'll probably be back any second."

"Perfect. You're no help either." Iona stomped back inside and I texted Mom as I followed Iona in. WHAT'S GOING ON? IONA ON RAMPAGE.

Iona stood in the living room, waving her hands over an explosion of parkas, ski pants, and four half-filled suitcases.

I checked my phone. Nothing. "I'm sure there's a good reason Mom's not here. How about I finish packing the boys so you can get ready?"

"Fine," Iona said, although clearly it wasn't. She fumed down the hall to her bedroom.

I stuffed the clothes into the oversize suitcases, wheeled them into the foyer, and checked my phone again. Still no response from Mom.

"Where are my goddamned boots?" Iona yelled.

I dashed out to my car and as I fumbled for my keys, dialed Mom's phone. This was crazy. Mom always answered her texts.

The phone rang four times before Mom finally answered. "Hello."

"Mom, where are you?" I said. "Iona is completely losing it."

"Miss Reyes?"

My heart missed a beat. "Who is this?"

"This is Denise Acampo, an ER nurse at Cedars-Sinai. Your mother was brought in a few hours ago."

A chill swept over my skin. "Is she okay? Can I talk to her?"

"She's in surgery, and we'll know more when she's out."

I jumped in my car and took off.

CHAPTER 8

There's no escaping Krell.

I'm parked in the CALINVA coffee bar going through the course catalog, because once again in studio class, Krell ignored what was on my easel while he counseled his favorites on how to attack specific problems in their work.

I was set up right next to David Tito for the in-class assignment, so I was forced to listen to every word as Krell and David went back and forth about color choice and perceptual color versus pictorial. Even Kevin, whose technical skills are the weakest in the class, got ten minutes of Krell's precious time to show him how removing paint in this one area could do more for his painting than adding it.

The catalog confirms what I already suspected. Krell teaches half the upper-division classes I need for my degree, so the only way to get out of his orbit is to change my concentration.

I scroll through the list of majors—ceramics, photography, printmaking, sculpture, nontraditional media—hoping for a spark or a revelation. Nothing.

I'm a painter. I have no interest in or feel for working in clay or textiles, metal or digital media.

As Mom would say, there's no around, there's only through.

Taysha plunks her rooibos tea down on the table and I casually close my laptop. "Did you ever consider majoring in something else?" I ask.

She squints at me. "Other than fashion design? Yeah, my other choice was dental hygiene."

At first I think she's joking, but she's serious, and I feel my cheeks get hot. Sometimes I forget how many other students at CALINVA are holding on by a string.

"You thinking about changing majors?" Taysha says.

I shrug.

"Krell's really getting to you." She reaches over and rubs my arm. "I could tell you it'll get better, but that might be lying."

Kevin sets a large white envelope on the table and drops into the chair across from me. "Mona in the office asked me to give this to you."

There's a big red Zoich logo on the outside, and a thought flashes through my head. *What if Krell contacted them? What if he told them my scholarship should go to Bryian?*

Kevin settles into his chair, and Taysha says, "Go on. Open it."

I'm being paranoid, I tell myself. Just because Krell hates my work doesn't mean he'd trash me to the Zoich, right?

I undo the flap and shake out a letter with a plastic card attached and four passes to the Broad museum. I scan the letter while Taysha examines one of the passes.

Dear Ms. Reyes, as a Zoich scholar we invite you to visit the Broad collection on a regular basis. Please use the enclosed entry passes . . .

"These are VIP passes," Taysha says. "You get in free— anytime you want, and you don't have to wait in line."

Bernadette, who's sitting at the next table, wheels around in her seat. "You're kidding me. I tried to get into the Broad in August, and the wait was three hours!"

"What's the card for?" Kevin asks.

I turn it over. "Free parking," I say, not quite believing it.

"Oooo. Your scholarship comes with some nice perks," Taysha says.

I hear the envy, and I know I'd be jealous if she was the one with free tuition and surprises like this.

The three of them start checking out the museum guide I didn't realize was in the envelope. I've only known them a few weeks, but I feel like Kevin and Taysha could become solid friends. Bernadette I'm not so sure.

"Who's up for a field trip?" I say, holding up the passes.

They each snatch a pass out of my hand and Bernadette charges right in. "What's the best day for you?"

"Sundays, I guess. I don't work that day."

"Great. Sunday." She looks to Kevin and Taysha, who both nod. "Okay," she says. "Who wants to drive?"

I hesitate, hoping someone else will volunteer. Because even though I cleaned out my car, what if there's something still in it, like a washcloth stuffed into a side pocket or a can opener rattling around the back that the second one of them saw it, they'd guess I'd slept there. They don't know me, and the only label I want is "artist."

Kevin raises a hand. "I'll drive."

The coffee bar echoes with the screechy sound of people pushing their chairs away from the tables, and we start collecting our stuff, realizing it's almost time for class.

"Pricks," Kevin mutters. He stares after two guys who just left a table littered with crumpled napkins and dirty cups. Then he walks over and clears it, separating their garbage into the trash and recycling cans.

I haul his backpack onto my shoulder and carry it over to him. I like that he cleaned the table, but can't resist teasing him. "Wouldn't have guessed you're a neat freak."

Kevin flashes me a self-deprecating grin. "My roommates would argue I'm not. But my dad has this saying: 'Always leave the campsite cleaner than when you found it.'"

"Sounds like a neat freak manifesto."

"Nope. More like a leave-the-world-a-better-place manifesto."

I smile to myself, knowing I chose right handing Kevin that pass, because right now he sounds like Mom.

CHAPTER 9

The Broad sits on a corner like an off-kilter white cube made out of perforated paper, but when we enter, the lobby swallows us inside undulating slate-gray walls. A narrow escalator disappears into the dark gray ceiling. Now that I see how big it is, I realize I should have pushed our visit back a week. I've got a truckload of assignments due tomorrow. But maybe what's inside will inspire me and be worth the time I'll lose coming here.

Bernadette and Taysha go right to the escalator, and Kevin and I hop on a few steps behind them. In the dim tunnel, it's almost impossible to tell how long the escalator is until we emerge into the light-soaked top floor.

"Nice," Kevin says. "Look at how they stretched the white waffle skin over the building so it acts as a translucent net to let in the light."

His curls bob around his face like soft brown springs, and it kills me how much they remind me of the Taylors' Labradoodle, but I'd never tell him that.

Taysha and Bernadette head over to Koons's huge shiny tulips while Kevin disappears around a corner. I walk the room and pass a dozen paintings that don't interest me enough to stop. Contemporary art is about ideas, but there are moments like now when I feel incapable of grasping its genius.

I can lose myself in a portrait like people lose themselves

in a book, wondering about the person it portrays. But this thing I swear is a car hood?

Maybe Krell can sense my lack of reverence and that's why he can't stand me.

I lean in to read the descriptive panel beside what looks even more like a car hood now that I'm directly in front of it. According to the museum staff, the piece "derives its form and materiality from the automobile." In other words, it's supposed to look like a car hood.

I roll my eyes, because I'll never understand why this is art, and as I turn away, catch Bernadette watching me. My neck prickles and I'm flooded with the feeling she was watching me the whole time I stood there.

I can't get out of the gallery fast enough. Disliking contemporary art is almost a crime at CALINVA, and I can't help wondering if Bernadette's so competitive she'd drop a casual comment about my disdain to one of the faculty.

I keep going until I reach a gallery on the other side of the floor that's dominated by a giant dining room table. Everyone in the room is caught up in the *Alice in Wonderland* effect of walking underneath Therrien's oversize table and chairs, but I stand to the side. *Seriously?*

It's a giant table and chairs. What's the big deal? I startle as Kevin plops his arm over my shoulder, and his slim, muscular body touches mine. "Sorry. I didn't mean to surprise you," he says.

His arm is draped over me as lazily as a dog flopped on a couch. "It's okay," I say, relaxing.

He tips his head so it almost rests on mine and whispers, "You really hate contemporary art, don't you?"

"No, I don't," I insist.

"Bull. Your eyes pass right over this stuff. No connection whatsoever."

I scan the room, making absolutely sure Bernadette isn't nearby.

"Don't worry. I'm not going to out you," Kevin says. He's smiling and I can't resist smiling back.

Kevin's not the type who plays mind games, so I decide to trust him on this one. "Okay, if I'm being honest, I feel like a lot of contemporary art is bull, but if you tell anyone, and I do mean anyone—"

"My lips are sealed. I promise." He slides his arm off my shoulder. "I bet you can find at least one piece in this place that you like—or feel is worth looking at for more than five seconds."

"Sure. You're on. Winner gets what?"

"A taco from the truck out front."

"Oh, big stakes."

We roam the third floor past the blanket woven of red metal strips and the Warhol silkscreen of the electric chair. Kevin seems to be watching me for the slightest flicker, and when we get to Koons's *Balloon Dog*, he takes my hand and makes me stop and look a moment longer. I gaze at our distorted reflections in the shiny blue steel dog that stands taller than us.

"Anything?" Kevin says.

"Nope."

"Is it because you don't like dogs—an emblem of loyalty and companionship?"

"It's a balloon dog," I toss back. "An emblem of circuses and scary birthday-party clowns."

"But Koons has transformed the humble balloon dog, and by enlarging it and giving it permanence has made us reconsider what we believe about it."

I double-check the gallery for Bernadette and she's nowhere in sight. "Koons," I hiss, "did not transform the humble balloon dog. That job went to the one hundred poorly paid assistants who slaved away in his SoHo studio manufacturing this blue dog—not to mention the four identical ones in orange, yellow, red, and pink."

"You believe that blue is the only true color for the balloon dog."

I'm shaking my head and trying not to laugh, because despite the ridiculous turn this argument has taken, I want to get my point across. "No, I'm saying that for me, the artist has to do more than have an idea and let someone else make it."

"You want to see the artist's hand in the work?"

"I want to feel like it meant something to them. It's hard for me to relate when a piece is essentially about an idea. I want to feel an emotional connection."

"So we can cross Koons off the list?"

"Yep."

Kevin lets go of my hand. "Come on," he says, and his knuckles brush mine. "Let's find an artist you can connect with."

Two rooms away, I find myself staring into a Basquiat. The faces of two horn players shine out of the dark. Scribbled words repeat on the black background, and a skull hangs between the men. I soak into the painting as Kevin explains that the words are song titles and a child's name. And in the dark, disjointed work, I see the echoes of the jazz the men play and the artist's personal rhythm.

"Am I wrong or do I perceive an emotional connection?" Kevin says.

"You are not wrong," I answer. We stand side by side taking a last look. "Damn," I say. "I owe you a taco."

CHAPTER 10

I t's after two when Kevin and I come out of the Broad, but Taysha and Bernadette are waiting to view Kusama's Infinity Mirror Rooms. The sidewalk is still packed with people trying to get into the museum, and the line for the El Gato truck out front stretches almost to the corner. But Kevin doesn't care how long he has to wait. "El Gato's tacos are legendary. We're not leaving."

"So, what about you? What did you like in there?"

"In the Broad? Nothing much. I'm not a big fan of contemporary art."

I smack his arm. "Are you kidding me?"

Kevin laughs and falls out of line. "Stop, stop," he says, holding up his hands in surrender.

We shuffle forward, and the smell of grilling onions, chilis, and meat makes my mouth water.

"Fine," I say. "So what does inspire you?"

Kevin reaches for his phone and taps the screen. "It's a sculpture called *Kinetic Rain*. I saw it when I was thirteen and we were going through the Shanghai airport. I couldn't stop watching it, so we almost missed our plane to Beijing."

"China? Wow. I've never been out of California."

"Dad was working on a hydroelectric plant, and I got to tag along."

The October sun is brilliant, but Kevin shields the screen so I can see the video. In a huge atrium, copper-colored raindrops the size of my hand slowly descend from the ceiling. I watch as they rise and fall, perfectly synchronized, moving as a wave, then a waterfall, then curve into a wing, and twist into a helix before they retreat into the ceiling. "How do they do that?" I murmur. "There must be a thousand of them."

"Twelve hundred actually."

Kevin plays the video again, pointing out the grid in the ceiling and the thin cables that raise and lower the raindrops. "A motor operates each drop, and all the motors operate off a computer program."

We move forward with the line.

"So this is why you came to CALINVA: to create kinetic sculpture?"

"Yep."

"But you must need to know a lot about motors and programming. How will you learn that when they don't teach it at CALINVA?"

"That's why I'm at Caltech."

I peer at him. "I've obviously missed something."

"I wrangled a special deal. Engineering major at Caltech, art minor at CALINVA."

"No wonder you're so normal."

"Normal. Ow. That hurts."

"No. It's a compliment! You don't get caught up in all the drama. Krell calls your work pedestrian and you don't—"

"Wait. Do you mean Krell *doesn't* like my painting?"

His face is so earnest that for a moment, I'm thrown, but then he bursts out laughing.

We've inched our way to the front of the line, and

Kevin nods at the menu board. "I'll have two fish and three beef."

"Five? You're having five tacos? The bet was for one."

"Have you seen how small they are? They're like two bites."

"Yeah, okay, you're right." I reach for my wallet, but he stops me.

"I'm paying."

"But I lost the bet."

"Yeah, but you admitted you were wrong and that was what I really wanted."

"Well, thank you, Mr. Walker."

"My pleasure, Ms. Reyes."

We put in our order and I grab a handful of napkins, then we move to the pickup window.

"You know, dealing with the whole Krell-CALINVA thing is not as hard for me, because I'm not talented the way you and Bryian are," Kevin says, very matter-of-fact.

His cutting himself down shocks me. "You're talented!"

"No, I'm inventive. That's different. And the art world doesn't see kinetic sculpture the way they do other art. Chances are, my work will never be installed in a top gallery or museum. At best, it'll be in a science museum or a corporate headquarters or a shopping mall in Dubai. So it doesn't matter if Krell doesn't like my stuff, because I expect him to dislike it."

There's so much to process here, I don't really know where to start. "I think you're wrong about the art world not valuing kinetic sculpture."

"Did you see any at the Broad?"

"No, but—"

"What about at MOCA?" and he points to the Museum of Contemporary Art down the street.

"No," I admit. "But there's that sculpture at the LA County Museum of Art—the one with the racetracks and tiny cars."

"One sculpture out of three museums. What does that tell you?"

I frown.

"It's okay," he says. "The shopping malls in Dubai are incredible."

"You've been to Dubai?"

"Spring break two years ago."

I can't resist teasing him. "How was the food?"

"Unbelievable. The *ghuzi*—they roast lamb with pistachios and rice—" He looks at me barely holding it in. "What? I like good food."

The man at the window calls out our number and Kevin grabs our order. The paper plate he hands me sags under the weight of my tacos. The tortillas are laid out like yellow flower petals piled with meat and beans. Bright white slices of radish and green limes dot the plate. "I'm glad you insisted we wait," I tell him.

Most of the benches are taken in the little plaza next to the Broad, so we perch on a concrete planter and balance our plates on our laps. We dig into our food, not talking except with our eyes.

Sauce drips down my chin. I wish I could feel the way Kevin does about Krell. I wish I could be immune to his attacks and just paint. But Kevin's not on a scholarship, so he can afford to relax.

He grins as he swipes slivers of lettuce off his cheek.

CHAPTER 11

I'd hoped the trip to the Broad would inspire me, but when I get back to the house, I face off with a blank canvas. The more I stare at it, the bigger and whiter and emptier it looks, so I shove it in the closet and pull out a smaller canvas board.

I've avoided painting since Krell reamed me the other day, but tomorrow he expects us to show up to class with a painting that doesn't have to be finished, but it has to be started.

I flip through my latest sketchbook, looking for ideas, but nothing grabs me. Then I dig one from high school out of the closet and sigh when I see CALINVA doodled all over the back.

I leaf through my drawings from last fall, shaking my head at how juvenile most of them look. A few pages later, I'm into sketches from last spring and can barely stand to look at them. Mom's fragile hand curled on her blanket. Mom floating in a cloud of dreams. The beach where I waded in and scattered her ashes.

I can't paint any of these. I might as well strip naked in front of the class.

The rest of the pages are throwaways from last summer when my hands were almost too cramped from cleaning to hold a pencil. Frayed scraps remain of pages I tore out:

pen-and-ink drawings I did at the hipster dog park in Silverlake and sold for twenty dollars apiece to overly proud rescue-dog owners.

By eight o'clock, panic's a monkey biting my shoulders. What am I going to do? I can't show up empty-handed to Krell's class and score another black mark for the girl who should never have gotten the Zoich in the first place.

The walls feel like they're pressing in, and I have to escape. I step onto the porch and the cool night air lures me down the steps. The broken sidewalks here trip me up even in daylight, so I walk down the middle of the street. Dead leaves crunch under my feet, but the sycamores are still thick overhead.

The houses are mostly bungalows with dried cornstalks lashed to their porches and peeling picket fences. Lights are on in most of the windows, and I slow when I glimpse a family moving behind the shades. They might be happy or they might be sad, but tonight those kids have a mom or a dad or maybe they're extra lucky and have both.

I'm almost to the corner of Mission Street when a Metro train clatters past the ice-cream place. Inside the store, people are lined up at the counter, bright as Popsicles, while outside on the unlit patio, a woman sits at a café table. Light from the window falls on the front half of her body, carving it out of the darkness. It could be a scene painted by Caravaggio if she wasn't sharing her cone with a tame white rat.

I can't believe it's Julie, because it feels like a weird coincidence that she's all the way down in South Pasadena, but then again I don't know where she sleeps. I turn to go back to the house, and I hear Mom's voice in my head. *It's not a coincidence, it's a sign.*

I roll my eyes at the heavens. *Seriously, Mom?* But a half block later I dig out my phone and pull up the pic of Julie. Her smile arrests me. What is it about her?

God bless you! I'm Julie. I have cancer. Please help.

I stare at her sign and her smile and the way she stands so straight, her head held high, and I can't make all the pieces work. I know without question she's sick, and probably in pain, so how is it possible that this woman who lives on the street exudes a presence in this shot I can only describe as radiant?

I feel a stirring in my gut. *I need to paint her.*

The feeling floods me, but I fight it off. Bring a portrait into Krell's class? Collin Krell who just sold a portrait for over a million dollars sight unseen?

Yeah, right. Not unless I want my ass handed to me.

I keep scrolling as I trudge back up the steps of the house and find a shot of the electric plant. Benita Newsom assigned us a study on color schemes for Color & Theory, so even though a part of me thinks that bringing Krell an urban landscape isn't a great idea, the painting could satisfy both him and Newsom, and I can't show up tomorrow with nothing.

Back inside, I start to sketch the pipes and cables and decide to play with a tetrad color scheme, using orange as the dominant color with accents of red and purple. The muscles in my shoulders tighten as I prep my palette and mix the paint, and even though I try stretching and windmilling my arms, they won't loosen up.

CHAPTER 12

The official title of Krell's class is Painting Strategies 101, but every few weeks he likes to borrow a practice from the upper-level classes—group critique.

I'm in my usual Monday-morning stupor, but it only takes a few seconds after I see the chairs rearranged into a circle for me to realize I totally forgot group crit is today.

Please, please, please do not call on me, I think as I rush for the empty seat next to Kevin.

"Ready to examine your peers' work formally, philosophically, and historically?"

Kevin's so chipper, I feel like smacking him with my travel mug. "I'm ready as long as someone else's painting is picked apart," I say.

"The point is not to pick a painting apart, but to conduct a deep inquiry that unearths a dialectic."

I glare at him.

The chairs are in a circle, because we, the students, are supposed to do all the talking. Still, Krell's seated at the front of the room like he's the king or the head inquisitor.

He reaches in his pocket and pulls out a crumpled piece of paper. "Tito and Reyes."

My stomach does a death spiral. Eighteen other people Krell could have chosen today, but he had to pick me.

"Stay cool," Kevin whispers.

Across from me, Bryian sits next to Bernadette, combing his fingers through the leather fringe hanging off the sleeve of her jacket.

"Our mandate in group critique is to understand a person's work as deeply as possible," Krell reminds us. "Mr. Tito will begin by describing the piece he's showing us today."

David Tito puts a shimmery gray abstract up on the easel. "I was inspired by Thomas Nagel's essay on consciousness 'What Is It Like to Be a Bat?' The painting is my attempt to express what I can never experience: the world through sonar or echolocation."

The painting is layers of almost invisible shadows and zigzag lines, pockets of dark, and pinpricks of light.

My skin feels like pinpricks of light are boring through my sweater. *Holy . . . I can't believe I have to follow this.*

Bernadette throws up her hand, shaking Bryian's off. "The artist's color palette of gray, black, silver, and white reduces the world to shadow and bursts of light."

She goes to take a breath, and Bryian leaps in. "Yes, and by negating our color experience, the artist challenges us to visually experience the unknowable."

Several people nod in agreement, but Bernadette scowls at Bryian. Hmm. Trouble in paradise.

I flip through my portfolio case in my head. The way to nail group crit is to show a piece with lots of detail or symbolism or a political stance so everyone can find at least one thing to say about it in the forty minutes it's under discussion.

Now Kevin joins the conversation about David Tito's canvas with a riff on the physics of echolocation, which I can't even begin to understand. Then the rest of the class adds comments about bats and sonar and how humans can or cannot grasp the experience of bat-ness and the limits of human sensory experience.

And the whole time, Krell sketches quietly in a notebook, looking up every so often to see who's speaking.

Shit, shit, shit, I think, watching the minutes tick by. I haven't brought anything good enough to show. I've got the painting I did last night, and some charcoal sketches, but nothing as polished or provocative as what they're discussing now.

Finally, Krell thanks David for creating a rich opportunity for discourse. David removes his painting from the easel, and Krell says, "Ms. Reyes, you're up."

I pull the canvas out of my portfolio, and as soon as I set the painting of the power plant on the easel up front, I know I'm in trouble, because the room is absolutely silent.

"I, um, am exploring the interplay of color, shadow, and texture." I babble on about repeating shapes, flat surfaces, and the texture of decay, wishing I could shut up, but I can't until at least one person says something.

I glance at Krell, and from the way his mouth puckers, things are going downhill fast.

Then Kevin raises his hand, and I'm so grateful I silently vow to be his friend forever.

"Mr. Walker. Does Ms. Reyes's canvas remind you of a notable American author, perhaps not Edgar Allan Poe, but John Dos Passos or Upton Sinclair?"

I suck in a breath and dig my fists into my pockets.

"No, can't say that it does." Kevin says it so lightly it's as if Krell's sarcasm went completely over his head. "I was going to say that the tetrad color scheme prompts the viewer to reconsider the aesthetics of the rusted pipes."

Krell sits back in his chair and drags a hand through his hair. "Yes, it's *pretty*, isn't it?"

My knees lock. "Pretty" is the ultimate condemnation. It means pastel landscapes sold at craft fairs to women who want to match the color of their guest bedroom.

"Pretty" is so mediocre it's worse than bad.

Bernadette and Bryian exchange a smile, and clearly the rest of my classmates are embarrassed for me, because Kevin's the only one looking up. His lips move. *It will be okay.*

Then, just when I think it can't get any worse, Krell stands and begins to circle the room. "Questioning. Provoking. Agitating. CALINVA's mission is carved into its very walls."

I know that what comes out of his mouth next will eviscerate me, and I grip the easel as the blood drains from my head.

"This piece, this pretty little craft project, is insignificant and utterly forgettable. ART should never be *insignificant*. It should never be *forgettable!*"

At last, Krell stops and looks from me to the rest of the class, and I brace myself for him to make an example of me.

"Ms. Reyes," he says, "until you risk failure, until you face the fear that there's nothing uniquely creative floating in the intracranial recesses of your mind, until you express your ideas in a way that is not literal but entirely unexpected so our experience of art is altered—until then, your paintings will be a waste of paint and canvas."

I can't feel the floor beneath my feet. I lift my painting off the easel and say, "Thank you, Professor Krell," in a voice so strained it's hoarse.

I take my seat. It's my own fault, I think, shoving the canvas into my portfolio case. But obviously Krell enjoyed humiliating me.

He dismisses class early, and people start to leave, but Kevin hovers over me.

"Krell hates me," I mutter.

"He doesn't hate you," Kevin says.

"Right, he doesn't hate me, he hates my paintings. But what does that matter when he's going to fail me?"

"Listen, I know you're upset, but it's going to be okay."

"Really?" I snap. "Easy for you to say. If you fail this class, you can get on your bike and ride back to Caltech. Your life isn't over."

Kevin jerks like I hit him. "I guess that's what it looks like," he says, and backs away.

Now I've done it. One of the few people I trusted to be my friend . . .

I turn toward the wall as if I'm getting something out of my bag, because I can't stop the tears welling in my eyes. How could I forget group crit was today?

This titanic disaster was my fault, but Krell didn't have to take me down in front of everyone.

I'm angry. Angry at myself. At Krell. At CALINVA for bringing me here, where apparently I don't belong.

I wipe my eyes and go to stand up when Krell says, "Ms. Reyes, a moment."

He's waited until everyone else has left, so what he's going to say must be even more awful than what he said in class.

I stand by my chair, because I need distance between us. Krell closes his notebook.

"I was surprised you chose to submit that particular piece for group crit," he says. "It looks more like an exercise for Color and Theory than an assignment for my class."

I don't even know what to say, I'm so pathetically transparent.

Krell doesn't wait for me to answer. "Clearly, you are struggling. I advise you to find a contemporary painter you connect with, someone whose work resonates with you on an emotional or intellectual level, and study it closely."

My throat's so tight I barely hear myself say, "So you want me to read about the artist and his work?"

"No, ignore what the theorists and critics say about them. Get yourself to a gallery or museum, find a piece that speaks to you, and transcribe it."

I squint at Krell. I've never heard the term, so I don't know what "transcribe" means, but I'm way too embarrassed to ask. "Okay?"

"Hmm. You're confused. The point is to think deeply about what the artist is saying and the nonconforming way they've chosen to say it."

I nod, still baffled, but trying to hide it in the face of his growing frustration.

Krell takes a moment, before saying in an embarrassingly patient voice, "You don't know what 'transcribe' means."

My cheeks burn as I shake my head no.

"It means to render a copy of another artist's work, perhaps in acrylics or pastels. You attempt to go below the surface beyond color choice and composition, always asking why the artist made the choices they did."

I manage to mumble "Thank you," but I don't think Krell hears me, because he sighs and says, "The point is, you have nailed yourself in a box, Miss Reyes, and you are in danger of it becoming your artistic coffin."

My artistic coffin. I nod good-bye, relieved he doesn't expect me to say more, and manage to get out of the room intact. I half expect Kevin to be waiting in the hall, and I'm grateful he's not.

Don't cry, don't cry, don't cry, I tell myself as I duck down the back staircase. The next floor down, I barricade myself in a bathroom stall. *This pretty little craft project . . . utterly insignificant . . . a waste of paint and canvas.* That bastard. I'm so sick of Krell treating me like my feelings don't matter, like my art is basically garbage.

I'm not nothing. I'm talented, more talented than at least half the people in that class, so why can't I make him see it?

I sob out my frustration until I'm limp. When I drag myself out of the stall, my eyes are swollen and my makeup's smeared, so the face looking back at me in the mirror appears distorted and bruised: a Francis Bacon portrait.

CHAPTER 13

I know I've messed up badly with Kevin, because even though I sit two seats over from him in Color & Theory, he doesn't look at me once. Or maybe everyone senses I'm shields up, because Taysha and Bernadette don't try to talk to me either.

Once class is over, I blow right out of the building. I march up the street past the homeless shelter and the alternative radio station. I'm eyes forward, thinking all I want to do is get through the next four hours at Artsy. Clean some shelves. Restock some displays. Ring up some sales and be done.

But fate's got it in for me, and who should be striding toward the opposite corner but Adam. Today when I can barely talk and my eyes are so puffy and red they're basically slits, that's when I run into him? I dig out my sunglasses and shove them on.

Adam's looking the other way, so I could wait until he's passed, but no, he spots me and waves. "Sabine, what's happening?"

Now I'm stuck. "Nothing much. Heading to work." The light changes, and I cross the street. He's eating an apple, and the sleeves of his snug Henley are pushed up, revealing sculpted biceps. I'm glad the lenses of my sunglasses are so dark, because he's a Rodin bronze come to life and I can't help sneaking glances at his forearms.

When I step onto the curb, he pauses chewing to smile. "When's the next sale at Artsy?" he says.

The flesh of the apple is so white next to his lips it's distracting. "In a few days. This sale's a big one. Two for one on paint, canvas, drawing pads. Time to stock up," I say, quoting the flyer.

"You're right," he says. "Time to stock up."

I tell myself to look away, but can't quite do it. Not when his dark, dark eyes are fixed on mine.

Finally, I break off eye contact and adjust the strap on my messenger bag.

Adam sticks his apple between his teeth and reaches into his backpack. He takes out another. "Honeycrisp. Want one?"

The red-and-green-streaked skin looks painted on, it's that perfect. I'm tempted, but for some stupid reason, I hesitate. *Oh, for God's sake, don't be ridiculous. Take it.* "Thanks. It looks delicious."

"It is."

I stow the apple in my bag and Adam says, "You mind if I walk with you? I'm going this way, too."

I like that he asks, that he doesn't just assume. "Yeah, that's cool."

We continue up Raymond past the Metro stop and the trendy restaurant in the converted train station. The scent of hot pizza wafts out, reminding me I didn't eat lunch, and it's too late to get something. But at least now I've got an apple.

"So how's it going with Krell?" Adam asks.

Even though today was mostly my fault, that doesn't stop me from saying, "Krell's a pig. I don't even want to tell you what he said to me in class, it was so awful."

"Sorry to hear that."

I soak in the only sympathy I've been offered today.

"Let me guess," Adam says. "He made an example out of you."

"How did you know?"

"When I was a first-year, he cut people down all the time."

I feel both relieved and pissed to be one of a long line of Krell's victims.

"It blows when the person you worshipped turns out to be a dick," Adam says.

"Right? I dreamed about studying with Collin Krell. I thought it would be amazing, learning from one of *America's top contemporary portrait painters*." I catch myself before I blurt out how I'd secretly hoped Krell would mentor me. "How did you survive him?"

"I kept my head down, studied Krell's paintings for clues to what he wanted to see in my work, and asked Hautmann to be my adviser instead."

Hautmann's work is all abstract. He's the last person I'd want as an adviser. I sigh. "I've never seen Krell's work, just photos of it, and you know how a photo tells you almost nothing about a painting."

"You didn't see his show at the Ankarian Gallery last February?"

I shake my head and force out a smile. Tears burble up in my eyes as I remember that day, and I blink them back. "I was supposed to, but something happened, so I never got there."

We walk in silence past the outdoor-furniture store. Adam pitches his apple core in a nearby trash can, and then he says, "Would you like to see the painting Krell's working on now?"

I brake in the middle of the sidewalk. "You're joking. The one that just sold for over a million without the buyer seeing it?"

"His dealer hasn't seen it either, but I have."

"You have?"

He pulls out a set of keys and dangles them in my face. "One of the perks of cleaning his studio. I get to see the master's work up close."

I don't expect the rush of envy that floods me.

Adam grins and pockets his keys. "Yeah, you want to see it."

"It's that obvious?"

"You're not that hard to read."

I study the sidewalk, avoiding his eyes. I can't deny it, so I don't even try.

"What time are you off?" he says.

"Seven?"

"I'll meet you in the CALINVA parking lot near the back at seven fifteen."

"Wait. You're serious about letting me into Krell's studio?"

"You deserve to have someone do something nice for you today."

He holds my gaze and I sense he isn't offering to do this only because he pities me. "But what if Krell catches us?"

"Krell's got a new baby. He's always gone by six thirty. Come on. When's the next chance you'll get to see a Collin Krell up close?"

All his work in LA is in private collections, and even though the painting will be unveiled at a reception in November, the party will be so packed I'll be lucky to get within ten feet of it.

And now Adam's offering to help me get a handle on Krell and I'm turning him down? Who am I kidding? "Okay, I'm in. See you at seven fifteen."

CHAPTER 14

I meet Adam at a back door near the loading dock. "You came," he says, and the delight in his voice makes me smile.

"I said I would."

The door lets us in by the main hall. Evening classes are in session, so Adam leads me to a service elevator in a back corridor. We ride up to the second floor and Adam doesn't take his eyes off my face and I'm trying to play it cool, but the skin on my arms feels like it's sparking.

"Krell's got the biggest studio at CALINVA," Adam says. "The board was so hot to snag the art world's rising star away from UCLA, they forced out two other instructors to pay him what he wanted."

I imagine Krell gloating about his salary the same way Iona Taylor did when she heard hers was twice what the other actors were getting for the reality show she's in.

The elevator opens and we tiptoe into the hall. Most of the studios are quiet as we go by, but loud African music pours out from one of them. "That's Ofelo," Adam says. "Around midnight the drums really start pounding."

We're outside Krell's door, and everything feels a little surreal. I can't believe we're stealing into Krell's studio. I'm hit with the same rush I'd get when Hayley and I used to sneak into friends' yards and party in their pools while they were away.

Adam goes to unlock the door. "You cannot tell anyone you've been in here," he says, his voice stern.

"My lips are sealed." I mime locking them and throwing away the key.

Adam doesn't smile. "I'm serious. Not even your friend with the purple hair."

The smile falls off my face, and for a moment I wonder how Adam knows Taysha and I are friends, but I realize he's probably seen us hanging out in the common areas while he works around CALINVA. "I promise I won't tell anyone." From what I remember from the student handbook, CALINVA doesn't have an explicit rule about going into a faculty member's studio without permission, but that doesn't mean we won't get in trouble if Krell finds out.

"Good." Adam opens the door and I scurry inside. He hits a switch and the fluorescents slowly brighten. The room smells of warm beeswax and oil paint.

My fingers start to itch as I take in the orderly disarray of the room. Couch, worktable, easels, sink, canvases stacked against the walls. Krell's inner sanctum.

Krell would shit himself if he knew I was in here. In the interview I read, he called his studio "an extension of [his] inner self," a private, closed-off space where he could express himself freely.

I brush my hand along the velvety back of a paint-speckled couch as I walk over to the huge worktable that anchors the middle of the room.

The top of the table is half covered with mason jars. Paintbrushes fan from their mouths like flower bouquets, and I run my fingers over the bristles. Krell has every type, size, and shape of brush from synthetic to natural hair bristles. "Must be nice."

"What?" Adam's across the room, standing by an easel with a large wood panel on it.

"There's at least two grand worth of brushes just on this table."

From here all I see is the back of the wood panel, but I can tell it's linden over a basswood frame. It's expensive, but the painting technique Krell uses requires a surface that doesn't warp.

As I walk over to Adam, I see dozens of photographs taped to the wall by the easel, headshots of a man I'm guessing is the one whose portrait Krell's working on. I come around the easel, and gasp, taking in the unfinished painting.

"It's so unfair," I murmur.

"What's unfair?"

"That a jerk like Krell has so much talent. What's it called?"

"*Duncan.*"

I nod at the photographs. "I'm guessing that's the real Duncan?"

"Yep."

Even unfinished, the painting is more subtle and complex than I could have imagined. The portrait is somehow realistic and abstract simultaneously, as the right side of the man's face disintegrates before the viewer. I peel a photograph off the wall and hold it up to the canvas. The look in the man's eye is unmistakably Duncan's.

The urge to touch the painting floods me, and I reach out,

"What do you mean?"

"You told me you studied Krell's paintings to learn what you needed for your art. What did you learn?"

He shrugs. "I can't put it into words, and even if I could I doubt it would help you."

I stretch, raising my arms over my head, reaching for what's beyond my grasp. "Yeah, you're probably right."

"Seen enough?"

"Yes," I tell him even though I could easily stand here another hour or two.

We pick up our stuff and duck out of Krell's studio. We're quiet as we make our way to the back door. Adam props it open and I expect him to follow me out, but he says, "I need to say good night here, I've got to go back upstairs to work."

I'm slightly disappointed, but I say, "Thanks. I really appreciate you showing me Krell's painting."

"Anytime."

The door shuts behind him, leaving me alone beside the loading dock. As I walk away, my phone buzzes and the screen lights up with the pic Adam took of me in front of Krell's painting. I shake my head at the look of rapture in my face.

It's like they say: Love the art, hate the artist.

I'm halfway up the block when Adam sends me a second pic, one of Krell's entire painting. I spread my fingers to enlarge it, but the details blur.

You really can't tell much about a painting from a photograph.

CHAPTER 15

I'm dreading Painting Strategies on Wednesday, knowing I have to face not just Krell and Kevin, but everyone else who witnessed my humiliation in class on Monday.

I get to class early and stake out a stool next to the easel Kevin normally picks. Yesterday, when I thought about what I said to him, I realized I needed to come up with a better apology than simply saying, "I'm sorry." Taysha and I talked it over, and this morning I set the apology for him on my lap and wait for Kevin to arrive.

My classmates trickle in, and it's like Monday never happened. No one's ignoring me or offering me pity smiles, they're basically going about their business.

I watch the door and can't help noticing how much sharper and edgier my classmates have become since the semester began. It's not just their painting, it's them. Bernadette's long blond hair is tipped neon pink, and the left side's shaved. Gone is her simple white tee; the black one she now wears under her slouchy overalls is shredded almost into ribbons.

Keiko's got ten more chains hanging off her ears, and somehow they make a plaid skirt with suspenders look angry. Birch sets his paint box down a few seats from me. His gold metallic shorts are shorter than any I've ever worn, and a new silver nose ring taps his upper lip. Instantly, I'm taken back to a fight I had with Mom junior year.

She was cooking me a veggie omelet while I thrashed through my wardrobe trying to create an artsy, edgy look.

"Why can't I get a nose ring?" I railed. "I look so boring. I'm practically invisible."

"And that's exactly how you will look as long as we live at the Taylors'."

I grabbed a granola bar, ignoring the omelet she'd put on the table. "It's not fair! I shouldn't have to dress to make them happy."

Mom took my face in her hands, holding fast as I tried to push away. "You don't need a nose ring to prove you're an artist. You've got talent, Sabine."

Looking around now, I realize Mom couldn't have imagined how CALINVA turned out to be as much a stage as the ones she used to play on—how if you want your art to be taken seriously, you've got to dress unconventional, unexpected, and unfettered, too.

Taysha takes the stool on my other side and shoots a nod at my lap. "Apology?" she says.

I glance at the door, but no Kevin, and turn back to her. "Can you help me change my look? I need to mix it up, but I have no money."

"No money is my specialty. Check it out. Kevin just walked in."

He grabs the stool next to me and sets down his gear. I hold out my foil-wrapped apology with two hands, it's that heavy.

Kevin takes it. "What's this?" he says, loosening the foil.

"I'm sorry."

"Funny, it smells like banana bread."

"Chocolate-chip banana bread, to be precise."

"I like precision."

Kevin smiles, but there's a coolness in his eyes. It's been a long time since I apologized to anyone, but what I've said so far isn't enough.

"I mean it, Kev. I was angry the other day, and I shouldn't have taken it out on you."

He nods, and his eyes warm as he carefully folds the foil back in place. "I didn't know you bake."

"Truth: I did not bake this bread. I made a deal with my landlady and she baked it."

One eyebrow goes up. "What did it cost you to regain my allegiance?"

"I have to clear out the sunporch and wash ten windows."

"You value my friendship highly."

"I value your friendship highly."

The smile that takes over his face is worth the hours with a bucket and squeegee it will cost me. Kevin, Taysha, Adam— without them, this place would be intolerable.

Krell comes through the door, chai latte in hand, and I force myself to sit up straight and face him. I screwed up, bringing in that stupid tetrad color study, but I have as much right to be here as anyone else.

"A quick announcement before we begin. I will not be here on Friday, but Fitz, our teaching assistant, will lead the class in my absence."

"Fitz? Who's Fitz?" Keiko mutters to Birch.

He sniffs. "You saw him at orientation before he turned invisible."

"Fitz is not completely invisible," Taysha says behind her

hand. "There have been sightings of him with Bernadette."

Are you kidding me? I tried three times to schedule meetings with Fitz to talk about how I could fix things with Krell, but the guy blew me off every time. Now I find out he's hanging with Bernadette?

Krell launches into his lecture, and everyone reaches for their laptop or notebook. "It is not enough to present the viewer with a dynamic image," he declares. "An image alone is not enough to make a subject iconic. It is how you paint, the brushstrokes and the physical energy you transfer to the canvas that move us!"

He strolls the room, pontificating about "inflection" and "psychic temperature" and "surface energy." His gaze skips over me and focuses on his favorites, Bryian and Bernadette, and now David Tito, as if they're the only ones worthy of his wisdom and the rest of us are filler.

Krell's not going to make an effort to teach me. Once again, it's abundantly clear that I can't rely on anyone but myself.

So maybe the best I can do is to take his advice and immerse myself in a work by a contemporary painter I respect. Like that Basquiat at the Broad, the one with the horn players?

I slide my phone out of my pocket and sneak a glance at *Duncan*. That's what I want to learn: how to create a portrait as evocative and mysterious and unexpected as his. I put my phone away.

It sucks that I'll never get the chance.

Unless . . . I could ask Krell for permission to copy his painting. Yeah, right. Like Krell would open his studio to me. It's back to the Broad.

It's disappointing on so many levels, not the least of which is that while I can study the Basquiat up close, the Broad won't allow me to bring in anything to work with except a small sketch pad and colored pencils.

Drawing won't make me the painter I need to become, only painting will.

CHAPTER 16

The next day Adam texts me. TAKE A LUNCH BREAK? SURE. I smile to myself because I'd hoped this thing with Adam wasn't just him doing a good deed.

I tell Kevin and Taysha I'll see them later, but don't tell them where I'm headed. I'm not exactly sure why, just that everyone at CALINVA gossips. I like how Adam's picked me out of all the first-years to hang with. Maybe it's stupid to think this makes me special, but I don't want to share.

Adam sends me an address not far away, a fifteen-minute drive south and west of CALINVA. But when the road I'm on crosses a ravine, I leave South Pasadena's tree-lined streets. Mercaditos replace wine shops and cleverly named toy stores, and the only shade in front of the tiny bungalows comes from palm trees shaggy with dead fronds and spindly poinsettias taller than I am.

When I get to the address Adam gave me, turns out it's a commercial building, not a restaurant. There aren't any windows in the front, so if it wasn't for the words RHODES GALLERY over the door, I'd assume it was an old machine shop.

Adam's waiting out front, his long wavy hair pulled back in a high bun. "You found it."

"It wasn't hard."

The sign says closed, but Adam presses the buzzer. "Florian's a friend."

66

A tall, trim guy in a pressed denim shirt opens the door. His balding red hair is cropped short, and I see in his eyes that he's expecting us. "Adam, come in," he says.

"Thanks for opening for us."

Florian's smile is welcoming, but I don't get the feeling he and Adam are super close. "So this is Sabine?" he asks. "Congratulations. I understand you're this year's Zoich recipient."

I try not to blush as I thank him. Adam has literally opened a door I couldn't have opened myself.

Florian gives a slight bow and says, "Enjoy the show," then disappears into a back room.

"I can't believe you told him about me."

Adam shrugs. "I'm doing Florian a favor. A couple of years from now you'll be looking for a dealer, and now you've met."

Now that Florian's gone, I look around the space. Skylights between the open rafters fill the windowless space with light. A dozen gleaming chrome sculptures dominate the cement floor. The polished steel is bent, layered, as if someone welded old bumpers together, then twisted and branched them like coral.

We walk among them, following a sinuous path formed by their outstretched branches as Adam talks about the relationship between flexion and extension, posture and composition. I glide my hands just above the surface of the metal as if I find them fascinating.

They're repetitive, boring even, as if the artist had only one creative thought, but I don't say that aloud. Adam's a grad student, and I don't want him to realize how little I know about contemporary art, so I act as if I agree with everything he says.

The path among the sculptures narrows the farther we

go. Adam takes my hand as we weave through the final ones, ducking our heads and contorting our bodies.

At the end, Adam gazes at the installation and murmurs, "The steel shapes the sculpture, which in turn shapes how we move in relation to it in an iterative process of engagement."

He sounds like copy lifted from an art show catalog, but when he squeezes my hand, I smile. I still don't love the installation, but I can try seeing it differently.

By now Florian's returned. We chat for a minute, praise the installation effusively, and thank him again for the private viewing. He lets us out the back door and we walk through the alley to the street.

"Hungry?" Adam says.

"Starved."

He leads me around the corner to a tiny place with a patio that's hidden behind an explosion of magenta bougainvillea. We order a couple tortas, take our drinks outside, and sit at a picnic table to wait for our food.

A half-dozen cats come running and Adam scoops up a tabby. "Here," he says, handing it to me. "This is Angelia.

"And this," he says, holding up a large black cat, "this is Diego."

"You must come here a lot," I say.

"I live around here, so my ex and I would eat here at least once a week. Neither of us liked to cook."

I fuss with Angelia while she nestles into my lap, so it looks like I'm smiling at her and not at how Adam let it drop that he's single. I don't have a lot of experience, but guys don't tell you they're single unless they like you.

Adam sets Diego on the table, and the cat stretches and purrs as Adam scratches behind his ears, then draws his hand along his skinny back all the way to the tip of his tail, showing me a nurturing side of himself I didn't expect.

Then the cashier comes out with our food, and Diego leaps down and disappears. I go to bite into the warm torta, and carne and beans slop out the sides. When I reach for a napkin, I can't help thinking this dish is messy and authentic, not styled for social media.

Adam names a bunch of galleries in the Arts District, asking if I've visited them, and I have to shake my head and confess that no, I haven't. The hope I had that he likes me dims. Adam's a grad student, light-years ahead of me, and now he'll see how unsophisticated I am.

But then he says, "Don't be embarrassed. Parking's expensive downtown. I probably wouldn't have gone to half of them if I wasn't bartending at an opening."

I smile and for the first time since we sat down I relax. I ask him about his favorite galleries, and when there's a lull in the conversation, I say, "You haven't told me what you're working on."

Adam glances from me to the street, then he dabs his mouth and offers me a sideways smile. "The theme is uncertainty. Things never play out the way we think they will."

"Story of my life," I mutter.

"Tell me more," he says.

I wave him off. "Another time."

He sips his limeade. "You know what you're going to paint for the First-Year Exhibition?"

"I'm avoiding thinking about it. Is it as bad as they say?"

"Nothing you can't handle." Adam gets up. "I could use some sriracha. You want anything?"

I shake my head then follow him with my eyes, taking

in his broad shoulders and how he draws himself up as he moves. He walks so straight and tall, so sure of himself, that even though I should look away, I don't.

He comes back and as he douses his food with the sauce says, "I have a confession—I saw your portfolio."

I peer at him over my drink. "The one I submitted with my application?"

"Yeah, I was cleaning the faculty lounge last spring and they had work by the Zoich nominees set out for the faculty to review. I remember seeing the encaustic portrait you did of the old lady."

He's not blowing smoke, I think. He really saw my portfolio. "My art teacher thought I'd get Krell's attention if I submitted a painting in encaustic instead of acrylic."

"It was gutsy. Not a lot of artists use encaustic. Acrylic's much more forgiving. When I saw it I thought, 'Whoa. This girl's got talent.'"

I feel the color rise to my cheeks, and can't help smiling. "Thanks, I needed that."

"Another rough day with Krell?"

"I've had worse."

Adam bends over and holds out a tiny bite of torta to Diego, who takes it and runs off. "You're very good at capturing what you see."

"I credit my mom for that. She learned to play guitar by listening to the greats, so when I said I wanted to paint she insisted I copy the greats. She memorized the free admission days for every art museum in LA and made sure I got there."

"She must be really proud of you."

My heart skips a beat, and I nod. I don't want to ruin this moment by telling Adam that she's gone.

"So you're a transcribing veteran," he says.

I sigh. "You know I'd never even heard that word until the other day when Krell ordered me to *transcribe* a contemporary piece."

"What's the problem? That should be a no-brainer for you."

I push a bean around on my plate, because I'm almost embarrassed to answer. "The problem is, I can't stop thinking about Krell's painting. That's what I want to transcribe."

Adam laughs. "*Duncan*? You know Krell would never agree to that."

"Right? Can you imagine me even asking permission to do it?"

He sips his drink, his gaze following something in the bushes above my head. "What if you didn't ask Krell?"

"What are you saying?"

"What if I were to let you in at night and you paint when Krell's not there?" Adam's face is completely calm, which tells me he's not joking, he's really offering to do it.

"No. No, that's nuts . . ." I say, even as the longing to paint *Duncan* swells in my chest. "I can't afford the materials. The wood panel alone would be a couple hundred, not to mention the oil pigments and beeswax."

"Yeah, I could probably scrounge you up some pigment, but even with your employee discount the panel wouldn't be cheap."

I knit my hands behind my neck as I search for another reason to give him. I can't admit to Adam that I'm afraid I'd get kicked out if Krell caught me. I don't want him to know how close I am to losing the Zoich.

I look at him carefully. "Why are you offering to help me?"

Adam has been fiddling with his unused fork ever since finishing his torta, rubbing his thumb over the tines, but now he presses down on them so hard the veins in the back of his hand bulge. Whatever Adam's about to say, he doesn't really want to say it.

"Krell's doing the same thing to you that he did to a guy in my class."

His face is a mix of anger and sadness, two feelings I know way too well. "How did he survive Krell?"

"He didn't. The guy took it and took it until the day Krell told him he had no business being here, he'd never be an artist."

"That's horrible," I say quietly.

"Guy dropped out. We never heard from him again."

The food I ate is a rock in my stomach. "So that's why you're trying to help me. Because you think I could be next."

He avoids my gaze. "No, of course not," he says, but he's not at all convincing.

I'm in more trouble than I realized and it's Krell's fault. He's such a prick.

"Even if I could afford a panel, I can't carry a copy of Krell's painting in and out of CALINVA."

"Yeah, I didn't think of that." Adam motions to the street. "We should go," he says, and picks up our plates and dumps them in a trash can.

I know that sneaking into Krell's studio to paint would be ridiculously stupid and insane, but I'm actually disappointed I can't do it.

We walk down the broken sidewalk to my car. As we pass a row of tiny bungalows, I ask, "Do you rent one of these?"

"Not exactly. My roommate and I share a dumpy RV

parked in a driveway." He shrugs. "Could be worse, right?"

For a moment I wonder if it shows—the nights I parked my car in the line of RVs along Silverlake Drive in the spot a retired teacher saved for me. "Yeah, could be worse."

When we reach my car, Adam relaxes against the fender. "We could lock the painting in Secure Storage," he says.

I realize he means my copy of *Duncan*, and my first impulse is *yes, but* . . . "What's Secure Storage?"

"It's part of shipping and receiving. We could stick the painting in an unused locker."

I unlock my car and swing open the door. What Adam's suggesting would work, but . . . "I don't know. I need to think about it."

Adam pushes himself off the fender and comes up beside me. I hold my breath as he leans over and kisses my cheek. "I'd hate to see Krell beat you, Sabine."

As I drive away, the kiss smolders on my skin, and I reach up to touch it, expecting it to feel like ash.

CHAPTER 17

Late at night, Adam texts me a shot of a wood panel. Apparently, Krell rejected it because of an almost invisible crack, but Artsy won't take it back, so it's been sitting in a storage room for months.

ITS YOURS, he says.

I glance at the painting of Mom on my bureau. Adam finding the panel I need, this is a sign, right?

Adam and I go back and forth, making plans. I'll start painting after work tomorrow.

I tell myself I wouldn't have to do this if Krell would do his job and teach me instead of eviscerating me. And with Adam's help, I'm going to show Krell he's wrong.

When I arrive at CALINVA, it feels different, as if someone changed all the lightbulbs to brighter ones. Taysha intercepts me after class. "Where did you disappear to yesterday?"

"No place special."

"Liar." She laughs.

I know my face betrays me, but she doesn't push it.

My phone buzzes and I slide it out, sure it's Adam, but it's Mona. "Mona wants me to stop by the admin office."

Instead of walking away, Taysha insists on tagging along. "I want to see what goodies the Zoich sent you this time."

74

The office is on the first floor right off the lobby. It's basically a glass box with a clear view of the lobby and the exhibition gallery by the entrance.

There's an awkward, bony-framed kid sitting on the lime-green couch with his portfolio by his feet, and I know by the anxious, hopeful look in his eyes that he's a high school senior here for an interview. He's me. Last year. Desperate to come to the school of my dreams.

Run, I want to tell him. *Apply to UC San Diego or Cal State Fullerton.*

Mona sits at her sleek white desk outside the president's office, where the blinds are shut. Mona always looks polished, from her straightened hair to her perfectly glazed bronze nails and immaculate white silk blouse.

"Hi, Mona. You wanted to see me?"

She cocks her head, her eyebrows raised as she holds up a pink "While You Were Out" slip. "This woman called, looking for you. She wanted to know if you were a student here."

I read *Iona Taylor* in Mona's big round handwriting and my stomach lurches. Why did I think Iona wouldn't find me? Taysha and Mona are exchanging looks, but I try to act nonchalant. "Did she say what she wanted?"

"No, she did not, and I informed her that I am not permitted to give out that kind of information. It violates the rules concerning student privacy."

It's obvious Mona has guessed this is *the* Iona Taylor, and it's absolutely killing her that she can't come right out and ask. "Thanks, I appreciate you looking out for me," I say, and take the message from her.

Taysha doesn't have anywhere near Mona's restraint, because the second we exit the office, she plucks the pink paper out of my hand. "Iona Taylor? I knew you grew up in Beverly Hills, but—"

I don't let her finish. "I might have grown up in Beverly Hills, but I didn't 'grow up' in Beverly Hills."

"Care to explain?"

"It's not the same when your mom's the help."

Taysha blinks like she's recalibrating what she thinks about me. I should have come clean weeks ago.

"You're telling me your mom works for a Platinum Mom!"

I squirm, seeing people turn around to look at us. "Worked. Just for a little while."

"What do you think she wants?"

"Don't know. Don't care." Crap. Taysha's never going to drop this.

"Iona Taylor's a piece of work. Did you see the episode where she tore into her assistant, Lacy, over losing her designer dress?"

"Nope. Missed that one," I toss back.

"She stormed around that big-ass kitchen of hers, yelling—" Taysha slams her hands down on an invisible counter and contorts her face into the one I'd see scream at Mom. "'VAL-EN-TIN-O, VAL-EN-TIN-O. Can you not hear me? Where's my VAL-EN-TIN-O?'"

My heart squeezes so hard I can barely breathe. "Yeah, sounds like Iona," I manage to force out.

Poor Lacy. I glance at the restroom because I need to end this, but Taysha will just follow me in, so I dive for my phone. "Oh, gotta take this. See you later?"

I walk away, mumbling nonsense like "yeah" and "okay" while I walk down the ramp as if someone's waiting for me outside. Then I duck around the side of the building behind what I think of as the flying chopstick sculpture.

The aluminum rods hover a foot off the ground. Strung on steel cables, they vibrate when a car goes by or a breeze hits.

I park my butt on the cement base. My stomach's churning, because what did I expect would happen when Iona figured out I had her dress?

I kept thinking I'd return it. Toss the box with it over the gate and drive off. But weeks went by and I didn't get around to it. And then when a cop warned me that I had twenty-four hours before my registration lapsed and I could lose my car to an impound lot, I did what I had to.

I took care of myself because no one else was going to.

I pull out my sketch pad and stare at the steel stairs spiraling up the outside of the building. My head begins to clear as I capture how the wide steps narrow and shrink the farther away they are.

Iona Taylor called CALINVA personally to track me down? That can't be right. Iona wouldn't waste her time trying to find me if she couldn't reach me on my old cell.

No, she'd tell someone else to call me. Like Lacy, her personal assistant, or more likely the girl who took Lacy's job after Iona fired her for losing the dress.

I tell myself not to freak. Lacy or whoever is probably about my age, desperate to break into the *industry*, and Iona's got her running around doing a thousand thankless jobs like scheduling her highlights and ordering bee pollen. She doesn't have time to go to the bathroom, much less track down the former housekeeper's daughter.

And even if this girl did track me down, let's be real. What would she do?

SKETCH #3

ALL OUR BELONGINGS, March 15

I chose a 6B graphite pencil because I wanted the lines crisp and sharp.

You'd think a sketch this simple would have been easy: boxes lined up in a garage against the wall. A dozen identical rectangles. Four in a row and three high. Perfectly taped and labeled REYES.

The cardboard was blank, negating the lives inside.

My pencil didn't falter until I went to draw the battered guitar case lying across the top row. I was always good at perspective, but when I tried to draw the curved black case, I lost it.

As I look at it now, the sketch is deceptive. Anyone seeing it would flip to the next sketch, thinking there's nothing interesting going on.

But me, I see the tiny Latina who met me when I showed up at the Taylors'. She took my hands in hers before I could stop her. "Miss Iona, she did not think you were coming back."

I shook off this stranger, so tired I could barely stand, and pulled out my phone to call Iona. Forty voice messages from her and I'd ignored them all.

Phones weren't allowed in the ICU, and what could I have told Iona? I didn't know when Mom would be coming back. But now I could tell her. Never. Mom was never fucking coming back.

I remember scrolling down to the oldest voice mail.

"Hi, Sabine, it's Iona. We're back from Telluride. Skiing was amazing. Haven't heard from your mom when she'll be back. The crew from *Platinum Moms* is shooting here on Thursday. Hair and Makeup is scheduled for six a.m. Crazy, right? So I need one of you to take the boys to school—"

Buried in the drama of Mom's accident, I'd completely blanked that Iona had snagged a starring role in *Platinum Moms of Beverly Hills.*

Oh God, I thought, and scrolled up seven messages.

"Sabine. You or your mom need to stop screwing around and call me back. I don't have time for this. We're filming every day this week. The producers sent a cleaning crew to the house, but I can't be expected to feed the twins and get them to school and softball and Mandarin and coding class—"

I skipped forward another fifteen. I knew I'd messed up bad by not calling, but . . . "It's been two and a half weeks, Sabine, and not *a single word* from you or your mom? This is so self-centered, so rude. You've put me in an impossible situation, and I'm done defending you. One of you needs to get back to me TODAY."

The last message had been days before.

"Hi, ah, Sabine? This is Lacy Efron, Iona Taylor's new personal assistant? Um, she asked me to let you know that your mom is in violation of her employment contract due to her unexplained absences, and ah, she's been officially terminated. She will be paid for the days she worked, but we need to know where to send the final check—"

The world, time, gravity stopped for a moment. "You took Mom's job. You work for the Taylors."

"*Sí. Sí.*"

There was air all around me, but I couldn't breathe.

Any normal human being would have known this was a crisis, that things with Mom and me were horribly, horribly wrong, but not Iona. She couldn't imagine we needed help, not when she was busy with Hair and Makeup and driving the boys to Mandarin.

"It's okay, it's okay. Don't worry," the new housekeeper cooed. "Your things, they are all packed. Very carefully. You show your mother. Nothing is broken." She hit a button and the garage door rolled up, revealing Mom's guitar case lying across a row of cardboard boxes.

The blood drained from my head. "What? No."

I'd begged Mom not to leave me, begged her to come back from her coma because I needed her. I was only seventeen. How could she expect me to take care of myself?

I looked up at the blue, blue sky, tears dribbling down my face. No. Mom, I pleaded silently. I can't. I can't do this.

"Where am I supposed to go?" I murmured.

The housekeeper shook her head helplessly at me and I buried my face in my hands.

I can't. Mom, do you hear me, I can't do this.

I started to sob. The new housekeeper looked on, wringing her hands while I cried so hard I doubled over, clutching my sides. When I finally stopped and caught my breath, the woman took my arm and guided me into my car. "You rest while I load your things," she said, and tucked Mom's last paycheck into my hand.

The check was only a few hundred dollars, a few hundred even though Mom had worked for the Taylors for over twelve years.

Every time I remember this I get angry all over again. Mom had been like a second mother to the twins, and this was how Iona treated her?

CHAPTER 18

At seven, Adam's waiting at the back door of CALINVA, holding a cardboard box.

I've had doubts all day about whether I should do this, so I approach slowly, telling myself I can end this now before any rules are broken. But then what will I do? Adam's the only person trying to help me keep my scholarship, and I can't afford to alienate him. I offer up a smile. "What's in the box?"

"I scrounged up some supplies for you. My roommate had some leftover pigment from a project he did last year."

I peek inside, and there are a couple dozen partially used tubes of pigment and a bunch of empty tuna-fish cans. At first, I'm puzzled. "Oh, I get it. The cans are for mixing." I reach in and read the labels on the pigment. It's imported from Germany. The good stuff. "Wow. You need to thank your roommate for me. This pigment's super expensive."

"He was happy to get rid of it. Called encaustic his nemesis. Ready to do this?"

I'm not. I shouldn't. But the image in my head of Krell's portrait dissolving into shards of color while still conveying the essence of Duncan makes me answer, "Let's do it."

"Good." Adam shadows me to the door. His keys rattle in the lock and he holds the heavy door so I can go first. We step into the barely lit hallway. My heart begins to pound as we creep into the back area where students don't normally go.

Secure Storage is double locked, but Adam's got keys for both. The room is dry and cooler than the hall outside. Deep metal lockers, big enough to slide in a canvas taller than me, line the walls. "The panel is over here," he says.

I peek through the ventilation holes in the steel door. The panel shines pristine white even in the faintly lit locker.

Adam spins the combination lock and slides out the panel, which looks about the same size as Krell's. I run my hand over the surface. "I thought you said it was cracked."

"I filled it with wood glue before I primed it."

"You did a really nice job. I can't even tell."

"Thanks, I'm known around here for my superior canvas prep," he jokes.

I pick up the box of supplies and Adam carries the panel over to the door. I open it and peer out. The atrium is echoey, and I hear voices coming from a floor above us, but there's no one on this one. I hold the door for Adam, then we sneak down the hall to the service elevator.

When I press the button, nothing happens. My pulse ticks up. We're away from the public spaces, deep in a gray cement hall, but I feel like a spotlight's trained on us.

"Adam, what do we do if we run into security? What do we say?"

His brows are knit and I can tell he's nervous, too, but he's trying not to show it, because he says, "I think we're okay. The service elevator's so slow, nobody uses it if they can avoid it. And security's not going to care about a blank panel."

He's probably right. Carrying around a blank panel or

canvas is nothing. People lug them around CALINVA all the time.

Finally, the elevator wakes up and rumbles down from an upper floor. "You're sure Krell went home?" I say.

"I checked his parking space before you got here. Empty."

We're insane for doing this. I should stop it right now. My mouth fills with saliva as I try out how to tell him. *Adam, I've changed my mind. I'm not sure I want to do this.*

The elevator opens and he steps in. Faded gray moving quilts line the steel walls like it's a padded cell, and a nervous giggle bubbles out of me.

"What's so funny?"

I don't want to admit how anxious I am right now. "Nothing. Just a stupid random thought."

Adam's making a big effort to help me, which I'm sure he wouldn't do if he didn't like me, and if I'm being honest with myself, if he didn't believe I'm in real trouble.

We get out on Krell's floor and I peek around the corner. The hall's empty and I don't hear anyone on this floor or the one below. Adam tells me to dig the keys out of his pocket. He tells me which one's Krell's and I put it in the lock.

The door swings open. The studio looks like it did the other night. Adam lays my panel on top of the worktable. I reach underneath the table and take out Krell's electric palette, which is a little like a griddle, and plug it in. My messenger bag is packed with the waxy medium I'll cut into chunks and melt with the colored pigment in the tuna cans.

Adam carries over the easel with Krell's painting and sets it upright by the table. One glance, and Krell's amazing, enigmatic portrait draws me over, hands linked behind my back as I fight the urge to reach out and touch it.

"The painting's going to Art Basel Miami right after the unveiling," Adam says. "It'll only be here for another month."

"Why is it being sent to an art fair when someone already bought it?"

"Krell's dealer wants the art world to see it so he can sell the next one Krell paints."

I can't stop staring at it. "What do you think is underneath?"

"You mean what do I think he's obsessed with?"

"Yeah."

Adam scowls and shakes his head. "Power? Fame? Money? Take your pick."

The way Krell treats people reminds me of Iona, the total disregard for anyone's feelings or needs but her own, so I'd have to say power or fame. But the way he paints? I wonder if it isn't something much deeper, more personal. "I don't know. Dogs playing poker?"

Adam laughs. "Women's underwear?"

"Ew."

"Satanic symbols?"

"More likely."

Adam adjusts the angle of the easel. "I'll be back in two hours to help you clean up," he says.

"You're not staying?"

"I have my own work to do."

"Yeah, of course." I don't let him see I'm disappointed. Silly to think he'd waste time lounging around here when he's got his own projects to finish.

"I'd invite you to see what I'm working on," he says, "but I share the studio with three other grad students and one of them lives there."

"That's allowed?"

He shrugs. "No, but I'm not about to kick the guy out. See you later." He walks out and the door clicks behind him.

I weigh the block of waxy medium in my hand. *Am I really doing this?*

Inside those layers of paint are secrets Krell won't share with me, because he'd rather cut me to shreds. My hesitation vanishes.

I dig into my pocket for my magnifying glass. Time to focus on why I'm here.

As the layers of Krell's painting emerge, I puzzle through how to deconstruct it. I peel the photograph of Duncan off the wall and go back and forth between it and the painting it inspired.

To understand the brilliance of an artist like Krell you need to look at the choices he makes. What he includes and what he ignores. What colors he uses, and how he employs line, light, and shadow. Even things like the length or energy of the brushstrokes, or the thickness of the paint, define his work.

I hold my magnifying glass over the areas where layers of color shine through, revealing more than I first thought.

The feeling that I'm a detective, an archaeologist unearthing buried secrets, makes me almost giddy. Reading his brushstrokes is like learning a new language. I've always tried to make mine disappear, but now I see I could use them to add power and depth.

You couldn't just teach me, could you? You had to tear me down.

Study a painting by an artist whose work you connect with. At least that advice was valuable.

I focus on how to begin the base. Krell's muted background isn't eggshell like I first thought. It's complex, layers of faint pastels that aren't quite blue or peach or the palest yellow.

I set out cans on the warm palette and drop in chunks of wax. As it melts, I shave in the pigment, and bounce on my tiptoes, seeing the colors on my palette match Krell's. Yes yes yes.

Unlike acrylics, encaustic takes time. Paint on a layer, wipe it off if it's not right, or fuse it with a warm blast from a heat gun before you paint the next.

The cloudy background begins to take shape, but I've only done one corner when Adam reappears.

"Oh, I thought you'd be further along."

He sounds disappointed, but I guess he's never done this kind of painting. Most people haven't. "Yeah, I hoped so, too, but you know, encaustic takes a while."

He's looking doubtful, like he's realizing he probably shouldn't have agreed to help me, but he says, "What do you think? You learning anything? You want to come back Monday?"

The thought of not coming back sends me reeling. I've only begun to solve the puzzle of Krell's painting, so—"Yeah, but I don't want to screw up your schedule."

"You're not. But we need to clean up before the night crew comes in." He picks up Krell's easel and carries it back to where it was, then unplugs the heat gun and wraps the cord.

I dip Krell's brushes in melted wax to release the pigment before I rub them with a paper towel. Despite how gently I rub, bristles come off in my hand. Damn. I can't use these.

Krell will see the wear on them. I've got to buy matching ones.

I'm running numbers in my head on how much this will cost me when Adam says, "We should go to 365 Mission sometime."

My neck starts to tingle and I stay turned to the wall so Adam can't see me grin. Yep. He likes me. "The art gallery? That would be cool. Everyone's talking about it."

"I was there Saturday night for the Amphibs album release, and Gavin Brown—" He pauses. "*Gavin Brown?*" he repeats, and I realize I'm supposed to be impressed.

I shrug, embarrassed I'm so clueless. "Sorry, who is he?"

Adam grins and shakes his head. "I forget that you're new to the art world. Gavin owns galleries on four continents, and 365 is just one of them. I ran into him by the bar and we started talking about the chromatic saturation of the music. Five hours later we're throwing back *soju* in Koreatown and he tells me he wants to see my studio."

"He wants to see your work! That's amazing. What if he offers to represent you?"

"I'll say yes, of course. And once he sells out my first show, I'll tell him about a young painter I know who shows enormous promise."

Our eyes meet and I blush. He squeezes my arm and gets back to cleaning up the studio.

The art world is all about connections, and being tight with Adam and this Gavin Brown? I picture a gallery, big white walls hung with my paintings.

I stick Krell's brushes back in the jars, careful to match how he's grouped them by size and shape. Then I kneel down to wipe a spot off the floor, and catch Adam rearranging them. "Is something the matter?" I ask.

He smiles like it's nothing. "Krell can be a bit anal about his brushes, that's all."

Adam gathers up my used paper towels and stuffs them in a trash bag. I take it from him and grab the box of pigment.

I'm not nervous when Adam carries my panel downstairs, because I'm still so pumped from the work I've done. We slide it into the storage locker along with the box of supplies, and Adam works the lock.

Watching him, it hits me that this is how I've wanted to feel all semester—that I'm energized and learning, and I won't let Krell make me feel bad anymore.

"Why so happy?" he says. "You're beaming."

"I didn't realize how much I needed this."

He squeezes my arm again, and what I see in his eyes makes my stomach swoop. "You're fighting back," he says. "That's great. I knew you wouldn't let Krell kill your spirit."

I look away, blushing but happy. Adam gets me in a way no one else at CALINVA does. He could be the reason I survive Collin Krell. The reason I hold on to the Zoich.

CHAPTER 19

By the time Adam and I get outside, night classes are letting out. We linger, saying good night, but the moment's not what I'd call romantic; Adam's hands are wrapped around the trash bag we need to dump.

"You working on Sunday?" I say, hoping he'll suggest we hang out.

He tosses the garbage into a dumpster and smiles at me, his teeth white in the shadows. "Yeah, I've got a gig, hauling equipment for a wedding photographer."

"Maybe some other time," I say, careful to keep it light.

"I'd like that."

The way he says it makes my heart skip. He comes in close and leans over me until his face is just inches from mine. Adam smiles and my lips part. *Yes, yes.*

He reaches up and sets his hand on my neck. I lean into it as he draws his thumb over my cheek. "I like you," he says, gazing into my eyes. "I didn't expect to."

My jaw actually drops. "Excuse me?"

"Sorry," he says. "That came out wrong." He frowns, collecting his thoughts, his hand still resting on my neck. "The first time we spoke, I wasn't looking to get involved—"

I hold my breath as he chooses his words.

"Things aren't quite resolved with my ex. I wouldn't

want to start something with you and then—"

I smile so he'll stop talking. "It's late."

He takes his hand away. "Yeah, I should get going, too."

He's looking everywhere but at me, so I ask, "What's on your mind?"

"I don't have to tell you we need to keep this a secret?"

"No, I get that if this got out it wouldn't look good for either of us."

He takes a step back. "Monday night? Same time?"

I hate walking to my car alone this late. There's hardly any traffic on the street after dark and late night is the only time a cop isn't parked outside the shelter. "You mind walking me to my car?"

Adam glances over his shoulder at the lot, which is lit like a football field. "You're not parked over there?"

"Nope. I couldn't afford a pass this semester. I'm up on Raymond."

He glances at his phone like he's checking the time, and then smiles. "Sure. No problem. I'm headed to the Metro stop anyway."

I step toward the lit walkway, but Adam waves me into the alley on the other side of the building. "This way's shorter," he says. We chat quietly as we exit onto Raymond and head up the street. Adam's keeping up the pace, and I realize he's probably eager to make the next train.

We're almost across from the shuttered florist shop that my car's parked behind when I say, "Thanks for walking me, but I can handle it from here."

"You sure?" he says, but I feel how much he wants to go.

"Yeah, my car's right over there and you've got a train to catch."

"Monday?" he says.

"Monday," I answer, and step into the street. I dash across, still feeling his touch on my cheek, and I know I shouldn't, not when there's an ex who's not totally out of the picture, but I imagine myself at his side at his first solo show at 365 Mission surrounded by everyone who's anyone in the LA art world.

I step onto the curb in front of the flower shop and a voice calls out, "Artist girl!" and I jump about a foot.

"Jesus!" I exclaim, and spin around looking for who's there.

A small voice comes from the doorway. "I'm sorry. I didn't mean to scare you."

I peer into the shadows by the shop's front door. Julie, the homeless woman, sits on a flattened cardboard box, a thin blanket over her knees. Sweetie is nestled on her chest.

"Julie, hi. Why are you out here and not in the shelter?"

"It's too nice to be inside tonight. Besides, I'm safer out here."

I shiver, because I know exactly what Julie means. I tried one night at a teen shelter in Hollywood, but felt more exposed in there than I did in my car.

"I saw you out walking the other night," she says. "You was lost."

It takes a moment before I realize she must have spotted me the night I saw her eating ice cream. "I wasn't lost. I live around there."

"Lost inside, not outside. Lost in here," she says, tapping her chest.

It rattles me how right she is about that, and I fumble in my messenger bag for the bottle of water I haven't opened. "Are you thirsty?" I say, showing her the bottle.

"Oh yes, I am. Thank you."

I set the bottle in Julie's grimy hand, and she pours some into a small plastic bowl for Sweetie before she takes a swig. I wonder what her story is. I'd like to ask her about herself, but she's not here to satisfy my curiosity. "Julie, I'm really tired. I need to go home. Stay safe, okay?"

She lifts the corner of her blanket and shows me a knife at least nine inches long. "Don't you worry. I'll be fine. Sweet dreams."

"You too." I take about two steps before I stop and turn around. "My name's Sabine."

"Sabine. Your mama chose a beautiful name for her girl."

And even though there's no way Julie could have known Mom, the feeling that she did floods me and I walk wobbly-legged to my car. I unlock the door, launch myself inside, and slam down the lock. When I glance up at the rearview mirror, the backseat stares back at me.

Memories I've tried to forget come hurtling back. The plastic knife, jar of peanut butter, and loaf of bread on the floor of the backseat. Washing underwear in a library sink. A cop banging on the window at 3:00 a.m. "You can't sleep here. Move your car."

I go to start the engine and drop my keys. *Dammit*. I scrabble around by my feet, getting more and more frustrated when I can't find them.

Stop. Breathe.

My heartbeat begins to slow and I start to catch my breath. I need to avoid Julie. She's triggering me.

But then Mom's voice comes through so clear it's as if she's listening. *No, baby, she's your spirit guide.*

The idea is so new-age-y, so Mom, I start laughing. Mom would talk about people, ordinary, everyday people who didn't look the least angelic, but who appeared when she was screwing up. *I couldn't shake them, baby. I'd try to ignore them, but they'd keep showing up until I got the message.*

I'm done laughing when I find my keys. Okay, fine. If Julie's got a message for me, then what is it?

I'm not sure what she's trying to tell me, but the first time I saw her I was compelled to take her photo. And the other night when I saw her again, I was swamped by the urge to paint her, but I chickened out and painted the urban landscape that got me reamed.

The engine starts and I shift into drive. The logical answer to my completely irrational question is: I have to paint her.

I need to paint Julie.

Portraits are my passion, they always have been, but painting a portrait of Julie to show to Krell, *one of the leading portrait painters of our time?*

It feels dangerous—no, insane! Krell will savage the painting's flaws and weaknesses, he'll shred me in front of the class.

But I can't hand in another painting that's safe. Krell told me to risk failure, and I guess that means I need to be daring and paint Julie.

I turn off the engine and walk back to where she's sitting. I crouch on my heels so we can look eye to eye. Julie's not surprised to see me, but she is when I ask if I can paint her. "This face? Why would you want to paint this ugly face?"

"To be honest, I don't know. But I don't think it's ugly."

She sizes me up, her mouth working, then says, "Would I have to go sit in that fancy school while you paint?"

"Not if you don't want to. I could paint you from the photo I took the other day."

She asks to see it again, and I show it to her. "Would it help you?" she says. "Painting my picture, would it help you?"

A sob rises in my throat, but I catch it and force it down. "Yes," I tell her. "It would."

"You go ahead, then."

We say good night and I walk back to my car, holding her permission to my chest like a gift.

CHAPTER 20

Krell's absent from Painting Strategies 101, so class is the most relaxed it's ever been. I text Adam asking if he can take a break, but he doesn't text me back, so after class I head for the student lounge. Bryian and Bernadette have taken over one of the couches, their giraffe-long limbs splayed over the arms and the table in front of them. They're both absorbed in whatever she's showing him on her tablet.

I veer over to where Taysha's working. A pile of earrings on midnight-blue paper backings sits on the table in front of her along with sheets of price stickers. "Nice jacket," she says.

"It was my mom's," I say, slipping off the cerulean velvet jacket she used to wear onstage.

"You should raid her closet more often."

Taysha's comment slides into a soft spot between my ribs, but still I smile through the pang in my chest, because when I put Mom's jacket on this morning, it was the first time that wearing something of hers made me feel close to her instead of infinitely lost.

I pick up a pair of earrings. Tiny origami cranes dangle from the silver wires. "You made these?"

"Yes, indeed. The whole bunch." Taysha waves her hand

over the pile. "They're not really my thing, but they sell like crazy. Do me a favor and peel the price sticker off that one."

"Sure." I sit down and scratch at the card stock with a fingernail, careful not to tear it.

Taysha hands me a new sticker. "Here. Put this on. It's almost the holidays. Time to raise prices." She watches me for barely a second, then pushes the rest of the earrings over to me. "You peel, I'll replace."

I smirk as I reach into the pile. "Why do I feel like you planned this?"

"Because you can see into my calculating soul."

We work in silence for a minute, then Taysha says, "Something's different about you."

The little square of card stock I'm holding pops out of my hand and I snatch it off the table. *Calm down. She has no idea what you're up to with Adam.*

"It has to do with Kevin, doesn't it?"

"We are not a thing, Taysha."

"You were pretty tight on that bench outside the Broad the other day."

"Okay, stop. Don't even."

"Fine," Taysha declares with a flick of her hands. "Maybe you'd be more interested in who got busted hooking up in CALINVA's hallowed halls."

"Ah, yeah."

"So Jorge—" Taysha sees I have no clue who he is. "Security guard, really tall, short black hair?"

"Nope, go on."

"Last night around ten, he's doing his rounds and he hears slamming noises coming from the library and thinks someone's destroying equipment. So he bursts in, and these two second-years are banging away. Chairs are turned over. Clothes are everywhere. Art journals cover half the floor."

"No!"

"To hear Jorge tell it, he's never seen an action sequence like this one. He made them hand over their student IDs, and the administration put them on probation. They can't even step into the library unless the librarian's present."

I laugh with Taysha, but at the same time, take this as a warning. With Jorge patrolling the halls at night, I need to be careful. The heat gun I need to use to fuse the layers of encaustic paint is as loud as a hair dryer. I don't want to tip anyone off that I'm in Krell's studio.

Class is about to start, so Taysha and I pack up. "Oh, before I forget," she says, "I could use some help next Sunday if you're free. I rented a space at the Rose Bowl flea market. It's how I pay for the extras, like, you know, *food*."

It sounds fun, but I was hoping to spend that Sunday in Krell's studio. *Duncan* will be gone in a few weeks, so I don't have a lot of time to work on it. "I don't know, Taysha. I'd like to, but I might be doing something."

Taysha smiles knowingly.

"Not with Kevin."

"Oh, with someone else?" she asks.

I feel my face turn pink, so I reach under the table and dig though my messenger bag. For a moment, I'm tempted to tell her about Adam, but it would be way too easy to mess up and let slip what he and I are up to. "You don't know him."

"So he's not in the program?"

"He's someone I met at Artsy." Which is sort of true.

"Mmm. The way you're blushing makes me think he must be hot."

"Yes." I feel my cheeks return to normal and I stand up. "But I'm not saying another thing about it. It's probably nothing and it's probably going nowhere."

Taysha gives me a look I can't read, then says, "Well, if you are free, and I'm not counting on it, I'll pay you fifty in cash and throw in a pair of earrings."

Fifty dollars I could put toward pigment or brushes or getting Mom's guitar out of hock. I'm late paying back the pawnshop, so I'm completely torn. "I'll check with my friend and get back to you."

"Deal."

Taysha and I pack up the last of our stuff and cross the lobby, skirting a group of students who've gathered in the center. Above us, people line the railings on the second and third floors.

As we climb the stairs to the second floor, an eerie quiet infuses the air. Class is about to start, but people aren't heading inside. "What's going on?" I whisper.

"Not sure," Taysha answers, and we squeeze into an opening along the railing.

Performance art in the lobby is a regular thing, so I wait for music or a dissonant crash of notes, but the silence intensifies.

Twenty students have formed a line across the cement floor below. Their arms hang limp at their sides and their eyes are focused on their feet.

The first student in line drops to her knees. She throws her arms up before she falls forward, flattening out on her stomach, her arms and legs splayed. Her eyes are wide open, but unfocused, and her mouth gapes.

She lies, silent and immobile, and what can really only

be a few seconds feels never-ending before she gets up and the next guy takes her place. Around us, there's sniffling and muffled sobs.

He was crazy talented . . . this day last year . . . feels so unreal . . .

Students hug each other as each person in the line below repeats the tiny drama. My hands turn to ice, and I wrap them in the ends of my scarf. "How did he die?" Taysha asks a second-year girl I don't know.

Her features contort before she forces out her answer. "He jumped."

"Sweet Jesus," Taysha murmurs, then crosses herself. "You okay?" she says, sliding her arm through mine. I squeeze her back and we hold on to each other as the last of the twenty students hit the cement.

Our instructor raps on her classroom door, breaking the spell. We file into class, shuffling as if we've survived a shipwreck, and half the period goes by before any of us speak.

I can't help wondering if he was one of Krell's students, someone creative and talented who couldn't handle the pressure of being at CALINVA.

I'm not him and I'd never do something like that loops in my head as if repeating it will make sure it never comes true.

CHAPTER 21

On Saturday, Kevin's banana-bread apology costs me hours of cleaning out old flowerpots crusted with dirt, sweeping away dusty spiderwebs, and washing the ten windows in the sunroom until the view of her garden goes from smeary to high def, but when I'm done, Mrs. Mednikov declares this is now my space to paint.

"Really?" I say, taking it all in. "Thank you!" I can't believe she's giving me this extra room when the rent she charges me is ridiculously low.

"Working late at night alone at school? It's not good for you."

I smile. "You're kind to worry, but I'm not alone."

She smiles back, curious, but restrained by her last-century good manners.

"I'm working on a project," I add. "It'll be done soon."

"That's good."

I'm relieved she doesn't pry. She's no fan of Krell's, but I have no doubt she'd disapprove of what I'm doing in his studio.

We haul an easel out of the garage, one that was left behind by another art student who lived here. I wash off years of dirt until the blond wood shines through.

There are still a few hours left until my shift at the

restaurant, so I set up the easel on the porch and place a small canvas board on it. I tape a copy of Julie's photo to the top and start to sketch in pencil on the white canvas.

But I've only just begun when I set down the pencil and rub my arms. It's cool on the unheated porch, but that's not the problem. In the unforgiving light of day, my "epiphany" that I need to paint Julie feels like a delusion.

With this next assignment, I have to redeem myself with Krell, but have I learned enough yet from working on *Duncan* to tackle Julie's portrait?

It has to be surprising and unconventional to satisfy him, and he came right out and warned us that this assignment is critical, because it will be hung in the First-Year Exhibition in the CALINVA gallery in December. "This will be the first time the entire faculty is exposed to your work," he said.

Then Taysha only made it worse when she whispered, "I heard the upper-level faculty decide who they want to mentor way before they ever have you in class."

I pick up my pencil. No pressure, I think, tapping it against my teeth. Just an assignment that determines the rest of my life.

I stare at Julie's photo and my gut says *paint her* while my head says *bad idea*.

Most of the fine art faculty paint abstracts, and the rest don't even paint—they create conceptual art. The only portrait painter is Krell. And even if I manage to change his mind about me, he'll never agree to be my adviser.

I toss the pencil in the corner and it bounces back and rolls at my feet like it refuses to be ignored.

The only paintings I've turned in to Krell so far have been still lifes and urban landscapes, things that even when

I worked on them obsessively, I didn't love. I can't do that anymore. I've got a little over a month to create the most important painting of my life and I need to trust in my passion.

The sun dips behind a cloud, casting the porch into shade. I blow out a breath and start to sketch.

CHAPTER 22

Today is Mom's re-birthday, and I'm sitting in the student lounge with a cupcake in front of me I can't bear to eat. My pencil hovers over my sketch pad, but it refuses to land. I can't draw myself out of my grief.

I knew today would be hard. Friday, October 23, has been staring back at me from the calendar all month and now it's here.

And it doesn't help that I'm way low on sleep. The last four nights, I spent hours painting *Duncan*, so I haven't gone to bed before 2 or 3 a.m. But you do what you have to if you want to live your dreams.

I rest my eyes on the blank paper, but I see Mom silhouetted in the kitchen window, touching her wrist as if she's checking her pulse, her fingertips resting on the word inked on her skin: SERENITY. Her lips move as she silently recites her morning prayer. *God grant me the serenity . . .*

Seven months until my birthday, today was her special day. She'd light the candles on the two cupcakes she bought and we'd blow them out together.

Last year she celebrated eighteen years sober. I remember her peeling the paper away from her cake and saying, "Not even born yet, but you made me rewrite my life. You're the best gift I ever got, baby. Nothing and no one will ever come close."

I sit very still because if I move even a finger, I may start crying, and in this room full of people I barely know, I couldn't bear it. People think home is where you live, but it's not. It's where you're loved.

Kevin joins me at the table and he has no idea how grateful I am that it's him and not someone else. I slide the cupcake over. "Do you want it? Turns out I'm not hungry."

"You sure?" He waits for me to nod before he peels off the fluted paper. "So how's it going?"

"I miss my mom," I say, surprising myself.

"I miss mine, too," he says. "You should call her."

My heart skips, because I'm still not ready to share that part of me with anyone other than Mrs. Mednikov. "Yeah, I should."

He asks me if I've thought about what I'm going to paint for the First-Year Exhibition and I feel my whole body relax. We've left the dangerous territory of my last year and are back on neutral ground. "A portrait. Of a woman named Julie. I saw her on the street and I can't get her out of my head."

"Sounds like you need to paint her," he says. "Any idea why?"

"Not sure. But maybe that's what I want to find out. What about you?"

Kevin pulls out a diagram and sets it on the table along with a tiny black box that turns out to be a motor. He walks me through his idea for a painting that will move and change, and his face becomes as animated as the tiny flipper things he's acting out with his hands.

When he's done explaining the piece, he says, "I have a theory for why the art world disrespects kinetic art."

This time I don't argue. "Tell me."

"Because it's art that follows the rules instead of breaking them."

It takes me a moment, but then I get it. "No breaking the rules of physics," I say, and Kev grins.

I see the same clarity in Kevin's work as I do in Krell's, the same conviction that his choices might not be popular, but they're his. Krell chooses to paint portraits, even though the stratospheric money and fame usually go to artists who do abstracts or conceptual pieces.

I envy Kevin's clarity. Deep in my gut, I feel I'm on the right path, painting Julie, but the path feels tangled and confused. What am I trying to say with this painting? When Krell asks for my artistic statement, what do I tell him?

Every night I spend studying *Duncan,* I feel the tiniest bit closer to the answer. Unlike Kevin, the only way I'll get clarity is to break the rules.

CHAPTER 23

I shiver on the sidewalk in front of Mrs. Mednikov's at dawn, waiting for Taysha. I pull the hood up on my sweatshirt and tug the sleeves over my fingers, wishing I hadn't agreed to help out at the flea market.

It was hard enough to leave my painting of Julie to go waitress yesterday, because even though the work had started to gel, it still felt off. And sure, it's Sunday and I can work on it later today, but I'm bummed about losing hours of sunlight.

I check the time on my phone and there's a missed text from Adam. GROUP HEADING TO LATE NIGHT GALLERY—WANT TO COME?

Damn, I can't believe I missed his text. But he sent it during my shift at La Petite Tomate so I couldn't have gone anyway. It's too early to text him back, so I put the phone away, thinking *Later*.

When Taysha pulls up, I crawl into the front seat of her van. She's in full makeup, with a cat's-eye sweep of liner I couldn't pull off at 6 a.m.

"Nice place," she says. "I'm in a converted garage."

"Yeah, I lucked out," I answer, remembering the sketchy rentals I checked out last summer—flimsy doors with eight locks, half of them broken, and bars on the windows.

"Thanks for getting up."

"Hey, I said I would."

"Good to see you're someone who keeps their word."

Five minutes later we're at the Rose Bowl, where Taysha flashes her vendor's badge and the guard waves us into the stadium's massive parking lot.

People are already setting up their booths, but Taysha smiles as she pulls into an empty space. "Getting up this early is painful, but it pays off." She points out how we're right by the entrance gate. "All the hipsters, stylists, and stars scoping out vintage have to pass right by us."

The first thing we haul out of the van is a shade tent. "It'll be an oven out here by ten," Taysha warns as we snap the legs into place.

Plastic folding tables and pop-up racks are next. Taysha pulls out tubs of clothing and handmade jewelry and puts me to work hanging up clothes.

The jackets and skirts look like they come from designer boutiques. Houndstooth jackets with snakeskin lapels. Plaid skirts with a galaxy of mismatched buttons that stretch from a hip to the opposite thigh. A coat with a corset sewn around the waist.

I hold up a black jacket with scarlet gores. A dramatic cut that bows to the past but feels now. "Where do you find this stuff?"

"Mainly at garage sales and thrift shops. I look for pieces that are well made, then I take them apart, recut them, dye them. The jacket you're holding used to be peach."

I shudder, imagining it, and note the price tag. "If you had a boutique on Melrose, you could charge five times what you're charging."

"True, but my dreams are way bigger than that. Designer to the stars with my own brand. All I need is the right A-list clients to get me started. You sure you won't introduce me to Iona Taylor?"

"I would not be doing you a favor introducing you to Iona."

Taysha laughs and whips out her phone. "Smile." I hold up a jacket as she snaps pics of the booth. She taps her screen. "There, now my fans know where to find me."

Taysha deserves a lot of credit. She knows what she wants and is out to get it. I'm glad she's concentrating in fashion, so we're not in competition.

We set the earring displays out front. Mixed with her origami cranes are dozens more styles carrying quotes about love or inspiration.

"Wow. You made all these?"

"Earrings pay the rent. I can sell thirty or forty pairs in a day easy. But necklaces, that's harder. Like this one." She unwraps a necklace and arranges it on a black velvet stand. Black-and-white rectangles that look like they're cut out of a graphic novel dangle from two silver chains.

"This is so film noir," I say. "It's like a crime story with a bunch of pages torn out."

"The earrings sold out two months ago, but the necklace is two hundred. If it doesn't sell today, I have to take it apart and make it into earrings."

"But it's perfect."

"Perfect doesn't matter if it doesn't sell."

I vow silently to find a buyer. The necklace is meant to be experienced the way Taysha created it. Taking it apart would destroy the magic.

The air smells of kettle corn by the time the gates open at nine. People flood in and Taysha's booth is soon packed with customers trying on her retro jackets. I'm in constant motion, pairing vintage sunglasses with jackets and showing guys how to knot ties that Taysha refurbished.

Earrings fly off the displays, and by noon we're low on shopping bags. During a lull, Taysha runs to the bathroom, and I message Adam. BUMMED I MISSED YOU LAST NIGHT— WORKING

Adam's helping shoot a sweet sixteen, so I'm surprised he messages right back.

ARTSY?

NOPE WAITRESSING

TOO BAD. FRIENDS WANTED TO MEET YOU

I smile to myself. Sounds like things with the ex are finally resolved. NEXT TIME.

Taysha returns with a bag of kettle corn and I pocket my phone. I'm dying to know what I missed last night, but scrolling for pics of the Late Night Gallery could prompt her to ask questions.

We're crunching away when she nudges me. *Look.*

My mouth falls open. "Oh my God, it's Krell."

CHAPTER 24

ollin Krell's coming our way, but he's not alone. Floppy baby legs dangle from a pouch strapped to his chest, and his wife strolls beside him looking like a Spanish movie star with her long black hair, big sunglasses, and full breasts. It's unsettling how normal he looks.

"His wife's name is Rachel," Taysha says. "She's a contracts lawyer and they met through his art dealer."

"And the baby?" I say, half joking.

"Bennett. But they call him Benny."

"How do you even know that?"

Taysha shrugs. "I pay attention."

I get busy tidying the booth. Krell's the last person I expected to see here today. He steers to the vendor across the aisle and hovers over boxes of Mexican tiles. Meanwhile his wife zeroes in on Taysha's earrings.

Taysha makes eyes at me as Rachel leans over the display. Her lips are a little thin and her teeth aren't perfectly straight, but other than that, Krell's spouse is gorgeous.

Why is she even with him? With her looks, she could probably get any guy she wanted.

Taysha shows her several pairs of earrings, but Rachel waves them away. Still, she seems eager to find something. She reaches for the display in the corner and I make out a spider tattoo on her inner arm.

Rachel could be a match for Taysha's necklace. I set the black velvet display stand in front of her. "Did you see this?"

She takes off her sunglasses and lifts the necklace off the display. "Okay if I try it on?"

"Go ahead." I angle the standing mirror so she can see herself.

The necklace flutters down on her chest, and Rachel plays with the panels, arranging them. "What's this made of?"

"Paper over aluminum, but the chain is silver."

"I'd like to show my husband. He's right over there," she says, pointing to Krell.

"Absolutely."

Taysha and I pretend we're not watching her show off the necklace to Krell. I nudge Taysha. "I swear she's going to buy it."

"That would make my day."

Rachel points to the booth. "Good. They're coming over," Taysha says.

I duck into the clothing racks and start straightening, because as nice as his wife is, I don't want to have to deal with Krell. But I'm close enough to overhear Rachel tell him she plans to pair the necklace with the dress she bought for opening night at Art Basel Miami.

Krell asks Taysha if she takes credit cards, then says, "I know you. You're in my painting class. Taysha Thomas."

"That's right, Professor Krell. Sabine! Look who's here, Professor Krell!"

I could murder you, Taysha. I emerge from the rack of clothes.

"Ah, Sabine Reyes." Krell turns to his wife, who's now juggling the baby. "This is the young woman who won the Zoich Scholarship."

Rachel smiles and her eyes linger on me as if I've been the

subject of one or more discussions. "Congratulations," she says, impressed.

"Um. Thank you."

My head is spinning, because Krell said I won the Zoich as if it was a positive.

"How's the crowd today?" he says as he signs the credit-card slip. "Good spenders?"

"Yeah, sales have been steady."

"Well, good luck selling out."

The Krells walk away and Taysha grabs my wrists. "Rachel Krell's going to wear my necklace at Art Basel Miami!"

We high-five, then Taysha turns to answer a customer's question. My eyes follow Krell through the crowd. *Who* are *you?* I can't believe how nice he acted, how he *bantered* with us like a normal human being.

Krell's savaged me in class, but the way he introduced me to his wife makes me wonder if Adam heard wrong and Krell actually voted for me, not Bryian, to get the Zoich.

The feeling that I shouldn't be stealing into his studio, that I'm being unfair to him, wells up. No, I'm not, I tell myself. He's putting on an act for his wife: the dedicated-instructor-turned-art-world-phenom who still makes an effort to get to know his students. If he gave me even a frac-tion of the guidance he gives Bryian or Bernadette, then I might feel guilty, but I wouldn't be learning a thing from him right now if I wasn't copying his painting.

What does it matter if Krell voted for me to get the Zoich? It doesn't change how he's treated me.

My shoulders pull tight, and I start rolling them to loosen them up. The customer Taysha was helping walks away.

"Have you ever been to the Late Night Gallery?" I say.

"No, but I know Birch from painting class parties there."

The next time Taysha takes a bathroom break, I do a search for pics of last night at the Late Night. The white-walled gallery is lit like the inside of a refrigerator while the parking lot's a party where blue and yellow spotlights carve out the figures of a front man, guitarists, and drummer against a warehouse wall. People are dancing, beer bottles dangling from their raised hands, and I scan the blurry pics trying to find Adam and his friends.

I want this—art and music-soaked nights with Adam and his circle of artist and musician friends, and an opening at every gallery in LA courtesy of a CALINVA degree.

Taysha taps me on the shoulder. "You okay?"

"Yeah, sorry. I zoned out there for a second." Krell isn't on my side, and if there's anything I've learned this year, it's that stars like him and Iona are out only for themselves.

CHAPTER 25

O ver the next few weeks, our assignments at CALINVA ramp up: essays, readings, art projects, and the infamous Cross Dis, a twenty-page paper comparing an artist and a writer with critical commentary on how their work reflects social issues. I'm buried, trying to keep up with what's due, put in my shifts at Artsy and La Petite Tomate, and make progress on my portrait of Julie while stealing precious hours most nights to immerse myself in painting *Duncan*.

There's only three weeks left before Krell's now completed *Duncan* goes on display at a reception at CALINVA, and I lose my intimate access to his artistic genius, so I blow off Kevin's invitation to celebrate Halloween at Caltech and spend most of the night in Krell's studio.

I barely see Adam before he rushes upstairs to paint. His landlord hiked his rent, and he's doing extra gigs with the photographer he works for so he can hold on to his place while completing his painting to show Gavin Brown.

The morning after Halloween I'm parked, bleary-eyed, on a couch in the student lounge, trying to form a coherent thought about Gerhard Richter's blurred photography paintings while Kevin's flopped beside me.

Kevin holds his head between his hands. He smells of

beer and the faint lines of painted whiskers stain his cheeks. "You missed a great party."

I nudge his coffee a little closer. "Yeah, I don't really do parties anymore, but I wish I could have seen you as Goldsinger's cat."

"Schrödinger's cat."

He's so pitiful, I'd like to give him a hug, but instead I pat his shoulder. "You explained it, but I still don't get it. How can the cat be alive and dead at the same time?"

"It's not a real cat," Kevin moans. "It's a paradox."

I sip my coffee, relieved he doesn't ask me about last night. Around eleven, my heart almost stopped when someone tried the door handle of Krell's studio. I'd just picked up the heat gun, but I hadn't yet turned it on, so I carefully set it down and texted Adam. He told me not to panic; it was probably the security guard, checking that all the doors were locked. We joked about it later when we were cleaning up, but I'm still not quite over it.

The thing is, I can't tell Kevin any of this, because he'd never understand why I was there. And I'm pretty sure he'd hate Adam if they ever met.

I can hear it now. *That guy's a poser, Sabine. He's so pretentious.*

Wrong, Kev. Adam's not a poser, he's got real talent. A major art dealer has scheduled a studio visit with him.

I cover my cheeks with my hands so Kevin won't see them turn pink as I remember Adam's hand on my back when we were saying good night.

Kev slurps his coffee, wincing at how even that small motion hurts. He slumps deeper into the couch. "Sunday, two weeks from now. I'm going someplace special. Want to come?"

I'm intrigued that he hasn't said where. "Maybe. Where are you going?"

His pained smile says he's not telling. "Here's a clue. It's transformative."

"Oh. Hell no. You're a Scientologist."

He laughs, then groans, then digs his thumbs into the pressure points by his eyes. "No, I'm Lutheran and I said transform, not convert."

"Fine, I'll go with you to this mysterious place as long as there's no conversion."

"Promise, no conversion," he says, crossing his heart. He closes his eyes. "Think I'll take a little nap."

I dig out my earphones, but before I have them in, Kevin's asleep. I get the feeling he likes me as more than a friend, and the last thing I want to do is mess things up with him.

A part of me feels bad, keeping secrets from him, but I don't need Kevin judging me. I'm doing what I need to do to stay here. Kevin doesn't have to worry about losing a scholarship, and he doesn't have to worry about Krell, because Krell doesn't mentor the sculptors; Ofelo does.

And I know what I'm doing with *Duncan* is right, because I see the progress I've made, how my technical skills are stronger, and the way I use color is more confident, more experimental. I'm close to a breakthrough, to discovering what will take *Julie* to the next level.

Plus, it's not like I'm going to keep doing this forever. In three weeks, painting *Duncan* will be past tense. Over and done.

CHAPTER 26

The next three nights, the security guard is back, rattling Krell's door handle and making me jump each time. Adam tells me to relax. He thinks it's Chuck, the new guy, trying to show his boss he's doing his job.

Adam's convinced Chuck won't enter Krell's studio. The security staff might have keys to get in, but Krell's intimidated most of them into staying clear of him and it.

The deadline for our Color & Theory papers is coming up, so this morning Kevin and I trade laptops during break so we can give each other feedback on our first drafts. Kevin tackles my thoughts on Lois Lowry's *The Giver* and Gerhard Richter's blurred photograph paintings, while I review his about Orwell's *1984* and Franz Kline's abstracts.

I'm only halfway through Kevin's paper when he's finished mine.

Kevin rests his chin on his hand and stares off into space. He's been growing a beard and it creeps along his jaw, curly and untamable.

"That bad?" I say.

He snaps out of his dream state and scrolls up the screen. "No, I think you're on the right track. I like how you compare the way Lowry and Richter use black and white to show the lost connection between people and their pasts. And I especially like when you posit that ambiguity in novels and abstraction in paintings both force the viewer to draw their own conclusions."

"That's a relief. I was afraid it was total bullshit." I spy Taysha run-walking through the lobby, making a beeline for our table. "Did you really just say 'posit'?"

"I could have said 'hypothesize,' but that would have sounded grandiose," Kevin replies.

I roll my eyes at him as Taysha drops into the seat across from us. She leans in, hands splayed over the orange plastic tabletop. "Mona in the administration office just told me one of the grad students got kicked out this morning . . . for stealing art!"

A grad student? "Did Mona say who?"

"No, she wouldn't tell me his name, but apparently this guy went through Ofelo's trash and pulled out piles of sketches, then sold them online."

My chest feels tight. Adam cleans Ofelo's studio, and I know he's hurting for money, but it couldn't be him.

Kevin takes off his glasses and rubs them on his shirt. "What an idiot. How could he think he wouldn't get caught?"

The punishment seems way too harsh for what the guy did. "I can't believe they expelled him. I mean, Ofelo threw the sketches away. He didn't care about them."

Now I wonder if that's why the security guard's been checking Krell's door every night; he's been looking for this guy.

"*Au contraire,*" Taysha throws back. "Ofelo intends to press charges unless the guy turns over all the money he got for the sketches or gets the drawings back."

"If I was Ofelo, I'd go right to the police," Kevin says.

"Hold on," I say. "I get why CALINVA kicked this guy out, but why is selling Ofelo's trash a crime?" It's barely out of my mouth before I wish I could take it back.

"Do I really have to explain it to you?" Taysha says.

"No, I get it. The sketches are Ofelo's intellectual property. Nobody wants their creative ideas stolen and sold behind their back."

Kevin hands me my laptop and reaches for his. "We should get to class."

I slide Kevin's laptop over and slowly pack my stuff. "Save me a seat," I tell Kevin and Taysha. "I'll be there in a sec."

HOW'S IT GOING? I message Adam, but he doesn't answer. The atrium's crowded with people heading to class, and I circle the room, hoping to spot him, but he could be working the loading dock or stretching canvases in the shop or miles away picking up supplies.

Color & Theory class has started when I slip in the door, but luckily Ms. Newsom doesn't notice I'm late, because she's focused on her lecture slides. I take out my laptop and start making notes, but I can't focus.

They kicked a grad student out for selling Ofelo's trash. Even if he stays out of jail, he'll never get accepted to another school. His reputation in the art world is finished, his future's over.

I check my phone, but still nothing from Adam.

The room feels ten degrees hotter than when I sat down, and I peel off my jacket and hang it over the back of my chair.

What I'm doing with Krell's painting isn't stealing, but Krell could argue I'm trespassing, violating his privacy, and copying a painting neither his dealer nor the collector who paid almost a million for it have seen yet.

Who am I fooling? Krell would be furious if he found out what I'm doing.

My armpits are damp and I push up my sleeves, trying to cool down.

That's it. I'm done copying Duncan. *I can't get caught. I could lose everything—my scholarship, CALINVA, this thing I've got going with Adam.*

I glance over at Kevin. He'd never understand what I've done. Taysha? Possibly. But Mrs. Mednikov would be so disappointed.

I'll tell Adam when he meets me here tonight. After he lets me into the building, I'll retrieve my copy of *Duncan* and then break it up and throw it in a dumpster somewhere.

The room cools down to arctic and I shove my jacket back on. This decision feels good. It feels right.

CHAPTER 27

It's been well over an hour and still no response from Adam. I know he's not that guy, the one who got kicked out, but I wish he'd message me back.

My shift at Artsy doesn't start for another half hour, so I'm up on the third floor, hoping to find him. The grad students share a row of studios along this one hall, and I go door to door, examining the ridiculous drawings and weird stuff they tape up in the place of name tags: a troll doll, PayDay candy-bar wrappers, and a smashed robot toy. None of this garbage tells me which studio is his.

Metal blares behind one of the doors, and I'm about to knock and ask whoever's inside if they've seen him, when I stop myself. Adam may be hard up for money, but he's got too much going for him to get involved in anything so stupid as stealing from the faculty.

I head off to Artsy, convinced there's a simple explanation for why he hasn't gotten back to me.

But hours later, he still hasn't returned my message. Adam's usually right on time to meet me, but tonight he's not. I fidget at the back door of CALINVA, convinced he's not coming. The Metro train rattles past, blowing my hair.

If Adam's gone, I'm screwed. I can't get into the locker to retrieve my copy of Krell's painting.

Unless . . . no one opens the locker. The painting could probably sit there for months before the staff decided to check what was in that particular locker.

And then what? The whole school would debate who copied Krell's masterwork, but it's not like CALINVA would dust it for fingerprints.

"Sorry I'm late." Adam strides out of the alley, and I'm so relieved, I run up, ready to fling my arms around him, but he walks right past me and shoves the keys into the lock.

I drop my arms to my sides. "I was worried. I heard one of Ofelo's grad assistants got thrown out."

He makes no move to turn the keys. "You thought I stole Ofelo's sketches?" His voice is barely above a whisper. "That's so insulting."

I never considered how what I said would sound. "I'm sorry," I sputter, "I didn't mean it that way. I knew it wasn't you."

Adam pinches the bridge of his nose and blows out a breath. It feels like forever before he looks up and says, "No need to apologize. I overreacted. Today was a real shit show."

I relax; we're okay.

He starts to turn the keys. "You ready to get to work?" he says.

Now. I need to tell Adam that this little experiment is over. "Yeah, um, maybe I shouldn't work on it anymore."

He tilts his head, curious more than anything else. "Why? You're almost finished."

"This thing today with Ofelo's grad student—it got me thinking. I shouldn't be doing this."

He nods, removes the keys from the lock, and pockets them. "Okay."

I expected a fight, so I'm happy he's okay with how I feel, but I'm still a little thrown. I'm deciding whether to say good night or ask if he wants to get coffee when he says, "Come on. I think we could both use a new point of view."

I trot along beside him around the building to the metal stairs that zigzag up the side. Three stories up, he stops and folds his arms on the railing. "Take a look," he says, and rests his chin on his forearms.

The flying chopstick sculpture is right below. Light slides up and down the thin aluminum pieces as they rock gently in the breeze. We stand side by side on the landing, elbows touching, taking it in.

"Looks totally different from up here, doesn't it?" Adam murmurs.

"Yeah," I say, watching the narrow tips weave together then apart. "I never noticed how the sounds it makes are almost like music."

A minute goes by and Adam says, "You're not doing anything wrong."

I look at him.

"You're not like that guy who stole Ofelo's work. You haven't taken anything from Krell and you're not forging his painting to rip him off, so you shouldn't feel guilty."

"I know," I say, but I guess I'm not very convincing, because Adam says, "Yeah, right." He taps my elbow with his finger. "No guilt. Didn't you tell me that transcribing Krell's painting had made you a better painter?"

"Yeah, I did."

"Then be proud. You did the right thing for your art."

It's true. I did the only thing I could do. It wasn't like Krell was going to help me.

"To be honest," he says, "I barely survived my First-Year Exhibition. The pressure almost killed me, knowing this one show would decide my future here and I had to be my best."

I slide my arms off the railing and wrap them across my chest. One exhibition decides everything. "Yeah, I have to show the faculty I'm good."

"More than good, actually. Exceptional." Adam's still absorbed in the flying chopsticks, but I can't focus. "Who's your biggest competition?"

"I don't know."

"Bullshit," he says gently. "You know exactly who Krell thinks is the best in your class."

I hate to say it, but . . . "Bryian, Bernadette, and David Tito."

"Your TA probably explained about the awards and faculty mentors?"

"Fitz hasn't explained jack," I snap. "Sorry, I'm not mad at you."

"Fitz is a worthless piece of crap." Adam turns and faces me. "The most important thing you need to know is the faculty hands out awards based on the work shown at the First-Year Exhibition, and they choose who to mentor the next year. So Krell isn't the only person you need to impress."

I dig my fingers into my hair and squeeze. If I want to keep the Zoich, I need a mentor to champion me. "God, I want this semester *over*."

Adam stretches out an arm, and I lean in and rest my head on his chest. "Hey. You've got this. You said it yourself: You're close to a breakthrough on your painting."

I want to believe him. I *am* close to a breakthrough, but I'm not there yet and the stakes are so high. I can't believe

I'm saying this, but . . . "I'm almost done with *Duncan*. It feels silly to stop now."

He nods. "Next semester will be easier," he promises.

We go back down and let ourselves into the building. When Adam slides my painting out of the locker, he says, "I can't believe your feel for Krell's work. If I didn't know you painted this, I'd swear he did."

He carries my painting into Krell's studio and places it on the worktable. I lay my jacket over the couch and pull out the materials I need.

I'm lost in thought when I sense Adam by my side. I glance up and he's looking at me with what feels like wonder. "You can be a great artist, Sabine. Don't be afraid to risk it all."

Electricity travels down my arms, and I stare into his eyes, waiting for his kiss. I lean in, sensing it's about to happen, but he steps back. "I shouldn't interfere with your work."

"Yep, good thinking," I answer, but what I want to say is, *No, please interfere.*

Adam cracks open the door and checks the hall. "I'll be down at nine thirty," he says. The door closes behind him, and I need to get started, but first I walk over and try the handle, making sure it's locked.

SKETCH #4

SELF-PORTRAIT, April 10

This drawing guts me every time I look at it.

I stand in the inky ocean, the water up to my knees, suitcases in both hands, my profile to the viewer. My long coat drags in the waves like a collapsed sail, and my belongings litter the sand: torn photographs of Mom, her shattered guitar, ripped sheets of music.

I drew the suitcases, scattered sheet music, and shattered guitar because I couldn't bear to draw the urn I'd carried into the surf. Even after changing it up, halfway through the drawing, I put down my pen, exhausted.

I remember closing my sketchbook when my art teacher sat down beside me at the table. I didn't want her commenting on what I'd drawn. Ms. Pensel had asked me to come to her classroom after school and I'd almost skipped out on her because I had to meet the rest of the cleaning crew in Tarzana by four.

"How's it going, living with Hayley and her family?" she said, her fingers drumming a large white envelope.

"We're getting along fine," I replied, omitting how I moved out when I overheard Hayley's parents talk about turning me over to Social Services.

"CALINVA's been trying to reach you."

I focused on the art projects dotting the walls, because I didn't want to tell her I'd already told CALINVA I wasn't coming. They didn't give me any money, so there was no way I could attend. "I haven't been checking my email."

Her eyebrows pinched, but she slid the envelope across her desk. "Open it."

I flipped it over and found the Zoich logo blazed across the front. "Oh my God," I remember saying.

Ms. Pensel pulled me out of my chair and threw her arms around me. "You won," she cried, her voice wobbling with excitement. "Didn't I tell you you could do it?"

I nodded yes, but whatever she said next I didn't hear; my ears had filled with static. I had a full ride to CALINVA. Tuition, books, art supplies, basic living expenses.

"How is this even possible?" I said when we were sitting down again. "I gave up hope a month ago."

"I never did. The portfolio you sent in—*squisito!*" she said, kissing her fingertips.

My phone buzzed and I glanced at the time. "Ms. Pensel, I need to go, but I want to thank you. Not just for helping me put my portfolio together for CALINVA, but for everything. The last four years—" My throat was closing up. She'd gone out of her way for me: scholarships, contests, invites to openings. My voice shook as I said, "I want you to know it means a lot."

"A student with your talent comes along once in a decade. What kind of teacher would I be if I didn't embrace the challenge of nurturing that talent?"

She hugged me good-bye and I took off across campus. The hell I was going through would soon be over. All I had to do was make it through the summer, and I'd be immersed in art, surrounded by people who lived and breathed it the way I did.

In the school parking lot, I set the envelope on the passenger seat, ducked behind a Suburban, and pulled on my Merry Mop pants and tunic. Barreling up the freeway, I set my hand on the envelope. *Look, Mom. I'm going to be okay.*

CHAPTER 28

The First-Year Exhibition is only a few weeks away, and Krell has us bring in our preliminary studies for the pieces we plan to show. The room is unusually packed for first period; no one has skipped class.

Wooden easels buck and scrape as my classmates drag them across the floor, looking for the spot with the best light to display their work.

Bernadette and Bryian have angled their easels in a corner of the room like they're defending the keep. Sheets of thick plastic cover both their paintings, while everyone else is busy unwrapping theirs.

I unpack the small acrylic study of Julie. I've started the actual painting, but it's two feet by three, too awkward to lug around. Plus, the study is more detailed and finished, so Krell will have a better idea of what the final painting will look like.

We all wait by our easels, stealing glances at our neighbors' work. Tensions have run high since the rumor went out that six gallery owners have accepted invitations to the show.

Krell goes around the room and everyone pretends to be busy, but they're listening in to what Krell says to the person who's presenting their painting to him. Bernadette is even more blatant, shadowing Krell like a stalker.

I twist my hair up off my neck and shove a pencil through it. I've been a wreck for the last twenty-four hours, and I replay Adam's pep talk from last night.

"Don't be nervous about tomorrow. Krell's going to see how much progress you've made."

I was wiping my brushes clean while Adam perched on the table beside me. "He hasn't looked at my work in days," I answered.

"You underestimate how far you've come. I bet you'll have a solo show lined up before you graduate."

His praise thrills me again, even though I fought believing him. "I doubt it. I heard the chances of getting a solo show are about one in a hundred?"

"Closer to one in two hundred, but you've got that level of talent."

I roll up on my toes and down a couple times, trying to quiet my nerves. I hate to run, but right now I could use a few laps.

Krell nods and points to areas on people's paintings, then waves his hand to suggest they delete something or spreads his fingers to suggest they expand it. My classmates' faces scrunch up in concentration.

The risks I've taken lately . . . I hope they've been worth it. I can see with my own eyes that my technique is better than ever, but Krell cares about more than technique.

I wish Kevin would joke with me, but he's caught up in making sure the motor attached to his mock-up is working.

His piece, *Unresolved*, is unique. Fifty narrow strips of canvas flip in random patterns so the painting changes every sixty seconds. Mathematically speaking, there are hundreds of ways to experience it.

Next to this, my study feels mundane. It doesn't matter that I'm a better painter. Kevin's challenged the limits of painting.

Now it's Kevin's turn and I shift from foot to foot as Krell questions him about color choice and directionality. "Are the two sides opposing forces or are they meant to reveal aspects of one another?"

I envy the way Kevin answers so calmly.

The last thing Krell tells him is, "Watch your execution. There's a real danger your piece will be perceived as cute or gimmicky."

Krell pauses to scribble in his little leather notebook, and Kevin wipes his forehead on his sleeve. He gives me a look. *That was brutal.*

"You're up," Krell says, turning to me.

Out of the corner of my eye, I spy Bernadette behind him. She'd walked away when Krell critiqued Kevin, but she's back, vulturing over Krell's shoulder.

He comes around the easel and I resist the urge to pick up *Julie* and hold it to my chest. Krell peers at my painting. "This is the homeless woman who stands out on Raymond."

"Yes," I say, surprised he recognized her.

"You're romanticizing the homeless." His voice is thoughtful, almost concerned.

"I didn't think I was doing that," I say quietly. "I thought I was capturing who she is." I hold up her photo and he takes it from my hand.

"Ms. Reyes, it is not enough to capture a person's essence in a portrait."

I try not to sigh. The hours I've spent with his painting have given me a sense of what Krell means. His portraits aren't literal portraits, but if I had to explain why they work, I couldn't. "I'm sorry, but I don't get what else I'm supposed to do."

I expect Krell to smirk and say something cutting, but instead he nods. "Think of it this way: Portraiture should force the viewer to contribute their own perceptions. How can you involve the viewer? Make them fill in missing information, question their assumptions about the subject, examine their prejudices?"

He hands the photo back to me. "You can render Julie perfectly, but how will you get people to really look at her?"

I stare back at him, thunderstruck. For the first time, I understand what Krell has been trying to teach me.

"Study portraits by Willy Steam, Francis Bacon, or Cindy Sherman," he says. "Steam, especially. You can't walk by one of his paintings without trying to fill in the blanks."

"Okay, yeah, I'll do that."

"All right, then. Good start."

He moves on to Bernadette, and I let out the breath I was holding in. At this instant, I feel as if the barrier between me and what I need to learn is lifting. My grasp is slippery, but I'm beginning to sense where I need to go from here.

What Krell told me to look for in Steam's and Bacon's and Sherman's work is what he does in his: arrests the viewer and gets them to question the story.

Now I have to find a way to do that in mine.

Across the room, Bernadette nods at Krell, her face serious. Her painting's uncovered, and I make out the figure of a man formed by hundreds of small brown paint strokes on the white canvas. *What?* I move closer, and goose bumps shoot up my arms.

What I thought was brown paint turns out to be thorns. *Actual thorns.*

"What you're doing with this piece," Krell tells Bernadette, "embodies CALINVA's artistic mission."

Questioning. Provoking. Agitating. *Crap, he loves it.*

Bernadette notices me behind him, and the smile she gives me feels like a challenge.

Everyone's been talking about the awards the faculty gives out after the exhibition, and how the instructors select a student to mentor based upon their work.

I wind my way over to Taysha. "Correct me if I'm wrong, but is Bernadette a stone-cold killer?"

Taysha cocks her head at me. "All-star girls' volleyball champion three years running."

"I should have seen that coming."

"Leopard can dye her hair pink, but she can't change her spots."

Adam tried to warn me about my peers competing for the faculty's approval. I return to my easel, my neck prickling.

Class ends and people start packing up. Kevin carefully rests his prototype in a cardboard box lined with foam. "You know what you need to do for Krell?" he asks.

"Yeah, I think so."

He shoves out his fist and we bump.

I need to look at Krell's painting in a different way—to look beyond the layers of color and brushstrokes for how Krell relates to the person he's painting and what he wants to say with his art. If I can figure out why he does that, I can get there, too.

I put *Julie* away, and before I walk out, I text Adam. SURVIVED KRELL'S CRITIQUE

KNEW YOU WOULD—TAKING RISKS PAYS OFF.

Yeah, sure does. If I hadn't spent hours staring at *Duncan*, I'd probably be hopelessly confused by what Krell told me to do today. I've got another week before Krell's painting leaves his studio, and I need to use that time well.

My painting can't just be good. It has to be extraordinary.

CHAPTER 29

I thought *Duncan* was a window into Krell, but it turns out it's not exactly transparent. The next few nights, I puzzle over what he is saying with his art while I try to capture *Duncan* with my brush.

Duncan is part of a series Krell's painted in which the faces seem to disintegrate, but no matter how hard I try, I can't explain why his faces shed pieces like autumn leaves. Trying to figure out what's in Krell's head feels like trying to see through milk.

And when I ask Adam what he thinks, he tells me I need to discover the answer for myself.

Krell could be saying anything, so I search through interviews and academic journals, only to discover that he refuses to reveal why. "Look at the work," he tells every critic or journalist who asks.

Saturday is supposed to be the day I fix my painting, but when my alarm rings, a thought pins me to my bed. If I can't figure this out, I might as well give up trying to be a real artist and go back to making dog portraits.

I force myself to get out of bed. I throw on Mom's old kimono and scuff into the kitchen. Mrs. Mednikov looks up from her *Paris Match*. "You do not look well, Sabine."

"I'm tired." I take a bagel out of the bag and stare at it. It's too much work to toast it.

"You should go back to bed."

"I can't. I have to work on my painting for the First-Year Exhibition."

"My art was my medicine," Mrs. Mednikov muses over her coffee. "When I danced, I forgot the pain in my feet and my aching back. I would lose myself in the music."

Her story could be mine. "I used to lose myself in my painting. But not lately."

"This instructor of yours, he's made you doubt yourself."

"He makes me question what I'm doing."

"It is good to question, but deadly to doubt. You cannot leap if you are afraid to fall. That is how you get injured."

I smile. "I wish my mom could have met you."

"I wish I could have met her as well. What would she tell you if she was sitting in this kitchen?"

"Stop moaning and go paint."

"Succinct, your mother."

"Yeah, she didn't waste words."

I reach for the knife, cut the bagel in half, and pop it into the toaster. Mrs. Mednikov and I watch a squirrel spring about the branches of the purple-leaved maple outside the window as we eat.

After breakfast, I huddle in a blanket on a wicker chair on the still-cold sunporch. My hands hug the coffee cup perched on my knees.

Look at the work.

Is Krell saying the truth about a person is elusive, that it can't be captured in a painting—because while he's painting someone, what is true about them is already changing or disintegrating?

I sip my coffee and a thought creeps up on me. I don't

need to know exactly what's in Krell's head, because he's gotten into mine. *Look at the work.*

He wants me to be involved—to contribute my perceptions, to question my assumptions.

Look at the work. *Engage.*

I peer at my unfinished canvas of *Julie* and the study I made for it. I haven't gone far enough. I don't want someone to just look at Julie, I want people to see they're wrong about her. That she's so much more than what they assume when they spy a homeless woman standing on a street corner.

I set down the coffee and stare out the windows. Bright yellow mums as big as my fist dot the garage wall. One is bobbing up and down, and as I follow it with my eyes a memory sweeps over me.

I'm walking to a convenience store with three kids from Advanced Art when we step around a woman pushing a shopping cart piled with mismatched bags. The two guys Josie and I are with snigger and start to crack crude jokes about her so loudly there's no way she can't hear them.

She's dressed so carefully, in a yellow skirt and matching jacket, and little white gloves that aren't the cleanest, and I know how hard she must work to look the way she does. As Josie and I walk by her, I want to stop and apologize for the two jerks I'm with. I sense this wasn't always her life, that she might have been a teacher or worked in an office, but something, an illness or an accident maybe, wrenched her out of that world.

I want to apologize, but my classmates are right there, so I don't. I'm too aware that if they knew how I sleep in my car, and shower in the gym, and stay late in the safety of the auditorium while the theater kids rehearse, they'd judge me just like they judged her.

It's so easy to judge, I think, to assume a hundred things about people that are untrue, or to blame them for their problems. It's the opposite of seeing them.

I throw off my blanket and scramble out of the chair. This painting isn't about me, I try telling myself. It's about Julie.

But the edge between a normal life and being homeless is razor thin. One accident can push you from one into the other, from being seen to being judged.

I turn the canvas sideways as an image forms in my head. Not one painting, but two on the same canvas, side by side.

One is in color. Julie the way I see her, realistic, but with her aura of bliss that confounds me. But the second panel is black and white. Julie with a dirty rat on her shoulder, the brushstrokes savage and unhinged. Her face is a black smudge, her identity muted. The second panel is the way the world sees her, the fears and prejudices and assumptions about her exposed.

Two images, same woman.

A title comes to me: *Seen/Not Seen*.

I'm trembling, because I've never felt so right about a painting before, and I grin, because right now I don't care what Krell thinks or if he likes it. This painting is mine.

SKETCH #5

HAYLEY & ME, July 30

I sketched us from the selfie Hayley sent me. In the drawing, we're smiling, heads together, sunglasses holding back our hair—two girls spending a hot summer day at a beach club, not a care in the world.

But when I finished sketching, I dragged a flat white eraser across my face. My features muted, faded into the paper, until all that was left were memories of our friendship.

I've drawn dozens of pictures of Hayley, and even though this is one of the better ones, I can't send it to her.

Hayley and I got together the last week before she headed east to Brown. We hadn't seen each other since graduation, but she invited me to the beach club.

I picked out two lounge chairs on the sand under a big canvas umbrella and waited for Hayley to arrive. She blew onto the beach, and I leaped up into a hug that felt more theater than real.

Hayley asked if I'd had any trouble getting past the guys at reception and I told her no, they remembered me from last summer. I didn't tell her I arrived an hour early so I could shave my legs in a hot shower and wash my hair.

Her phone kept buzzing, and in between texts she told me about who was with who and the parties I'd missed and graduation night at Disneyland.

She asked how it was living with Mom's cousin Dolores, and I told her fine, but left out how I made Dolores up so Social Services wouldn't get its hands on me.

Hayley asked how I was staying so skinny, and I told her about the diet where you eat for eight hours and fast for sixteen, but left out that I could only afford two meals a day, so it wasn't hard to stay on.

She told me how she and her roommate were decorating their dorm room. I told her about the room I was moving into at Mrs. Mednikov's, but left out how I hocked Mom's guitar to pay the first month's rent when I didn't get my check from the Zoich in time.

When we ran out of things to say, Hayley asked if I wanted the staff to bring us some lunch, and I said I was craving a seared ahi salad.

I left out how the women I'd cleaned with all summer spoke no English so there were entire days when I barely spoke.

I left out how no one knew my name anywhere I went. How no one knew I was an artist, how no one had told me they loved me or told me they missed me in months.

I left out how I spent my birthday taking in a free movie at a cemetery so I'd be surrounded by happy people.

I left out how this summer left me feeling erased.

CHAPTER 30

My breakthrough on *Seen/Not Seen* has me so excited I have to fight the urge to bail on Kevin. There are so many assignments due this week, and only a few nights left in which to learn from *Duncan*, so giving up most of Sunday, the one day I have free to paint, is killing me, but I promised Kev I'd go on his mystery trip.

During the ten minutes while I wash up and brush my teeth, Kevin worms his way into Mrs. Mednikov's kitchen. I emerge from the bathroom to find them chatting over coffee, a brown paper bag by his elbow that I suspect is full of the kolaches Mrs. Mednikov baked last night.

My face must convey my confusion. Kevin told me he'd message me when he got here. "Good morning?"

Mrs. Mednikov looks pleased with herself, but Kevin's not so sure. "I hope you don't mind," he says. "Stephania invited me in."

Stephania? Even I don't use Mrs. Mednikov's first name.

"I spied him creeping up my steps like a stray cat," she says, deadpan.

Kevin waves his finger at her like they've been playing mah-jongg together for years and he knows her tricks. "All I did was put the newspaper on the step, and the security light came on."

They're both much more awake than I am. "I'll be ready in five."

"There's no hurry," Kevin calls as I retreat to my bedroom.

When I come out, Mrs. Mednikov tells me he's outside warming up the car. "I like your young man," she says.

"He's not my—" She thinks he's the guy I'm spending my evenings with, an assumption I don't want to correct just yet. "Yeah, I like Kevin, too."

Kevin's got the Kia's motor running, and he's even stuck a pillow in my seat so I can sleep. "Front seat's pretty cramped, but—"

"Trust me, I can sleep anywhere." I settle in and prop the pillow against the door. "A two-hour drive? This had better be worth it."

"I can't promise, but I think you'll thank me when we get there."

When I wake up, the sun's up and I'm stiff from leaning against the car door. Kevin brushes crumbs off his jeans. "You're awake."

"Almost." A sign along the highway says we're in Santa Barbara.

"You weren't lying when you said you could sleep in the car."

I freeze for a sec before I remember our conversation. "Ugh. Was I snoring?"

"I wouldn't say snoring. More like snorting."

I bury my face in my hands. "Embarrassing."

"Nah. I'm just jerking your chain. You don't really snort— it's more like a snuffle." He imitates me, snuffling delicately like a cartoon character.

"You tease your sisters a lot, don't you?"

"All the time. And that's why I'm their favorite brother."

"Aren't you their only brother?"

Kevin smiles, and I harrumph and reach into the crumpled paper bag between us. It's almost empty, but a few prune pastries are left. "I guess you liked the kolaches."

"Especially the poppy-seed ones. I haven't had any that good since I was in Poland."

"Of course you were in Poland." I lick jam off my fingers and the last exit in Santa Barbara sails by. "We're not stopping in Santa Barbara?"

"No, but we are minutes from our destination. Be patient."

"I'm not patient."

"Clearly."

Kevin turns up the music. It's guitars and mandolins, folky and contemporary at the same time. The sky is clear and hills rise up on the right, dry and yellow, aching for rain. I crack the window and cool air blows across my face.

In a few miles, Kevin turns off the highway and I glimpse the ocean as we turn onto an access road. We pass a few scattered houses before Kevin pulls into a gravel parking lot. "We're here."

We get out of the car by a grassy lot. There's not much to see. A group of trees a little way off. An elementary school across the road. "O-kay."

"It's worth it, I promise." Kevin pulls a backpack out of the trunk. "This way," he says, and heads for the end of the parking lot.

We follow a dirt path into a grove of eucalyptus. The path dips up and down, and our footsteps are muffled by dust. Seagulls cry overhead, and I smell the ocean even though I can't see it.

We walk for about a mile before Kevin slows and holds up a finger. Sun filters through the trees, striping the yellow-gray bark. Bright blue sky fills the gaps between the trunks. Everything is hushed and even the gulls are silent.

As beautiful as this place is, I wonder why we drove two hours to get to it. Then an orange butterfly wobbles into the sunlight. I follow the monarch with my eyes as another flutters into the clearing, then another.

Kevin taps my arm and points to a nearby branch, and I gasp and walk forward. This branch, and every branch nearby, is weighed down with butterflies—hundreds, maybe thousands of butterflies.

Their wings are folded, exposing tan undersides veined with black. Still and silent, the butterflies look like leaves, until one stretches, and then ten more pop orange.

"Do they live here?" I whisper.

"Just for the winter. They come down from Canada."

A dozen paths wind through the grove, and we explore them silently. My heart slows, matching the rhythm of the place.

Mom would have loved this. I picture her, sitting cross-legged on a fallen log, humming a melody under her breath, her fingers picking out chords on an invisible guitar. I glance at Kevin, grateful he feels no need to speak.

We stay until we hear the squeals of excited children, then we walk out of the grove, not speaking until we reach the cliff's edge and see the ocean below. The water is gray-blue striped with green. White foam swirls and sloshes below the cliff.

"My mom would have loved this place," I say.

Kevin's quiet, as if he's waiting for me to tell him more

about her, but instead I ask, "Why did you bring me here?"

He blows out a breath, and I'm surprised by how different, how much older he looks from two months ago. How did I not notice?

He's smiling, but not happily. "Caltech messes with my head, and sometimes I need to get out of there before I lose it."

"But you're so smart."

"Everyone in my class was valedictorian of their high school. One of my roommates interns at the Jet Propulsion Lab and the other won the Intel Science Fair."

"I don't know what either of those is, but they sound really impressive."

"Yeah. They are. The competition is . . ." He shrugs. There are no words.

I wrap an arm around his waist and he leans into me. "I didn't know it was that bad at Caltech. When you're at CALINVA you act like everything's cool."

"Everything *is* cool at CALINVA. But if I don't get my engineering grades up, you're not going to see me around next semester."

"No! Why not?"

"The only way I could get my dad to agree to let me enroll part-time at CALINVA was to promise I'd get A's in my classes at Caltech."

"And?"

"It's not looking good."

"Oh, Kev, I'm so sorry." I look into his face, and our eyes connect, and what I see is an opening, an opening to *more*.

I drop my arm from his waist and grope for something to say. I knew Kev liked me, and I should have been more careful not to give him the wrong idea. "Maybe you'll surprise yourself and ace the finals."

Kevin's eyes flicker as he registers that I've pulled back, but he acts like what just happened didn't happen. "Yeah, it's not impossible if I put in the hours."

The tone of his voice has changed. He could be talking to anyone.

A sadness I didn't expect washes through me, and it takes a moment before I grasp what it's telling me: I care about Kevin more than I realized.

I've been so caught up with Adam, I've been blind to what I have or could have with Kevin. And now I've hurt him even though I didn't mean to.

Kev's silence feels endless. "You want to head back?" I ask.

"Sure," he says, patting his stomach. "I could use something to eat."

We walk back to the car. I hate to imagine CALINVA without Kevin making me laugh and keeping me from flying out of orbit.

But what if my future is with Adam, the two of us taking LA's art world by storm?

CHAPTER 31

We're not even through Santa Barbara when Kevin pulls off so we can eat at a legendary taco stand. Either Kevin's a really good actor, or he's not as wounded as I thought, because he's his usual famished self.

The place is tiny, whitewashed, with turquoise trim around the door and windows and zigzag roof, and the line of customers is out the door.

"Look, they make their tortillas fresh." Kevin points through the window at the woman working the tortilla press.

"Do you eat tacos every day?" I ask.

"Almost. I have to make up for the eighteen years I lived in a place where guacamole comes in a squeeze bottle."

"No, that's just wrong."

"Hence my quest to eat as many tacos as I can before I go back to Kansas, land of the squeeze bottle."

I clamp my hands over my ears. "Stop saying 'squeeze bottle.' Don't make me picture it."

Kevin mouths the words in front of my face. *Squeeze. Bottle.*

I jab him with my elbow.

Our eyes connect, and we gaze at each other for an inexplicably long moment until Kev says, "Okay, okay, I'm done," and we flip back to the menu board.

We order chorizo tacos for me and posole extra spicy for Kevin. A table opens right as our order comes up and I dive for it. Kevin digs into his posole while I assemble my tacos. When I look up, his face is red and he's wiping his nose on a napkin.

"Hot enough for you?"

He nods, eyes closed, and I'm not sure if he's happy or hurting.

"Real sexy," I say. "The snot. It's a big turn-on."

Kevin mumbles something.

"Save it," I tell him. "You should consider performance art. Watching you eat has changed my experience of Mexican food forever."

He takes a last mouthful and drags his wrist over his sweaty forehead. "Man, that was good."

The sleeve of his tee rides up, revealing the tattoo on his bicep. "Aw, you've got a tattoo of the BFG?"

Kevin hooks his sleeve with a finger and pulls it back. "Yeah, my sister Toby used to call me the Big Friendly Giant because I'd read her to sleep when we were little. Not gonna repeat what she calls me now."

"How old is she?"

"Fifteen. Toby's 'testing boundaries.'"

I laugh. "Yeah, fifteen's not pretty."

"What about you? What's the story behind your tattoos?"

"No tattoos," I say. "My mom always joked that the wrong tattoo was like a bad relationship: easy to get into, and impossible to get out of. She made me promise I'd wait until I found a design that had real meaning for me, and now . . ."

I pick a slice of jalapeño off the table and drop it on my plate, not sure how the sentence ends.

Kevin smooths his sleeve back down. "Back at the grove, you said your mom would have loved it. Does that mean she . . ."

He leaves his question unfinished, but I nod, and my eyes fill. "Last February."

"Jeez. I'm sorry."

"Thanks, it's been rough."

He reaches over and squeezes my hand. My fingers wrap around his.

"Can I ask . . . ?"

"How? Hit-and-run."

I know Kevin's thinking it's horrifying what happened to her, to me. It's all over his face and the way he's taking me in, so I'm surprised when all he says is, "And your dad?"

"Not in the picture. Not now. Not ever."

He pauses, weighing what I said. "I've never heard you mention any brothers or sisters."

I shrug and give him a half smile, because I can't say it aloud. I'm alone.

His eyes pinch as if he's in pain. "How did you . . . did someone take you in?"

"Hayley, my best friend; her parents let me stay with them." I stop there. Kevin doesn't need to know what happened next.

He squeezes my hand one last time before he lets go. Then he takes a long drink of his soda, giving us both space to recover. The truth is heavy and now he's carrying some of its weight.

When he's done, he looks at me over his cup and his brown eyes are soft. "Tell me something about your mom."

It's an invitation I didn't know I wanted. I dab the last traces of hot sauce off my mouth. "Her name was Crystal, but she went by Crys, and before she had me, she was a singer-songwriter. If she'd been at the grove with us today, I think she would've been inspired to write a song about it."

"Yeah? What about?"

I mull over this for a moment before I answer. "About butterflies traveling thousands of miles to go home. About having the faith to start an impossible journey."

"You really love her."

My heart squeezes hearing him say "love" instead of "loved." My love for Mom will never be past tense.

"Yeah, I do," I manage to say, but I'm not sure he can hear me.

A helpless look comes over Kevin's face. He doesn't know how to make this better.

I have to turn things around, so I say, "I'm picking up her guitar tomorrow! This bachelorette party left me an outrageous tip last night, so I can finally ransom it."

"Is it an acoustic?"

"Yeah, custom made."

"Who do you have to ransom it from?"

I could kick myself for saying that. It's embarrassing, being so desperate for money I had to pawn it. "A guy who does repairs. It was a small— The neck got chipped and I didn't want it to get worse."

"I'd love to see it once you get it back."

Once again, I sense I've missed something. "Do you play guitar?"

"Guitar, mandolin, banjo, but I doubt I'm anywhere near as good as your mom."

"Probably not," I say, and toss him a grin, "but I'd like to hear you anyway."

People crowd against our table, waiting for their orders. I sweep our crumpled napkins into a pile. "We should probably let someone else have the table."

Kevin stacks our plates. "Yeah, I should get back. Physics test tomorrow."

On the drive, wind whips through the car. Kevin listens to music, and I watch the ocean fly by the open window. The highway follows the rocky coastline, and my breath catches.

We're not far from where I waded in to sprinkle Mom's ashes, and I see it again, the trail of white ribboning away from me on the water.

My anger flares. *Why did it have to be her, God? Why not somebody else?*

"What are you thinking about?"

It's the first thing Kev's said in a half hour, so it's a real question. "How angry I am at God."

He looks from me to the road, before he says, "For what happened to your mom?"

"It isn't fair. She'd made up for every bad thing she'd ever done. She lived clean, ate right, and never crossed a line . . . and a guy mowed her down with his car like a stray dog. He didn't even stop."

Everything I need Kevin to say is in the look on his face and the hand that reaches for mine. What happened is horrible, and unfair, and completely indefensible, and what he has to offer me is this: that I am not alone.

We stay like that for a few miles, and I squeeze his hand before I let go.

Kevin turns off the freeway, heading east on a two-lane

highway through orange groves and fields of cabbage and brussels sprouts. I steal glances at him. CALINVA would be so different if I didn't have Kevin to talk to.

I try to picture Adam and me talking about Mom, but I can't. We talk about our work and Krell and the LA art scene, but now that I think about it, Adam never asks about my life outside of school.

"You'd better nail that physics exam," I say, only half joking.

Kev gives me an easy smile. "I'll do my best."

It's midafternoon by the time he drops me off outside Mrs. Mednikov's. I say thanks and good-bye, but before I can cross the street, Kev calls me back. I grin and shake my head as I saunter over to the driver's-side window. "What now?"

He hooks a finger on the strap of my bag. "I'm good at keeping secrets, just so you know."

"Yeah, I figured that out." I'd never have told him a tenth of what I did otherwise.

He drives away and I wander back inside the house. Kevin thinks I'm like him, that my secrets are merely things I want to keep private, not things I'm scared to let out. I doubt he's ever had to hide who he is, and I'm sure he's never had to hide what he's done.

People say sharing secrets makes you closer, but not mine.

CHAPTER 32

Pawning Mom's guitar was like cutting out my heart, but I'd sold everything I could to make it through the spring and summer, and I needed my first month's rent for Mrs. Mednikov. Today, I get that piece of my heart returned.

After Color & Theory, I have just enough time to run over to the pawnshop, liberate Mom's guitar, stow it in my car, and make it to Artsy before my shift.

The pawnshop is two blocks west of CALINVA, and a continent away from the boutiques on Colorado Boulevard. The black-painted steel bars over the front door are peeling, and a thick coat of dust blurs the jewelry in the windows. Inside, the walls are lined with abandoned guitars, and the glass counters are full of cast-off wedding rings. If you're shopping for broken dreams, this is the place.

I tug my tee down in front, exposing the lacy trim on my purple bra. Steve, the guy working the counter, was very helpful to me last August, which I'm pretty sure wasn't because he loved the red roses on Mom's guitar.

The man behind the counter buzzes me in, but it turns out he isn't Steve. His bulbous nose is shot with red capillaries, and his graying hair is tied back in a stringy ponytail. His faded short-sleeve shirt is almost transparent from being washed so many times.

"Can I help you?" he says as he focuses his watery gray eyes on me.

"Is Steve here?"

"Not today. You sure I can't help you?"

I set my pawn ticket on the counter. Gold watches on faded green velvet gleam dully through the glass below. "I'm here to pick up my guitar."

"Name."

My hand tightens around the thick wad of cash in my jacket pocket, and I give him my name.

"The loan was due on the first," he says.

"Yeah, I know I'm a few weeks late, but I have the money." I pull it out. "There's four hundred I borrowed and the hundred and fifteen in interest."

He counts out the money twice, turning the bills so they face the same way. He tests the twenties with a special pen, looking for fakes, and shuts the cash in the register.

"So can I have my guitar?"

"Absolutely. As soon as you pay the rest of what you owe. One-month interest, late fee, storage fee. Total's seventy dollars."

"Seventy?" The twenty in my wallet's got to last until my next waitress shift on Friday. "I don't have that."

The man flips over my pawn ticket. "Reread the terms of our agreement. On the first of December you'll owe the seventy plus five dollars interest on it, and another thirty-five dollars late fee and storage fee."

"Okay." I stuff the pawn ticket back in my pocket. This wasn't the way things were supposed to go. "Can I see it?"

The man's mustache sags over his mouth. "Promise you won't try to run out with it."

"Yeah, no, I won't. I just—"

"Wait here."

There are cameras in the corners, and if I had to guess I bet there's a loaded gun hidden by the register.

The man returns with the battered black guitar case. He lays it ever so gently on the counter, then steps back like he's trying to give me privacy.

My eyes smart as soon as I see the white line of words that run clumsily down the case. THE SMALLEST BIRD SINGS THE PRETTIEST SONGS. My heart opens and is submerged.

I run my hand over the words, then carefully flip open the clasps so they don't make a sound. The blond spruce body nestles in folds of dark crimson velvet. My eyes trace the red roses that twine from the pick guard under the strings and up the fingerboard to the headstock.

"Go ahead and play it if you want."

"I wish," I tell him. "I can barely pick out a tune. My mom, she—"

He nods, freeing me from saying any more. I close the lid. He picks up the case and sets it behind the counter.

"Thanks, I appreciate you letting me see it," I say, and start for the exit. I have my hand on the door when I turn back to the guy. "You won't sell it, will you?"

"Not as long as you keep paying down your debt."

Out on the sidewalk, the sun half blinds me, and I flip down my shades.

Rent. Car insurance. Food. Gas. Phone. No way I can squeeze out another $110 in two weeks.

I hoof it toward work, stopping only to throw my portfolio in the back of my car. Two hands on the hatchback, I shove it closed. Should I sell the car and get a bike?

My stomach lurches, imagining it gone. It's my life raft. I can't give it up.

Nope, the car stays. For now.

So what am I going to do? I can't lose Mom's guitar again.

I storm up the street. Add another waitress shift? I'm barely getting my class assignments done now. I'd be better off selling something, but there's not much in my closet anyone would want except Iona's boots.

If Taysha's right, Hollywood Redux would probably give me at least two hundred for them, but not with the torn heel. Damn. The only shoe-repair guy I trust to fix it is way over on the west side.

Nothing's ever easy, is it?

CHAPTER 33

It's one of my last nights working on *Duncan*, and from the moment I pull out my brushes, I struggle. I prop my painting up on an easel right next to Krell's, but I can't get the shapes or textures right, can't get a rhythm going, can't even match the spruce blue that Krell used on the man's shoulder. By the time Adam appears to help me tidy up, I've already started cleaning my brushes.

Adam snaps open a garbage bag and drops my used paper towels in it. "I thought I saw you over on Fair Oaks today," he says.

Great. He saw me by the pawnshop. "Oh yeah?"

"I was riding by on my bike, and I called your name, but you didn't turn around."

I'm tempted to say it wasn't me, but I'm so freaking tired of pretending to be "artist poor" and not "real poor."

"I was trying to get my mom's guitar out of hock, but I didn't have enough money."

"That blows. Here, let me help." He shoves his hand deep in his jeans and pulls out some crumpled bills. Two fives and a bunch of ones. "How much do you need?"

"You're sweet, but a lot more than that."

"Tell me how much. I could borrow it from a guy I know."

"You shouldn't borrow money to give to me when you're worried about rent."

"Let me help. It feels like this is important to you."

Adam's been so good to me, I can't let him do this. "Thanks, but really, I don't need you to give me the money. I've got this."

"All right. But if you change your mind . . ."

"I'll let you know."

I check the worktable to see if I've missed anything, and I have. There's one last can of blue paint over by the easels.

I scoop it up with my hand, but as I turn, my foot hits a waxy spot on the cement and I'm falling. My hand hits the table, and the can flies out of my fingers.

I come down hard on my thigh while the can bounces off something onto the floor and rattles toward the wall. I lie there, dazed, trying to catch my breath.

"Oh shit," Adam says, his voice tinted with panic. He's rushing around, and I hear him tearing paper towels. "Are you all right?"

I nod and sit up. My thigh hurts, but— "I don't think I broke anything."

Adam's not even looking at me. He's too busy trying to stop the rivulets of waxy pigment flowing down Krell's canvas. A dark blue streak cuts across Duncan's cheek.

"Oh no," I murmur.

"Get me some clean rags. Now!"

I scramble to my feet and dig out a pile of rags from Krell's stash under the sink. I hand them to Adam. "What should I do now?"

"Pick that fucking can off the floor and wipe the paint off the cement."

I wipe the floor while Adam swears behind me, a nail-gun fire of anger.

Once it's clean, I go back to where Adam's working and

start collecting the used rags and paper towels and shoving them in the garbage bag. I work around him, trying to stay out of his way while I check to make sure I got every drop of paint off the floor.

I'm sick, seeing how my copy's undamaged while Krell's painting is a mess. The only blue on mine is a blob on the unpainted edge.

Adam steps back and he's managed to lift off the worst, but we have to get the blue scar off Duncan's cheek. Adam looks from the rag to the man's face. A muscle in his jaw twitches. "Do you carry any Q-tips?"

I dive for my bag. "Yeah. I've got them right here." My hand shakes as I hand him the little box.

He takes a deep breath, exhales, and leans forward. Then he twirls a Q-tip, barely touching the canvas, a surgeon removing a layer of cells.

I try not to move or even to breathe. He's so angry and I deserve it. We are screwed if he can't fix this.

The dark blue streak gets smaller and smaller until I can't see it from where I'm standing. "Give me your magnifying glass," he says.

I strip the glass and chain from my neck and dangle them in front of him. Adam snatches the chain out of my hand and peers at the canvas. A minute passes while he studies it, then he steps back and drops onto the couch.

He drags his hands through his hair, and I hang back. Silent. Motionless. Ready for him to tell me how stupid I am.

But then he laughs. "We dodged a bullet. A big freaking bullet."

I swallow, but can't answer. The air is still dense with anger and I quietly pack my bag. Adam holds out the chain with the magnifying glass and I pluck it from his fingers.

"I'm sorry. I'm such a disaster," I say.

Adam peels himself off the couch. "You're not a disaster. You slipped. It wasn't your fault."

There's a slight disconnect between what I hear and what I feel, like when the audio and video are off by a millisecond. The atmosphere hasn't cleared, so why is Adam taking my hands?

He threads his fingers through mine. "Take a deep breath." Together we slowly inhale. "And let it out."

I give Adam a smile because he's trying to reassure me, but I'm almost sick imagining what might have happened if I'd ruined Krell's painting.

Adam pulls me closer. Time slows and the room dissolves as he gazes at me. My pulse quickens, sensing his kiss. "Your painting's almost finished," he says. "You've come to the end of this experience. Has it been worth it?"

"Yes." I exhale the word, because I can't speak.

Our lips brush, and my breath catches. "We should celebrate with a bonfire," he says. "Thursday night."

"Sounds romantic."

His lips dive for mine, and we shuffle until the wall's against my back. Adam presses into me as he draws my hands over my head. I'm pinned, but I don't want to be free.

We devour each other with kisses. I want to hold him, feel the muscles under his shirt, but when I try to slide my hands out of his, he won't let go.

"Don't be in a rush," he says.

We smile at each other. He straightens up and leans his head back, lips out of reach. The tension from not kissing him is almost unbearable.

"Thursday. I'll borrow my friend's van," he tells me, "and we'll take your painting out to Dockweiler Beach."

"Wait, what?"

"You know you can't keep it. The first time one of your friends saw it, you'd be screwed, trying to explain why you have a perfect copy of a painting that no one—not even any faculty member—has seen."

I sigh. It's only a copy of someone else's work, so I shouldn't be proud of it. "I didn't think of that."

"Sucks, I know, but since it must be destroyed, we will build a bonfire, consign your artwork to the wild conflagration, and celebrate its creation and demise."

"A ceremonial bonfire. That's perfect," I say. I move forward for one more kiss, but Adam releases my hands and steps back.

"We should get it back in the locker before the night classes let out," he says.

"Yeah, it's getting late." We really do need to get out of here.

We do a final cleanup of Krell's studio and carry the board down to Secure Storage. I can't stop smiling, imagining Adam and me feeding it into the fire. The night will be cold and clear, and we'll have the beach to ourselves. Adam and me. The ocean and stars. Firelight and a blanket on the sand.

We stow the painting and leave through the back door before the night classes let out. Adam pulls me into a shadow and we kiss briefly before he pulls away. "I'll see you Wednesday? You only need one night to finish, right?"

I'm tempted to tell Adam I'm done with Krell's painting, because I'm a little freaked that our luck may have run out, but instead I say, "Yeah, Wednesday." Adam disappears into the dark, and I touch my lips, which are ever so slightly swollen.

CHAPTER 34

E ven though Krell's painting looked perfect when Adam and I locked up, I wake up feeling we missed a spot. We were rushed and panicked while we cleaned it, and in the daylight something might be visible that wasn't last night.

I'm almost nauseous worrying about it, and frustrated that I can't get into Krell's studio until tomorrow night. When I show up for Krell's class on Wednesday morning I'm convinced he's found a smear or a splotch that Adam and I didn't.

But Krell's his usual provocative self as the crit session for Bernadette's thorn painting begins.

She's a lot further along, and now what emerges from the canvas is a man in an overcoat and bowler hat. The only actual paint on the canvas besides the white background is a bright green apple in the middle of the man's face.

Kevin's sitting next to me and I tap his shoe with my foot. He turns, and I whisper, "Is it just me or did she appropriate René Magritte?"

He squelches a smile, letting me know that what Bernadette's done is obvious to anyone who's taken a semester of art history. She's used one of the most famous images of Surrealist art to make her painting seem deeper than it is.

Bernadette faces the class, one hand on her hip like a Valkyrie daring us to cross her. She sweeps her hair over her shoulder and says, "We always want to see what is hidden by what we see . . . but humans hide their secrets too well." Then she makes air quotes so we know she's quoting Magritte.

The class launches into a discussion of how Bernadette's use of thorns defines the man in her painting, but also keeps the viewer at a distance, protecting his secrets. The discussion turns into a debate about what we know or will never know about a painting or a person.

As a strategic move, Bernadette's painting is effing brilliant.

It's everything CALINVA's faculty goes nuts over: an unexpected medium that expresses a philosophical inquiry.

Now it's even more clear that not only does *Seen/Not Seen* have to be perfect and arresting, but my artist statement has to be compelling if I want to compete with what Bernadette has created.

I glance at Bryian, and for the first time in weeks, he's not smiling or nodding proudly as his girlfriend talks about her work. His eyes are tense, and I'd bet money I don't have that Bernadette didn't share with him what she was going to say. Hmm, Bryian's scared, too.

After the crit ends, Kevin leans over. "You seem worried."

"How am I supposed to compete with that? The faculty's going to fight over who gets to be her adviser."

I half expect Kev to tell me I'm wrong, but he nods and says, "You're probably right. Bernadette's going to get a lot of attention."

"So what do I do?"

"Just keep going, I guess."

I stand and haul my messenger bag onto my chair so I can pack my stuff. "I wish I could just focus on my art. I hate worrying about who's the best, who'll get their pick of advisers, who'll get a dealer—"

Kevin signals me with his eyes to stop talking, and I hear, "Ms. Reyes?"

I go rigid, knowing Krell's right behind me. I turn and say, "Yes?"

"If you're free, I'd like to see you in my office." Krell's expression isn't angry, but it is serious.

Oh God, Krell knows.

CHAPTER 35

The walk to Krell's studio is agony. As soon as we start down the hall, his dealer calls, hot to nail down the final details for shipping the *Duncan* painting to Miami on Monday. Krell's cool, and if he's found anything wrong with his masterwork, he isn't giving it away to his dealer. Not that I would if I were him.

When we enter his studio, my eyes flit to his painting, but it faces away from me so I can't see what he's discovered. Krell sits down at his big worktable, snaps his fingers to get my attention, and points at the stool across from him.

Sweat trickles down my sides, and I don't want to look at him while he's on the phone, so I train my gaze on a white coffee cup near my hands. DEFACE CONVENTION, it dares in bright red letters.

I'd like to take off my jacket, but if I move, he might look my way, and I struggle to keep my face neutral. My thoughts are lightning strikes: Krell found some damage, security caught Adam and me on tape, I'm going to be expelled.

Krell sets his phone down on the table and switches it off. *Oh God, this is it.*

His fingers drum the paint-specked tabletop. "You're probably wondering why I asked you here."

I can barely hear over the wind in my ears. My mouth

is cotton dry, and my tongue sticks to my teeth. "Yes."

"Your scholarship is at risk," he says. "Did the financial aid office explain that the Zoich is performance based?"

I nod yes. "Ms. Gonzales went over that with me."

"Then you know it's critical you turn in outstanding work. That's why I want to check in with you about your work in progress. I'd hate to see you lose the Zoich."

For the first time since I walked in here, I look right at him. "What did you say?"

His mouth twists in annoyance. "I said, I'd hate to see you lose your scholarship. I've championed you from the beginning."

That can't be true. Adam told me you wanted Bryian to get it.

"Your instructors agree that your technical and observational skills surpass those of your classmates. Your potential is undeniable, but other students are ahead of you creatively."

"Bryian and Bernadette," I say with a sigh.

He nods. "You saw how compelling her piece is."

"Yes."

"And I assume you've noticed that Bryian has spent this semester experimenting and challenging himself with different approaches to express his ideas."

I have to admit that even though Bryian's copied other artists, he's never repeated himself all semester. His work is getting looser and more daring. I couldn't identify who he'd impersonated this week, but now I wonder if his latest and best work was actually all him.

"Yeah, I can see that."

Krell leans in, and I know he's about to deliver the death-blow, so I'm not ready for the gentle, not entirely condescending way he says, "The portrait you're working on now could turn this situation around. Have you revisited your painting since we last met?"

My voice sounds like it's coming from far away. "Yes. I took your advice and—" I pull out my phone. "Do you want to see where I'm going with it?"

Krell motions for me to pass him the phone, and for the next twenty minutes we talk through what I'm trying to do with the two panels. He comments on how he feels my use of contrasting styles, colors, and brushwork can succeed in forcing the viewer to question their assumptions about Julie.

"But consider how you can take the idea even further by exploring dimensionality. Currently, the two panels are the same size, so the viewer may interpret that as the images carrying equal weight or validity."

"Oh, that's not what I'm trying to say. But making one smaller, wouldn't that be too obvious?"

"Mmm. Agreed. The solution should be unexpected."

I've never played with dimension beyond size or shape, but the layering Krell does with the Strata or going 3-D like Bernadette did with those thorns are other ways of approaching it.

We're almost done talking when Krell challenges me not to use black paint on the second panel.

"Think about the energy in Monet's railway paintings," he says. "The locomotives look black, but Monet built the blackness out of red, blue, and green so it has depth."

I walk out of his office, my head spinning. I've been wrong about him. Not wrong about everything; Krell's still an asshat, but now I wonder if his harsh and obnoxious comments were intended to help me.

I don't think Krell was lying about wanting me to keep

my scholarship. Adam must have heard wrong when he said Krell wanted Bryian to get the Zoich. Or maybe Krell was all set to vote for Bryian and changed his mind.

I can't continue sneaking into Krell's studio. Right now it feels completely wrong.

For the first time, I consider what Krell would have said if I'd asked him if I could copy his painting. The answer almost makes me sick, because there's the tiniest chance he might have said yes.

CHAPTER 36

The regret and confusion I feel after my meeting with Krell dog me through Color & Theory. I'm supposed to be such a talented observer, but I've been blind as far as he's concerned.

As I walk through the atrium, a woman calls, "Sabine," and I whirl around, wondering who's so excited to see me, but I don't recognize her. She dashes toward me, arms outstretched, her long black hair swinging. "I can't believe it's you!"

Her lips are bright red against her pale skin, and everything about her—the cut of her black pants and chartreuse swing coat, the perfect arch of her eyebrows—feels like a warning.

I take a step back, but before I can get away, she wraps my arm in both of hers and is walking me across the lobby. She's smiling, her head bent toward mine, but her voice is anything but friendly as she says, "I'm Iona Taylor's personal assistant, Tara Speer. I think you know why I'm here, so where would you like to have this conversation?"

The exhibition gallery's empty, but Tara feels so dangerous I need to get her out of the building. "There's a bench outside."

"Perfect. Lead the way."

She marches me down the entrance ramp, her grip tight on my arm. "I am not your average PA, Sabine. Not some simpering twenty-year-old who does coffee and dog-grooming runs. I've been doing this awhile, so I know how to dig into problems. How to investigate and rectify discrepancies."

Just as I imagined, poor Lacy lost her job. Iona must have tired of sweet young things trying to break into Hollywood, so she hired Tara as her personal assistant.

When we're outside, I nod to the right. There's a small courtyard cut into the side of the building where there's a bench no one uses.

Thankfully, no one's sitting there today.

Tara releases my arm and we both sit down. I'm not surprised she doesn't waste time on pleasantries, but launches right in. "You picked up Iona Taylor's Valentino dress from the dry cleaner on February twenty-first, the same day you retrieved her Zanotti boots."

I nod yes. Tara's not at all what I expected, and I don't know how I'm getting myself out of this.

"Iona wants them back."

"I don't have them."

She screws up her face like she's in pain. "I really hoped you wouldn't say that. You know how much that dress cost, don't you? Six thousand. And the boots were seventeen hundred. That's grand larceny, Sabine. Iona could have you arrested."

The street is swimming before my eyes. I'm trapped.

"What did you do with the Valentino?"

"I sold it."

"Great. Just great. Did you sell it online? Take it to a consignment store?"

"I took it to Hollywood Redux in the valley."

She whips out her phone and taps the screen. "Over on Victory. There's a chance it's still there. How much did you get for it?"

"Four hundred."

She snorts. "Four hundred dollars. Too stupid to get a good price."

How dare she judge me? "I needed the money. You don't know what happened that day, do you?"

"No?"

"Iona didn't tell you about Mom going to the hospital? She didn't mention how she fired Mom while she was dying, packed up our things, and kicked us out?"

I watch Tara's face shift as what I've said sinks in, but her feeling sorry for me lasts about two seconds before she says, "Oh, I get it. You think that selling her dress was justified. You think Iona deserved it."

"Yeah, I did and I still do. I was seventeen. I had no mom, no money, no home, and I was sleeping in my car, because of her."

Tara smirks, probably because she's thinking that it doesn't matter if I was justified. If Iona files charges, I could go to jail. "How much did you get for the boots?"

"I lied. I still have the boots."

"Are they in decent shape?"

I shrug.

Tara shakes out her hair. "Here's what we're going to do. I will see if I can get that dress back from Hollywood Redux, and if I do, you will repay me what that costs. And you are going to return the boots and write the most abject, obsequious, groveling apology of your life and send it to Iona."

I hate the idea of pretending I'm sorry. "What if Hollywood Redux already sold the dress?"

"You'd better pray they haven't."

Tara refuses to leave until my cell number is in her phone. "I'll be in contact," she says, and strides off.

Iona hired herself a bulldog, and Tara's not going to stop until she's satisfied. There's no escaping her.

I'm late for work, so I haul my messenger bag onto my shoulder, and I'm not paying attention as I hit the sidewalk and almost bump into two of my classmates having a smoke break.

They glance back and forth at each other, and I realize they might not have heard every mortifying detail of my conversation with Tara, but they heard enough.

A block from Artsy, Tara's text comes in. DRESS GONE— BETTER START WORKING ON YOUR REPAYMENT PLAN.

CHAPTER 37

A t work, I put my jacket and bag in the back room and throw on my green Artsy apron. The store is crowded with moms and kids buying card stock, glitter, and paint to make Christmas cards, so my manager assigns me to the cash register up front.

I ring up sales, wondering how the hell I'm going to come up with the money to pay Iona back. Unlike Krell, Iona has zero interest in my leading a productive, artistic life. Every time I think things are getting better, I find out I was wrong.

As I bag candy-cane-striped paper and Santa Claus rubber stamps, Mom is in my head. *Karma isn't some anonymous, mystical force, Sabine. It's the energy you create from your choices. Bad choices breed bad endings.*

Customers keep coming and a kid who can't be more than five or six melts down in front of me. He wants the twenty-four pack of colored pencils and his mom will only spring for twelve. She drags him out of the line and over by the greeting cards, where he sobs and flails his arms, and she stands over him, waiting him out.

Right there with you, buddy.

By the time I get through the rest of the people in line, the little guy is back in front of me. His arms are sagging and his face is drained. He pushes a twelve pack of Crayola pencils up on the counter.

"Sorry about that," his mom tells me.

"It's hard when you want something you can't have."

She smiles wearily and steers her son out of the store.

Artsy is empty now that it's dinnertime. I rest my elbows on the counter and thump my forehead with my hands.

Karma's on my ass and I have to get her off. It burns that I have to write Iona an apology and return her boots after what she did, but I don't want Tara showing up again.

I reach into the drawer below the cash register and take out the key to the display case of the Lascaux acrylics. My coworker Romy's upstairs in the custom frame and canvas department, so I'm alone on the floor. I walk over and unlock the case. I remove a tube of Phthalo Turquoise Blue and carry it over to the cash register. Then I scan the paint as a sale and pull fifteen dollars out of my jeans. For a second, I weigh whether I deserve an employee discount. Nope.

The paint goes back in the display and I lock the case. There. My debt is repaid.

Not so fast, Mom whispers in my ear. *It's not enough to pay for what you stole. You have to make amends.*

Barney, my manager, comes out of the back office. He stops partway down the main aisle and fusses with an end-cap of glitter glue. I could walk over right now and confess what I did.

I wipe my sweaty hands on my butt. What would confessing get me? Out of a job, and a truckload of hurt if word got back to CALINVA.

No, the best way to make amends to Artsy is to be better at my job. To clean shelves without being asked, to tidy displays, and to be the friendly, helpful, customer-centric employee Artsy loves.

I go over to Barney, who's still trying to clean up the end-cap. Handfuls of glitter pens are thrown around the shelves. "I can do that."

"Every year it gets worse. From the week before Thanksgiving to Christmas Eve, this place looks like Elf Revolt at Santa's Workshop."

"I won't let them beat me, sir," I say, and give him a salute.

My manager thanks me, and I scoop up pens and start to slot them. Green, red, gold, silver, and Hanukkah blue. If only I could sort out my life as easily as I can art supplies.

I can repay Artsy, but what about Krell? Invading his studio and copying his work without permission? If I confess, I'll be out of CALINVA in a hot minute.

The glitter pens are all in their proper slots, but I find a tub of yellow poster paint that needs to be put back where it belongs. I stroll toward the front of the store as the door swings open.

Adam walks in, wearing a battered black leather jacket that even unzipped shows off his broad shoulders and trim waist.

I'm not prepared for how his smile latches on to me and pulls me down the aisle. When I get to him, he reaches for me, but drops his hand when he sees my manager looking at us.

"I thought we were meeting at CALINVA," I say.

"We were, but I couldn't wait to show you something."

CHAPTER 38

My manager lets me off early, and Adam and I walk down Raymond toward CALINVA. The first block is well lit, and even though it's midweek, the bars and restaurants are busy.

Adam clasps my hand, but he's scanning the street as if there's someone he's trying to avoid. His stride is longer than mine, so I have to walk fast to keep up.

When we cross to the next block, Adam slows. The patio furniture store is dark, and the outdoor display of fountains and gazebos behind the ironwork fence looks like the remains of a cemetery in a gothic novel.

Adam's never chatty when we're in a public space, so I'm used to his silence.

"I'm so glad to see you," I tell him. "I almost lost it today."

"What happened?"

"First, Krell called me in—"

His hand spasms, almost crushing mine. "Shit. Did he find something?" An ugly look comes over his face.

"Yeah, that was my first thought, but—"

"So he didn't find anything."

"No, he—"

Adam blows out a breath. "That's a relief."

"I know."

"So what else was going on?"

I decide to skip over my meeting with Krell. "My past has come back to haunt me."

"You've got a past?" he jokes.

I don't laugh. Adam stops and turns me toward him. "Are you in trouble?"

"Definitely."

"What did you do?"

I wish I hadn't said anything, but now it's too late. "I sold something that didn't belong to me."

He gives me a sideways smile. He's both amused and intrigued. "But you didn't steal it?" he says.

"No. I didn't take it, but I didn't return it either when I realized I had it."

"You must have had a good reason."

Adam sees me so clearly. He knows I'd never hurt someone for no reason. "I did. I was desperate."

"Why, what happened?"

I've never told anyone even part of the story, but I feel in my heart that Adam won't judge me, so I lay out what happened with Iona, her tossing me out, me selling her dress, and the six grand I owe her. Adam does all the right things, cursing Iona and insisting she deserved everything I did to her. Then he wraps his arm over my shoulder. "You're unbelievable. I had no idea how strong you are, living on the street like that."

I lean into him. No one's ever said that to me before.

"Whatever happens," he says, "I'm here for you."

"Thanks." I nestle closer, taking in his warmth. "I can't tell you what that means to me."

He looks over my head and mutters, "There's a homeless woman staring at us." I turn. Julie's in the park across the street with the guy who sells Jesus poems for a dollar. She waves at me like she wants me to come over.

"Hi, Julie!" I wave back, pretending not to understand what she wants. Adam's creeped out, and I don't blame him. The palm trees they're standing under slice the light across their faces, so Julie and the poet look like ghouls.

Adam tugs me along. "That's the woman you're painting?"

"Yes."

"How's that going?"

He listens, not interrupting once, while I describe the second panel, the idea of seen and unseen. I've never felt closer to Adam than I do tonight.

We cover the last two blocks to CALINVA and Adam goes ahead of me around the building. We sneak in the back door, and even though we've done this dozens of times without getting caught, I'm still on the lookout while Adam's striding through the halls and unlocking doors.

I need to tell him I'm done with *Duncan*, but he's so fixated on getting into Secure Storage I can't find a way to say it. It's not until he opens the locker and slides out my copy of *Duncan* that he starts to relax.

He gazes at my painting. "Promise me that if anyone ever tells you you're not talented, you won't believe them."

The look he gives me next is so intense, so awestruck, my heart swells with pride for how I've grown. "I promise." How could I have made it through this semester without him?

"This is it. Tonight you complete this painting and tomorrow we light its funeral pyre."

"Funeral pyre. I like that. It sounds heroic."

"Your work deserves to be honored." Adam scans the painting. "The only part left to do is this small area on the shoulder."

"Actually, I don't want to work on it anymore."

Adam's face shifts, and for a second, he looks pissed, but before I can ask what he's mad about, his features relax and he says, "Oh. I guess I read you wrong."

I fold my arms over my chest, because even though his expression appears calm, the tone of his voice is slightly hostile. "What are you saying?"

"I didn't think you were a quitter."

The dig hurts. Still, I'm done. I've wronged Krell and it's time for this to be over. "Why does this even matter to you?" I say quietly. "I thought the point was for me to get what I needed from Krell."

Adam shakes his head. "You're right. I'm sorry, I don't know why I said that. You're not a quitter. You're the last person in the world anyone could call a quitter."

He slides the painting back in the locker. His features are tense like he's gritting his teeth, but then he turns, his eyes bright, and says, "Ready for my surprise?"

I'm thrown by how he's acting tonight, and I don't know why he was so put out, but it seems like his little storm might be over. "Can't wait," I say, and take his outstretched hand. We ride up to the third floor, and Adam scopes out the halls and waves me forward. He turns down the hall with the grad student studios and leads me to the door with the flattened metal robot toy duct-taped to it.

"Is this your studio?" I ask.

Adam nods. "Sean said he was moving out today to go live with his girlfriend." Adam puts his ear to the door and listens. "All clear."

We walk in and Adam flips on the light. As the fluorescents warm, he points to a huge canvas leaning against the wall. "My magnum opus."

"This is your painting, the one you've been working on all semester?"

It's at least eight feet long and six feet high. I move closer, taking in the hundreds of scribbled white squares on the black canvas. They float, but are all connected. A maze or a language without words. They are black-and-white photos scarred with acid, or a house of staircases leading nowhere.

My mouth goes dry, and a wave of curiosity and discomfort washes over me as I stare at the canvas. "So this is *Infinite Uncertainty.*"

"You remembered."

I walk along the painting, taking it in in pieces. My skin prickles up my arms, and I struggle to understand what my body's telling me. It's not until I walk the length of it that I realize what is setting me off.

This painting doesn't feel like Adam. I'd never have guessed he painted it, and it makes me feel I know nothing about him.

Maybe it's me, I think. I'm the one who's off kilter tonight.

He walks over and slides his arm around my waist. "What do you think?"

I don't tell him what I'm feeling, but share my impressions of a maze, language, vandalized photos, house of staircases.

"You're very poetic." His breath is warm on my neck as he murmurs into my ear. "You should write the description when it goes on exhibit."

"If you want me to."

"Gavin Brown's coming to see it next week."

He throws this out like it's nothing, but I squeal, "No way! That's incredible."

Adam squeezes my waist, and I turn for his kiss, but he says, "Let's go up to the roof."

My heart races as we walk to the staircase. I've only been to the rooftop garden during the day, but I can imagine how romantic it is at night.

The mustard-colored steel door is locked. Adam pulls out his keys, ignoring the sign: ACCESS PROHIBITED AFTER DARK.

We step outside. I expect it to be dark, but the raised planters are dotted with solar lights, and a huge skylight thrusts out of the roof, a jagged iceberg spilling light.

Because this is CALINVA, nothing up here is built with right angles. The sides of the raised planters tilt and their tops bulge with mounds of floppy grass planted over the feet of crooked Japanese maples. The planters divide the rooftop into oddly shaped spaces that hide lounge chairs and tables.

We walk through the garden, our arms around each other's waist. Adam gives off faint scents of musk and paint, and his hip is muscle over bone beneath my hand. My skin is hot under my shirt, and I sneak my hand up and unbutton it down to my bra.

We're four stories up, and Pasadena is spread out before us. The Metro rattles past, its silver sides streaked with reflected light.

"It's beautiful out here," I say.

"You can see even better from up top." Adam points back to where we came in. That half of the building is one story higher. "You game?"

"Absolutely."

We climb the ladder bolted to the wall, and the metal clangs as we go. Adam's first and he reaches for me and helps me over the last step.

To the north, the dome of city hall is lit up against the sky, and to the west, houses twinkle in the hills along the arroyo.

On the south side, an art deco fountain bathed in colored lights splashes outside the power company.

We walk over to the edge. It's a five-story drop, and there are no railings. Adam's so relaxed, it's like the height doesn't bother him at all, so I pretend I'm good with it, too. He slides his arm around my waist. "You're really something," he murmurs.

I turn and lift my face to his.

"Not what I imagined at all."

I feel myself swept forward, and I cry out as my feet touch air. I grab for Adam as he swings me around so we're face-to-face. I clutch his shoulders, body trembling, my toes clinging to the edge of the roof.

He looks into my eyes, and I watch the tiny muscles around his eyes and mouth move as if he's arguing with himself. My thighs feel like they're about to cramp, and I'm terrified my toes will slip. Adam leans in to kiss me, and I duck my head. "Please, can we move back a little?"

He smiles and tightens his hold on me. Light catches on the silver cross dangling from his ear. "Trust me. I won't let you get hurt."

I stare into his eyes, wishing he'd just scoot back. "Please, I know I'm being silly but—"

Adam waits a moment longer before he spins us around so he's between me and the edge. "Better?"

He doesn't wait for an answer. His lips crash into mine and I am tossed by a wave of desire. My hands dive under his shirt, and my breath catches, feeling his lips on my ear, my neck, my breasts.

We are so lost we struggle to surface when we hear, "Whoever's up here, I know you're here. This area is off-limits after dark. The administration takes this rule very seriously, and the penalty can be a suspension up to one semester."

Adam and I drop to a crouch. We huddle together and spy the security guard strolling away from us through the garden.

My blouse hangs open and I race to button it. "Why the big deal?" I whisper.

"A student jumped last year."

I'd forgotten about him. Adam signals to me to keep quiet.

"I don't want to bust you, but I will," the guard declares. "If you are not off this roof before I finish this cigarette, I will stand by the door and you will not get past me."

Adam jerks his head at the ladder. We stay low across the roof and keep the guard in sight. We scramble down, and the guy keeps his word. His back stays turned and we slide through the door.

Adam races me out of the hall, pushing me to the left. "Take the elevator," he says, dodging to the right. Behind me, I hear him clamber down the stairs.

I make it to the ground floor and push through the back door. I'm shaking from the adrenaline when Adam grabs my hand and pulls me over to the loading dock.

We lean against the wall, chests heaving as we try to catch our breaths. "Nothing's ever boring with you," he says.

"I could say the same for you." I search Adam's face in the half-light. I feel I've barely penetrated his layers, and it might take me longer to figure him out than it took me to figure out *Duncan*.

He raises my hand and kisses the tips of my fingers. "Tomorrow we send off *Duncan* in style, and then . . ."

I realize that our relationship has shifted to a new plane, and I have to wonder where tomorrow will take us.

CHAPTER 39

The next morning, I hang around in the main hall after Drawing 101, hoping to run into Adam. My body hums at the thought of seeing him. It's eight long hours before we're supposed to meet and the day cannot go fast enough.

I prop myself against the wall with my sketchbook and pretend I'm working on an assignment while I sketch his face.

Bernadette goes by and her eyes lock on my feet, and it dawns on me that she's checking out my shoes. *Great. The rumors have started.*

I go back to drawing Adam, rounding his lips and adding the tiny cleft in his chin.

Taysha comes up to me. "What are you smiling about?" she says, and before I can slap my sketchbook shut, she tips it toward her. "Mmm, is that Mystery Man?"

I blush and try to make my face a blank, but I can't.

"Don't even try to lie," Taysha says. "He's gorgeous. This is the guy you met at work?"

"Yeah," I say, a little surprised Taysha doesn't recognize him when she knows everyone including the cashier at the CALINVA snack bar. Still, it's not like Adam's in any of our classes.

"He's a painter, right?"

"How'd you guess?"

"Those smoldering, soulful eyes."

I bite my lip, because as soon as Taysha says "smoldering," I'm finally ready to spill.

"Guessing from your face, I'd say things have progressed."

I can't resist any longer. "Promise me you won't say anything to anyone."

"When you say 'anyone,' you mean a certain anyone from Kansas."

I ignore her. "We're having a bonfire at the beach tonight."

"Romantic . . . You really like this guy."

"I've never been with anyone like him before. He's not just interested in me, he loves my art—"

She sighs and shakes her head. "Girl, you need to guard your heart, because this man looks like he could pulverize it."

Taysha walks off to class, and I settle back against the wall.

Only a few more hours, and it will be just me and Adam under the stars, burning the evidence of what I swear will be my last act of wrongdoing ever.

CHAPTER 40

I barely make it through my shift at Artsy, I'm so excited. Adam and I are meeting where we always do, by the back door at CALINVA. Any minute now, he'll drive up to the loading dock in the van he borrowed from the photographer he works for and we'll be off.

The sun set a couple of hours ago, and it's a lot colder tonight than it was yesterday. I button my jacket, glad I've got a hoodie on under it. Hands crammed in my pockets, I can't wait to warm them over the bonfire we're going to build.

I wait by the door, shifting from foot to foot. Adam's late, but he could be inside already, getting the painting out of the locker, so I text him to let him know I'm here.

"Come on, Adam," I mutter when ten more minutes go by with no response.

I can't decide whether to stay where I am or duck into the loading dock and get out of the wind. My hair's blowing into my face, so I pull out a hair band and tie it back. Fingers crossed Adam remembered his promise to bring a couple blankets, because we'll need them.

Somewhere nearby a church bell bongs out the time. Seven thirty. Fifteen minutes late isn't *that* late. Maybe Adam had to run a last-minute errand for Ofelo or one of the other professors like Hmong.

I pace and check the time on my phone. Why isn't he answering? After a half hour, I'm panicked. Maybe Adam got caught by security. Krell's painting was sent out to be professionally photographed today, but security might not know that. No, they'd see a guy trying to sneak a million-dollar artwork out the back.

I walk to the edge of the parking lot and scan it for a white van. Lots of Priuses, no vans. Okay, maybe Adam's stuck in traffic. The 210 freeway can be a parking lot this time of night.

My fingers and feet are just about frozen when a figure moves in the shadows. My heart races. "Adam?"

"No," a small voice answers. Julie steps into the circle of light by the huge black dumpster. Sweetie's perched on her shoulder and Julie pets her absentmindedly. "You're looking for your friend, but he isn't here."

At first, I wonder how Julie knows who I'm waiting for, but she's seen Adam and me together and she might have even seen us here.

"How do you know he isn't here?" I say.

"Green mountain truck's not there."

"He doesn't have a truck." He told me weeks ago he sold it because he couldn't afford it anymore.

"Yes, he does." Julie turns to watch the Metro clatter past, and I get the feeling she's standing guard over me.

I zip my hoodie up to my chin and tuck my hair inside the hood. Julie's in a ripped down jacket and tonight she's wearing shoes. I check if she's got socks on. Yes, but they're cotton. I should bring her a pair of wool ones.

It's freezing out here. How long am I supposed to wait?

A couple more minutes tick by and I can't pretend any

longer. Either Adam's in trouble or he blew me off. As soon as I think that, I feel it in my gut.

Adam blew me off.

He never said he'd ended his relationship with his ex. I assumed it was over, but he never actually came out and told me it was.

A flash of his phone screen pops up in my head. REYES. That's what he typed in with my phone number. REYES, not SABINE, REYES. Like I was just another contact. Like I could be anyone.

Now all the little signs I ignored, signs that this girl who is probably a student at CALINVA is still very much in his life, the signs that should have made me put on the brakes . . . they're blazing.

The way his mood would run warm then cool like he couldn't decide if he was in or out.

The way he'd disappear then reappear. How he always worked on Sundays.

And right now he's probably with her, so he's left me waiting out here in the dark. He couldn't even text me to say he couldn't make it.

I haul back and kick an empty soda can by my foot. It flies through the air and bangs into the chain link along the train tracks. "Prick!" I can't believe I've been so stupid.

Julie backs away from me, shaking her head. "I don't like anger."

I walk toward her, holding up my hands in surrender. "I'm sorry, Julie. I'm sorry," I say, but she keeps moving away.

"Anger's poison," she says. "It'll kill you."

"Okay. I hear you."

"Go home. Cool down."

"Yes, I will, Julie, I promise. I'm going now."

Julie melts into the darkness and I pick up my bag and throw it over my shoulder. I shove my hands deep in my pockets as I walk to my car.

We're done, Adam. We are so done, but I'm not going to be a baby and demand that you explain why you blew me off the next time I see you. No, I have way too much self-respect for that.

Adam's going to open the locker, and then I will kick that freaking painting to pieces if I have to.

CHAPTER 41

Things will look better in the morning. Mom used to play that on repeat. Anything bad happened with friends or at school and Mom would drag out her promise that once the sunlight touched my problems, I'd barely be able to see them anymore.

Yeah, well, sun's up, Mom, and things aren't looking any better.

I drag myself out of bed and shove open my closet. I thrust my hand into the mess inside and pull out the first thing I touch. The Henley's faded and there's a rip by the wrist, but so what.

The jeans I wore last night are by the bed. I pull them on and reach into the pile of shoes in the corner for my Converse. One of Iona's boots tumbles onto my foot.

"Funny, karma, real funny." I shake my head and nudge the bootie away. "So I guess what you're saying is this thing with Adam, it's payback."

If I hadn't been so pissed at Krell, I wouldn't have gotten so close to liar/cheater/swine Adam.

If I'd returned Iona's things instead of letting my intense loathing of her stop me, I wouldn't be facing years of paying her back.

Maybe things aren't better in the morning, but they're a lot clearer.

I snatch Iona's boots off the floor and rummage around for a box to put them in. Then I tear a page out of my sketchbook and start to compose my apology.

~~Dear Bitch on Wheels.~~

Tempting, but no. Cross it out.

Dear Iona.
~~*So sorry for the misunderstanding.*~~

Yeah. Like she'd believe that. Cross it out.

So sorry I didn't return these boots sooner.

True statement. I am sorry, because they've brought me nothing but grief.

If you send me the bill from the shoe-repair place I will pay you back.

And I will. Eventually. That place is superexpensive.

I set down the sketchbook. Tara, her personal assistant, wants me to apologize for not returning her dress, but I'm at a total loss. Is there a single normal human being in existence who'd give it back after what Iona did? Someone would have to be a total saint to turn the other cheek on her. And I am no saint.

I pick up the sketchbook.

I was a mess when Mom died.

It was wrong for me not to return your dress when I found it.

I can acknowledge I screwed up, but I'm not evolved enough to apologize for it, and if that means karma's not satisfied, then I guess that's too freaking bad.

I hope you can forgive me.

But I'm not holding my breath.

I find a nicer piece of paper, write the apology in my most penitent handwriting, and lay it on the tissue-paper-wrapped boots, then seal the box. In between classes, I'll drop this at Pack 'n Ship, and be done with it.

Even though doing this means I won't get Mom's guitar back anytime soon, maybe it will slow the flood of bad luck dumped on me this week.

Once again, I'm probably late for Krell's class. I twist up my hair, grab my stuff, and bolt out the door.

CHAPTER 42

When I get to class, the room feels unnaturally bright, as if I'm hungover. I tiptoe between the easels to my spot, and notice that people aren't just looking to see who's late, they're checking me out.

I stick the box with Iona's boots by my feet and take this week's assignment out of my portfolio.

"Are you feeling okay?" Kevin whispers.

Once again, I lie to Kevin, who deserves to hear only the truth from me. "Sinus headache." I offer him a weak smile. "I'll be fine once the drugs kick in."

Kevin nods, but Taysha sees right through me.

After class, she drags me into the bathroom, whips a hairbrush out of her purse, and shoves it into my hand. "Brush now."

I let my hair out of the clip. Fluorescent light is cruel, but it's not the lighting's fault I look this bad. There are dark purple half-moons under my eyes, and my hair looks like I was attacked by crows.

The brush catches on a mass of tangles. Taysha finds my makeup bag and plunks lip gloss, concealer, mascara, and gum on the shelf above the sink. "Tell me what happened last night."

"He didn't show." I stop the tear before it's even out of my eye. I'm not crying over this guy.

"From the way you look, I'm guessing the jerk didn't call either."

"Nope. Didn't call, didn't answer my texts." I shake my head. "I'm so stupid. You know how he listed me in his contacts? 'Reyes.' Like I'm one of his bros."

Taysha rolls her eyes.

"You don't have to say it," I tell her. "I was an idiot to trust him."

"Did he break your heart?"

"No, I wasn't *in love*—but he made me feel . . ."

Taysha waits for me to finish my sentence, but when I can't she tries. "Beautiful?"

"Not beautiful exactly." One glance at Taysha's confused expression and I scramble to explain. "Okay, yes, he did make me feel beautiful, but it was more than that. He made me feel special. Like I had enormous talent. That I'm worthy to be here, at CALINVA."

"First off, you're crazy talented and beyond worthy to be here. Second, why would you give this random guy power over how you see yourself?"

"He's not some random guy. He's a grad student at CALINVA."

"Ooooh."

I see in her eyes that all the pieces are clicking into place, and I pray she won't ask why I kept Adam a secret, because I'm too embarrassed to admit that I liked being his chosen one.

She wets a paper towel and holds it out. "I'll finish your hair while you do your face."

It's been forever since someone brushed my hair. I close my eyes at first and pretend it's Mom. I lean in to the brush, loving each slow and steady stroke, the careful way Taysha frees the tangles strand by strand.

She works a French braid on the back of my head and asks me questions about Adam. I dodge enough of them that she finally says, "You ready to talk about something else?"

"Sure."

"You may be amused to know there are some interesting rumors floating around about you."

I force out a chuckle that sounds ridiculously fake even to me. "Oh yeah? Do tell."

"So my personal favorite is that you're the leader of a bling ring of rich kids who break into celebrity homes and steal designer clothing."

"Wow. How cinematic, and yet untrue."

"Clearly. If it was true, you wouldn't be wearing this." She pokes a finger through the hole in my sleeve.

It feels like a miracle that the rumor's so outrageous; still my heart thuds in my chest. "What else?"

"You lifted Kylie Jenner's purse off her chair at La Petite Tomate and sold it on eBay."

I struggle, but keep smiling. "Again, not true. Any others?"

"Just one more," she says quietly.

My heart stops. "Tell me."

"It involves Iona Taylor and a pair of designer boots." The look in Taysha's eyes says she wants to help.

I nod, and rest my hands on the sink to steady myself. "What else did you hear?"

"That Iona tossed you out on the street after your mom—"

I suck in a breath and focus on the ceiling. "You can say it: She died. She was run over and the guy never even stopped."

"Oh, baby, I didn't know." Taysha curls me into her arms and hugs me fiercely. She blankets me with "so sorry so sorry so sorry," and I surprise myself by how intensely I hug her back. I feel her caring flow into all the empty parts of me, and ever so quietly she says, "How can I help?"

She means it. She's not saying it to say something, and I wonder why I took so long to confide in her when she's so much more deserving of my trust than Adam was.

"So have you ever tried making a Valentino knockoff?" I joke.

"Not yet, but I'm up for putting my skills to the test." She makes a mean Iona face and mouths the word VAL-EN-TIN-O.

She's trying to make me smile, but I can't. My head feels so, so heavy. "This is such a mess."

"We'll find a way," she promises.

I'm calm now, but I'm not quite ready to let go of her. "Does Kevin know about the rumors?"

"I don't know what he's heard, but you should talk to him before they get any worse."

"I don't see how I'm going to get through this semester. Everything feels impossible right now."

Taysha loosens her hug and steps back. She takes hold of my shoulders. "You cannot be wrecked. You are a survivor."

At last I smile.

"Now, promise me you will change out of that nasty getup you're wearing before Krell's reception tonight."

The entire school will be there for *Duncan's* unveiling. Students, faculty, administration, guests, Adam, and the girl-friend he never mentioned. Just thinking about him makes me angry all over again.

"I don't think I should go. Stay out of sight. Let the rumors die down."

"Oh no no no. You *will* be there. You need to get your

face and name in front of the faculty. Remember what I said about the faculty choosing who they mentor?"

"Okay; okay, fine."

Taysha slides her hands down my arms until she's cradling my fingertips. "You cannot be wrecked. Remember that."

"I will. I promise."

"Now, I really need some coffee before next period."

We go down to the coffee bar, and once I've got the biggest cup they sell, I spy Kevin sitting to the side with a calculator and a textbook thicker than any I've seen around here. His cheeks are usually pink, but right now they're pasty white. He's scruffy and not in a good way.

"Hey," I say.

"Hey yourself. You feeling better?"

I want to get to him before the gossip does. "Yeah, the hatchet-to-the-brain feeling's gone."

"Good to hear it."

It's very un-Kevin for him not to invite me to sit with him. "You seem really busy."

"Intro to Engineering test in"—he checks his phone— "two hours and thirty-five minutes."

"I'll let you alone. Maybe we could talk later?"

"You going to Krell's thing tonight?" he says.

"Yeah."

"Good. We'll catch up then." Kevin ducks back into his book and I look around for Taysha. I don't see her, but I do see Bernadette chatting up our rarely sighted TA, Fitz, and two tables over, Bryian glaring at the back of Bernadette's head.

So much for that romance.

For the first time, I actually feel sorry for Bryian. Apparently, we both trusted the wrong person.

CHAPTER 43

I traded my Friday-night shift at La Petite Tomate for Sunday brunch so I could attend Krell's reception at CALINVA, so I can't fall back on that as an excuse for not showing up.

I push through the glass doors and start up the long concrete ramp to the main entrance. The floor-to-ceiling windows on my left look out over the street, while on my right, and level with my head, a long glass wall runs the length of the gallery.

The party for Krell is packed. I pause partway up the ramp, struck by an impulse to turn around. Adam's somewhere in there, his girlfriend probably orbiting him like a satellite.

You hurt my feelings, but you didn't break me.

I cannot be wrecked.

I check my reflection in the window overlooking the street. Normally I don't bother with eyeliner, but tonight I want Adam to regret how he toyed with me. My eyes are dark-rimmed and enormous, and the deep-cut, midnight-blue halter under Hayley's cast-off leather jacket . . . Let's just say I can hold my own with any of the girls here.

I start back up the ramp and take in the crowd. The entire school's come out, and according to Taysha, the guest list includes trustees, art dealers, critics, and some of LA's biggest collectors.

Krell's painting hangs in the center of the long wall that runs the length of the gallery, and even though the piece is five feet tall, I see only the top over people's heads.

When I push through the glass doors into the lobby, the sound of people talking and laughing hits me like a wave. The art gallery is so full, I have to wade in slowly.

Krell stands by his painting of Duncan, and I get glimpses of him between the layers of adoring fans. His wife, Rachel, and the dean are chatting nearby, and Rachel is wearing Taysha's necklace.

I scan the crowd for Adam and feel myself relax when I realize he isn't here. Still, it's early.

Taysha's hanging with some of the first-years, so I head in that direction. Tonight her smoky-purple hair is a cloud, and as the sea of people around her parts, I get a full view of her outfit.

The blouse crisscrosses over her breasts, and the left and right sides are different prints that both command attention. One long dolman sleeve is a bold black-and-white tribal, while the other is hot orange, green, red, and white. Taysha's claret-colored leather skirt is belted high up on her waist. The look is fierce and uncompromising.

When I get up closer, I realize what I see in the colorful print. Coke. Fanta. Heineken. Sprite. The colors and logos are blown up, layered, distorted, and sliced into irregular shapes. "You designed this print yourself, didn't you?"

"Indeed I did. I wanted to honor the creativity of African tin artists while making a statement about corporate colonialism."

"The fashion-design faculty must be blown away."

"I've raised some eyebrows, but I'm looking beyond the

faculty. There could be a designer or a collector or even a blogger here tonight who can boost my profile."

"So you must be pumped Krell's wife is wearing your necklace," I say.

"She is?" Taysha grabs me by the wrist and the next second she's wrestling us through the crowd until we've got a good view of Krell and his wife.

Rachel's low-cut neckline is the perfect frame for the necklace. Taysha whips out her phone and starts snapping shots of Rachel. "It looks incredible."

A moment later, Rachel spies Taysha and waves her over. I hang back as Rachel introduces Taysha to a man who takes in her outfit from neck to hem before he motions with his finger for her to turn so he can see the back.

The crowd is pressing in on all sides, so I retreat to the wall. More people have arrived, but still no Adam.

Krell is to my left, standing in front of *Duncan*. People approach him, wanting to talk, and he smiles politely and answers their questions, but as soon as they walk away, his gaze drifts back to his painting.

You'd think he'd be puffed up with pride, surrounded by adoring colleagues here to worship his genius, but he seems distracted.

When I follow his gaze, something catches my eye: a slash of dark blue on the edge of the board.

My stomach flips, and I whip my head around. No, I've got to be imagining this.

I ease by a cluster of faculty engaged in debate, and move in closer to the painting until I stand at an angle to it. Arms crossed, I tilt my head as if I'm contemplating *Duncan* for the very first time. My heart skips a beat.

I'm not seeing things. A blue blob on the edge of the painting in the exact spot I remembered.

But the area on the shoulder that I didn't finish looks done. This doesn't make sense. I run my eyes over it again, and it feels off.

Now I stare at the painting, focusing on areas where I struggled. By the left eye, under the chin, a spot on Duncan's neck. The flaws are almost invisible, but not to me.

How? How did my copy get here?

Adam locked it in Secure Storage. I saw him take it off the easel.

My heart's jumping in my chest. This has got to be a mix-up. Someone must have spied my copy in the locker and thought it was Krell's.

I catch myself shaking my head. *Stop it.*

No, even if someone got into the locker, which would mean getting past the combination lock, Krell's original would still be in his studio. He'd know if it hadn't gone out to be photographed.

I have to find Adam. I rise up on my toes, but still no sign of him.

Maybe the original was sent out to the photographer, but it hasn't come back yet. No, that makes no sense. The photographer knew the painting had to be returned in time for the reception.

I whip out my phone. WE NEED TO TALK—NOW. The room's so loud, I set the phone on vibrate and hold it tight.

Or maybe the original came back from the photographer and was put in another locker in Secure Storage and that's when the mix-up happened. Someone assumed my copy was Krell's original.

When I find you, Adam, I will kill you.

No, first we will fix this and then I will kill you.

A finger taps my shoulder and I wheel around so I'm face-to-face with Natalie Fung from admissions. "Sabine! How's it going? Are you enjoying your first semester?"

I can barely think, my pulse is so loud in my head. "Ah, it's going great, Ms. Fung."

"Call me Natalie."

"Natalie." My eyes are darting from side to side, but luckily so are Natalie's.

"How do you like your classes? I believe we put you in Painting Strategies with Collin Krell?"

"Yes, that's right."

"I hear he's really demanding, but his class is transformative."

I force out a smile. "Yeah, nobody's the same after it."

"I'm looking forward to seeing your painting in the First-Year Exhibition. Are you excited?"

"More nervous than excited. I've still got a lot of work to do on it."

Natalie tips her wineglass to someone behind me. "I'll let you go. So glad we got a chance to catch up and I can't wait to see your new work."

The crowd is even thicker than before. People are still arriving, many of them older than students and better dressed than faculty. Art collectors, critics, dealers, all here to see the new Krell before it wings off to Art Basel Miami then disappears into private hands.

I check my phone, but still no answer.

Adam's tall, but not so tall he towers over people. *Come on, Adam, where are you?* I work my way through the throng, from the front of the room to the back, looking for him.

If I knew the grad students, I could ask them if they've seen him.

After two circuits of the room, I give up. He's not here.

Because he's sick. He's working a wedding. He's trying to avoid me.

Well, avoiding me is not going to happen.

I make my way out to the lobby. Adam could be hiding in his studio until he thinks I've left or the party's too packed for me to make a scene. I start for the stairs and hear Kevin behind me. "Sabine!"

I rearrange my face into a smile before I spin around. "Hey, did you just get here?"

"Physics lab ran late. You leaving?"

"No, no, I'm coming back," I say, and wave a finger toward the bathrooms. Kevin looks like he just showered. His oxford-blue button-down is tucked into his jeans.

"I could wait for you," he offers.

"No, you go ahead. I'll meet you in there."

"All right."

The nicest guy I've ever known goes to join the party, and I duck into the ladies' room. I wait a minute, check that the hall's empty, and dart to the stairs. Once I get to the third floor, I head to the door with the flattened metal robot taped to it.

Adam's studio is locked. I put my ear to the door and listen for movement or music or voices. Nothing. I tap lightly. No response. Tap again harder. Still nothing.

Adam, where are you? We're in such deep shit.

The metal robot taped to the door grins at me, and it's all I can do not to rip him off and crush him under my heel. I hammer the steel door with my fist, and the banging reverberates off the concrete floor and walls. A couple seconds later, a door nearby wrenches open and I take off running.

I spin around the corner and catch my breath. If I don't go back to the party, Kevin will come looking for me.

And yeah, he's waiting for me near the doors of the gallery with a couple bottles of grapefruit soda. David Tito comes over, and we hang out together, and while I laugh at people's jokes and clap for Krell during the speeches, I'm not really there. I'm neck-deep in the worst trouble of my life.

CHAPTER 44

This weekend, everything I want is beyond my reach: answers, friends, and the reassurance that my first semester at CALINVA won't be my last. Adam's ignoring my voice mails, Taysha's at a swap meet in the desert, and Kevin's locked in a marathon engineering project at Caltech and his group won't free him until it's over.

I throw myself into homework and painting *Seen/Not Seen* every minute I'm not at Artsy or rushing plates of steak frites to half-drunk customers. I keep busy, trying to shut out the crushing question of where the hell Krell's painting is.

The only explanation I can come up with is that *Duncan* is in one of the other lockers in Secure Storage.

I'm so pissed with Adam that Sunday evening, I'm standing out in front of the Rhodes Gallery. It's just after closing, but there are lights on in the back, so I press the buzzer, hoping Florian's still here.

He cracks open the door. "Oh, hello," he says, and opens it wider. "It's Sabine, isn't it?"

He doesn't invite me in, but I'm relieved he remembers me. "Yes, thank you for answering the door. I know you're closed."

"You seem upset."

I didn't think through what I was going to say on the drive over and now I fumble to explain why I'm here. "I wondered if you'd heard from Adam. He was supposed to meet me a few nights ago, but he didn't show."

Florian gives me a sympathetic smile. "He's not answering his phone?"

"No, he's not," I answer, and I realize Florian sees me as the desperate girl who got dumped. "We're working on a project together. I thought since you're friends—"

"I wish I could help you, but I'm afraid I only met him that one time."

"But you . . . I thought you knew him. He told you about me."

"We'd corresponded online."

"Oh." I don't know where to go with this.

The sun's gone behind the hills, and the lights are coming on down the street. It's disorienting: the shift in how the neighborhood looks in the artificial light.

Florian is still holding on to the door. The keys are in the lock, he's probably exhausted after dealing with people all weekend, and I'm holding him up.

"Thanks for talking with me," I say.

"My pleasure."

I turn and start down the steps, and I sense Florian's still watching. I look over my shoulder, and our eyes meet.

"I have a feeling you'll hear from him soon," Florian says. "Adam was very eager to impress you. I probably shouldn't tell you this, but he offered to pay me to open the gallery so you could have a private showing. Of course, I couldn't accept his money. . . ."

Whatever Florian says next I can't hear over the whooshing in my ears. Somehow I manage to say good night and walk to my car.

Adam who has no money, Adam who should know how tacky it is to offer to pay a gallery owner for a showing . . . Adam did that?

The streetlights are cutting shadows into the buildings along the street, deepening the cracks in the sidewalk, sharpening the tips of poinsettia leaves.

I get into my car and start the engine. I drive past the restaurant where we ate and go one block more, then veer into a residential street. Cars line either side of the narrow street and I cruise along, looking for the hulking shape of an old RV in a driveway. I only get a few blocks before I realize how futile this is.

Adam will show up tomorrow at CALINVA. Right now I'm wasting time I could spend painting.

CHAPTER 45

barely sleep Sunday night, and the next morning I'm at CALINVA by half past eight. When I drove by the building on my way home from waitressing, my copy of *Duncan* was still hanging in the gallery, but now it's gone.

Screw me.

I hit Adam's number, and it rings twice, and then: "The number you have dialed is no longer in service."

Nausea floods me, but I tell myself not to panic. The jerk probably didn't pay his bill. He was hurting for cash.

Then why would Adam have offered to pay Florian for a private showing?

I can't wait for Adam to show, so I run-walk to the back of the building and Secure Storage, even though I'm not exactly sure what I'm going to do when I get there.

The door's shut but not locked, so I knock as I open it. "Hello?"

Two guys are examining a large abstract laid out on the huge worktable. From the look on their faces they don't see a lot of students down here. "Can we help you?" one says.

"Mmmm," I mumble, and stroll around the room, peeking into lockers and trying to buy time. My copy of *Duncan* isn't propped against the wall like I'd prayed it would be, and the locker where we stored it is empty.

Helpless is my best strategy. "Um. Collin Krell's my instructor and he told the class to study his painting this weekend, but my sister got sick, so I had to go home to Visalia, and now Krell's going to ask us about it, so I was hoping you might let me see it?"

The guy shakes his head. "Sorry, it already left for Miami."

The earth crumbles beneath me, but somehow I manage to get out, "Wow, okay."

"Hope you don't get in trouble."

"Thanks, I'll try asking my friends what it looks like."

I walk out of the room but can't hear my footsteps. What did I think was going to happen? That I'd open the locker, find Krell's painting, then somehow magically switch the two?

Right now a painting known as *Duncan*, which is in all probability my copy, is in a crate halfway to LAX. And when it gets to Miami, it won't be just a stupid, innocent copy anymore. No, once it's hung at Art Basel Miami, the king of international art fairs, my copy will be a full-blown forgery.

I'm coming for you, Adam.

CHAPTER 46

I'm jumpy as a cat in class, twisting and untwisting my pen cap, because Krell looks like he hasn't slept in days. His eyes are sunken, and he hasn't shaved, which is a first. Maybe he realized over the weekend that the *Duncan* at the party Friday night wasn't his and he's freaking out.

Taysha's right next to me, and she'd know before anyone if a scandal was brewing on campus.

"Does Krell look okay to you?" I whisper.

"He looks like a wreck. Benny had an allergic reaction Friday night, and Krell and his wife spent the weekend in the emergency room."

"Poor little guy."

"Benny's better, but the doctors are still trying to figure out what caused it."

So Krell was preoccupied with Benny, but he had to have felt something was off when he saw my copy of *Duncan*.

As class drags on, I'm beginning to believe that as of this minute, no one, including Krell, suspects there are two *Duncan*s. Those two guys in Secure Storage would not have acted so cool if I'd walked into the hottest story at CALINVA.

I scoot out of class as soon as it's over.

No one answers when I knock on the door of Adam's studio. The smashed robot taped to it grins mockingly at me.

Okay, Adam. It's 11 a.m. Monday. Where are you?

He's not in class, so he's probably working somewhere in the building. I start my search on the loading dock and work through the support areas. There's a set of stairs that lead to the basement, and as I start down them, I run into an older man I've noticed a few times around the building. He's wearing the same coveralls Adam wears when he's working.

"This level's off-limits to students," the guy says, and circles his finger in the air, ordering me to walk right back up the stairs I'm coming down.

"Sorry. I'm looking for Adam."

The man screws up his face so his eyes almost disappear. "Adam?"

"He's a grad student, but he works here part-time."

"Don't know the guy."

"Tall, dark hair, wears a silver earring shaped like a cross."

"Never seen him," he says in a way that tells me to stop asking and get going.

My neck pinches as I walk up the stairs, but I tell myself that maybe this guy works in the basement and Adam never goes down there. It's a big building. If Adam spends most of his time doing errands for the faculty, their paths wouldn't cross. Right?

I roam the halls, peeking into open classrooms and unlocked studios. Finally, I'm back on the third floor outside Adam's studio. This time when I knock a male voice calls out, "Come in."

Now, some answers.

Clearly, I've interrupted this guy who shares Adam's studio, because the paintbrush he's holding is wet. He peers at me through big black glasses, his face squashed between the tan porkpie hat pushed down over his hair and the mossy beard under his chin. "Yeah?" he says.

"Hi, I'm looking for Adam."

"Adam? Huh."

He fills his brush with paint from his palette, then turns back to the canvas in front of him.

It's Adam's.

I march across the room. "What are you doing to Adam's painting?"

The guy squints at me as if I'm nuts. "Um, this is my painting."

"No, Adam brought me here and showed me this painting. I know it's his."

"I don't know any Adam."

"Yeah, you do. He's a grad student. He shares this studio. He's been at CALINVA for almost five years."

The guy leans to one side, his mouth slack like he can't figure out what to do with me. "Only four of us work here, and I don't know him."

My mouth goes dry as sawdust. "Are you sure? Tall, dark hair, silver cross in one ear?"

He shakes his head like he can't even believe I'm still standing here.

"Then I guess I was mistaken." I walk into the hall and collapse against the wall, slide until my butt hits the floor. What the hell just happened?

My head drops into my hands and I peer out between my fingers. Adam lied when he told me he painted that painting. He lied about this being his studio, lied when he said he'd meet me the other night.

My lungs empty and I force air into them. There's so much that doesn't add up.

Julie said he had a truck, but Adam said he didn't. Still, Julie could be wrong.

The janitor didn't recognize him, but I saw Adam fix that light in Krell's classroom.

Adam has to be a student here. He has keys to the entire building and he used Ofelo's account number at Artsy.

If there's one person who can tell me for sure if Adam's a student here or not, it's Mona. My heart thuds in my chest as I head down to administration because I don't have Taysha's talent for getting Mona to spill. I approach her desk, biting my lip as if I'm embarrassed to bother her.

One eyebrow goes up when she sees me. "You look like you want something."

"You've been here awhile, right?"

"Eight bliss-filled years."

I can't rush her even though the suspense is killing me. I sigh and crush my sketch pad to my chest as if what I'm going to ask might be crossing a line.

"Okay, what is it?"

"I met this hot guy Friday night, and he told me he was a student here, so I wondered if I show you his picture, maybe you could tell me his name?"

Mona smiles. "Probably. I try to know every student here by sight, but I make an extra effort when it comes to the hot ones."

My heart is beating so hard, I'm afraid Mona can hear it. I flip my sketchbook open to Adam's face.

She presses a fingertip to her temple and studies the page for way too long. "You'd think I'd remember a face like this."

Shit, no. The blood leaves my cheeks, but I can't let her see me panic. "I can't get over his eyes . . . the way he looked at me."

Mona frowns sympathetically and hands me back my sketchbook. "Sorry I can't help."

"Well, thanks for trying." I get halfway to the door before I turn back around and look at her. "Do you think he lied to me about being a student here?" *Please say no.*

"It wouldn't be the first time."

I want to break into a run, but I hold myself back even though it takes all my strength not to. I manage to make it across the lobby to the ladies' room and throw myself into a bathroom stall.

I lock the door but can't let go of the lock.

Oh, my God. Oh my God. Oh my God.

That lying, lying liar.

Adam lured me into painting a secret copy of Krell's painting. He had the combination to the locker, the keys to Secure Storage. Adam was the only person who knew about the two paintings, and he promised we'd destroy the copy.

But then he didn't show.

I'm such a freaking idiot. He played me. The bastard played me. How could I have trusted him?

Now I know which painting is en route to Miami. Mine.

I dig the heels of my hands into my eye sockets. I've watched enough crime shows to figure out that I'm an accessory to a million-dollar art theft. It doesn't matter that I didn't intend to commit fraud or steal Krell's painting. Adam's disappeared, and it's like he never existed.

Getting thrown out of CALINVA isn't the worst thing that could happen to me. There's a chance I could go to prison.

CHAPTER 47

Taysha has saved me a seat in the front row for Color & Theory. Benita Newson conducts the class as half lecture, half debate, and expects you to speak up if you want to pass. Taysha insists that even if we have nothing to say, Newson will give us points for looking interested.

Kevin slips into the room at the last minute and heads for the back, his engineering book tight against his chest like a shield.

I want this day to be over.

Benita's tunic is woven wool, angles and blocks of red, orange, and black. When she moves she's a Cubist painting snapping to life. She jabs the air with a finger and says, "Cultural appropriation. Why is this a concern for artists?"

Taysha throws up her hand. "Because it's theft. When members of a dominant culture steal the elements of a marginalized one, they reduce the group's own culture to a stereotype."

My neck starts to itch and I twist my hair into a bun to get it off my skin.

"All right," Newson says. "But all artists steal ideas and motifs from other cultures. Isn't that what we call inspiration?"

For crap's sake, could you people stop saying the word "steal"?

"With inspiration, the artist uses elements to experiment or add layers of meaning. Van Gogh took ideas about color and composition from Japanese woodcuts, but he didn't try to paint exactly like them."

I shove my sweater down my arms, but my shirt's so damp with sweat I can smell it. I fold into myself, hoping the people beside me can't smell it, too.

The discussion keeps going, but I can't bear to listen. I can't defend copying Krell's painting without permission, but I never intended to steal his ideas.

I should tell Krell, warn him that the *Duncan* on its way to Miami is a fake. There's still time to stop it from being exhibited or to warn whoever bought it that the original has gone missing.

He'll be angry about the copy, furious actually, but he's got to appreciate me coming forward, right?

When class lets out, I head for Krell's studio. He holds office hours in the morning and usually paints in the afternoon, so he should be there.

Sweat trickles down the backs of my legs. *You're doing the right thing. You need to come clean before this explodes.*

My legs turn wobbly as I come around the corner into the hall that leads to his office, and I feel like I could vomit. And as soon as I see the sheet of paper taped to his door, I know this is not going to play out the way I'd hoped.

Due to a family emergency, office hours are canceled today and tomorrow. Professor Krell will return after the Thanksgiving break.

Should I go to the administration? No, they'd toss me out of here so fast. Krell will be furious, but he'd at least see that I didn't intend to forge his painting. I was following his instructions to transcribe a painting that moved me, even though I did it in a stupidly misguided way. I'm not guilty of forgery. I'm guilty of terrible judgment and a total disregard for him and his work.

I thump my forehead on the doorframe, even though part of what I feel is relief. *Shit*. Krell won't be back for a week, and this isn't something I can confess in an email. I need to explain how it happened. How Adam's the real criminal here.

I'm just Adam's idiot patsy. And I'm going to pay the price.

CHAPTER 48

I've avoided thinking about Thanksgiving, but when CALINVA starts to clear out after class on Tuesday, I can't pretend it's not happening anymore. Taysha gives me a long hug as we say good-bye in the lobby. "You sure you don't want to come out to Riverside with me? My moms love a full house."

It's tempting, but I'm not sure I can hold it together between the crisis with Krell and the unavoidable reality of my first Thanksgiving without Mom. The last thing I want to do is fall apart in front of Taysha and her family. They don't need their holiday ruined, hosting a blubbering, inconsolable mess. "Thanks, I really appreciate the invite, but I volunteered for extra shifts this weekend and I desperately need the cash."

"If you change your mind—"

"I'll text you."

Taysha walks off, and I go to grab a yogurt from the coffee bar off the lobby, but right when I get there, the cashier rolls down the metal gate and flips off the lights.

The cavernous cement lobby's empty except for me, the security guard, and Mona in the admin office. My footsteps echo eerily, and I speed up to get out of there.

My shift at Artsy starts in twenty, so I head up Raymond

Street. Kevin's flying home today, or maybe he left already. I know he was swamped, but I thought for sure he'd say good-bye.

Passing the homeless shelter, I spy a poster for their free Thanksgiving dinner. The turkey's shaped like a hand cut out of paper, and a memory of Mom stops me dead in my tracks.

She's ladling out sweet potatoes, a crazy paper turkey hat bobbing on her head.

Every year, we'd spend the day serving people at the Episcopal church. I loved it when I was ten, hated it when I was twelve, and blew if off to go out to dinner with Hayley's family when I was fifteen.

"Don't come," Mom told me the next year. "I know you don't want to."

I ran to phone Hayley to tell her I could join them again, thrilled Mom finally got that she couldn't force me to help the less fortunate. But I hadn't finished dialing when I put down the phone.

An hour later, I walked into the kitchen wearing a paper turkey hat shedding orange glitter. "Please, Mom. I want to come."

And right there on the sidewalk, I can feel Mom's arms around me and I sink into the memory of being loved. Loved so hard and so stubbornly, my selfishness couldn't even dent it.

When I open my eyes, I'm gripping the iron fence. I promised Mrs. Mednikov I'd help her with her dinner, but I bet she'd let me volunteer here for a few hours before it.

I push open the gate and walk into the concrete courtyard out front, where a half-dozen men mill about. Wrinkles etch their faces, even the ones who seem young. Their clothes are powdery gray, the colors muted from layers of dirt.

"Hi, guys."

An older man in a wheelchair makes a beeline for me. "You can't go inside until supper."

His crossed eyes throw me off, and I want to be respectful, but I'm not sure where to look.

A man in a frayed plaid coat comes over to us. "Homer, can't you see she's here on business?" He motions to a doorbell. "Go push that button. They'll let you in."

"Ah, thanks."

I'm buzzed into a narrow entry where the floor is speckled gray linoleum and the walls are yellow and nicked. Light filters through small windows above my head that cage the sky behind chicken wire.

A woman in knit pants and a purple cowl-neck comes out to greet me. "Good morning?" Her dark eyes sweep over me as her smile warns me not to waste her time.

"Hi, my name's Sabine. I wondered if you need any volunteers for Thursday."

"Thank you for offering, but we already have so many volunteers right now, I'm turning people away."

"Okay, well, another time maybe."

"Contact us next week if you want to volunteer for Christmas."

"Thanks, I'll keep that in mind." I turn to go, but remember the socks I have for Julie, and reach in my messenger bag. "I don't know if you know Julie, maybe she doesn't come in here, but I have these socks for her."

The woman takes the socks from my outstretched hand. "I know Julie. She stops by for breakfast most days." She rubs the wool between her fingers. "Cashmere?"

"They're soft and really warm." I see she wants a better explanation. "They were a gift. I never wear them. I thought—"

"I'll give them to Julie the next time I see her. I'm sure she'll appreciate them."

I barely get out "Thank you" when the woman's expression goes hard.

"Wait a minute. Sabine. I remember Julie mentioning you. She said you're painting a picture of her."

I grip the strap of my bag, sensing trouble. "Yes, I'm an art student at CALINVA."

"Why?"

"I'm sorry. What do you mean, why?"

"I think it's a fair question. You're painting someone who's vulnerable, someone who people often look down upon. I think I'd like to know if you're doing this to 'enhance your artistic cred.'"

I shrink under her gaze. "No, I'm not, or at least I don't think I am. I saw Julie on the street and then our paths kept crossing, so I wanted to paint her. I promise you I asked her if it was okay and she said yes."

The woman is still eyeing me, pushing me to explain.

"You don't know me, so you probably think I'm rich since I go to CALINVA, but for a while I lived in my car. I know what it's like to have people's eyes move past you, judging you but not really seeing you, and I . . ."

I can't go on and I shouldn't have to. I don't know this woman, and I don't owe her an explanation.

"Sabine," the woman says quietly. "I'm sorry. I assumed wrongly."

"It's okay. I get it. You're trying to look out for Julie."

"Do you think I could see your painting when it's done?"

For a moment, I'm stunned. "Yes." I dig into my bag and pull out a flyer. "There's a show at CALINVA in two weeks. You can come to the opening reception and bring Julie if you want."

The woman studies the flyer as she walks me to the door. "I apologize for not introducing myself. I'm Florence Harris. And I would very much like to come to the exhibition. I doubt Julie would agree to, however. As you may know, she's very uncomfortable indoors."

"Yeah, she's told me that."

Florence Harris lets me out, and I wave good-bye to the men in the courtyard and continue back up the street. I can't help feeling I might have made a mistake inviting her to the opening since there's no guarantee I'll still be at CALINVA when it happens.

CHAPTER 49

Wednesday night, I fall into a hard and dreamless sleep, but a call comes at 2 a.m. I fumble for the phone, and my eyes struggle to focus on the too bright screen.

NAME WITHHELD. Normally, I'd assume it's a wrong number, but for some strange reason I answer.

"Hello?"

"Did I wake you, Sabine?" Adam sounds like he couldn't care less.

I sit straight up. "You played me, you prick."

There are street sounds in the background. People passing by? A bus?

"True. But admit it: You were happy to be played. You got what Krell wouldn't give you, and sticking it to him—that's just a bonus."

"Where's his painting?" I demand.

"Hard to say. A portrait by a contemporary master like Krell can end up anywhere: China, Russia, Bahrain. A Swiss art vault. A drug lord's villa."

I shudder and pull my blanket around my shoulders. Krell's painting has gone underground. Stolen art almost never resurfaces, especially when crime lords are involved. The Rembrandts and ten other masterpieces stolen from the Gardner Museum decades ago have never been found despite a ten-million-dollar reward.

Adam continues, "When I picked you for my partner—"

"I'm not your partner."

"I could not believe my luck. A highly talented student, the only one in her class who'd even attempted encaustic painting, desperate to hold on to her scholarship in the face of Krell's unrelenting abuse."

I'm horrified at how easy I was to figure out, how transparent.

"Now imagine how surprised I was to discover you weren't the naive, innocent girl I'd assumed. You're like me. You steal, but not just for the money. You wanted to get back at that woman."

The words take my breath away. It was an accident Iona's dress was in my car. *I'm not like you,* I want to say, but I can't. "You won't get away with this, Adam, or whoever you are. When Krell gets to Art Basel, he'll realize the painting's a fake."

"Yes. The area on the shoulder I was forced to complete. Clumsy, I know. At first I was angry you refused to finish it, but as I imagined how this would play out and what options I had, I realized you'd pointed the way for me to get what I ultimately wanted." He takes a sip of whatever he's drinking.

I have no idea what he's talking about, but the tone of his voice makes me squirm. "I'm going to Krell and I'm telling him everything."

"Of course I can't stop you, but you should ask yourself: Will Krell appreciate my honesty when he has to return the nine hundred thousand he got for the painting? Will it stop him from getting my ass thrown out of CALINVA?"

I have no comeback. The painting's gone and confessing won't bring it back. I'll be the only one around for Krell to blame.

"And before you try calling his dealer, consider this: Barry Ankarian has no reason to believe you, not when the truth would screw his million-dollar sale. And a few years from now, when you're angling for your first gallery show, he'll warn his friends you don't appear to be 'all there,' and they might want to stay far, far away from you." Adam lets that sink in before he says ever so quietly, "So, is confessing really worth the price?"

I hang my head, hating myself for my silence.

"I promise you, Sabine. Next semester will be easier."

He hangs up and I set down the phone and pull the blankets tight around me. I lie awake, thinking I can't fix this.

Adam could be anywhere. He could live for years on what he got for Krell's painting. Maybe not in the US, but in Mexico, Costa Rica, Thailand.

There's just enough moonlight to make out Mom's painting on the bureau. I gaze at her face and remember her saying, "I didn't hit bottom because of what life did to me. I got there because of what I did to myself."

I don't know how far away bottom is, but I'm careening through space and it's going to hurt like hell when I hit.

CHAPTER 50

On Thanksgiving morning, I swear I've just fallen back to sleep when the *whack whack whack* of furious chopping makes my eyes snap open. From the sound of it, Mrs. Mednikov is dicing pounds and pounds of onions or maybe celery.

Ugh. I know I promised her I'd help with Thanksgiving dinner, but right now I can barely lift my head. Adam's call has flattened me, and I wish I could disappear and not come back until the mess with Krell is over.

Mom looks down from her portrait. "I know, I know. You don't have to say it," I tell her, and drag myself out of bed. "The only way out is through."

I pluck Mom's paper turkey hat off the dresser. It's wrinkled, and most of the glitter's gone, but I stick it on my head and scuff into the kitchen. *Today sucks, but I will get through it.*

"Good! You are awake!" Mrs. Mednikov says, and heaves a bag of russets into my hands. "The potatoes need peeling." She raises an eyebrow at the paper turkey perched on my head. "You are wearing a hat."

"My mom liked to wear this on Thanksgiving."

"Very festive, but perhaps something dressier when the guests arrive?"

"Oh, I guess you want me to change out of my pajamas, too?"

Mrs. Mednikov's been baking for days, and the kitchen counters are crammed with gingerbread, dinner rolls, rye bread, and pie. We prep Russian potato salad and wedge it in the refrigerator under a bowl of pickled herring. Then I help her wrestle a pork roast into the oven with the turkey, because what if there wasn't enough to eat?

A half hour before the guests are due, she shoos me out of the kitchen to get dressed. Fresh out of the shower, I sift through my closet for *dressier* until I find a blouse I've never worn. Loose silk with sheer gold, crimson, and cobalt stripes, I touch the fluttery ends of the sleeves, remembering how Mom beamed when I slid it out of the tissue last Christmas.

An ache fills my chest. She spent way too much and I told her I wanted to save it for a perfect occasion, and she said, "Wait too long for perfect, and you'll miss great."

I slide my arms in the sleeves. The silk is light as air on my skin as I button it on.

When I walk back to the kitchen after drying my hair, Kevin's there. His sleeves are rolled up to his elbows and he's mashing a big pot of sweet potatoes.

My heart swells, and I throw my arms around his shoulders. "What are you doing here?" Kevin glances over his shoulder at me, and green sunbursts halo his irises. How did I not notice his eyes are hazel, not brown?

"I'm on kitchen duty. I came in the wrong door and she nabbed me," Kev says, and jerks his elbow at Mrs. Mednikov. "I'm not a serf, you know."

"You want to eat, you can help," she throws back.

"She thinks she's a czarina," he mutters.

Mrs. Mednikov gives me a look. *This one I like.*

Me too.

The doorbell rings, and Mrs. Mednikov slaps a spoon in my hand. "The gravy. Do not let it burn." Then she's gone.

"I thought you were going home," I tell Kevin as I start to stir.

"Too much going on between lab reports and the First-Year Exhibition next weekend, so when Stephania invited me, I canceled my flight."

Mrs. Mednikov didn't ask me about inviting Kevin, but I smile to myself and decide to give her a pass. "How's *Unresolved*?"

"It's living up to its name."

"I'm sorry."

"No, it'll be fine. My roommate's helping me with the mechanical stuff." Kevin points to the open door of the sun-porch. "*Seen/Not Seen* is looking good."

I left the canvas on the easel after working on it yester-day. "Yeah, almost done. I hope it's enough to impress the faculty."

"I wouldn't worry. I think you're solid."

The front door opens, and Mrs. Mednikov's joy can be heard all the way to the kitchen. "Peter! Chelsea! Welcome! Oh, Tobias, what a big boy you are."

I peek into the living room, where she's kissing the cheeks of a young couple and their toddler. Peter's a tall blonde with a port-wine stain across his temple. He rented from Mrs. Mednikov several years ago. Chelsea's a small, freckled Madonna whose ginger hair is braided like a challah on top of her head.

Chelsea takes in the paintings that cover almost every

inch of the living room walls. "Art students did all of these?" she says.

"Yes. I give one month rent-free in return for a painting," Mrs. Mednikov answers. "Can you pick out your husband's?"

"Shouldn't be hard." Chelsea puts Tobias on her hip and strolls around the room while his dad and Mrs. Mednikov watch.

It's hard to take my eyes off this happy family, the nods and glances and smiles that go back and forth between the couple, a deep silent conversation that only they truly understand.

Someday, I could have that.

I turn back to the stove and stir the gravy. *Where the hell did that come from?*

Guests continue to arrive, and Mrs. Mednikov frees Kevin and me from the kitchen. She puts her arm through mine, and we circle the room with a tray of tiny glasses of vodka. From the guests' smiles and knowing glances as she introduces me, I sense they've already heard about me.

An older man, a collector of rare books, looking dapper in a burgundy tie and navy vest, raises his glass. "To our beautiful hostess," he says, and we toast.

Her guests are as vibrant and varied as the paintings on the walls. Men and women of different ages: a music composer for documentaries, a rose collector, a trustee of a local dance company, a chess master, and a man who designs bridges.

Kevin sits on the floor with Tobias as the little boy stacks yellow, red, and blue plastic blocks on the coffee table. Kevin removes the top block from Tobias's tower and hands it to Tobias, who puts it right back on.

"Did you pick out your husband's painting?" I ask Chelsea.

"On the first try." She points to the dark blue abstract whose brush marks crash like a turbulent sea. "I know him so well, how could I miss?" She raises her glass to Peter's, and they clink.

I think back to the disconnect I felt with the painting Adam claimed was his. I knew it wasn't. I knew in my gut, but I ignored it.

Kevin plucks the top block off Tobias's tower, but this time he covers his eyes as Tobias puts it back. When Kevin uncovers his eyes, he acts shocked that the block has reappeared, and Tobias screams with delight.

I steal glances at Peter's port-wine stain. It's beautiful in a way, a map of an imaginary island. And the fact that he doesn't hide it, but instead he parts his hair so it's exposed, makes me like him even more.

Mrs. Mednikov refills Peter's vodka glass, and he gives me a wink. "Has Stephania chosen a painting of yours yet?" he asks.

Before I can answer, Mrs. Mednikov interrupts. "I would like the painting Sabine is working on now, *Seen/Not Seen*. It is very powerful."

"I didn't know you liked it that much," I say.

"Now you know."

Peter smiles and raises a pale eyebrow. "Can we get a preview?"

"No. It is not ready," Mrs. Mednikov declares. "But you may view it at the First-Year Exhibition next Saturday."

"I guess we're going," he says as Mrs. M turns to another guest.

"Don't feel you have to come," I tell him.

"Stephania's an unstoppable force and I've given up trying to resist her." Peter sips his vodka. "What did you think of Collin Krell's newest painting?"

It's an innocent question, but for a split second I freeze. "Um, it's genius."

"One of those paintings you wish you'd painted?"

My cheeks get hot as I laugh. "That happens to you, too?"

"Happens to everyone," he says.

Mrs. Mednikov sets the vodka on the table and invites us all to take our seats. Kevin sits across from me. The table's lush with gourds and red and gold mums. Light catches on the facets of the delicate crystal that survived the trip from Eastern Europe decades ago.

Kevin and the bridge designer mirror each other as they talk, their hands shaping arches and sweeps of steel. I can't hear over everyone talking, but I know when Kevin describes *Unresolved* because his hands flick back and forth like the panels of his painting.

The sun sets and the first round of toasts is followed by three or four or maybe five more. I lose count. We eat, and with each course, Mrs. Mednikov brings out dishes I didn't even know she'd made.

The conversation roams from art to literature to politics. The woman with the dance company invites me to sketch a rehearsal. Kevin and the chess master debate openings in chess-speak. The composer makes a hand puppet out of napkins and keeps Tobias giggling until he crashes on his dad's shoulder. They lay him on the couch facedown, and the book collector sings a Russian lullaby over him, gazing at Mrs. Mednikov while he does.

We are an odd assembly, like a sculpture of found objects: a clock, a kettledrum, a kitchen whisk, that once they're put together remind you of an elephant or a pagoda.

Taking in this makeshift family, I'm flooded with longing for Mom. Tears judder in my eyes, and when I glance across the table, Kevin is looking back. *I'm here for you.*

I don't know how he knows what I'm feeling, or how he knows what I need, but I curl my hand into a fist and lay it over my heart.

We gaze at each other, and smile. The air shimmers with the raucous harmony of this table, these people.

For a long time, I didn't believe that I could ever be happy again. But at this moment, I see that real joy is possible.

CHAPTER 51

At one point, Kevin disappears into the kitchen and doesn't return. I get up, wondering if he left, before I spy him through the open door to the sunporch. He's lounging in a wicker chair, talking on his phone.

Light from the kitchen falls across his back. On his phone screen, a girl a few years younger than us, whose cropped hair is badly dyed, is chatting at him nonstop.

Kevin senses me behind him and turns. He unhooks his earphones and tugs me onto the chair arm. "Hey, Toby, this is my friend Sabine."

"Hi, Sabine!" She gives me a little wave, but a sinister glint has entered her eyes.

"Hi, Toby."

"Give her the phone, Kevs. I want to talk to Sabine in private."

Now I'm intrigued. I reach for the phone, but Kevin hugs it to his chest. "You don't have to talk to my kid sister. I can tell Toby you're busy."

"No, I want to. How else am I going to learn your secrets?"

"Okay, but don't say I didn't warn you."

I carry the phone down the steps into the yard. *Whoa.* I haven't drunk this much in a long time, and I'm a little unsteady on my feet. "So what do you want to talk about, Toby?"

"I've heard about you and I know you're after my brother."

I catch my toe on the stone path and lurch forward. "I am?"

"Yes, Ms. Just a Friend from School. Showing up late at night with bagels? Inviting him to help you track down the Korean-Mexican fusion truck? Kevs may be dense when it comes to how girls hook guys, but I'm not."

Kevin's seeing someone?

My stomach goes sloshy, imagining him and a girl sharing kimchi. How did I not know? How did Taysha not know? Doesn't matter, I tell myself. Kev deserves to be happy. "Yeah, you're onto me."

I wander into the driveway and peer out at the street. Someone is strumming a guitar nearby, not playing a song exactly, but trying out the strings.

"Listen," Toby says. "You'd better treat my brother right, because if you hurt him like that cockroach-lipped Chantal, I will take you down. Maybe not me exactly, but I know how to access the dark net."

"Did you just threaten to have me murdered?"

Her mouth drops open. "No. Not murdered." It takes her a moment to recover her steely-eyed bravado. "I'd have them break your hands!"

The porch light snaps on and I turn back to the house. Kevin's holding a guitar I didn't know he'd brought.

"So, Toby, I hate to disappoint you, but I am not the girl seducing your brother with Korean-Mexican fusion. Kev and I are just friends. But I will help you exact revenge if she hurts him."

"Why didn't you just say it wasn't you?"

"Curiosity, and a bunch of vodka shots. You want to say good night to your brother?"

I walk the phone toward the house, and the first notes of a song send ripples down my spine. Kevin sings so softly I can barely hear him, but the lyrics of the song are tattooed on my heart. I sing along in my head, hearing the ache in Mom's voice.

"Cruel wind at my back and holes in my shoes . . ."

Mom hardly ever talked about leaving Oregon for LA, but on the nights she sang that song, I'd learn one or two more things about Grandma Betty, who turned her back on us.

I step onto the porch, and Kevin looks up. I hold out the phone and he strums a few more bars before he takes it from me. As he says good night to Toby, he fails to notice I'm frozen in place.

Red roses twine up the neck of the guitar he's playing. It isn't a copy of Mom's guitar. It's Mom's.

I shake my head, openmouthed. "I can't believe it. How did you know?"

"'Broke Down in Stockton'? It's a classic."

He's talking about the song, not the guitar. My silent confusion prompts him to try again. "Oh, wait," he says. "Did your mom play that song?"

"Yeah, she did." Nothing makes sense. How the hell did Mom's guitar get here?

"God, I'm sorry. I should have asked before I touched her guitar, but when I saw the case, I wanted to see how the repair turned out."

A sick feeling floods me. If Kevin didn't bring me Mom's guitar, then who did? The only person who knew I'd pawned it was Adam. I'm nauseous, imagining him creeping around the backyard early this morning and dropping it off on the porch.

"It's okay. I'm not mad," I tell Kevin.

"The guy did an amazing job matching the wood. I can't even tell where he fixed it."

I sink down on the chair beside him. It could be the endless vodka shots or my lack of sleep, but I'm so damn tired of lying about everything.

"The guitar wasn't being repaired. I lied, because I was too embarrassed to tell you I pawned it."

One thing about painting portraits is you learn to really look at someone's face. If you're not blinded by how you feel about them, you can catch small shifts in their expression that reveal more than they'd ever admit.

And what I see in Kevin's face tells me he's heard people talking about me, and he's tried to ignore it, but he can't any longer. I'm ready for him to ask me about Iona and the dress when he says, "Is it true you were homeless?"

It takes a second for it to register with me what he's asked. "Yes. For about six months after Mom died."

"I thought you said you lived with your friend."

"I did, but it didn't work out."

"Why didn't you say anything before?"

I shrink even farther down in the chair. "Because once you tell someone you were homeless, that's how they see you forever. I don't want someone looking at me and wondering if I lived in a crappy motel or a tent on the sidewalk next to heroin addicts and hookers, which I didn't. I want people to see me as I am now, as an artist."

He's quiet for so long that it's obvious he doesn't know what to say. He thought he knew me, but now . . .

"I'm sorry you had to go through that," he says.

My heart squeezes at the gentleness in his voice. His fingers are laced together, and he's not quite looking at me. He knows there's more I'm not telling him.

"People are talking about me and Iona Taylor. I should probably tell you the whole story."

"You don't have to tell me anything you don't want to," he says.

"No, I do."

He's mostly quiet as I share Mom's final days, and what happened after with Iona, how I chose to sell what wasn't mine, and how it's come back at me.

"But you knew what you were doing was wrong," he says, leaving the so-why-did-you unsaid.

"I can't defend what I did. I knew it was wrong, but I needed to hold on to my car, and I was still unbelievably angry about how Iona treated Mom and me."

He's not looking at me, and any second now he's going to get up and go in, thank Mrs. Mednikov for a lovely dinner, and drive off, never to trust me again.

"I don't know what I would have done if I was you," he says quietly. "I'm not exactly sure how I'd handle things if I was thrown out on the street."

I let out the breath I didn't know I was holding in. Kev's not absolving me, but he's trying to understand. If he had any fantasies about what a good person I am, they're gone now.

"We've been out here awhile," he says, and goes to stand up. "We should probably rejoin the party."

I reach out and touch his arm. "Wait. I need to know. Are we still friends?"

"Of course we are," he says. "Yeah, you made a mistake, but you're a good person. And now you're back in school, you're safe, you've got your scholarship and a place to live. You'd never do anything like that again."

Kevin's trying, but when he meets my eyes, I see that as sorry as he is for what I've gone through, he wishes I'd told him all the rumors were lies.

CHAPTER 52

Long after the guests leave with groaning bags of leftovers, long after the dishes are washed and Mrs. Mednikov has gone to bed, I take out Mom's guitar.

Last week I imagined what it would be like to have it back. To wake up in the morning and see the black case tucked safely in the corner by my bureau. I'd vowed I'd never let it out of my hands again no matter how desperate I got.

But now her guitar is on my lap, and when I picture Adam opening the case and handling it, I'm sick. I feel in a drawer for my softest tee and use it to rub his touch off the shiny blond spruce, the mahogany sides, and up the neck.

The cotton glides over the wood, erasing Adam's fingerprints, but not his taint. I'll never be able to look at Mom's guitar again without seeing him.

How did he get his hands on it? The pawnshop drilled into me to hold on to my ticket. "You need this to redeem your guitar. Do not lose it," Steve said when he handed me the pawn ticket for the loan.

I reach for my wallet, but when I thumb through it, the ticket's gone. Adam must have gone through my wallet some night in Krell's studio while we were cleaning up. And he found out from the ticket where I live, because my license doesn't have Mrs. Mednikov's address on it.

But why? Why screw up my life and then turn around and give me back Mom's guitar? Guilt? He said he liked me.

I'm polishing the brass tuning pegs when the answer pops into my head: Adam didn't leave me Mom's guitar because he felt guilty. He did it to warn me that I'm as guilty as he is. He knows I'll never sell it or give it away, and every time I look at it, it will remind me of how I got it back.

Mom tack-stitched a small pocket to the velvet lining of the guitar case so she'd have a place to keep her picks. I slip my finger inside, expecting to find a plastic pick, but instead I discover a folded paper ticket.

"Great. Paid in full," I mutter when I see the big red stamp across it.

I screwed Krell over but can't pay him back. My debt will never be paid in full.

I could confess before *Duncan* goes on exhibit in Miami. But even though it's the right thing to do, it won't get his painting back, or the months he spent on it, or the hundreds of thousands of dollars he'll lose when the sale falls apart.

If I confess, we both lose, but if I keep quiet, this could all go away. The buyer gets a not-so-genuine Krell, Krell keeps his money, the gallery's reputation is spotless, and I start second semester a sadder but much savvier girl.

Mom tut-tuts in my head. *Good luck with that magical thinking, honey. Let me know how that works out for you.*

Maybe Adam did commit the perfect crime, but it's also possible he screwed up, and if he does go down for it, he'll try to take me with him. And since he's still around, he could be watching me right now.

I get up and snap the curtains closed.

I realize I need to arm myself—not with a gun, but with

evidence that shows he exists, and that he lured me into painting the copy.

Someone has to know who Adam really is. How he got keys to CALINVA and Ofelo's account number at Artsy. There's got to be something I've missed that connects Adam and CALINVA. Adam knew Ofelo's habits, his schedule. He could have stolen Ofelo's account number like he stole mine.

I have no photos of Adam, and I curse myself for wiping his fingerprints off Mom's guitar, but at least I have the sketch I made. I dig out a sketch pad and jot down notes as I try to remember as much as I can about him.

And the more I write down, the more embarrassed I am at the lies I believed and the things I refused to see.

Adam made sure no one at CALINVA saw us together. Never gave me an email address. If he had a truck, he parked it where I'd never see it. Never showed me where he lived.

He never spoke about family or friends. Never even named the photographer he supposedly worked for. The people and places he did talk about . . . he could have picked them up on the internet.

He planned everything down to the very last detail. Keys to the building. Ofelo's account number. Me—his naive, pissed-off accomplice.

The only person I know who saw Adam and me together at CALINVA is Julie, and who'd believe a homeless woman?

I flip through the notes, thinking maybe I won't need any of this. Maybe Krell will be too busy walking the show and schmoozing with the luminaries of the art world to clue in to the fake, and Adam and *Duncan* will fade into the sunset, leaving me free of them both.

Turns out I'm a natural at magical thinking.

CHAPTER 53

I work and paint nonstop the rest of the weekend, doing day shifts at Artsy and evening shifts at La Petite Tomate, and fitting in time with *Seen/Not Seen* in between. The art store is as frenzied as my manager promised, but the tips from happy revelers at the restaurant will more than cover my car insurance for the next month.

The nonstop pace keeps me from obsessing about Adam and Krell. I don't know what I should do once Krell gets back, and every time I start to think about it, my thoughts tornado around my head until I almost can't breathe.

Kevin texts me updates about his battle to get the bugs out of *Unresolved* before Friday's exhibition. I'm relieved we're still talking, but can't help wondering if it's because he feels sorry for me, CALINVA's messed-up orphan.

Sunday night, I don't have to waitress, so I'm deep into painting the double portrait. While the rest of my life feels like it's about to crash, *Seen/Not Seen* is soaring. On the left half of the canvas where I show Julie the way I see her, my brushwork is so measured and precise it almost disappears, so she looks strangely regal as she holds up her head and her handmade sign, despite her dirty clothes and bare feet.

Tonight I attack the right side, the one that will picture Julie the way others might see her: feral and unknowable.

I've thought and sketched and talked about this other half for so long, and now it's time to make it real.

I squeeze a line of black paint out on the palette before I remember Krell daring me not to use that color, and I reach for my tubes of scarlet, cobalt nickel green, and ultramarine blue. I'm not sure I'm ready to abandon black, but I can at least try.

I load my brush with paint and slash the white canvas. My strokes are loose, bold, and unrelenting. The band of fur Julie wears around her head darkens until it forms a charred crown. Her face is blurred, her identity erased. Sweetie perches on her shoulder, rat teeth bared, her fur spiky and electric shocked.

I paint the sign Julie holds. HI, MY NAME IS JULIE. I HAVE CANCER. PLEASE HELP. Then I XXX over the words, obliterating her message. When I step back from the canvas to take it in, the panel is both scary and unapologetic.

I love what I've done, but is it enough? Krell challenged me to explore dimensionality, but where do I go from here? Is there a way I can use dimension to add a layer of meaning or force the viewer to reflect on what I'm saying?

I play with ideas for what I could add to the surface, but I don't want to come across as copying Bernadette. My solution has to be unique. It's late when I give up and crawl into bed.

I'm dead asleep when the answer wakes me. It's still dark out, but I drag Mrs. Mednikov's toolbox out to the porch. I flip the painting over and pry out the staples holding it to the supports. When the canvas is free, I cut it in half, separating the two portraits.

I set the first aside, then pick up the black-and-white

one and tear at the unpainted edges, trying to shred them. I twist the canvas, ball it up until it cracks, but it's not enough. Finally I drag a screwdriver down the face of it, gouging the paint.

When I hold it up, it's everything I want to say about how false and mistaken this image of Julie is.

I smell coffee, and when I turn around Mrs. Mednikov is watching me from the doorway. "A breakthrough, yes?"

"Yes." I roll the two pieces up so I can take them to work. My coworker Romy can help me fix the canvas to new stretchers. This is it.

CHAPTER 54

K rell cancels Painting 101 so he can meet with us individually before the First-Year Exhibition. A sloshy feeling hits me when I note the time of my end-of-semester conference. I need to tell Krell about *Duncan*, but I'm afraid I'm too much of a coward to do it.

Our work is due no later than 10 a.m. on Friday, and by Tuesday everyone's feeling the pressure. Self-medicating. Bursting into tears or hysterical laughter. It's actually a relief to walk out of CALINVA and go work in Artsy's pre-Christmas mania.

Taysha texts me around six. I NEED HELP. COME BY AFTER WORK?! she pleads. When I call her back, her voice is ragged, and now I know why she wasn't in class for the last two days.

I show up with Mrs. Mednikov's goulash still steaming under the foil cover. Taysha's apartment is a small studio behind a garage. When she unlocks the door, her eyes are slits and her hair is a half-blown dandelion. She's layered in sweaters, and fingerless gloves cover her hands.

A space heater rattles in the corner, but the cement floor makes my feet go cold.

The bed's on a platform over a worktable with a sewing machine on it. Clothes hang from a makeshift rack. I set the goulash down on top of the microwave. The kitchen is a sink, a toaster oven, and a refrigerator that could fit inside a dishwasher if the place had one.

"I'm sorry," Taysha says. "I know you've got your own work to do, but I'm freaking out."

"No, it's fine. I'm in good shape. *Seen/Not Seen*'s almost done."

"I have to finish the *Zoetrope Coat* tonight. David Tito's filming it tomorrow so I can make the deadline for the LA fashion scholarship."

"Okay, we'll get it done."

Taysha scrubs her face with her hands. "I lost it when CALINVA announced the tuition increase. I had to bust my ass last year to get enough grants and scholarships to be able to come, and now?"

"I know. It's crazy, right?" I can't think of how to respond, embarrassed my scholarship protects me from tuition increases—as long as I hold on to it. "So, how can I help?" I say, turning to the fabric laid out on a folding table. I recognize the black wool as the body of Taysha's coat and the hand-painted panels that are the insets.

"The sleeves, the collar, and the bodice are done. I painted all the panels, except the last one." Taysha grabs her sketch pad and flips the pages until she gets to the one she wants and holds it up. "If you paint the final panel, I'll sew the rest into the skirt and then finish sewing the pieces together."

I take the sketch from her and my stomach sinks. I wish she'd asked me to do anything else.

Taysha sees me hesitate. "What's the matter?"

Me painting her design on the fabric is not cheating, I tell myself. It's her idea. I'm just executing it. "Nothing. It's all good."

Taysha lays out the fabric for me. Her sketch is to scale and she's worked out all the colors. I mix the paint to match the sketch and think through how to begin. Taysha's sewing machine growls, and the backs of our folding chairs almost touch.

"How was Thanksgiving?" she says.

"It was really nice. Mrs. Mednikov invited a ton of people for dinner and Kevin came."

"Kevin? I thought he went home to Kansas."

"Nah. He had too much work." I pause before adding, "But I think there's a girl."

The sewing machine stops. "Pray tell."

I start painting a corner of the pie-shaped panel, and the sewing machine hums along thoughtfully as I fill Taysha in on my conversation with Kevin's sister. When I describe the midnight food-truck runs, there's an edge in my voice that surprises me.

"Hmm. I have to wonder if Toby got the story right," Taysha says. "She wouldn't be the first fifteen-year-old to invent a romance."

"Well, someone's been bringing him bagels."

"How are things between you and Kevin?" she asks.

I go to answer, and the words catch in my throat. "I'm not sure where Kevin and I stand exactly. We had a long talk about what happened with my mom and my problems with Iona . . ."

"And?"

"You know Kevin. He was perfectly nice, trying not to make me feel bad, but the way he looked at me—it was like he wasn't sure who I was anymore."

"You're afraid of losing him."

Her words hit me harder than I could have guessed. "We're not together, Taysha."

"Do you know how you really feel about him?" Taysha says quietly. "Because it looks to me like you're avoiding the question."

I turn back to the panel. "You're probably right," I murmur.

Thoughts roll in my head like waves while I paint. I'm not sure I can trust my feelings when it comes to Kevin. I had Krell all wrong, Adam all wrong.

So how do I really feel about Kevin?

My knees don't buckle when I see him, I don't lie awake thinking about him, but when I walk into class and he's not there?

Kevin's the spot of red in a green painting that brings it to life. He changes how I look at things, and he makes me feel *seen*.

Kevin would never lie to me. He'd tell me the truth, even if it was hard for me to hear. And he'd try to be kind.

I imagine him walking through the butterfly grove with someone else, and my heart squeezes. "I really like him," I admit to Taysha.

She smiles as she bites through a thread. "Thought so."

We go back to work, and I'm painting in the tiny details when Taysha asks if Tara's gotten back to me about repaying Iona. "Not yet. I still don't know how I'm going to come up with the money."

"Maybe you don't offer her money."

"I offer her what instead?"

"A big-ass portrait."

I start to laugh. "You're insane."

"Don't laugh! I'm serious. Iona Taylor's a diva, and what do divas want? They want to be *seen*! I bet if you offered to paint a life-size portrait of Iona, she'd snap it up."

What Taysha's saying starts to sink in. Everyone wants to be seen a certain way. Iona wants people to see her as a star. "That's not a terrible idea. Especially if I could paint her in that dress. I bet there's a pic of her wearing it online."

"More like a thousand. She wore it on the red carpet."

By midnight, we're both exhausted, but Taysha's finished the coat—the outside, at least. "I can line it after David photographs it. See what you think."

She puts her arms in the sleeves and hands me her phone. "I need to see if it works," she says, and starts to twirl. The *Zoetrope Coat* flares and the panels emerge from the folds. Like a flip-book, a story unfolds: A girl rises from the ground, her wrists in chains, then she surges into the air and the chains break. Fist raised, she transforms from captive to superhero.

I beam, watching Taysha spin on the screen. "It works, it's amazing," I say.

"I'm going to make T-shirts," she says. "I'll pay you royalties for using your artwork."

"No, no way," I tell her. "Your design. You own it. I was just the hands."

"Then let me dress you for the exhibit." Taysha reaches into the clothing rack and pulls out a dress. "You think that girl Kevin's supposedly seeing will show up in anything that can compare to this?"

"No way." I pull off my sweater and slip the sheath over my head. The brown leather is as thin as paper and it shapes to me. It's a riff on flapper style, if flappers wore brass buckles on their hips. "Are you sure?"

"Pass up the opportunity to show this off to a roomful of artists and tastemakers? I'd be a fool to do that."

I carry the dress out to my car and lay it gently on the seat. It's late, but knowing Iona, there's a good chance Tara's still up, doing what assistants do. So I text her.

About a second later, she calls me. "I assume this is about your repayment plan."

I'm tempted to be snarky right back, but I force myself not to. I need Tara to sell Iona on my idea. "I have a proposal."

"Let's hear it."

"The dress is gone, which is my fault, and there's no way I can give it back. But . . . what I *can* give Iona is a little of how it felt to wear it."

"And how do you propose to do that?"

"What if I paint a life-size portrait of Iona in the dress? I could base it on photos of her on the red carpet. She can hang it on that big wall in the living room, and every time she walks in there, she can see how amazing she looked that night."

Tara says, "Interesting," and I can hear her amusement, as if she knows what it's costing me to offer this. "This would be a realistic portrait?"

"I'll even match her lipstick."

"I'll share this with Iona and get back to you. But not tonight." *Click.*

Okay, then.

As I drive back to Mrs. Mednikov's I think about Iona wanting to be seen. I've spent weeks thinking about how people judge Julie instead of seeing her, and how people would label me if they knew I'd lived in my car, but I've never once thought about why Iona is so desperate to have the cameras on her.

Mom always seemed to make excuses for Iona's behavior, but now I wonder if she saw what was underneath it. I remember her telling me that if I looked past my feelings, I'd see people more clearly.

I park my car but don't get out. Maybe it's because I'm so tired that I can finally take in how the reason I'm probably in the messes I'm in with Krell and Adam and Iona is because I couldn't look past my anger and fear and hurt. My feelings blinded me, and only now am I starting to see clearly.

CHAPTER 55

On Friday, I deliver *Seen/Not Seen* to CALINVA for the First-Year Exhibition, and as I carry my canvas up the entrance ramp I feel like it's weighed down with the irony that this could be my first *and* last exhibit.

Yesterday, Romy helped me mount *Seen/Not Seen*. The portrait of Julie as I see her is stretched taut over wood supports, while the black-and-white one hangs down from it like a discarded snakeskin tacked to the wood frame.

I'm glad I took a risk and played with dimension like Krell encouraged me to. The painting says everything I want it to say.

The white gallery walls are empty for now. The staff has leaned several canvases against the blank spaces, testing how to arrange the show.

Damn, I missed Kevin, I realize, spying *Unresolved*. Things have been so crazed this week, I've barely seen him.

Bernadette's painting isn't here yet, but I'm sure it will grab the choicest spot: the middle of the long back wall where a piece can be seen from every corner of the room.

Not surprisingly, three staffers are clustered around Bryian's painting. Everyone's talking about the enormous Asian baby biting the head off a toy North Korean soldier while other soldiers wait their turn. The official title is *Our*

Benevolent Leader, but Kevin calls it *Totzilla*, and the rumor, which some of us think came from Bryian himself, is that Kim Jong-un has threatened "a merciless attack that will silence Bryian, the American imperialist warmonger."

A bow-tied staffer dashes over to help as I carry my painting through the double glass doors. "Interesting," he says as he takes it from me. "Name?" His red gingham shirt and the cresting wave in his gelled hair make me think of the Lollipop Guild from *The Wizard of Oz*.

"My name or the painting's?" I answer.

He chuckles and takes the canvas from me. "Yours."

"Sabine Reyes."

"We have Reyes!" he calls out, and another staffer checks me off a list as bow-tie guy walks *Seen/Not Seen* deep into the room before setting it down.

Then he steps back and studies it, looking back and forth between *Seen/Not Seen* and the other paintings they've set in place. I can't tell if he likes it, if he's impressed, or if he sees hanging it as just another task he has to get done.

"Do you care where it hangs?" He lowers his voice and his eyes glitter behind thick black glasses. "Usually people want to be hung near a friend or away from a piece they . . . well, you know . . ."

Loathe?

It's tempting to take over, but Krell warned us that behaving like a diva with the staff could get our work stuck in a dark corner. "Nope, I trust you guys to decide what works best."

The look that comes over his face tells me not everyone listened to Krell's warning.

"But there is one thing," I say. "And I understand if you can't help with this, but a friend of mine can't make it to the show, so if you could hang my painting so she could see it through the window, I'd be really grateful."

He smiles and digs a Post-it out of his shirt pocket. "I'll see what I can do," he says as he scribbles a note and slaps it on the painting.

I exit the gallery and head right for the coffee bar. I've given *Seen/Not Seen* all I have, every bit of imagination and conviction I possess, and if that isn't good enough for Krell and the scholarship committee, then I don't know. My final conference with him is this afternoon, so I won't have to wait to hear his judgment.

When I return, half the gallery is hung and the staffers are in a corner. The four of them are mounting Taysha's *Zoetrope Coat*, attaching clips and stringing wires to the walls and ceiling so the twelve painted panels on the skirt are visible.

Taysha's going to be thrilled.

I glance around, and in the middle of the room a canvas that can only be mine hangs from the ceiling so it faces the street.

Did they really do that? I dash around to the front, and yes! Julie will be able to see her portrait from outside. "You guys are amazing! Thank you so much!"

The team looks up and one of them nods at his buddy. "It was Marco's idea."

I blow Marco kisses and he gives me a thumbs-up.

Then I pause to appreciate the moment. Six months ago, I was barely surviving, and now I stand here with a painting I know is good and it's hanging in a real gallery.

"Ms. Reyes." Krell strides over to me. "Ready for your critique?"

It's the first time I've seen him in days, and my stomach flips. *Do the right thing: Tell him the truth.*

But confessing won't help. It will only make things worse.

Krell peers at me. "Is everything all right?"

"Yes, yes, everything's fine."

"Then let's begin with your artist statement."

I know it cold. *Seen/Not Seen* is about the chasm between perception and reality, the damaging or ennobling nature of assumptions. Who are we if the truth depends on how people see us and everyone sees differently? If assumptions form the lens through which we see someone, can we ever grasp that the lens is faulty?

My delivery is cool and polished, and Krell does not interrupt, but cups his chin in contemplation. When I'm done he says, "You've made significant progress, and this painting is evidence of that. If a student paints no differently at the end of the semester than they did at the beginning, they haven't learned a thing from me."

Significant progress. My heart flutters. I knew it, but it means so much more hearing Krell say it. "You taught me a lot." Including things he'll never ever know.

"You've been an especially challenging student to teach."

My mouth drops open; no one's ever said that about me. "I have? Why?"

"When the semester started, you were almost defiant in your unwillingness to accept criticism."

"Oh." My face heats up, remembering how shocked I was the first time Krell dissected my work, taking apart my painting in front of these people I barely knew. "I wasn't used to being critiqued. I always got praise from my teachers."

"Hmm." Krell pauses, weighing what to say next, but I know he's probably thinking they were wrong not to challenge me.

Now I see how staying at Beverly Hills High with Ms. Pensel instead of going to the visual-arts magnet school didn't prepare me well for CALINVA.

"Then when you failed to show for our first appointment—"

I interrupt him. "I was late. I messed up the time and was too embarrassed to talk to you about it. I'm sorry, I should have apologized."

"Yes, you should have," he says, but not in a mean way. "I assumed your behavior and reluctance to accept criticism were due to arrogance. Students who don't have your talent . . . they *have* to ask difficult creative questions, the kind you were able to avoid before you came here. As your teacher, I felt I had no choice but to attack your unshakable belief in your talent so you could grow artistically."

I shake my head. So that's why Krell acted like such a dick—because he thought I was too arrogant to listen. If only I'd talked to him . . .

"Are you pleased with what you've achieved?" he asks.

I gaze up at *Seen/Not Seen*, surprised by how the painting affects me. I see differently, and I paint differently. "Yes. I won't ever look at my art the same way."

"Good. Then this semester has been a success. Well, I see Kevin Walker is waiting for his review. I assume you're attending the opening this evening."

"Yes, thank you, Professor Krell."

"Good luck tonight, Ms. Reyes."

Krell walks up to Kevin and asks for his patience before going over to confer with the gallery staff. A moment later, they switch the placement of two paintings, and for reasons I could never explain, the flow of the paintings on the wall feels better and Kevin's *Unresolved* now pops.

Kevin hangs back, waiting for Krell to finish with the guys. His hands are hooked behind his neck, and even though he's standing upright, he gives off the impression he could collapse any second. He strolls over to me. "You look happy," he says. "Your critique with Krell must have gone well."

"I'm so relieved." I stretch like I'm reaching for the ceiling so I don't reach for him. "You look fried."

"Finally got the computer program working about four this morning."

"Krell's going to love it."

"Hope so."

"I'm ready for you now, Mr. Walker," Krell says.

"See you tonight?" Kev asks.

"Wouldn't miss it," I answer.

I linger to watch Kevin's painting come to life. As the narrow strips of canvas flip, the strokes of color fly up, fall down, and cross. The painting seems to argue with itself, speeding up, slowing down, contemplating, and then exploding in the simultaneous movement of six, eight, or twenty strips.

Before I walk out the door, I take one last look around the gallery. I want this—

. . . hanging out with Kevin . . .

. . . being a part of this creative family . . .

. . . and I want it to go on through this year and the next.

I want to do my second-year show and third and fourth.

I want to work like a dog and see the progress in my work that I see in *Seen/Not Seen*.

My gaze drops on Krell for a moment. As long as people believe that my copy of *Duncan* is the original, this will be mine.

CHAPTER 56

When I arrive at CALINVA for the show, the gallery is lit. The staff must have rigged a spotlight on *Seen/Not Seen*, because my painting is perfectly visible from the street. I come up the ramp, hoping I can be with Julie when she sees it, but knowing I might not. I'm nervous she'll be disappointed or confused by the two portraits.

My classmates are inside the gallery already, and I squeeze through the crowd waiting for the doors to open. The hall vibrates with the excitement of friends and families like the final moments before popcorn kernels explode. Mrs. Mednikov's catching a ride with Peter and Chelsea, so they'll be here soon.

Taysha's surrounded by a group of about twenty people wearing matching tees with her superhero design on the front. Older women who must be aunties and little girls who could be nieces are hugging her and snapping selfies. Even as I grin at the crowd, I feel a pang of envy.

And scattered around them are young women wearing jackets Tay designed, which also makes me smile. Leave it to Taysha to bring out her fans.

The gallery curator unlocks the door to let me in. "Have a good show," someone calls out.

"Thanks," I call back. Kevin's way across the room and I head for him.

I pass Bryian, who's pacing in front of *Totzilla*, but honestly, I don't know what he's worried about. The painting went viral a few days ago when a Hollywood comedian launched a Kim Jong-un limerick challenge.

Bernadette fusses with a video screen perched on a pedestal, and I brake to a stop. Her backless dress is so sheer, it's almost transparent. The smoke-colored pleats flow to the floor, shadowing her long bare legs and Doc Martens. Bernadette's out to be remembered.

David Tito must have seen me staring, because he's at my side. "What do you think of her painting?"

I look for the thorn man, but Bernadette's canvas is pure white except for one green apple.

David whispers, "She scraped off the thorns."

"I don't get it. I thought the thorns were the whole point?"

"Check out the video. She recorded the construction and deconstruction like it's performance art."

We both shudder. "That girl will do anything to win," David says before he walks away.

I half expected Kevin to wear a suit, so I'm not surprised by his pressed button-down and thin black tie. "Like the tie, Walker," I say.

Kevin punches my arm like a middle schooler. "Not too shabby yourself, Reyes," he says, taking in the leather dress Taysha created.

He hooks his thumbs into his jeans, suddenly shy, and I silently thank Taysha.

"How's *Unresolved*?" I say.

"Working. I think. Next couple of hours could prove me wrong." Kevin flips a switch and his painting starts to evolve.

I'm about to ask if he's doing anything after the show, when the curator claps his hands.

"Attention, everyone. The doors will open in two minutes, so please take your place by your painting. And artists, remember: Enjoy the show!"

All thirty of us clap, and I dash over to *Seen/Not Seen*. This is it. My first gallery show. I run my tongue over my teeth and recite my artistic statement in my head.

Krell's the first one in the glass doors, and he ushers the crowd through the entrance.

As people flood in, I pick out faculty members, including ones I haven't studied with yet. Taysha made me memorize the names and faces of the painting faculty so I'd pay them extra attention when they came over to see *Seen/Not Seen*.

Please please please let them love Seen / Not Seen *so they vote for me to keep my scholarship.*

I stand beside my painting, but no one approaches my side of the gallery. A crowd swells around Bryian's *Totzilla*, and another gathers around Bernadette. A group wearing tees printed with math formulas or the Caltech logo stands transfixed in front of Kevin. His engineering friends, I guess.

His hands are raised, and he's miming how the flaps swivel, and I get caught up, first in watching him, and then in the girl gazing at him rapturously.

That's her. The girl who brings him bagels late at night.

Damn. I'd hoped she wasn't pretty, but she is. Her long hair shimmers in the studio lights, and her features are delicate, and of course her skin is perfect. I'd like to think that's makeup, but probably not.

I'm so absorbed I don't notice the man with cropped silver hair until he's right in front of my painting. I smile and he nods hello, and settles in front of *Seen/Not Seen*.

Expensive sport coat, designer jeans, manicured nails? He can't be a working artist.

I steal glances at him, sure I've seen him before. His dark brown eyes have a quiet intensity as if he sees through the layers of pigment into the heart of my painting. I don't know whether to speak or stay silent. He could be a critic or a dealer, someone who could change the trajectory of my life with a few words, or he could be nobody at all.

Then he asks about *Seen/Not Seen* and I recite my artistic statement, conscious of how his gaze goes back and forth between me and *Seen/Not Seen* as if he's trying to make the connection.

"How representative of your work would you say this painting is?" he asks.

I'm so surprised I blurt, "I don't know."

He stifles a smile, so I fumble for a better answer. "When I arrived at CALINVA, I painted what I saw. Now I try to paint what I want to express."

He nods and the smile that graces his face is respectful. "It will be interesting to see where you are as an artist a year from now."

He walks away, and for a moment, I feel a champagne shiver bubble through me. He walks over to Krell, who's chatting with his dealer, Barry Ankarian, and slaps Krell on the shoulder. That's when I finally realize why he looks familiar. He's the art dealer Gaereth Wattleberg—a sensation in the global art world.

Gaereth Wattleberg liked my painting.

I hold my breath as they talk, hoping that Gaereth Wattleberg, *the* Gaereth Wattleberg is telling Krell how impressed he is with *Seen/Not Seen*. How he's interested in seeing how I grow as an artist. If they'd only look my way, I'd know they're talking about me.

But instead, Krell points out Bryian and Bernadette, and walks Wattleberg and Ankarian over to *Totzilla*.

My hand balls into a fist and my first thought is: It doesn't matter how hard I've worked or how far I've come, Krell still worships Bryian and Bernadette. But then I tell myself it's okay. Krell will support me when it comes to keeping the Zoich, and that's what I really need from him right now.

I don't notice Florence, the woman who runs the shelter, until she says hello. Among all these people determined to appear hip and dramatic and cutting-edge, Florence is normal and real. "Thanks for coming," I say, and I mean it.

"I wouldn't miss it for the world," she says. "I'd like to introduce you to Casey Stiner, one of our shelter's trustees."

Casey is tall and slender, with a serious smile and black hair bobbed in a way she probably paid a lot to make look effortless. As we shake hands, Casey repeats my name and looks right at me with azure-blue eyes that I bet cut right through bullshit.

"This is the painting I told you about," Florence tells her.

"So this is Julie." Casey stands back, appraising my double portrait. "Why paint Julie?" she says, her tone stopping just short of a demand.

I explain how Julie and I met, but Casey's not as interested in me as she is in the painting. Her eyes dart back and forth between the two portraits like she's weighing an argument while Florence gazes at the canvas quietly.

When I finish, Florence says, "I think Julie will be happy when she sees this."

"You do? I'm so glad you said that. I was worried she wouldn't."

"You honored her humanity and showed her with dignity."

Casey touches her collarbone, deep in thought, and I sense she's about to say something when Mrs. Mednikov, Peter, and Chelsea appear.

Mrs. Mednikov exclaims over the painting, demanding that Peter and Chelsea observe this element and that element. The circle of people in front of *Seen/Not Seen* begins to swell, keeping me busy answering questions and explaining my artistic statement.

From the corner of my eye, I spy Mrs. Mednikov talking with Florence Harris and Casey Stiner. She frowns and flings her hand out dismissively, making me wonder what the hell is going on. Peter stands to the side of them, grinning, so when I catch his eye I mouth, *What's up?*

He slides through the crowd until he's beside me. "Your landlady is negotiating your first art sale."

"You're joking."

"Not at all. She overheard that Casey woman say she wondered if you'd donate your painting to be auctioned at a gala for the homeless shelter. Stephania told her in no uncertain terms that she owns your painting and that if the shelter wants to auction it, they should get a wealthy trustee to buy it from her first."

I burst out laughing. "Did she name a price?"

"She's asking two thousand, but I think she'd settle for seventeen fifty. Given the quality of the work and the size of the canvas, it's a fair price for an unknown artist."

"You're serious."

Peter nods at Mrs. Mednikov. "Look. They're shaking hands. Congratulations. Well done."

I'm still shaking my head when Mrs. Mednikov strolls over looking like the cat that ate not just one canary, but an entire aviary. "You heard that I sold your painting?"

"Yes, I can't believe it."

"The deal is not quite done, but almost," she says. Mrs. Mednikov shows me the business card she's holding. "She's a lawyer for rich criminals."

I glance at the card. "So I guess she can afford to buy my painting."

"The money will go to you, you understand."

"But it's your painting."

She reaches for my hand. "I will rest better if I know you will not struggle so much."

My eyes fill. "Oh, Mrs. Mednikov." For the first time in months, these are happy tears. It's not just the rent or car insurance the money will cover, it's knowing someone actually cares.

She whispers something in Russian and kisses both my cheeks. Then Peter and Chelsea escort her away.

I can't wait to share the news with Kevin and Taysha. I'm so high from the sale, I finally start having fun, greeting faculty by name and answering questions, chatting up bloggers, and taking selfies with Taysha fans.

A couple hours later, the crowd thins, until all that's left are my classmates, several of whom are flopped on the floor, their laughter burning like methane.

Taysha and I lean on each other. "We survived," she says.

"You have a good night?" I ask.

"Yeah, I made some good contacts. You?"

"My landlady might have sold *Seen/Not Seen*."

"What!" Taysha slaps me on the head. "When did you plan on telling me?"

"Ow. I'm telling you now."

Just then Krell reappears. He stands in the center of the room, and we all go quiet.

"Congratulations, everyone, on a fine show," he says. "Your hard work paid off, as the faculty was very impressed with the caliber of your work. But they weren't the only ones. I understand that a sale is pending for Ms. Reyes's painting, *Seen/Not Seen*."

Krell pauses and beckons to me. My exhausted fellow students peel themselves off the floor until they're standing. I smile and nod as everyone claps, surprised at some of those clapping hardest, like Bryian and David Tito, people I didn't expect would be happy for me.

"But Ms. Reyes is not the only one to experience success this evening. One of your peers has been offered representation by the Ankarian Gallery. Bryian, will you please step forward."

We start clapping for Bryian, and Taysha bumps me. "Check out Bernadette," she says.

Bernadette's clapping, but her face is as pink as her hair. "Oooo. They are never getting back together."

"Bryian'll be lucky if he makes it to the parking lot alive."

Krell waves us to silence. "I wish I could stay and celebrate, but I've got a plane to catch. Your final assignment, a self-portrait, is due when I return next Friday from Art Basel Miami. Until then, create!"

CHAPTER 57

The buffet in the back of the room, which I never got a chance to even look at, is trashed. Kevin comes back from it, holding up a lonely Wheat Thin. "I'm starving, but this is all that's left. You want to get a pizza?"

"Aren't your friends waiting for you?" *Isn't that girl waiting for you?*

"Nah, they're holding a big D and D party. They took a break to come to the show."

Yes! I resist the urge to fist pump. "Pizza sounds amazing."

We grab our stuff and head out. "So, tell me all about the sale," Kev says. I launch into the story of Casey Stiner, expert negotiator, meets Mrs. Mednikov, indomitable old lady, but my eyes are on Bernadette, who's ahead of us as we start down the ramp.

She's thrown on a black motorcycle jacket, and her fog-gray dress billows behind her as she heads for a burnt orange Maserati parked right outside. Too bad Taysha's already gone, because she'd know exactly who the guy is who drives Bernadette away.

Kevin and I come out of the building, and we're about to head into the parking lot when I see Julie standing across the street. She's wrapped in a striped blanket, looking up at CALINVA.

I reach for Kevin. "Hey, I know you're starving, but I can't leave just yet. Why don't you go without me?"

Kevin looks from me to Julie and shakes his head. "No, I'm not in a hurry. I'll stay."

The street's empty of cars, so I dart across. I haven't spoken to Julie since the night I scared her, so I slow as I get close, afraid she might run away.

Sweetie's curled around Julie's neck, nestled in the folds of the blanket. "Hi, Julie, I haven't see you in a while."

"Florence said I could come see my painting."

"I'm glad you came. Why don't we cross the street so you can see it better?"

"Who's that man standing over there?"

Kevin's spotlit by the entrance. "He's my friend Kevin."

"He has a good aura, not like that other one."

I shiver, knowing she means Adam. "Yeah, you're right, Kevin's a good guy." On impulse, I ask, "Is the other one—is he around?"

Julie reaches from underneath her blanket and pats my arm. "You're safe now," she says, and a weight lifts off me. I'd love to believe Adam is far, far away.

We cross the street together and I guide Julie to a place on the sidewalk that gives us the best view of my painting.

"That's me," Julie says, breaking out into a huge smile. "And you even got Sweetie in there."

She studies the painting, her eyes moving over the canvas, and I wait, afraid of what she'll say about the ragged, black-and-white portrait attached to it. When she speaks, her eyes turn sad. "That part there hanging down. That's *old me*. I like how you showed she's not part of me no more."

I dig my hands deep in my coat pockets. I can't find the

words. Julie seems like such a gentle soul, but I get the feeling, and I could be wrong, there's something dark and violent in her past she ran from. Her need to be in the open. Her fear of anger. Her wanting to help.

I start thinking about how to share some of the money I'll get for the painting with her. "A woman wants to buy it," I tell her.

"She does? My painting?"

"She thinks it can help raise money for the shelter."

"And bring blessings upon the world."

It's so Julie, her saying that. I look over at Kevin, watching us and he's smiling. "Julie, is it okay if I leave you now? My friend's waiting."

"She must be so proud of her girl."

Julie's eyes are glued to the painting and I'm thrown, because I have no clue who she's talking about. "Who's proud, Julie?"

"Your momma. She's got to be proud tonight."

I sway on my feet and suck in a breath. "Thank you." I pat Julie's bony shoulder through the blanket and then say, "Be safe," and walk toward Kevin, carefully putting one foot in front of the other, because I hope, I really hope Julie's right.

When I reach him, he tosses his head at Julie. "She likes it."

"Yeah, she does."

"Still up for pizza?"

"I'm starving."

As we walk to the car, Kevin says, "You think we could find her later?"

"We might. Julie usually stays right around here."

"So if we pick up an extra slice, we can bring it to her."

I didn't see the glow around Kevin when Julie mentioned it earlier, but now I do. The way I feel about him at this moment, the light he radiates, it isn't a mere aura, it's an aurora borealis.

CHAPTER 58

I smile through my shifts at Artsy and La Petite Tomate on Saturday, reliving the exhibition, Julie's joy when she saw *Seen/Not Seen*, and the hours Kev and I lingered over pizza. It feels like Christmas lights are wound around my heart, and their blinky brightness fills my chest.

Taysha's soaring, too, and she messages me nonstop.

9K VIEWS OF ZOETROPE COAT!

12K!

15K! INDIE ACTOR WANTS TO BORROW 4 SUNDANCE FILM FEST.

Kevin sends me shots of his self-portrait as he works. He's a smiley-faced blue robot gobbling down tacos. WHAT DO YOU THINK?

RESEMBLANCE IS UNCANNY! I message back.

I don't have time to think about my self-portrait until after I finish the brunch shift on Sunday. By the time I get back to Mrs. Mednikov's, my hair reeks of bacon, but there's only a couple hours left of sunlight, so I make some coffee and go out to the porch to start in on the assignment.

A canvas board waits on the easel and I face off with it. The empty white square stares back defiantly. I spill my drawing pencils out on the little table and pick through them, because it might sound silly, but the right pencil makes a difference.

My hand circles the canvas board, and the charcoal pencil hovers over the surface. Round and round it goes, but won't touch down.

"Argh!"

The terrier next door starts yapping and won't stop. *Oh, shut up, would you?*

I pick up the makeup mirror I brought out and try a frown, a glare, a soulful gaze, a tentative smile. Painting what I look like is easy. But a self-portrait isn't a mirror. I'm supposed to go deeper and reveal what's under the surface, my true self.

I swap out pencils, choosing one that's easier to erase. My hand sweeps over the canvas, barely brushing it before my head falls back and I stare at the ceiling.

Who the hell am I?

Last year, I would have said I'm a talented artist, I'm a good person, I'm honest, I'm loyal to my friends.

But would a good person have set Krell up so his painting was stolen?

I've pushed away thoughts about Krell all weekend, but now I check my phone. It's seven o'clock in Miami, and the opening reception at Art Basel is about to begin. The booths are up and the artwork's on display. Krell's probably walking the exhibition hall right now.

He knows his painting like he knows his own face, so the only way to explain why he didn't realize the *Duncan* at his reception was a copy is that he was distracted when he saw it.

But he'll be at the art fair for almost a week. At some point, he will look at *Duncan* and realize something about it is off.

I pick up my cup, but the coffee's stone cold, so I throw open the screen and toss it on the lilies. Krell's not blind; he'll see where I didn't get it quite right. Not to mention the part on the shoulder Adam must have done.

And then? When he clues in that the painting's a forgery?

A ridge of pain takes hold of my shoulders, and I slowly roll my arms and move my head from side to side, trying to work out the cramp.

What an idiot I was, letting Adam convince me Krell would stay silent. Krell's not going to do that. He'll go right to Barry Ankarian, and Ankarian will have to pull the painting from the show and concoct a convincing story to head off the scandal so it doesn't sink his gallery.

The pain's dug in. *Dammit.* I fold one arm over my chest and pull with the other, trying to force the cramp free.

Krell might be in shock, but Ankarian will be pissed. Because even if the insurance pays out, he'll have to tell the buyer what happened.

I picture him at Krell's reception, eyeing the crowd, sorting us into those who are worthy of his attention and those who are not. With an ego like his, he's not going to let this go. Not when he'll have a million reasons to hunt down the person who painted the copy.

And of course, the investigation will start at CALINVA, because no one outside it even saw *Duncan* until the day before Krell's reception when it was sent out to be photographed.

I stretch my arms out in front of me, only now seeing that my fingertips are black from my charcoal pencil. I spit onto a paper towel and try to wipe off the residue, but it clings to my skin.

Krell will narrow down the suspects to painters with the strongest technical skills. I run through the first-years. Me, Bernadette, and Bryian will be the top suspects, but I don't know the upper classes or grad students well enough to guess who else they'll target.

Whoever's in charge of the search will probably check security tapes to figure out which of us got into Krell's studio when he wasn't there. I try to picture the halls. I don't remember any security cameras, but that doesn't mean there aren't any.

My chest tightens as I recall one by the back door on the pole with the security light. *Shit.* I'm on tape going in a door that students don't normally use.

No, wait; that's good. If there's a tape, Adam's on it, too. It proves he exists.

But Adam's gone, and my fingerprints are all over the painting. I'm so, so screwed, but there's nothing I can do.

I shut my eyes and count to five as I breathe in, hold the breath, and slowly release. Again. Again. My heartbeat begins to slow.

God, I want this over.

When I open my eyes, it's no surprise the canvas in front of me is still blank. But I'm clued in to who I am: a liar.

And unless I admit that, I'm stuck.

Fine. "I'm a fraud," I whisper. I say it again, a little louder. "I'm a cheat."

My pencil circles the board twice then touches down. A vision forms in my head and flows through my fingers, and a sketch emerges: my face as Raphael would draw a Madonna with lowered eyes and a gentle smile. From the neck up, I appear innocent, happy even.

But the hands I draw hold open the doors of the wood cabinet that is my chest. A bluebird wheels out of it, fleeing the burning house that consumes the inside.

Mrs. Mednikov steps out on the porch, cat-quiet in her slippers. I'm tempted to cover my drawing, but I've never done that with my art before.

Her tea smells of orange and cinnamon, and when I glance over my shoulder, she's taking in my sketch.

"This drawing. This is how you feel?" she says.

I answer the only way I can. "Yes."

She's never hugged me or squeezed my hand, but I feel her embrace in the tender way she says, "I pray the end of your trials is near."

"Me too," I say. Me too.

CHAPTER 59

The painting moves swiftly as if it demands to be painted. It tells me which colors to use, where to throw light and deepen the dark, how to angle my brush, and how long, short, strong, or delicate the strokes should be. I work until the sun begins to set, then put the canvas aside to dry.

I roll my shoulders and shake out my hands. The portrait's so honest, just looking at it makes me nervous.

One last look around, and I gather my dirty brushes and go inside. I'm washing the brushes out in the kitchen when my phone lights up and it's Kev. My lips curve into a smile. "Hi. I didn't expect to hear from you."

"Hey," he says. "Are you busy?"

I wipe a wet brush on a paper towel, checking the bristles for any paint I've missed. "Depends."

"There's this party . . ." He says it like he's sure I won't want to come. I get it. I've turned him down before.

"You sound like you want to go," I say.

"It's the Geminids, this is your chance to see them."

Clearly, he's talking about an indie band. "I don't know them," I say.

"I promise, you'll love the Geminids. Biggest meteor shower of the year."

I smile so big at his excitement, my cheeks crease. "So where's the party?" I say, imagining a kegger on some rooftop at Caltech.

"Mount Wilson."

I picture the mountains just north of Pasadena. Mount Wilson's where all the TV towers are. "Okay. I'm in."

"Great! I'll be there in twenty—oh, and dress warm. It's going to be freezing up there."

Mount Wilson is up an old highway that winds into the mountains, but we've barely left town before it feels like we're hours away. There are no streetlamps and hardly any other cars. The forest hugs the road on both sides, but I glimpse the valley below through the gaps between the pines. "It looks like someone shook a jar of gold glitter over Pasadena," I tell Kev.

He doesn't answer or maybe he didn't hear me.

Something changed in the half hour between his calling me and showing up at my house. He's bobbing his head and nodding along to the music that's playing, but he feels far away.

What's going on? I wonder. I pick up the CD lying on the console and flip it over to see what we're listening to: a bluegrass band, Mandolin Orange.

"Kevin Walker partying on a school night," I tease. "Did you blow off physics study group?"

"No, that's tomorrow," he says quietly.

I don't get it. He was so excited an hour ago. "Did something happen before you picked me up? You seem upset."

Kev makes eye contact with me for the first time in miles. "My dad called. He's stopping by."

"He's coming to see you?"

Headlights flood the inside of the car, and we duck our eyes until they pass.

"He's doing a layover on his way to Korea," Kev says.

"Sounds like he misses you."

"Dad hates LAX and he hates layovers. He'll do just about anything to avoid both those things."

I think back to what Kev told me when we went to see the butterflies. "Do you think this has to do with your grades?"

"That. Or the cancer's back." Kev tries to sound matter-of-fact, but his voice catches.

"Kev. I didn't know." I rest my fingers on his sleeve, unsure if he wants to talk or not. "Can I ask what kind?"

"Bone cancer. He's been clear five years, but that's no guarantee."

A hollow opens in my gut as I picture Mom bandaged and unconscious, becoming a ghost before my eyes. "Are you close, you and your dad?"

"We got close. After Dad lost his arm, he started taking me with him when he had to travel outside the US."

China. Poland. Dubai. Now I know why Kevin's traveled everywhere. "It's different when it's just you two, isn't it?"

"Yeah. Yeah, it is." Kev slaps the steering wheel with the palm of his hand. "I don't want to think about any of this tonight, okay? Tonight I want to hang out and watch the Geminids put on a show."

"All right. I'm good with that." I've seen Kev stressed, but this feels different. I'm praying his dad's visit doesn't mean he's sick again.

We drive deeper into the mountains, and patches of snow glow under the pine trees, caught in our headlights.

Kevin begins to hum along to Mandolin Orange, and I smile to myself because I can feel his mood get lighter. The guitar, mandolin, and bass are a perfect soundtrack for the night-quiet highway.

After we turn onto the road for the observatory, I catch Kevin singing under his breath. He wasn't shy about singing in front of me on Thanksgiving, so I pretend not to listen. His voice drops down so I can barely hear him. *"I'm a fool for the finest girl, but she's no fool for me. . . ."*

My heart doesn't know which way to go, if he's singing about me or someone else. Like the girl at Caltech or the one at home who broke his heart, Chantal.

I don't want us to just be friends, Kevin. I want you to sing that song to me.

When we finally get to Mount Wilson, the small parking lot is almost full of cars. We park and get out, and the cold combs through my hair.

Kevin pulls his beanie down over his forehead. "You want your hat?" he says, and tosses it to me, then tucks a blanket under his arm.

The white dome of the big observatory peeks through the trees, along with smaller rounded top towers. Kev and I start down a paved path where pine cones as big as my boot lie scattered. All around us, the mountains are dark and deep. We walk beside each other, hands stuffed in our pockets. Our arms bump every few steps, and I wonder what would change if I reached for his hand.

The night is still except for the wind rustling the trees. The quiet seeps into us and makes us whisper. Kevin points out two slender steel towers. "Most of the telescopes here are for nighttime observation, but those two track the surface of the sun. The astronomers make a pencil drawing of the pattern of sunspots every day."

"That seems so bizarre," I say. "Can you get any lower tech than that?"

"I know, right? But supposedly the drawings give them better data."

As we get closer to the buildings, the quiet is broken by bursts of laughter or cheers. We pass a small museum, which is closed for the night, and take a walkway that leads left to the domed observatory.

People have set up portable telescopes on tripods along the path. They cluster around the instruments. The unexpected scent of hot coffee draws my attention to a folding table loaded down with paper plates of cookies and bags of chips.

"How's it going?" Kevin asks one of the guys.

"The show's just starting," he replies. "The hundred-inch is open tonight if you want to see it."

"I've got a clear view of Jupiter over here," someone calls out.

Kevin steers me over to a scope. I peer through the eyepiece at a gray-striped ball. "This is so cool. Isn't Jupiter supposed to have a big spot on it?"

"Red spot's not visible tonight," someone says, "but if you look to the left, you can see two of the moons."

The moons are shiny pinheads. Kevin guides me to another scope. "I can't believe it," I say, peering into the eyepiece. "Saturn really does have rings."

Kevin beams at me, then scans the sky. "Come on. Let's find a good place to watch for meteors."

The night is washed with stars. We leave the party behind

and veer off onto a quiet walkway. "We really lucked out," Kevin says. "The night's clear, and the moon's not up."

We come to a bench, and he sets down the blanket. He takes another look at the sky before he places his hands on my shoulders and gently turns me. Then he leans over my shoulder until our cheeks are side by side.

The heat radiating from his skin makes my pulse flutter. I don't trust myself to look at him or move my head even a little. He points to Orion and swings his hand to the left. "See those two bright stars?" he says. "Those are Castor and Pollux in the Gemini constellation."

I stare at the stars, which blaze like far-off candles. My skin sparks as Kevin's curls tickle my cheek, and I can barely concentrate on what he's saying.

Kevin circles his hand in the direction of the constellation. "The meteor shower will look as if it radiates from there, hence the name Geminids. But we're the ones passing through the debris field of the extinct rock comet 320 Phaethon. Chunks of cast-off rock hit our atmosphere and ignite."

I try to imagine the sky the way Kevin sees it. "So it's like a cosmic dodgeball game."

He laughs and moves around me so we're standing shoulder to shoulder. He scans the sky above us and I take my hand out of my pocket, hoping he'll reach for it.

Then a silver streak cuts across the sky. "I see one!" I cry.

Kevin looks to where I'm pointing. "Good eyes. I'm glad I brought you."

I blush, but I'm sure he can't tell, it's so dark out. "Me too."

A minute or two later, another star streaks by, then

another. The meteors start coming faster until it's like a fireworks show. I bounce on my toes counting one, two, three, four at once.

"This is amazing!" I grab Kevin's arm. "We need to make wishes."

"Okay." Kevin closes his eyes like he's thinking, and I jiggle his arm. "No. You have to keep your eyes open."

He breaks into a grin. "I didn't know there was a protocol."

I grin right back at him. "I can't believe your sisters didn't teach you it."

He weaves his fingers into mine and we turn back to the sky. I pin a wish to each falling star. I wish for Kevin's dad to be okay and my troubles with Krell to end. I wish for the faculty to applaud my vision in *Seen/Not Seen*. And I wish for Kevin and me to be more than friends.

Each meteor that streaks by, I tag it, silently repeating my wishes again and again.

Then the sky goes still, and Kev and I wait, our breaths making little clouds. Nearby people are clapping. "Do you think it's over?" I say. "Did we pass out of the debris field?"

He moves around in front of me until we're standing face-to-face. He gazes into my eyes, and I hold my breath as his arms circle me and slip down to my waist. "I don't think it's over," he whispers. "I think it's just beginning."

I'm trembling as I reach behind his neck and draw him close and rest my lips on his.

Our kisses are sweet and star-blessed, and they feel so different and right, because now I'm kissing Kevin, the guy I should have been kissing all along.

CHAPTER 60

B efore Kevin said good night, he asked if I'd proofread his paper for Color & Theory. With Krell out of town and his class canceled, we meet in the student lounge before Newsom's class and swap laptops. We're stretched out on a couch, shoes off, our feet resting on a coffee table. Every so often Kev traces a circle on my jeans with his pinkie and we smile at each other.

His paper on how the chemistry of pigments has changed over the ages and revolutionized art is so engrossing, I can't believe I'm reading history and liking it. When I get to the end, I've got a handful of comments, but Kevin is only half-way through mine.

I take out my phone and scroll through the news while I wait for him to finish. Art Basel Miami opened yesterday, and I've been holding my breath, praying Krell won't notice *Duncan*'s a fake.

Today, Krell's on everyone's radar. Four interviews already this morning and they all feature photos of him and Barry Ankarian standing in front of *Duncan*. Every time I see the words "masterpiece" or "magnum opus," I feel sick. People are calling *Duncan* a turning point in Krell's artistic career.

I zoom in. The cameraman's floodlights are trained on

the painting, making the flaws so obvious, I don't get why Krell doesn't see them.

I twist a strand of hair around my finger until it hurts. The patch Adam painted on Duncan's shoulder? It's a big, messy blob. At some point in the next three days, Krell's got to notice it.

Kevin looks up from my laptop. "What's going on, Sabine?"

"What do you mean?" I say, pretending I didn't catch the serious tone in his voice.

"You've been really tense the last couple weeks. Is it all the stuff that's due or . . . that other thing we talked about?"

I peer at him, unsure what he means, but instead of explaining, he peels off his glasses and starts wiping them on his shirt. He's so determined not to look at me that I realize he must be talking about Iona. I force out a smile. "Actually, I think I've come up with a way to fix the thing with Iona Taylor."

"Oh yeah?" His expression brightens. Kev might be even more eager than I am to have this disaster behind me.

"Yeah. I offered to paint her portrait since I can't replace the dress. Her assistant thinks it's a good solution. I'm just waiting to hear back from her."

Kevin leans over and gives me a quick kiss. "That's great. I'm happy for you," he says, then goes back to reading my paper.

I go back to my phone and pull up the last photo of Krell with *Duncan*. Can't he see how the subject's eye isn't right? All those months he spent painting, he's got to.

My head starts to throb. Maybe Krell has noticed the flaws but he's in denial. He could be telling himself that those areas that look off, they're his mistakes. Why think someone might have forged his painting when no one else had seen it until the reception at CALINVA two weeks ago?

I press my fingers to my temple. This could all be over by Friday. Krell will be back in LA. The art fair will be winding down and *Duncan* will be crated up, ready to go to its permanent home.

Right. I'm either the greatest optimist the art world has ever seen, or I'm lying to myself.

The rest of the day I sneak peeks at my phone. Krell goes from one interview to the next, chatting up reporters, critics, and bloggers from the US, Europe, and South America. The words "breakout" and "rising star" seem to appear in every profile.

I'm wrung out from reading all this, so when I get back to Mrs. Mednikov's and find an envelope on my bed, my first thought is, Damn. What now? I wave the envelope at Mrs. Mednikov, who's standing a few feet away, sprinkling paprika into a pot on the stove. "It's from a law firm."

Since Tara hasn't gotten back to me about painting Iona, I guess that's a no-go. It wouldn't surprise me if this was Iona's next move: to sue me to get back the cost of the dress I sold.

Mrs. Mednikov wipes her hands on a towel and comes over. "Why are you nervous? Look. Stiner," she says, tapping one of the names on the return address. "The woman who bought your painting."

"Oh. Right. I can't believe I didn't see that." This has nothing to do with Iona. It's good news.

Mrs. Mednikov stands over my shoulder as I tear open the envelope. A pale yellow check peeks out of a folded piece of creamy stationery.

I gasp. "My first sale." I run my fingers over the numbers on the check. "Pay to the order of Sabine Reyes. One thousand seven hundred and fifty dollars."

"I tried to get you more," Mrs. Mednikov says. "But this lawyer, she is tough. If I were to commit a crime, I would hire her to defend me."

I raise an eyebrow and scan the letter that came with the check. "Any idea what kind of crime you'd commit?"

She smiles, considering the question. "It would be a crime of passion. A murder, perhaps. Very dramatic."

"Remind me not to make you angry."

"I doubt you would be foolish enough to cross me." Mrs. Mednikov gives me a wink and retreats to the kitchen.

Stiner has sent detailed instructions on where and how to send *Seen/Not Seen*. The woman leaves nothing to chance.

I pull out my phone, take a pic of the check, and send it to Kevin with a one-word text: SCORE!!!

This windfall means I could give some money to Julie and start paying Iona back if I have to. I could even treat Kevin to Korean-Mexican fusion. I pull up my bank account to check the balance, which I hardly ever do since I live off my tips day to day.

When the screen comes up, I see the balance and shake my head. This isn't my account. It can't be. There's over six thousand dollars in there.

I log off and try again, because what if there was a glitch or I put in someone else's information by accident?

The same screen comes up. Oh shit.

Six thousand dollars. No. This . . . this . . . this is wrong.

I click over to a screen that shows deposits. Oh no no no. Two deposits for three thousand each? The first on the day that Adam went missing. The second a few days later.

I exit the screen and shut the door to my room. My hands are trembling, and I lean into the wood. Six thousand? That's exactly what I told Adam I owe Iona.

No way he did this to be nice. He's way too calculating.

Oh God, I took money from Adam. Even if I didn't know it, the money's been in my account for days.

What the hell do I do now? I shove my hand over my mouth because I can feel the vomit rising inside me. I can't call the bank. Start an investigation that could lead right back to me?

I don't want the money, but I can't give it back. Who would I even give it back to? Krell?

I can stuff it in a bag and leave it outside the homeless shelter. Let it do some good. But that won't solve the problem, because even if I get rid of the money, there will still be records showing it was in my account.

Take a deep breath, take a deep breath, I tell myself, trying to force down the nausea. No one but you and Adam and the scumbag who has Krell's *Duncan* knows it was stolen.

I melt against the wall and let it hold me up. You've got to hold on, I tell myself. It's almost over. The nightmare's almost over.

But then the phone in my hand buzzes, and I shriek like I've got a wasp on me and fling it onto the bed.

For a moment, I'm sure it's Adam, that thinking about him has made him swoop out of hiding to taunt me. I lean over the bed, and the phone buzzes again.

"Are you all right?" Mrs. Mednikov asks through the door.

"Yes. Yes, I'm fine. Sorry for the noise."

The stupid thing's not going to stop until I turn it off or answer it. I curl a finger under the phone and flip it over.

There's a pic of the Komodo food truck and NEXT TIME YOU'RE BUYING.

I exhale. It's only Kev. YOU KNOW IT, I promise before I turn off my phone.

The check from Casey Stiner slides off the bed onto the floor. I pick it up and set it on the bureau by my portrait of Mom. The way Mom's bent over her guitar it's like she's staring at the check at her feet.

I'm disappointed, Sabine.

I drop on my bed and bury my face in my hands. *I know I messed up, I know it, but I told you I wasn't ready. I told you I couldn't do it alone.*

And I'm back in that moment in the hospital when she let out her last breath, and I realized she was utterly and completely gone.

My heart tears loose, but Mrs. Mednikov is right on the other side of the door. Shoulders shaking, I hold in my sobs and let the tears fall.

None of this would have happened if you were here, Mom. You'd have figured out what I was doing with Krell's painting and made me stop. You'd never have let me be so stupid.

Please, Mom. I'm so, so lost, and I know I need to fix this, but I swear I don't know how.

CHAPTER 61

Adam's money is still dragging on me as I walk up the entrance ramp to CALINVA the next morning, but I stop for a moment to look at *Seen/Not Seen*. I'm so proud of what I've done. Not just because Julie loved it, or Krell was impressed, or Casey Stiner bought it, or even because Gaereth Wattleberg, *the* Gaereth Wattleberg thinks I'm an artist to watch. I'm proud because I pushed myself to go further, and I got people engaged, got them to reconsider who Julie is.

As I soak in Julie's portrait, I see what I can't believe I didn't see before. Every painting is the painter, their inner life splayed across the canvas. This is even more of a self-portrait than the one I just painted.

The disconnect I feel between who I thought I was, who others think I am, and the truth is right in front of me. Only in my case, it's reversed. The real me hangs off the canvas, ragged and torn.

Suddenly I can't stand that the painting is here where my friends and classmates can see it. I'm about to go ask Marco when the exhibition's being taken down when I see Keiko coming up the ramp, practically standing on tiptoe to see through the windows, and I realize my classmates are so excited to see their own paintings, they couldn't care less about mine.

I walk in the lobby and start looking for a familiar curly head, because I could really use a dose of Kev today, but then I spy David Tito, Bryian, and Birch outside class on the second floor and remember it's Tuesday and Kevin's not here, he's over at Caltech. Damn.

There's a strange current in the air that I pick up on even before I step off the stairs. People are huddled in the hall outside our classroom with their phones out, comparing screens.

David Tito waves at me to join him and Bryian, and their faces are tense. "What's going on?" I ask, leaning my portfolio against my leg.

"There was a fire last night at Art Basel," David says.

"Oh my God, was anyone hurt?"

"They reported that about twenty people were treated for smoke inhalation. Here's a video," David says, and hands me his phone.

I tap play, and the video pans across an exhibition booth filled with paintings and sculptures as smoke pours toward the ceiling. People are screaming and shouting, and the image jumps around as the person holding the camera runs for the exit. I play it again, trying to spot Krell or his wife or get a glimpse of Barry Ankarian or his booth, but the image is way too jumbled and blurry.

I hand David back his phone. "Does anyone know if Krell and his wife are okay?"

"Taysha's talking to Mona right now," Bryian answers, his thumbs flying over his screen.

I crane my neck to see down to the admin office. Taysha's leaning over Mona's desk, and it seems as if they can't get out a sentence or two before Mona's forced to pick up the phone again.

This can't be good.

Bryian nudges me to get my attention. "Here's a shot from outside the exhibition hall." Smoke pours out the doors onto a crowd of people dancing among palm trees and huge spotlit sculptures. The music cuts off, and people run down the steps into the park below as sirens begin to wail.

A reporter comes on, saying, "Despite the highly flammable artwork on exhibit, and toxic smoke produced by burning acrylic and fiberglass, the swift response from Miami firefighters last night ensured that there were no casualties and property losses were limited to a handful of works. The show will be closed today for cleanup and reopen on Wednesday."

"This is good news, right?"

Bryian winces. "Yeah, try telling that to the artist who just lost a year's work."

Taysha scurries out of the office and is still crossing the lobby when she calls up, "Krell and his wife are fine. They were at the party on the patio when the fire started."

All around us people look up, relieved.

Taysha hoofs it up the stairs, so she's breathing hard when she reaches us. "Mona said the only person she knows who was injured was Barry Ankarian."

"Is it bad?" Bryian asks. The concern in his voice is genuine, and even though I'm not used to seeing this side of him, I'm not surprised. Barry's his dealer now, too.

"No, Ankarian will be fine. He suffered a broken wrist, that's all. There was a rush for the exits and he tripped."

"He's lucky he wasn't trampled," Bryian says.

"Yeah, it could have been a lot worse." Taysha scrunches her mouth as if she can't decide whether to confide in us, and

I realize that something must have happened to Ankarian's booth.

The weight I've been carrying for days lifts and I instantly feel ashamed, but that doesn't stop me from blurting, "What aren't you telling us? Did Ankarian's booth burn down?" I hold my breath, hoping Taysha will say the booth and Krell's painting are ashes.

She shakes her head. "No, his booth didn't burn, but there was 'an incident,' and Mona refuses to give me any details."

The weight settles back down on my shoulders. *An incident*, whatever that means. I'm not safe, but the exhibition hall in Miami is closed today, which means one less day to worry my fake will be exposed.

"You think the fire was an accident?" Bryian says. "Like a neon piece blew?"

"Doubtful," David answers. "Neon's inert. It's more likely someone wired something wrong and caused an electrical fire."

"Maybe it was deliberate." Taysha sounds so certain, all of us turn to her. "An act of terror? Miami's been hit before."

She and I stare at each other, sick at the thought, but David disagrees. "Nah. A terrorist would have taken credit for it. I think arson's more likely," he argues. "There's got to be a hundred million in art in that building, and it's all insured."

"That would make sense," Bryian says. "If a dealer had a painting that wouldn't sell or he knew was fake, he could take out insurance on it, hire someone to set a fire, and problem solved."

My neck pinches as he says "fake," but this can't have anything to do with Adam. Ankarian's booth didn't burn.

"What the hell!" Bryian holds up his phone. "Krell's painting was tagged!"

I gasp, taking in the just-released photo. Red spray-painted letters shriek MURDERER across Duncan's face.

Murderer. My pulse quickens as my eyes trace the bloodred letters. Duncan's features are almost obliterated by the vandal's work. "You can't fix this. The solvent an art restorer would have to use . . . it would destroy Krell's painting."

"This—a normal person would not do this," Taysha says. "No wonder Mona's keeping her mouth shut."

"Were any other paintings hit?" Birch asks Bryian.

"Not in Ankarian's booth."

I press on a spot between my eyes, trying to counter the pressure building in my skull. There's got to be a rational explanation. "Why? Why would someone choose Krell's painting out of all the art in Ankarian's booth to tag?"

"Envy?" Bryian suggests. "Everyone's calling *Duncan* a masterpiece. Maybe Krell has a rival out there we don't know about."

Birch frowns. "Nah. My guess: a commentary on Duncan Pyne."

"Wait, who's Pyne?" I knew Duncan was a real person, but I didn't realize he was somebody.

"He's a UCLA researcher who manipulates GMO grain. He tries to spin it that his goal is to relieve hunger in developing nations, but his mutant grain is actually murdering the earth."

David looks slightly annoyed. "Technically, all grain other than ancient grain has been genetically modified by man."

"Whatever, science guy," Birch mutters.

Nausea wedges at the back of my throat. I'd love to

believe the attack on *Duncan* is about Pyne and that the tagger's an eco-activist trying to bring attention to the cause, but a fake was vandalized? Coincidence? I don't think so.

This has to be Adam or whoever Adam paid or tricked into doing it.

Bernadette's been on the fringes of the conversation, but she picks this moment to jump in. "This spray-paint thing is so Banksy, I wouldn't be surprised if Krell and Ankarian planned it to up the prices of Krell's work."

She's referring to the artist Banksy shredding his *Girl with Balloon* the minute it sold at auction for a million four. Supposedly the painting's now worth even more half-destroyed.

Bryian glares at her, his eyes filled with disgust. "That's so messed up, Bernadette. Only you would think like that."

Bernadette glances around, hoping one of us will back her up, but none of us do. She huffs away and joins another group outside the classroom door.

Ms. Newsom finally appears and we file into class. As I take my seat, I am more and more certain this was Adam's work. The red paint obliterating the badly rendered shoulder and mistakes I made on *Duncan*'s eye?

But the tagger writing MURDERER? The word is so . . . so attention grabbing. Unless that's Adam's game: Distract the viewer. Get them to focus on Duncan Pyne. The pressure in my head takes hold right behind my eyes. What am I not seeing?

CHAPTER 62

With Krell still in Miami and no class first period, I take my time getting to CALINVA the next morning. I need to stop by Secure Storage before Color & Theory because Marco, the guy who helped hang *Seen/Not Seen* for the First-Year Exhibition, wants to go over Casey Stiner's instructions for how my painting will be shipped to her office.

I haven't been in Secure Storage since the day I went looking for the real *Duncan*. Despite the fact I have a legitimate reason to be here, when I step inside my shoulders tense like I've returned to the scene of the crime.

I glance sideways at the steel locker where Adam stored my copy of *Duncan*, but no, it hasn't miraculously reappeared.

Marco stands at the big worktable, stretching a tape measure over an acrylic. He peers over his glasses at me, and the metal tape measure rolls up with a snap. "You've created quite a stir."

I set my portfolio and messenger bag next to the worktable. "I have?"

"Indeed. In the seven years I've been here, you are the only student to sell a painting during a First-Year Exhibition. Don't think the faculty didn't notice."

I try to hand him Stiner's letter, but he waves me off. "Ms.

Stiner emailed us instructions as well. Here's the bad news: A properly constructed crate for a painting the size of yours runs about two hundred."

"Ouch." My shoulders sink as I mentally subtract the money from the legit amount in my bank account, not the six grand that doesn't belong to me. "When do I need to pay you?"

"Never. The good news: We found you a *previously owned* crate." Marco beams, and points to a nearly new wooden crate leaning against the wall.

"You guys are the best," I say, and hold up my hand, inviting him to high-five. He slaps my hand and says, "You can tell Stiner that her driver can pick the painting up on Friday," then reaches for his tape measure. Clearly, we're done.

"Thank you." I go to grab my bag and portfolio case, when a guy saunters in carrying a cup of coffee. The smell of cigarettes pours off his gray-green coveralls. "Marco, you hear the latest about Miami?" he says.

"No, what's up?" Marco answers.

I slowly pick up my messenger bag.

"Listen to this: *ArtHype* is saying the tagging of Krell's painting could be a slam at Krell, not Duncan Pyne."

I lift the strap of my bag over my head and set it on my shoulder as my pulse takes off like a rabbit.

Marco peers at this guy, his head twitching in disbelief. "They're saying Collin Krell is guilty of murder?"

I feel like I'm about to be sick and I snatch my portfolio off the floor. Adam did this; I'm sure of it.

"Blows your mind, right? Yeah, they were contacted by"—he rolls his eyes as he air-quotes—"multiple sources who claim CALINVA hushed up that kid's suicide last year after Krell verbally abused him into diving off the roof."

I'm trying to hold myself together, but I can't get out of that room fast enough. "Unbelievable," I hear Marco mutter as I reach the door.

When I hit the hall, the walls feel like they're closing in. I dash into the lobby, keeping my head down, hoping to get outside without anyone stopping me. I skirt around people, and they're all talking about Krell.

"Man, you'd really have to hate Krell to go to *ArtHype* like that."

"To come right out and declare Krell's a murderer! I bet it was second-years. They despise him after what happened to that guy last fall."

"What the second-years just did, attacking Krell, that is not going to play well with the administration. They better pray they don't get kicked out."

I can't breathe. I need to get out of here. The ramp is so close, I'm only steps away when someone clamps onto my arm. "Sabine!" he says, and I jerk away before I register it's Kevin.

"Kev. Ah, hi."

"Sorry. I didn't mean to startle you." He's hunched over, rubbing his palms together like he's a fugitive on the run. "My dad's here—"

I suck in a breath and scan the lobby, trying to control my panic. "Where is he? I don't see him."

Kev nods at the plate-glass wall between us and the gallery. "He's looking at the show. Could you come meet him?"

His dad stands in front of *Unresolved*, a roller bag and backpack at his feet. His arms are crossed, and even from here, the tilt of his head and slumping shoulders announce that he's not pleased.

As much as I want to help Kev, I really want to get out of this place. "I'm sorry. I forgot something and I need to go home and get it right now. If you're still here when I get back . . . ?" I take a step toward the exit.

The hope in Kevin's face dissolves. "Yeah, yeah, sure. He'll be around for an hour or so before he has to catch his next flight."

I hate myself right now, but that doesn't stop me from saying, "If I'm not back before he leaves, text me the gory details, okay?"

Kevin gives me a limp smile. "Later."

I throw myself through the glass doors and plunge down the ramp. But I'm barely halfway down when a glimpse of Kevin and his dad stops me. I don't have to hear a word of what they're saying to know the visit's not going well.

I can't abandon Kevin when he never asks me for anything.

I shake out my hair and twist it back up. Chin up, I enter the gallery as Kevin reaches out and hits the switch to activate *Unresolved*. The canvas strips begin to flip, and I hang back so his dad can see the pattern break and re-form before I interrupt them.

"So the pattern's random?" his dad says. His tone is curt and unimpressed, like Krell on a bad day.

"No, actually, each strip of canvas corresponds to a musical note," Kevin answers. "Each is a key on the piano. The program is translating a jazz piece right now."

His dad's salt-and-pepper hair is buzz-cut, and I wonder if that's one reason Kevin leaves his long.

I edge closer, unsure if this is a good time to interrupt.

Mr. Walker's narrowed eyes bore into the canvas. "How long did you spend tinkering with this?" he asks.

Tinkering. I can't believe he said that, as if what Kevin's done isn't brilliant and inventive.

"Six weeks, more or less."

"How's your engineering grade?" his dad snaps, and even I flinch.

"Decent." Kev seems like he's keeping his cool, but I know he's upset.

"Be specific!"

Kev mumbles something, and his dad replies, "Seventy-four? You've never had a seventy-four in your life!"

"Yeah, well, the highest grade in the class was an eighty-two. Caltech's a few notches higher than Kansas State, Dad."

His dad puffs up his chest, and clearly it's time for the bomb squad to take over.

"Kevin," I call out, "is this your dad?"

They both turn to greet me. Side by side, Kevin and his dad are variations on a theme. Same eyes, nose, and mouth, but the sharp edges of his father's features are muted by Kevin's clear plastic frames and long brown curls.

I go to shake his dad's hand and my fingers wrap around metal. I lock my eyes on Mr. Walker's while I absorb the unexpected heft and smoothness of his bionic hand. "Hi. Sabine Reyes."

"Kurt Walker."

Before I can get another word out, Kevin jumps in. "Sabine did the double portrait by the window. It sold the first night of the show."

"Congratulations," Mr. Walker says. "I expect that's a coup for an unknown."

Unknown. That stings, but I force myself to smile. "A big coup," I reply, telling myself that of course I'm an unknown. I'm a student. There's zero shame in that.

And it's obvious that the issue Mr. Walker's got right now is with Kevin.

"What do your parents think about you attending CALINVA?"

I blink hard, blindsided by the question.

"Dad! Sabine, you don't have to answer—"

"No, it's okay," I tell Kev, and hold up my hand to quiet him. "It was just me and my mom, and I lost her last spring, but she would have been overjoyed I'm here. She sacrificed a lot to give me opportunities to develop my talent."

Kevin's smile holds both sadness and respect. *You're awesome,* he mouths.

His dad stumbles through an awkward apology that I tell him isn't necessary, then he makes a show of checking his watch. "You said something about mac and cheese?"

"Yeah," Kev answers. "The mac and cheese truck's two blocks over from here."

"Care to join us, Sabine?"

I glance at Kevin. *Just tell me what you want me to do.*

"Sabine has class, Dad," Kevin says.

"Color and Theory," I add. "Otherwise I'd love to join you."

Mr. Walker and I say our good-byes, and then Kevin walks me partway across the room before he leans in for a quick kiss. "I'll come over after work, if I survive."

"You'll survive. Your dad loves you, Kev. He just doesn't understand all this."

I take a couple of steps toward the lobby, remembering

how Mom insisted art was practical, because it challenged you to come up with unconventional solutions. I stop and call back, "Kevin isn't wasting his time here, Mr. Walker. He learned a lot, working on *Unresolved*. The programming and mechanical problems he had to solve blew me away, and I bet you'd find them intriguing."

Both Kev and his dad look slightly stunned by my outburst, but Mr. Walker gives me a thoughtful look and says, "Thank you, Sabine. I'll take that under advisement."

As I take a last look at Kevin and his dad, I realize I'm not the only one who has a Krell in their life.

CHAPTER 63

The lobby is still crowded when I leave the gallery, the tension an electric storm crackling around my head. A news van pulls up in front of the building, so I give up on going outside and instead head for the coffee bar, figuring I could use a cup to steel me for Color & Theory. When I get in line, who's in front of me but Bryian.

"You heard about *ArtHype*?" he says. Heat's pouring off of him and red blotches cover his neck and face.

"Yeah. It's pretty messed up."

He glares at a group crowded around a table in the back. "Look at those second-years. They're smiling like they just pulled off a coup."

I recognize them from the performance-art piece they did a few weeks ago. As I watch, two of the guys high-five over something on their laptops.

"Son of a—" Bryian crumples the napkin he's holding.

"Bryian. Bryian," I say a little louder. "I don't know what you're thinking, but—"

He throws his backpack down and I grab his wrist. "Bryian, don't," I say, but he wrenches free.

He moves through the room like a bull dodging tables to get to the second-years. The ones who see him coming elbow their friends to look up. When Bryian reaches them, his voice is shaking. "You happy about this? You think you're crusaders, meting out justice? This is not justice. It's just a fucked-up form of revenge."

He slams an empty chair against their table, and they half jump out of their seats. "You know nothing, NOTHING about why people choose to kill themselves!"

There are bursts of scattered applause as Bryian spins on his heel and walks back to where I'm standing. He doesn't say a word to me, just jerks his backpack off the floor and stomps out.

I follow him into the hall, carrying our coffees. "Bryian, wait up." He stops and I hold out his cup. "Are you . . . okay?"

His chest heaves as he takes it from me, but I can tell he's trying to calm down. "Sorry about the scene back there," he says.

I nod so he knows I get it. "That felt like it was personal." Bryian and I aren't close, but I can't leave him like this. "Did you lose someone?" I ask gently.

His face sags, and he bobs his head up and down, his eyes stripped of their usual arrogance. "My dad. He . . ." Bryian sighs with his whole body. "He had everything. Success. Respect. Us. We loved him, but it didn't matter because you can't love someone out of depression. It's a disease." He points back at the coffee bar. "I know Krell can be a bastard sometimes, but blaming him for that guy's suicide . . . that's bullshit."

Bryian says he needs to clear his head, and I go sit on an empty bench, hunched over coffee that I don't even want anymore. What's happening with Krell is so hideously awful it's almost impossible to take in.

The second-years are still hanging around the café, but

they're a lot quieter than they were before Bryian lost it. I wasn't here last year so I don't know what Krell said to the student who died, but I do know how angry and frustrated and scared Krell's comments made me feel. Still, I never, not once, thought about throwing myself off a building.

Krell said some horrible things to me, and his teaching style really sucked at times, but he wasn't trying to push me out. He was pushing me to try harder, and I did.

But if that boy was depressed and trying to hide it, Krell might not have had a clue that he was sick and needed help. Krell's not innocent: I'm sure he added to that kid's pain, but to call Krell a murderer feels wrong.

There's a scuffle by the admin office, where a security guard is telling a guy with a huge video cam he has to leave. I burrow into my scarf. *Vultures.*

Adam's got to be celebrating. No one could possibly look at *Duncan* now and guess it's a fake. And the controversy he's kicked up? Everyone's completely focused on that.

Wait. A realization resonates through my chest. What did Adam say when he called that night? Talking about Iona's dress, he said I was a thief just like him, because I didn't want what I stole. I kept her dress to get back at her.

Maybe taking *Duncan* wasn't about the money. Maybe what Adam really wanted was this: to hurt Krell. Accuse him, get CALINVA to punish him, and the art world to turn on him.

But why does he hate Krell so much, if he didn't go to CALINVA? Unless . . . unless he was Krell's student before . . . at UCLA? Or somehow he was friends with the guy who killed himself, and like the second-years he blames Krell?

People are starting to spill into the lobby as the next class is about to begin. The second-years walk by, and I wonder if Adam used them the way he used me, because he knew that if he gave them a chance to get back at Krell they'd take it. Tag the painting and let the second-years do the rest.

I smooth my scarf up around my cheeks. When it comes to exploiting other people's anger and fear, Adam's a true artist.

CHAPTER 64

I can barely concentrate in Color & Theory, because I can't stop thinking about Adam using me and the second-years to do his dirty work. He's so sure he pulled off the perfect crime, but when he tagged or got someone else to tag a million-dollar masterpiece with "Murderer," he guaranteed the police would get involved.

He probably thinks he's safe since he's basically a ghost. Still, all those nights he spent wandering around CALINVA? Someone other than me has to have seen him.

The painting's probably in the hands of the police right now, and if they pick up clues that point to Adam, they could point to me, too.

After class, I pound up Raymond toward Artsy. *Effing Adam, putting that six grand in my bank account. He thinks I'm too selfish or afraid to turn on him?*

The scarf around my neck is choking me, and I tear it off and stuff it into my bag. Yes, Adam had my number: desperate, weak, and easy to manipulate.

The light turns red just before I step off the curb. I wheel around and smash the button, which does nothing. I am not going down for what he did. There has to be a way to fix this. I have to prove he exists. Adam's smart, but he's got to have left some kind of trail. Julie saw him.

I sweep the park across the street but don't see her. Now that I'm thinking about it, I haven't seen Julie since the night of the exhibition. Not on the street or on the bench she likes in the park.

This is not good. On so many levels.

What if she . . . No, I just saw her a few days ago. She will show up, she *will*, but in the meantime . . .

I draw in a long breath and let it out. I go down the list of everything I know about Adam, and it hits me—he got my guitar out of the pawnshop. He could be on their surveillance tape.

I check my watch and I've got fifteen minutes. The light changes and I dash across the street toward Fair Oaks.

My portfolio case flaps alongside my legs, threatening to trip me, but I make it to the pawnshop in record time. I'm breathless as I burst through the door. Steve with the slicked-back hair and moist lips looks up from behind the counter. "The devil chasing you or something?"

"Yeah, something like that," I say. I dig into my wallet and take out my pawn ticket. "One of my friends surprised me by paying off my loan, and then left my guitar on my porch."

"Nice surprise."

"Yeah, it was, but I want to know who it was so I can thank them."

"Why don't you ask them?"

"I did, but they've all denied doing it, so I thought maybe you might remember who came in a couple weeks ago and picked up a guitar with roses painted on the neck."

Steve picks up the pawn ticket and reads it. "I remember the guitar, but I wasn't working the day it got picked up."

I slump against the counter. "Darn." Then I look at the

surveillance camera as if this is the first time I've seen it. "Oh, wait. Does that camera mean the person who picked up the guitar might be on tape?"

Steve frowns, only mildly put out by my asking. He invites me behind the counter to look at an ancient computer screen.

It's early in the day, but the smell of beer seeps out of his skin. Steve's slowly rewinding the tape, and it's tight behind the counter with the two of us. He's not a small guy, and I pray he'll keep his hands to himself.

"You must go to that art school," he says.

I'd like to say no, but my portfolio case is right there. "Yeah."

The tape's wound back, and Steve fast-forwards through the day Adam retrieved my guitar. People jerk on the screen, handing over watches and cameras for cash.

"What's your major?" Steve says.

"Painting."

"You paint any naked men?"

It takes all my strength not to bolt. "Nudes? Nope. That's an upper-division class," I say as casually as I can.

Steve checks the time stamp on my ticket. "Should be coming up soon," he says, just before Mom's guitar appears on the screen. "Was I right or was I right?" He chuckles.

My jaw drops. *What the . . . ?* It's not Adam. I close my mouth before Steve sees I have no clue who that girl is who's paying for my guitar, that girl who looks uncomfortably like me.

Long hair cut like mine, artsy blouse over jeans, messenger bag and portfolio.

"So who's your friend?" Steve says. His hand grazes my ass and I edge away.

"That's Trish," I say, throwing out the first name that comes to mind.

"She looks like you."

"Yeah, people always say we look alike." I scoot out from behind the counter and gather up my bag and portfolio case. "Thanks for helping me. I really appreciate it."

I make a show of checking my watch. "Oops! Late for work!" Then I fling myself through the door and hustle up the street, not looking back.

Adam's thought through every detail, even finding a girl who looks like me to pick up my guitar? I slow as I turn the corner, filled with a nauseating certainty that if I went through CALINVA's security tapes, Adam's face wouldn't appear. When we walked the halls, he always carried my painting in front of him like a shield.

The only person I know for sure who's seen Adam near CALINVA is Julie. I have to find her.

CHAPTER 65

When I walk in from work, Kevin's sitting at the kitchen table with Mrs. Mednikov, and he's operating on her toaster with a screwdriver. A half-eaten piece of pear crumble lies next to the toaster's metal cover, clear evidence she bribed Kevin to fix it.

It's a moment of normal, of how my life could be if I straightened it out. "Hi. Sorry I'm late."

Kev tilts his head back and I give him a quick kiss. He tastes of pear and brown sugar, and the vanilla ice cream melting on the plate. I scoop up a forkful and drop it in my mouth.

"What's wrong with the toaster?" I ask, surveying the knobs, screws, and small metal pieces carefully laid out on the tabletop.

"This morning it burned the toast to cinders. To be safe, it needed repair." Mrs. Mednikov is almost imperial in the way she rises from her seat and glides into the living room.

"She's shameless!" I whisper.

Kev smiles after her. "It's an easy fix," he says, working the screwdriver. "All I have to do is turn this calibration knob toward the solenoid to shorten the toasting cycle."

"No more cinders?"

"Cinders averted."

I scoop up another bite of crumble. "You know that's mine," Kev says as I lick a drop of ice cream off my lips.

"I know," I say, and scoop up a large forkful and guide it to his mouth. His lips close around the fork as I slide it away, and we can't take our eyes off each other.

He puts down the screwdriver, plucks a curved metal piece off the table, and sets it in place. "Hand me that screw?" he says, pointing.

I hand it to him.

"I heard what happened with Krell today," he says.

"Ugh. Let's not. Can I declare this house a no-Krell zone?"

"Okay. Sure." Kevin's movements are certain as he begins to reassemble the toaster. "Thanks again for trying to rescue me today."

"Anytime," I murmur.

"Sorry my dad was such a jerk."

"No worries. How'd it go with him after I left?"

"You'll be pleased to know he asked several detailed questions about the engineering problems I ran into with *Unresolved*, and we actually had a decent conversation. Not that it changed his mind." Kev slides the metal shell back over the toaster and replaces the final screws.

"I'm sorry to hear that."

We both look up as we hear the creaking of Mrs. Mednikov's feet on the stairs. Kev puts down the toaster and reaches for my hand, then gently draws me into his lap. He's in that quiet place you hit after you spend all your energy being upset.

I wrap my arms around his neck and gaze into the green-and-gold-brushed depths of his eyes. "Now I get why you were so nervous about seeing your dad. He's not exactly crazy about you going to Caltech or CALINVA."

Kev tucks his arms around me, cradling me so I melt into his chest. "He's an engineer. He'd feel a lot better about Caltech if it didn't cost twice what Kansas does."

Kevin's lips are on mine, sure, ginger, and sweet. I want to lose myself in his kisses, but before I can I need to know, "Is he making you transfer?"

"He didn't say."

It's not the *no* I'd hoped for, but it's better than *yes*. "You've got to be relieved he's not sick."

"Yeah, when you get down to it, that's the only thing that matters."

He's not fooling me. Kevin can say that all he wants, but like me, he has a dream coiled up inside him like a spring and he wants to stay where he is.

I slide off his lap. "Come," I whisper, taking his hand. I lead him to my room and guide him onto my bed. Light from the house next door filters through the window, casting the shadow of Mom's dream catcher onto the wall.

Kev kicks off his shoes, and I toss mine in the corner before I slide onto the quilt next to him. He hands me his folded glasses and I set them on the tiny bedside table. We lie facing each other, legs entwined, our heads sharing my pillow.

He slips his hand under my shirt, and I shiver as his warm fingers travel slowly up my spine, following the crest and valley of each vertebra.

My fingers brush his cheek. This is nothing like the desperate, racing hunger I felt with Adam.

Kevin draws me closer, pressing his lips to mine. I never knew before now that kisses possess their own vocabulary, but tonight his say "tender," "wounded," "hopeful."

And I answer them back, and everything I say through mine is real and true. *Let me love you, let me be there for you, let me take away your hurt.*

We begin to shed our clothes as if they're walls we can't allow to stand. I read his body with my hands as he reads mine. When we are naked and lying in each other's arms, we are both trembling.

"Are you sure?" Kevin asks. "We don't have to—"

I set my finger on his lips and slide my leg over his. This is the only thing in my life I'm sure about.

CHAPTER 66

The next morning, Kevin pedals off to Caltech before I peel myself out of bed. I slide over into the still-warm spot where he lay. The mattress holds the shape of his body and I nestle into it, imagining I'm still in his arms.

I bask in wanting him *and being wanted by him*, marveling at how foreign and delicious it is, like a food I've never tasted until now.

Outside, the neighbor's marmalade tabby trots along the fence, her orange fur brightening and dulling as she moves from sunlight to shadow. Her ears prick up, following the raucous, discordant calls of wild parrots who've claimed a nearby tree.

I press my pillow to my mouth. "I'm in love." I dare myself to say it again without the pillow. "I'm in love with you, Kevin Walker."

The words float in my ears, fragile and evanescent. I imagine whispering them in his ears, his face turning to mine. . . .

Boom. Something hits the fence, and I jerk upright as the sound of barking and snarling tears through the quiet. Heart racing, I lean into the window, looking for the tabby, but she's gone.

I sit back down on my bed. The electric charge of

adrenaline has shot me back to the real world.

I need to get up and deal with what's in front of me. It's nice to pretend everything's perfect between Kevin and me, but if he finds out what I did, I could lose him.

Hoping this will all go away is just *magical thinking*, as Mom would say.

The only chance I've got of putting things right is to find Julie. I'm pretty sure she saw Adam and me enter CALINVA together, so at the very least she could back me up that he's real. Sure, it's a long shot, her knowing something about Adam that could help me track him down, but how else can I clear my name?

I get dressed and head out early. Julie's not out on Raymond Street, and it looks like breakfast at the shelter's over, because Homer and his buddies are milling around the courtyard outside.

Most of them turn to look at me as I come through the gate. "Hi, everybody!" I stride past the group, and I'm just about to hit the door buzzer when I hear, "Hey you, artist girl."

"Yes?" I smile, looking for signs that the man in the tattered green camo jacket who's coming toward me is sober, sane, and harmless.

"You paint that picture of Julie?"

His hair is silver against his ebony skin and nothing I read off him tells me he's a danger. I smack the buzzer. "Yeah, I did. What do you think?"

"I like it fine. Julie looks good."

His praise is so genuine, so real, I almost don't know what to say. "Thank you for telling me. I'm really glad you like it."

The door release buzzes, and I slip into the hall, where

Florence is waiting. "Perfect timing," she says. "Come back to my office. I've got something for you."

We pass a big room full of long tables where the smell of sausage lingers in the air. Red and green streamers cross the ceiling, and an artificial Christmas tree is plunked in a corner. The decorations on it cluster in spots, leaving whole branches bare.

Florence's office is small and buried in files and boxes. She digs through a pile on her desk, pulls out an envelope, and hands it to me. "You showing up here saves me having to mail this."

I peek inside. "Two tickets to the gala?"

"For you and your plus-one. Courtesy of Casey Stiner."

"Wow. I can't believe this. It's so nice of her." I picture Kevin and me walking into the ballroom at the Langham in our fancy clothes. If only . . .

"So, Sabine, you stopped by for a reason. What is it?" Florence steps back into the hall, my signal to stop marveling at the tickets and tell her why I came.

Florence has no reason to suspect me of anything, but for some crazy reason I don't want to appear overeager. "Um, I haven't seen Julie around. Not since last Friday."

"Neither have I, but that's not unusual."

"I'm worried about her. Do you think she's okay?" I feel stupid saying this. "I mean, I know she's sick, but . . ."

"I believe I'd have heard if she was in trouble. An officer friend keeps an eye on my regulars."

"I'd like to give her some of the money I got for the painting, but I don't know the best way to do it."

Florence nods. "You're worried cash could make her a target out on the street."

"Yeah, I thought maybe I could cover some of her medical bills."

"Sabine, I'm sorry to have to tell you this, but Julie has refused treatment."

"No. Why would she do that?"

"Treatment's painful. Debilitating. It would require a hospital stay." Florence frowns at the ceiling as if she knows she's breaking a rule before saying, "I've located a sister of hers who lives outside Phoenix and would take Julie in, but she needs convincing to go."

"I don't understand. Why doesn't Julie want to be with her family?"

"Sounds like that's hard for you to imagine."

Florence is trying to turn this conversation to me, but I don't want to talk about myself. "It is. Did something happen in Julie's past?"

"You know I can't answer that." We exchange looks. Florence has told me way more than she should have, and now she's drawn the line.

"So if I see Julie first . . . ?" I ask.

"You let me know." Florence goes to open the exit door for me. Santa beams at us from a poster for a Christmas dinner and toy giveaway taped to the door.

I point to the poster. "Do you still need volunteers?"

"We do," she says, "but there's another way you could help that we could use even more."

"What is it?"

"We offer day camp over the holidays for families with schoolchildren who stay at our shelter. Could you organize some art activities?"

My chest floods with sadness, remembering how alone I

felt last spring break. Until then, I didn't realize how much I counted on being at school to feel halfway normal. "Yeah, I'd love to."

"I'll send you the dates," she promises.

Walking to CALINVA, I scan the street for Julie, but she's not in any of the doorways. The thought flies through my head that Adam got to her, but I bat it away. Julie's smart. She sized him up fast, and if he ever tried anything with her, I'm pretty sure she'd cut him.

CHAPTER 67

Julie's in my thoughts all morning. Every time I over-hear someone talk about Krell, I worry I won't find her, so it's almost eerie that she's waiting on the sidewalk when I leave CALINVA. I slow down as I approach her, afraid my eyes are playing tricks on me. "Julie, hey, I'm glad to see you."

She's layered a thick red sweater with an even thicker orange one despite how warm it is today. Even though she's smiling, her hand's laid across her stomach, so she's either hungry or in pain.

"Have you had lunch?" I ask.

"No, can't say that I have."

Julie's face is puffy, but those sweaters are swimming on her. I've been so caught up in my own drama, I haven't noticed she's getting worse. "Let me treat you. What would you like to eat?"

Her eyes brighten. "Chicken salad," she says like it's the food of the gods.

"A chicken salad sandwich?" I speed through a mental list of restaurants where I could get one.

"Not a sandwich, just chicken salad."

The nearest deli I know is blocks away on California Street. "How would you like to take a ride?" I say.

The two blocks to my car, Julie shuffles beside me as if all her joints hurt. The scuffing of her dragging feet makes me feel guilty and weirdly angry. She shouldn't be sleeping on cold cement every night, so why can't she accept her sister's help?

We reach my car, and before I even get my seat belt fastened, the car fills with a cheesy, moldy smell. It's not her fault, I tell myself as I quietly crack open the windows.

Driving over to the deli, I ask her where she's been, but Julie ducks the answer and instead talks about Sweetie, who's tucked in the kangaroo pocket of her sweater.

Julie waits in the car while I go inside. I return with cartons of chicken salad, a big one for her and a small one for me, along with packets of saltines and two forks. There's an empty table in front of the deli, but the other customers will probably stare at us if we eat here, so I drive to the park down the street.

As we walk over to an empty table, I steal glances at Julie. Her bony wrists stick out of her sleeves, and her pants flap around her legs. I swear they weren't this loose before.

I unpack our lunch, weighing whether to ask her about Adam's car or her sister first. Julie's in bad shape, and talking about Adam is probably less likely to spook her. I stack saltine packets in front of her, thinking whatever she doesn't eat now she can save for later. Yeah, right, Sabine. As if a few crackers are going to save her.

"Julie, I need your help."

"That's why I'm here." She scoops some chicken salad onto the lid of her deli carton and sets it on the table. Sweetie scurries down her arm and goes right for it.

I pick up my carton and prop my elbows on the table.

I trust Sweetie, sort of. "That man, the one you warned me about—"

Julie cuts me off. "He's gone."

"I need to find him."

"You shouldn't court danger." She eyes me like I'm about to do something stupid.

"I swear I won't go anywhere near him. But he broke the law, and I want to help the police find him."

She considers this while she chews. "You got a question for me?"

"You told me he has a truck. You said it was green."

"Not green. Gray."

"But you called it a green mountain truck."

"It is. The license plate's got green mountains on it."

I pull out my phone and search pictures of license plates until I find one with green mountains. Colorado. "Like this?"

Julie nods and crumbles a cracker into her chicken. "That's it."

"So it's gray with Colorado plates." I take out my sketchbook, and we begin to play a version of twenty questions. I know I'm pushing her hard, and I try not to act frustrated. Julie can't tell me the model, but by the time we finish I'm fairly certain we're looking for a Ford pickup with two doors, running lights, and a scratch on the passenger door. All I've got of the Colorado plate is an X and a J in no particular order.

Julie drops her fork in her empty carton. Sweetie's cleaning her whiskers. I put away my sketchbook, and now the hard part begins.

"I saw Florence today," I tell her. "She told me your sister wants you to come live with her in Arizona."

"You interfering in my business?" Julie sits up tall and Sweetie runs up her arm like she's been called. Then they both glare at me.

"I'm sorry, I'm not trying to interfere, but—"

"But what?"

"Don't you want to be with your family?"

She strokes Sweetie between the ears. "I got my family right here."

"I don't get it. If I had someone who wanted me—"

"You're not me. You don't know what I want or what I deserve. You don't know my story." Julie swings her legs around the bench and gets up. "Thank you for my lunch."

I scramble to my feet, but she's already walking away. "You're right, I don't know your story, but I bet that whatever the 'old you' did that you're so ashamed of, you've already paid for it."

She stops for a moment but doesn't turn around.

I wait, sensing either Julie's going to take down the wall she's put up or she's going to walk away.

She walks away. *Damn.*

I snatch our trash off the table and head for a nearby can when my phone rings. It's Tara. Terrific. Wasps circle the mouth of the trash can, so I stand back to toss my garbage. "Hi, Tara. What's up?"

"Good news. Iona's accepted your offer to paint her portrait."

A week ago, I'd have jumped for joy, but today the thought of a month spent gazing at Iona's overly made-up face as I paint her is almost more than I can bear.

There's an easy way out and that's to hand Iona the six

grand Adam gave me. All I have to do is tell her: *I sold a painting, so I can send you the money.*

It's so damn tempting, but I'm not stupid enough to believe it was an accident that Adam gave me *six* grand, the exact amount I owe her. He wants me to pay Iona back, and I'm betting it's because if I get arrested for stealing her dress, any reasons I have to stay silent about my part in *Duncan*'s theft won't matter anymore.

If I offer Iona the money, I play right into Adam's hands again.

"I'm waiting, Sabine."

"Sorry, I got distracted. That's great, Tara. Thanks for arranging this with Iona." And even though I toy with saying *I bet it wasn't easy*, I don't.

"Iona starts shooting the new season the first week in February. Can you get the portrait done by then?"

It will suck up every free minute I have over winter break, but I guess that only matters if I'm not arrested for art theft. "Yes, I can."

"You sure?"

"I promise," I say through gritted teeth.

"Talk soon." Tara hangs up and I head for my car.

Krell's coming back tomorrow, and all I've got to show him is a drawing of Adam and a poor description of his truck. I wish I had more, but if Krell recognizes Adam from the drawing, it might be enough.

Adam insisted Krell wouldn't want to know *Duncan* was a fake, but with everything that's happened, I have to believe that he would appreciate learning the truth.

Wouldn't it be better to know your masterpiece was stolen and not destroyed, so you could hold on to a sliver of hope that you could get it back? And wouldn't you want information that could help find the person who stole it and used it to attack you?

It's even possible Krell would be so grateful I came forward that he wouldn't insist CALINVA kick me out.

Yeah, that's likely.

Julie's friend the Jesus poet is splayed out on the bench nearest my car, so I circle back around, hoping he doesn't turn and look my way. He may be an expert on redemption, but apparently I'm going to learn those lessons the hard way.

CHAPTER 68

When Kevin comes over tonight, we don't even pretend that we want to talk. We kiss, and grope, and stumble all the way from the kitchen door to my room, where we fall on my bed. We are buttons and zippers and sleeves, a mess and tumble. And later, when we are panting and fumbling to uncap a water bottle, the water douses our faces and necks, and we can't stop grinning.

We lie back, hands clasped, and Kevin's curls tickle my forehead. His arm is hot and damp against mine. He draws up the sheet, and I push it down with my foot.

"I have a surprise," I tell him.

"Yeah?"

I reach into my messenger bag and pull out the two tickets. "Will you be my date?"

"A gala." He tosses his head back and forth like he's weighing whether or not to say yes.

"Oh stop," I say, giving him a shove.

He laughs as he rolls into the wall. "Of course I'll be your date," he says, and sits back up. His elbow rests on his bent knee, and his face is tilted toward me.

He's so beautiful right now, his features relaxed and his long limbs stretched out. In the soft yellow light of my room, he looks otherworldly, like a Greek hero in a

Maxfield Parrish painting. I reach for my sketch pad.

"What are you doing?" he says when I flip to a clean page.

"Capturing you."

"You've already captured me," he says.

I can't help smiling. "Not this way."

I start to sketch, but even though his body is still, the angle of his head keeps shifting as his eyes explore my room. "Okay, you need to focus on one spot."

He settles down and at last I pencil in his profile: the tilt of his head, the slope of his nose and cheeks, the lidded oval of his eye. I shadow Kevin's cheek, and squiggle in the beard he's growing.

As I work the details around his eyes, my skin starts to prickle. There's an intensity in his focus as if he's questioning what he's seeing.

I shift my gaze until it aligns with his. My completed self-portrait. He's disturbed by it just as Mrs. Mednikov was. I reach for a softer pencil to deepen the shadows. "What do you think about my self-portrait?" I keep sketching like it's no big deal.

"The bluebird, that's your mom, right?"

My breath catches and my eyes meet his. "How did you know?"

He shrugs. "Look around."

My room is half hers. Her portrait with the embroidered birds, the dead songbird of *Appetite*, THE SMALLEST BIRD SINGS THE PRETTIEST SONGS trailing down her guitar case.

My eyes spill and I swipe my cheeks with my hands. Kevin lays his hand on my knee and a minute goes by where neither of us speak. We both know I'm lost.

When he finally breaks the silence, his voice is so gentle

I almost don't catch what he's saying. "Why is the house on fire, Sabine? Please tell me what's going on with you."

I want to confide in him, to tell him everything, but this, what we have, is so new it could snap under the weight of my confession. "Everything's so hard without her. I don't know who I am, if I'm making the right choices, if I'm reading people right."

"Does this"—Kevin lifts his hand off my knee and it hovers over my skin—"have anything to do with me . . . us?"

I weave my fingers through his and squeeze tight. "No, no, this has nothing to do with us. You . . . you make this bearable."

"Just bearable?"

"Infinitely more than bearable."

We fall back on the bed, and Kevin cups my face in his hands. We gaze into each other's eyes before he sets his lips on mine. He kisses me as if he believes we've gone to a new place where at last I've shared my secrets.

But as I kiss him back, I can't stop thinking, Don't leave me, Kevin. Don't leave me when you learn who I really am.

CHAPTER 69

I lie awake half the night, watching Kevin sleep, knowing that when the truth comes out, it could wreck us. The sun is just coming up, and I mute my alarm before it goes off, holding on to these last few minutes of peace.

Kev's curls splay across my pillow and I wind one around my finger and stroke the silky hair with my thumb.

I was so blind about Adam. So desperate for approval. All he had to do was toss me a little praise, and I ate his lies up like ice cream. Even when I knew in my gut things were off.

Kevin turns toward me and I pull up the blanket and tuck my body into his. I close my eyes as he nestles me up against his chest, and I match my breathing to his, wishing we could stay like this for the rest of the day.

I'm close to falling asleep again when a dog starts barking and Kevin groans. He gropes around on the floor and silences his phone. I pass him his glasses.

"Thanks. You think Krell will be back this morning?" he says.

I slide out of bed and grab my jeans off the floor. "Who knows, but I'm not chancing it," I say, tossing Kev his jeans.

He leaves the house before I do. I kiss him good-bye, and when he pedals off, I linger on the stoop, watching until he disappears around the corner and hoping it's not the last time I do.

I'm going to confess to Krell after class. I pour out a bowl of granola, knowing I need to eat, but the cereal takes forever to chew. Still, I shovel it in, because I need to be strong. I owe Krell the truth.

He might not believe me that *Duncan*'s a forgery, but I'll remind him an X-ray can prove it. He'll see I'm not lying when whatever he painted in the strata beneath *Duncan* doesn't show up on the film.

My self-portrait's tucked in my portfolio, so I get to my seat in class without anyone commenting. My whole life could change after this class, and I'd really like to avoid any drama just yet.

But as soon as my self-portrait goes up on my easel, Taysha looks it over. "Something serious going on here," she says.

"It's been a long semester."

"You know it."

Birch plunks down in the seat on the other side of me, the one Kevin usually takes, but before I can ask him to move, Kevin takes the empty seat next to Bryian.

Krell's back, like he promised he would be, but instead of striding to the front of the room, he walks in, head down, lost in a cloud of thought so thick you can almost see it.

We wait, our self-portraits on our easels or in our laps, for Krell to acknowledge us. No one chugs water, or checks their phone, or messes in a bag at their feet.

Krell sets his latte on the table up front, and when he finally takes us in, he blinks as if he didn't register we were here until that very moment.

"Welcome back, Professor Krell," Bernadette says.

He nods, and even that seems hard for him.

The granola's a brick in my stomach. It's awful, seeing him like this.

"We're really sorry about what happened at Art Basel," Bryian offers. "We hope the police find whoever did that to your painting."

Krell's gaze darts to the ceiling. "Thank you. Your concern is much appreciated."

"Will they attempt to restore *Duncan*?"

Krell can't seem to bear to look at us. His eyes are fixed on the ceiling. "*Duncan* has been examined by a restoration expert who believes it is unlikely it can be returned to its former state."

A minute goes by while we all sit in silence before Krell returns his attention to us and launches into his lecture.

"Self-portraits are an ironic art form. We look into the soul of the person we know best, but oddly that may be the person who perplexes us most. We try to control how the viewer perceives us, but our subconscious can defy our efforts and reveal much more than we intend. Self-portraits are mirrors and windows, and sometimes they are wells."

Then the air seems to go out of him, and instead of standing or pacing like he usually does, he slips into a chair at the front. His mouth is flat, and his brows sag as if they're too heavy to hold up.

Taysha and I exchange glances. "Someone's philosophical today," she murmurs.

"Bernadette," Krell says, "could you bring your portrait up?"

Back in September, I might have enjoyed Krell's misery.

His masterpiece ruined. His reputation destroyed as the art world paints him as a monster who drove a student to kill himself.

But right now what I feel is more complicated. I can't believe I feel sorry for him, when he brought so much of this mess on himself by treating people the way he did, but I do, and I hate the part I played in it.

Bernadette's neon-pink hair is topped with a crimson head wrap, and she's tucked a row of pink silk roses into a fold in the velvet.

"I see Frida Kahlo's made an appearance," Birch says under his breath.

Bernadette sets her canvas on the easel, and I don't have a decent view, but people around me are coughing into their hands and making eyes at each other. I lean to one side so I can see.

She's painted herself from behind, crouching naked over a pile of splintered bones. *What the . . . ?*

"Tell me those are not real bones," Taysha says.

I clamp my teeth over my knuckle so I don't laugh.

"Of course they're real," Birch mutters. "The question is did she herself trap and kill the animal they belong to."

Taysha considers this. "Too small for a deer," she says.

"Probably a dog," Birch replies. "Once I heard her say she hates corgis."

I kick Birch in the ankle. *I'm warning you. Stop.*

Krell calls Bryian up to the front, and Bernadette clips his canvas with hers as she carries it back to her seat. Birch nods in her direction. "The other day, I saw her coming out of the Humane Society."

I roll my eyes, and Birch shrugs. "Just saying."

There's a knock on the door and the dean sticks her head in. "Professor Krell, can I talk with you outside?" Krell steps into the hall and closes the door behind him.

I look at my portrait once more, imagining what Birch will whisper about me when I'm up front. House on fire? Birch'll have a field day with that, but he can't go too far or Taysha will shut him down.

A minute later Krell returns. He asks Bryian to take his seat and he stands at the front, hands on his hips. Krell's eyes slowly sweep the room as if he's trying to capture the moment.

I squint at Taysha. *Any idea what's going on?*

She shakes her head no, but right as she leans in to whisper something, Krell clears his throat.

"The administration will issue an announcement this morning, but I wanted to tell you in person that I am resigning my position as department chair effective immediately and plan to take an indefinite leave from teaching."

No. He can't be doing this. Everyone around me . . . we all gape at each other, hoping we heard him wrong.

"Rumors will abound regarding my decision; I urge you not to give them credence. As a working artist who has secured several new commissions, and as a new father, I have made a choice I believe works best for my art, my family, and ultimately, the students at CALINVA. That said, I have enjoyed our time together profoundly, and my only regret is that I will no longer have a front seat to observe your creative endeavors."

What? No! I don't care what Krell says about his commissions or being a new parent, I can't believe he really wants this.

Bernadette stands up. "We won't let the administration do this to you, Professor Krell. We'll start a petition. . . ."

He raises a hand to silence her. "Bernadette, your belief that I was forced to resign is mistaken and that is all I intend to say on the matter. Bryian, if you would come to the front, please."

My heart is pounding so loudly in my ears, I'm surprised no one else hears it. Maybe Krell wasn't forced to resign, but I doubt he would have quit if I'd come forward a week ago and confessed.

When I painted *Duncan*, I gave Adam the weapon he needed to take down Krell. If I'd told Krell that my copy of *Duncan* was shipped to Miami and the original was gone, there wouldn't have been a Krell painting at Art Basel for Adam to tag.

Adam would have had to find a way to take down Krell without me.

Bryian struggles to hold it together up at the front as Krell comments on the creative choices Bryian made on his self-portrait. We all knew Bryian was counting on Krell to be here for him and mentor him, so he's probably in shock.

The ripples of what I've done, the choices I've made, keep expanding, slamming everyone around me.

Krell calls my name. It takes all my concentration not to step on the bags and paint boxes and portfolio cases beside everyone's stools as I carry my portrait up to the front. I place my painting on the easel and turn to face Krell.

I try to keep my face composed as I look him in the eyes, sure he must see the guilt in mine.

But he must not, because he focuses his gaze on the painted girl whose open chest reveals the burning house inside. I expect Krell to complain that my style isn't bold or experimental enough, that I've reverted to my old ways, but he doesn't. Head propped on one hand, he looks at me almost tenderly and says, "You would not have painted this six months ago. You aren't trying to impress the viewer with your virtuosity. It's the most honest thing you've painted all semester."

I'm not sure he hears me thank him, because I barely hear it myself. Air fills my head and I'm almost dizzy as I go back to my seat. I plop down on my stool and Taysha wraps an arm around me. "Great job," she whispers.

I smile back, but inside I'm ashes.

CHAPTER 70

I sit through the rest of class, but I don't hear a word Krell says.

Adam won. He forced Krell out and I helped him. I could have come forward weeks ago. I could have stopped Adam, but now it's too late.

A few seats over, Bernadette is sniffling and Bryian's biting the skin around his thumb. A fluorescent bulb starts to flicker, so I duck my head, trying to keep the strobing light from making me feel sicker than I already do. I'm dying inside, full of disgust at Adam and at myself.

Taysha leans over and whispers, "Seems like you're taking Krell's leaving awfully hard."

I give her a broken smile. "Yeah, who'd have thought I'd be upset?"

Krell's leaving CALINVA, so does it really matter anymore if I come forward about Adam? Would it be stupid to confess when my confession won't change what's happened?

There's a chance the police are so focused on the tagging, no one realizes *Duncan*'s a fake. They might never find the tagger, or if they do, he could insist that Duncan Pyne, not Krell, was his target.

Say nothing, and there's a chance I can go on with my life, my scholarship secure. I keep my friends at CALINVA, my cozy room at Mrs. Mednikov's. I spend the next three years living my dream, and when I graduate, I might have a dealer and a slot in my first group show.

I look over at the portrait on my easel and the house in my chest consumed by fire and realize I'm still lying to myself. Until I come clean, until I confess what I know to Krell and my friends, I'll continue being this girl whose lies are destroying her from the inside. I will always be scared of being exposed and losing Kevin and this new family I've created.

I need to tell Krell what happened to *Duncan*, not just for him, but for me.

I pull my sweater tighter around me because the room has turned incredibly cold. My fingers are ice and I slide my hands into my sleeves. *I'm afraid, Mom.*

I close my eyes and her voice in my head is quiet and clear. *I know, baby, I know, but the only way out is through.*

The way out is right in front of me. I open my eyes, taking in Kevin and Taysha, my rivals, Bryian and Bernadette, and this room where I was ridiculed and embarrassed, but ultimately learned so much.

After class, I ask Kevin and Taysha if they have a few minutes to talk. What I have to tell them is so combustible that I make them come with me to the roof. The garden's empty except for a couple of grad students grabbing a smoke, but I lead my friends to a far corner.

It's warm and sunny and the blue sky is cloudless, while inside my chest a storm is roiling. I'm not sure what I expect from telling them, but I can't keep going on alone.

We drop into tangerine-colored plastic chairs, and the look on my face must be desperate, because Kevin and Taysha draw their chairs up so close our knees almost touch.

"What's going on, Sabine?" Kev says. "Why did you bring us up here?"

I hug my sketchbook to my chest, but the cardboard cover can't protect me. "Promise me you won't tell anyone what I'm about to tell you."

"What's this about?" Taysha asks.

"It's about Krell. But you have to promise this stays with us."

Kevin glances at Taysha, and she nods back. "Go ahead," he says.

"I think I know who's responsible for setting the fire at Art Basel and vandalizing Krell's painting."

They look at me like I've lost it. Kevin shakes his head. "How could you possibly know anything about that?"

Taysha shoots a look at Kevin. *Hold off.* "What is it?" she says. "What do you want to tell us?"

"There was this guy . . ." I open the sketchbook to Adam's portrait and turn it so they can see. There's no going back from here, but I feel myself circling the truth, trying to avoid telling them what I've done. "I don't know his name. I know what he looks like, and that he drives a gray pickup with Colorado plates."

"Where did you meet this guy?" Kevin says, trying to place him. "Did he model for your drawing class?"

Taysha stares at me. "That's the painter you went out with."

"You went out with this guy?" Kevin says.

"Only a couple of times."

His lips curl as he studies Adam's face. "How could you go out with him and not know his name?"

"Because he told me his name was Adam, but it wasn't."

Taysha's shaking her head.

"I know you warned me about him, but how was I to know that everything he told me was a lie?"

"What did he tell you?" Kevin says.

"He claimed he was a grad student here, and he had keys to the whole building, and he took me to one of the studios and showed me a painting he said was his, but later I met the student who actually painted it."

"So this guy was running around CALINVA pretending he's a student. That doesn't prove he has anything to do with the fire or vandalizing Krell's painting," Kevin says.

"He hates Krell."

"So does half the school."

"That number seems high to me," Taysha mutters.

"The point is," Kevin says, "where's your proof?" He's angry, and I'm not sure what's made him madder: that I hung out with a scumbag or that I didn't tell him about the guy before.

I suck in a breath as if I'm diving into the deep end, and dig my fingers into my hair.

"What are you hiding, Sabine? What don't you want us to know?" Kevin snaps.

"What the hell, Kevin?" Taysha reaches for me, but I wave her off.

"Is this why you've been so upset lately?" Kevin says.

I nod, and try to find my voice. "I'm involved. In this mess with Krell and Art Basel. I'm involved."

"No, how are you involved?"

There's no way out but the truth. "That was my painting in Miami. Not Krell's. It was a copy, not the original."

"Oh no! No no no!" Taysha folds her arms over her chest, but Kev sucks in a breath and closes his eyes, which hurts so much more. Taysha can't believe I'm capable of crossing the line like this, but Kevin totally accepts that I am.

"Go on," he says. "Tell us how it happened."

I start with the day Adam approached me at Artsy, and tell how I went from visiting Krell's studio to copying *Duncan*, then Adam going missing, and my painting being swapped for Krell's. I explain how I had nothing to do with the vandalism at Art Basel and am as shocked as they are about how it's hurt Krell.

Kevin has barely looked at me since I began my story, and now he can't stop shaking his head. "I can't wrap my head around why you'd do something so stupid. Going into Krell's studio behind his back, and painting a copy without permission."

My face goes so hot, it feels sunburned. "I don't know. I was scared, I was an idiot."

Taysha jumps in. "He played her. Sabine's a victim here. That guy manipulated her."

Kevin ignores her. "Was that really it?" he says, his voice breaking. "Why didn't you come forward when you knew the paintings had been switched? You didn't even try to fix the situation."

"Yes, I did! I tried to find Adam, I asked people if they knew him. I quizzed Julie about his car, and I figured out he had an accomplice."

"Yeah, you."

This stings worse than if Kev slapped me, and I count to five before I answer. "Not me, a girl who looks like me. I saw her on tape at the pawnshop paying for my guitar."

"Wait. You said . . . No, sorry, you let me believe *you* picked up your mom's guitar."

His cheeks are red and blotchy. This is one lie too many, and Kevin's sympathy's run out.

"Kevin, stop it." Taysha's gripping the arm of my chair. "Can't you see she's trying to turn this around?"

The muscle in his jaw twitches and anger's blowing off him like smoke.

"Please, Kevin. I need your help. I don't know how to get out of this mess."

His voice is so calm, so carefully constructed, I feel him forcing himself not to snap. "The answer's pretty clear since you only have one option."

"What's that?" As if I don't already know.

"Confess. Show Krell the guy's picture since he'll probably recognize him. How about hire a lawyer before you have to turn yourself in to the police."

Even though I've been thinking the same thing, it sounds a hundred times worse coming from Kev. "I hoped you'd say something different."

"I guess I could have lied and told you what you wanted to hear, but that hasn't proven to be an effective strategy so far, has it?" he says.

I've got no witty comeback, and we must all sense we're done talking, because Kevin and Taysha move their chairs back and I stow my sketch pad away. Kevin's the first to get up.

"Call me later," he says. "Let me know how it goes."

"Kevin?" I jump out of my chair, but he's disappeared around a corner. No kiss. No hug. No looking back.

Taysha puts her arm around my shoulder. "Give him a few days," she murmurs.

"Sure," I say, but my insides are ruins. I swallow back

my tears, because if I let go now, I'm not getting off this roof.

"You got a lawyer you can call?"

"Ironically enough, I've got a direct line to one of the best criminal lawyers in LA."

"Not the one who bought your painting?"

"Yeah, that's the one."

Taysha walks me back to the lobby and offers to drive me home, but I tell her no, I've got to go to work. Each block I walk feels like ten, and I'm barely conscious of where I'm headed until I'm standing next to my car in the alley. I climb into the backseat, curl up in the corner, and stare at the brick wall outside the window.

Tears trickle down my face, and I dig into my pain, letting it loose until my chest is heaving. I rage at Adam and God and fucking fate, and drivers who hit people and run away. And I rage against myself when there's no one left to blame. I made my own choices. Adam didn't force me to copy Krell's painting. I wanted to.

My clothes are soaked with sweat when I finally lean my head back against the seat. The sky beyond the sunroof is faded blue.

Help me, Mom. I'm so messed up. Help me.

I see her cradling her wrist, her thumb rubbing the word inked into it. When her eyes meet mine, they're disappointed, but still loving. *You can't fix the problem if you're not honest about how you've messed up. Time to come clean, baby.*

I wipe the last tears off my cheeks. My hand shakes as I dig my phone out of my bag. I steady my breathing and dial, but I'm still thrown when the phone only rings twice before a receptionist answers.

He rattles off the firm's name, but my mouth is so dry I can't speak before he rattles it off again.

My thumb hovers over the end-call button for what feels like forever, but at last I hear myself say, "I'd like to speak to Casey Stiner. Can you please tell her Sabine Reyes is calling and I need her help."

CHAPTER 71

Casey Stiner drives me to Krell's house. We idle at a crosswalk while kids walking home from school dart in front of her car to catch up to their friends.

Turns out Casey was classmates with Rachel Krell at law school, a fact I learned when we met and I revealed *the chain of events that led me to seek legal counsel.* Sitting as I am now in her passenger seat, that chain of events feels locked around my wrists.

The neighborhood streets are lined with sidewalks, and small but meticulously renovated Craftsman houses. Casey pulls up in front of Krell's compact contemporary, where the lawn has been replaced with a drought-tolerant display of plump succulents and silver-gray lavender.

"Remember, stick to the facts," Casey says. "No commentary, no why-you-did-this-or-that."

"Right."

She releases her seat belt, but I can't seem to move my hands.

"I know you're nervous," she says, "but you're doing the right thing."

"What if I end up going to jail?"

"Then I will get you out as fast as I can."

Krell opens the door, and his face pinches when he sees me. "Casey, Ms. Reyes."

I grip the shoulder strap on my bag tighter, unnerved by his red eyes and bent head. What happened to the man whose posture was defined by arrogance?

"I wouldn't disturb you, Collin, but Sabine believes she has information that can help shed light on the events at Art Basel Miami."

Doubt deadens his voice. "Come in, by all means."

We walk through a sunlit living room. It's like stepping into a minimalist canvas, the dove-gray walls and couch the color of pencil lead punctuated by spots of color: a fluffy white area rug, a sea-blue vase, a copper bowl.

Rachel joins us at a long table. Makeup-less, her eyes are small and unremarkable, except for the suspicion glittering in them.

Krell offers us coffee, but we say no. He and his wife link hands, and I force myself to make eye contact with them. It's almost unbearable seeing what I've threatened: the happy family, the cozy house.

Casey taps my hand. *Go ahead. Tell him.*

I try, but the truth is a wad of wet paper in my throat. My mouth opens and closes, but no sound comes out. When Rachel can't stand it anymore, she gets up and brings me a glass of water, and I gulp the whole thing.

I dab a last drop from my lips. "The painting in Miami wasn't *Duncan*; it was a copy."

Krell looks right at me; he believes me.

"That's impossible," Rachel says. "Collin never shows his work in progress to anyone before it's done."

Krell ignores her. "How?" he says, meaning how do I know. "Because I painted it."

Rachel gapes at me like she can't believe I said this, but

Krell nods and starts to smile. "I knew it. I knew something was off the night it was unveiled, but I told myself I was imagining it."

"How could you?" Rachel says to Krell. "How could you show her *Duncan* when you wouldn't show me?"

"I didn't show her!" Krell says, but I see in Rachel's eyes that she doesn't believe him.

"It's true," I tell her. "He didn't know I saw it."

Rachel rises out of her chair and slams her hands on the table, and I jerk back as Casey leans forward to block her. "You entered his studio without permission!" Rachel cries. "You forged his painting!"

Casey squeezes my hand, and in a very quiet voice says, "Let's all take a breath, why don't we, and process what we've heard."

Rachel eases back into her seat, but her eyes are narrowed on me like a cat about to pounce. Krell lays his hand over hers, but she pulls her hand into a fist, and I sense she's about to fire questions at me when Benny lets out a cry that sends her down the hall.

When she's gone Krell says, "Why did you do it, Sabine?"

I'm not sure I know why anymore, and I stick to the most basic facts. "You advised me to find a painting I connected with and you said I should transcribe it."

His expression shifts as he moves from confusion to disbelief to tamped-down anger. "As I recall that particular conversation, I told you to visit a museum or gallery. . . ."

"Yes, that's true, you did. . . ."

"You broke into my studio."

"No, I did not break in." I open my sketch pad to the drawing of Adam. "This man let me in."

"Who is he? One of the janitorial staff?"

"You don't recognize him?" Casey says.

"No."

My heart sinks. "Are you sure? I thought he might have been one of your students when you taught at UCLA."

"No, not that I recall, and my studio classes were small enough that I would remember."

I can't believe Krell doesn't know who he is. It makes no sense.

"Collin, we believe this man stole the original *Duncan* and substituted Sabine's copy before the painting was shipped to Miami. We also believe he either vandalized the copy or hired the person who did," Casey says.

"So he's an art thief. Doesn't the FBI have files on art thieves?"

"Consider the evidence. He didn't quietly disappear with the original. He orchestrated a stunt to wound you personally."

Krell picks up the sketch and squints at it. He covers the bottom half of Adam's face with his hand, then the top, then covers the hair. "What's his name?"

"He called himself Adam," I answer. "He said he was a grad student and he talked about you like he'd taken classes from you."

Krell gets up, and when he returns, he's carrying charcoal pencils and a large sketch pad. The room goes quiet as he begins to draw, working from my sketch. The only sounds are the scratching of the charcoal on the paper, Rachel murmuring to Benny in a nearby room, and the rhythmic thud of a rocking chair.

Krell goes back and forth between my sketch of Adam and his own, roughing in the face and head. But then he draws dreads sprouting from Adam's head and hides his cleft chin beneath a short beard, There's no zigzag scar through his brow. The nose and mouth are Adam's, but when Krell draws the eyes, they are wide-open, the irises huge and the whites shocking.

It's not Adam, but the similarity is disturbing.

Casey signals me with her eyes to keep quiet as Krell sets down the charcoal. His face is tense as he quietly says, "Rachel, can you come here a second?"

When she comes to the table, Benny is in her arms. Krell flips the sketch around so she can see it, and she gasps. "It's that boy."

Krell nods. "Aiden Bellasco."

Rachel falls into the chair next to him. She lays her head on his shoulder and whispers, "It wasn't your fault."

I huddle in my chair as tragedy settles like dust over the room. I'm unsure how all the pieces fit together yet, but I know deep inside that Adam must have loved Aiden to be so angry with Krell.

"Who was he?" Casey asks.

"He was my student," Krell answers. His face is anguished as he tells the story of a young man who was struggling. Although he was immensely talented, his behavior became increasingly erratic. Krell can barely look at us as he says, "I encouraged him to take a leave of absence so he could get the help he needed, but not long after, he jumped off the roof of the CALINVA building."

None of us says a word. We can't.

I picture Aiden hitting the pavement and I'm swamped with a feeling of sorrow. He must have been in such pain to make the choice he did.

And Adam . . . he must have been so angry. Of course he'd blame Krell for Aiden's death. Why wouldn't he when Aiden's own classmates were so sure it was Krell's fault?

Benny waves his tiny hands and Krell holds out a finger for him to clasp. I believe Krell was telling the truth when he told us how he tried to help Aiden.

But Adam didn't see this . . . or he couldn't see it.

Casey's the first to speak. "Given the family resemblance, it's likely that 'Adam' is a relative, a brother or a cousin. Your lawyer will want to inform the authorities." She pushes back her chair as if we're done here, but Rachel holds up a hand to stop her.

"Not so fast. I have some questions," she says, turning steely eyes on me. *How did I meet Adam? How did I end up in her husband's studio? Did Adam offer me money? Did I know what he intended to do with my copy?*

I clutch my chair, barely holding on against the barrage. So when Rachel demands to know why I didn't come forward sooner, I snap back at her, "I was afraid. I thought I'd go to jail!"

"Jail's exactly where you should be," she throws back. "How can you live with yourself?"

I glance at Casey. *Please get us out of here.*

"Rachel," Krell says softly. "She didn't have to help us."

"She hurt you! She hurt us!"

Casey signals to me to get up. "We should go," she says to the Krells. "I expect you'll want to relay this information to the investigators on the case. Sabine's provided me additional information that may help the search."

Rachel glares as Krell walks us to the door. He offers me his hand. "Thank you for coming forward, Sabine."

"I'm sorry. I never meant for any of this to happen."

"Yes, I can't imagine you did," he says, and shuts the door behind us.

Once Casey and I are buckled inside her car, I lean my head against the window. "Rachel Krell's going to make sure I'm kicked out of school."

"Probably, but it's the end of the semester. They might let you finish." Casey pulls away from the curb. "As information about the forgery and the theft leaks out, and it will, rumors will start flying. You don't want your face all over social media, so be careful who you talk to, and *no press*."

"Okay. I got it."

"I'll try and work a deal: your testimony for immunity from prosecution."

"Thank you, Casey."

She lists a dozen other things she'll do to keep me safe, but I barely follow what she's saying.

The streets go by, tiny green lawns lush under sprinklers. Big wreaths with gold or red velvet bows hang from doors that never see snow. Christmas is out of place in LA.

"I need to warn you," Casey says as we near Mrs. Mednikov's, "the board will probably pull your painting from the auction."

"No, why?"

"We can't expose a donor to the scandal that will be attached to it."

"Great. Another shining example of how everything I touch turns to shit."

Casey lets that go by.

"Sorry," I say.

She bends her head toward me and takes her eyes off

the road for a moment. "The people I defend . . . their lives implode even if they're innocent. The ones who rise from the ashes are those who find a new purpose. You can have a satisfying life post-CALINVA, but it won't be the one you imagined."

"Are you saying I should give up painting?"

"Not at all. But think about what art and being an artist mean to you as you go forward."

She pulls up in front of my house and my landlady is pruning her roses with a huge pair of shears. Mrs. Mednikov looks up as I get out, and at first she smiles, but then her lips part as if she sees the bad news wafting off me.

CHAPTER 72

Mrs. Mednikov's elbows rest on the kitchen table, her hands locked as if she's praying. Our cups of tea sit between us, untouched. She's been silent through most of my confession, barely looking at me, her fingers splayed over her mouth.

"I can be out of here today," I say.

"And then what? You will sleep in your car?" she snaps.

I pick at the chipped polish on my thumb. Mrs. Mednikov's known about me this whole time, but she's been too kind to say anything. "I could stay with a friend."

"Your rent is paid! You will not go anywhere tonight." She mutters angrily in Russian, and my stomach clenches.

Mrs. Mednikov stands and snatches our cups off the table.

"I can wash them," I offer, but she turns her back on me. "No, I do not need your help," she says, and dumps the cold tea in the sink.

She scours the cups, and I slip out to the sunporch, sensing she can't bear to be near me right now. I sit motionless in the creaky wicker chair until I hear her leave the kitchen.

She doesn't have to say it, but I've disappointed her, and that's way worse than making her angry.

I see Mom pacing our apartment after Nordstrom's

security made her come and pick me up the time Hayley and I tried shoplifting. She won't speak to me, or even look at me, and I hear myself trying to apologize over and over while Mom holds up her hand to *stop*. And finally she can't hold it in any longer and yells, "I don't care if you're sorry. Did you learn anything from this? Have you changed?"

Now the question sifts through me. *Yes, Mom, I've changed. I was a house on fire, now I'm burned to the ground.*

I've torched most, maybe all, of my relationships, and if I'm lucky, I'll have a chance to earn back some of them. Might as well start now, I think, and tap out a message to Kevin and Taysha.

IT'S DONE.

Taysha's comes charging back. R U OK?

DRAINED, I answer.

TELL ME EVERYTHING.

TOMORROW OK?

I carry my phone into my bedroom and lay it beside my bed. I curl up, not expecting to sleep, but sleep drags me down to the bottom of the ocean. And nothing and no one comes to pull me out.

CHAPTER 73

I don't hear from CALINVA during the weekend, so I assume it's like Casey said and they're letting me finish the semester. Two exams and I'll be done, so I cram for both of them every free moment I'm not working.

A security guard intercepts me in the lobby on the way to my first exam. Heads turn and I feel dozens of eyes trained on my back as he escorts me to the administration office.

The president's door is closed, but Mona takes me right in, and who's sitting on the couch inside but Rachel Krell, one leg crossed over the other. She's fierce, dressed like she's going to court. She glares at me, refusing to say hello.

The air is whooshing in my ears, so I can barely hear the president when she asks if what Rachel Krell has told her is true.

I nod yes, certain that my silence is the only force holding back Rachel's anger.

The president hands me a letter, but I can't read what's below the CALINVA letterhead because the small black type swims like guppies. "This terminates you from the program, and this," she says, handing me a second letter, "cancels your scholarship."

This must have been what Rachel Krell was waiting for: to see my face as I lose what I value most, because she gets up and leaves.

Strangely, the loss doesn't hurt the way I thought it would. I've been released from my body, and I float over the scene, taking it in but not feeling it.

The president walks through specifics, noting that it is unclear if I'll get credit for my classes since I left before the instructors turned in the grades.

I sign a document promising not to give interviews or discuss CALINVA or the Zoich on social media, and in return, they agree not to comment publicly about my part in the crime. I turn over my ID card and the guard escorts me from the building.

I plunk myself down on a cement planter not far from the entrance to wait for the airy feeling in my head to dissolve. My first and last semester at CALINVA is over.

My hands are ice, and I raise my face to the sun. *God grant me the serenity to accept the things I cannot change . . .* I picture Mom with her hand resting on her wrist, and for the first time, I understand why blowing out the candles on those stupid cupcakes was so important to her.

My wrist is white and blank, a perfect canvas. I trace the blue veins with my finger. "Serenity" was Mom's guiding light, but there's got to be a word that can be mine.

CHAPTER 74

Despite CALINVA's official promise of silence, my fellow students are all too eager to share the rumors about what I did. By noon a pic of me wearing Taysha's leather flapper dress is everywhere, and I'm the talented but pathetically gullible art student linked to the scandalous desecration and theft of a contemporary masterwork.

That a lot of what they're saying about me is true doesn't make it easier to handle. The only thing that makes it bearable is that Kevin's meeting me in the park during a break from his physics study group.

The park isn't crowded even though it's lunchtime and the sun is warm. Lawn bowlers cluster outside their tiny clubhouse, the light bouncing off their immaculate white sweaters and pants, while only a few yards away, the blanketed forms of sleeping men and women form gray islands on the thin grass.

I scan the benches and picnic tables under the palm trees and magnolias for Kevin. I spy him before he sees me.

His red mountain bike leans against a picnic table and he's sitting on top. His back is turned, but even from across the street, I see his foot tapping along to music that must be coming through his earphones.

He's bent forward, and his elbows rest on his jeans. I

keep walking until I can see his profile. *Look up, Kev. Look up.*

I could call to him, but I hold off because I need to see him look for me. If he stands up and waves, everything will be fine.

But I'm right in front of him before he finally sees me, and I stop a few feet away, expecting him to smile or step off the table and maybe not wrap me in his arms, but at least close the gap between us.

He seems to know what I am hoping for, because he barely glances at me as he pulls out his earphones and shoves them in his hoodie pocket. "You okay?" he says.

I sit down next to him, avoiding a sticky spot rimmed with pollen. "I'll survive. Casey Stiner thinks she can keep me out of jail."

"That's good."

"It's probably better than I deserve."

He doesn't contradict me; in fact, he doesn't say anything, and I squirm in his silence. "I'm sorry I lied. I'm sorry for a lot of things, actually."

Kevin still won't look at me. His eyes are locked on a bald patch in the grass as if it's the only safe place around. When he does speak, his voice is hoarse. "I care about you, Sabine, more than I've cared about anyone in a long time, but I can't trust you."

I curl into myself. It kills me, hearing him say that. "I swear I will never lie to you again, Kev."

"It's not just the lies. I can't handle how you treat people."

"What do you mean?"

"How about the way you screwed over Krell and that woman whose dress you sold. It's not like you didn't know what you were doing was wrong. You chose to hurt them."

Suddenly I'm freezing, and I glance at the sky, expecting to see clouds blocking the sun, but it's clear blue. "But I'm making amends, and I'm trying to turn things around. Doesn't that matter?"

"It matters, but what I can't wrap my head around is your need to get revenge in the first place."

"You don't understand wanting to get back at someone who hurt you?"

"No, I don't."

"You're telling me you never wanted to get back at someone who made you feel worthless. Not even Chantal?" He shakes his head, but I don't believe him. "Seriously, you never thought of taping a sack of dog crap to her locker?"

I expect him to at least break a smile, but he doesn't. "I might have thought about hurting someone, but I'd never actually do it," he answers.

"Wow." I shake my head, the heat rising inside my clothes. "You totally believe that. Obviously what I did was messed up, but you don't know that you'd never cross that line, because you've had the privilege of never having your entire life go up in flames."

He whips his head around and he's pissed, but not as pissed as I am.

I shove my finger in his face. "You thought I was fixed when I got my scholarship. Since I had money, a decent place to live, I wouldn't screw up again. But I wasn't *fixed*, because the single most important thing I lost can never be replaced.

"You know the real reason I didn't tell you about the mess with Krell? It's because I knew you'd judge me. I regret everything I've done more than you will ever know, and I wish you could try just a little to understand what it's like to be lost and utterly alone."

I hop off the table and Kevin doesn't even try to stop me. I walk away, my heart tearing away from my chest. This hurts so much worse than losing my scholarship or my place at CALINVA, maybe because what Kevin and I had was what I really wanted most of all.

CHAPTER 75

A news van for KTLA is parked on the street outside the shelter when I drive up the following week. *Crap.* I shade my face as I pull into the driveway, and a uniformed officer orders the dozen or so photographers and reporters out of the way so I can park.

I park on the far side of the shelter's van and turn off the engine. I take a deep breath, knowing the news media can't see me unless they are willing to risk ticking off a cop for trespassing.

Casey Stiner called a minute ago, so I dial her back. "I hope this doesn't mean the police want to question me again," I say when I get her on the phone.

"No, they seem to be satisfied for now."

"That's good to hear."

"Actually, I called to let you know they located Gabriel Bellasco in Croatia."

I look around even though I know he's a continent away. In one week, Casey learned that Aiden's older brother, Gabriel, is twenty-nine, ex-military, and a hacker.

"Let me guess," I say, "Croatia has no extradition treaty with the US, so we can't force him to return."

"Correct. But the good news is he can't reenter the US without us knowing, so you can sleep knowing you're safe."

"What about that girl, the one in the security tapes? Do they know who she is?"

"Not at this time. Bellasco was alone when he arrived in Croatia, and the theory is she was a student like you who he conned into helping him. The police have set up a tip line, and their hope is one of those leads will pan out."

It's no consolation that someone else was as easily duped as I was.

I thank Casey for looking out for me, then climb out of the car. Last week when we turned over the six grand Adam gave me to the police as evidence, she made sure I was identified as a victim of his crime. "The police will hold it until they close the case, which could take years, but then you could get it back," she explained.

I don't want the money, but maybe I'll feel differently when I'm still struggling to pay rent and car insurance on minimum wage and tips.

When I get inside the shelter, Taysha's setting up. She said she'd help out the first day of Christmas holiday camp, but she's come back every morning since.

This week, she's been in charge of the tweens, while I've wrangled fifteen first- through fifth-graders. We started with colored pencils, then watercolors, and now papier-mâché masks. Every day, I've had to rush home from the shelter to scrape off paint and glue before my afternoon shift at Artsy.

Tay thinks I'm hiding out by coming here, and she's partly right. Here I get to focus on keeping these little guys from destroying the place, and I forget about my own drama. It's been a week since I saw Kevin, and he went home to Kansas without even a text.

Florence opens the doors and the kids rush in. Taysha sits

at the end of the table, surrounded by giggly tweens. I teased her that she's got a sweatshop going, because the girls have spent whole mornings making earrings for their friends. Rolled paper beads, Sculpey, origami.

I walk around the table, tapping the balloons the kids covered with papier-mâché, checking that the gluey newspaper strips are dry so we can paint.

Yesterday we started by blowing up balloons, which quickly turned into a balloon fight with flying, farting balloons before Florence appeared and restored order. Today the kids are painting their masks. The girls have grabbed the pink and yellow paint, declaring they want to be princesses or superheroes, while the boys slap on bright red and blue slashes and argue over who gets to be which top Mexican wrestler.

I park myself next to Raymond, whose big ears, buzzed hair, and pointy little chin make him look like a Christmas elf. Raymond leans over his mask, his tongue sticking out in concentration. He's stolen my heart the way he makes sure he knows where I am at all times. All week, I've caught him looking up, checking if I'm there. And each time I smile at him. *See, I'm still here.*

I know what it's like to need a touch point, someone or something solid when everything else has crumbled. If I can do that for Raymond this week, it makes every minute of the wrangling and noise and cleanup of putting on these art lessons worth it.

Florence strolls by the table. "I thought you'd like to know: Julie got off okay."

Florence and I were worried Julie would refuse to get in her sister's car when she drove out from Phoenix to take her back. "Did you meet her sister? Is she nice?"

"Nice and . . . relieved. She'd been looking for Julie for eight years."

Florence and I share a smile. It's not a perfect ending. Julie's still sick, but at least now she's with someone who cares about her.

Florence sets a sheet of paper by my elbow. "What's this?" I say, picking up what looks like a page copied from a career guide, because it's titled "Art Therapist."

"It's a little something to think about."

I scan the description. "You need a master's degree, and I don't even have a bachelor's, plus I've never taken a single psych class."

"Yet."

She looks so damn sure of herself. "I don't know if I even want to go to college anymore."

Florence frowns at me like I'm being ridiculous. "You know, I have not always worked in Social Services. For years, I ran a very successful business."

I'm stunned. Florence never reveals anything personal. "I didn't know that."

"I loved running a business, until I stopped loving it, because it did not satisfy this," she says, and raps her heart with her fist. "The fact that you are here suggests that you, too, need this."

"Miss Sabine, look!" Raymond says, grabbing the arm I was leaning on, and I fall forward, catching myself right before I face-plant in El Diablo.

"Whoa, Raymond!"

"Do you like it? Do you like my mask, Miss Sabine?"

"I'll let you go," Florence murmurs, and wanders off. I fold up the paper and take a second look at the name and phone number Florence wrote on the bottom. Underlined next to it she's written: *Career counselor at Pasadena City College.*

It feels too soon to think about my future, since I'm still dealing with my past. Casey's optimistic I'll come out of this ordeal okay, but if I've learned anything this year, it's that I can't take anything for granted.

Taysha pops by my table. "You're still coming for Christmas, right? Because my moms want to know if you have any food allergies."

Mrs. Mednikov has barely spoken to me since I confessed, so it was a huge relief when Taysha's family invited me for the holidays. "No food allergies. I'll eat anything they serve and I'll do cleanup after."

SKETCH #6

IONA January 5

I flip through the photographs Tara sent me, landing on a three-quarter shot of Iona in the black Valentino dress. Iona's smile and stance are practiced as she poses for the press. Chin up, hand on hip, one leg forward, she owns the red carpet. The lace drapes, exposes, suggests, and conceals her curves, so her body appears tall and slim. No wonder she loved that dress.

This shot may be the best, I think, but then I flip to the next: a candid taken in the limo moments before Iona stepped out to greet the crowd. She looks out the window, and the expression on her face is somewhere between fear and doubt, as if she isn't sure she should be there.

Iona wouldn't want anyone to see this, and I wonder why Tara sent it. I lean in, studying this person who I lived with for years but never really saw, and a memory hurtles back from a fall day when I was ten.

I went looking for Mom in the Taylors' house. It was time to leave for school and I was careful not to make noise as I padded down their stairs. Someone was crying quietly in the kitchen, and Mom was soothing whoever it was. I peeked around the corner and Iona was holding on to Mom, her head on Mom's shoulder, while Mom patted her back. I had never seen Iona act this way, and I retreated to our apartment over the garage. When Mom reappeared I remember asking if Mrs. Taylor was okay. "Everybody has tough times, baby. So it's important to be kind."

I turn back to the shot of Iona on the red carpet. This time I will be kind.

CHAPTER 76

T he street into the hills above Altadena is a straight shot
north for several miles, but then it narrows and begins
to wind. Stuck to my dashboard is a Post-it with a man's
address and his assistant's phone number, but not his name.

Maybe Mona was screwing with me by pretending she
didn't know it. When I saw CALINVA pop up on my phone
a few days ago, I almost didn't answer, and Mona's hello
was so icy, I considered hanging up. But then she told me a
woman was trying to track me down for an interview.

"I don't do interviews," I replied, thinking this was about
the scandal.

"Not that kind of interview," Mona snapped. "This is for
a job."

The road curves around the side of the hill, and the
houses up here are planted farther apart. A couple still have
their Christmas decorations up even though we're halfway
through January.

When I called the phone number, the woman said the
artist she worked for needed someone with my skills, and
I'm still wondering what she meant.

I find the address I'm looking for and steer past the mail-
box down a driveway cut into the hill. The drive flattens into
a circle in front of a one-story house.

This better be for real. I'm tempted to drive away. I've already been contacted by dealers who wanted me to *touch up* paintings they said were in bad shape. The money they offered was way too much to be legit.

But none of them went through CALINVA to reach me.

I pull up to the carport under the sprawling limbs of an oak. The matte-brown L-shaped house is a classic midcentury with clean lines and long triangular windows under the low roof. I take my portfolio out of the car and walk to the ocher red door. I'm five minutes late. *Damn.*

It doesn't matter if you don't get this job, I tell myself. You mostly came because you were curious. Right now I work enough hours at Artsy and La Petite Tomate to cover my expenses.

An Asian woman wearing a black tunic and loose khaki pants opens the door. Her black hair is fastened into a short ponytail, and a chunky turquoise necklace circles her neck. "Ms. Reyes?"

"Yes, sorry I'm late."

"Five minutes in LA isn't late."

I step inside and huge black-framed windows offer a panoramic view of the canyon. A fire road zigzags up the opposite slope, a mustard-colored cut through the silvery gray-green brush. "Wow. This view is amazing."

"Surprising how serene the location is considering its proximity to downtown." The woman smiles at my portfolio. "Good. You brought your work." She motions to me to follow her. "I'm sure you have questions, and I apologize for the mysterious nature of the invitation, but Willy is a very private man. He did not wish to expose himself to anyone whose purpose in coming was questionable."

We start down the hall. Long angled shelves of art books offer their covers to us.

Willy who? I run through every Willy I can think of in the art world, and as we emerge into a huge room at the back, I see two enormous portraits.

Holy shit, it's Willy Steam.

Several eight-foot-tall portraits fill the wall opposite me. The faces look like mosaics assembled from brightly colored shapes: diamonds, squashed circles, and triangles. Oversize photographs of the people he's painted hang next to the acrylics.

The paintings draw me to them. How Steam has captured these people using abstract shapes I can't even begin to understand.

I come close to the canvases and then back up again. *How does he do that?*

A soft *thunk thunk* makes me wheel around. "Mr. Steam. Hello."

Steam shambles forward with his walker, but seems too young to shuffle this way. He commands my attention with his piercing blue eyes and streaked mane of hair. His eyes take me in, assessing me, sizing me up.

"Sabine Reyes. Thank you for coming. I wanted to meet you." He chokes and his words break up as he speaks, but his eyes are fiery.

I fumble through thank-you-glad-to-meet-you-too, and follow him as he crosses the room to a pair of chairs positioned by the wall of windows. I take the chair he offers me. "I brought my portfolio," I say.

Steam falls back into his chair. "Don't need it."

This has got to be some kind of joke. Why am I here? "I don't know what you know about me."

"I know you paint so well you fooled Collin Krell."

Heat rises into my cheeks and I pop out of my seat. "I'm sorry. I made a mistake coming here."

"You're mighty indignant for an art forger," he calls after me.

"I am not a forger. I copied his work without permission, and that was a huge mistake."

"What if I asked you to paint a copy of something?"

"I'd say no."

"What if I asked you to be my hands?"

I stop at the doorway.

Steam lifts his hands off the arms of the chair and holds them out. He tries to hold them steady, but his fingers jerk and twitch like they're playing a frenetic song. "Parkinson's. I can barely hold a brush."

His confession makes me gasp. What would it be like to have so much talent, so much vision, and not be able to express it? I go back and sit down. "Tell me what you need."

"I begin a painting by taking a photo and breaking it into a grid. I'd need you to lay the grid out on the canvas." He rushes to finish as his chest seizes. Coughs rack his body, and his face turns red.

He tries to explain but can't get out the words, so I say, "I guess we'd talk through what shapes and colors to use in each square on the grid."

He nods, so I continue. "Then I'd paint in the square, and we'd change it if it isn't working?"

"Yes. Exactly." The coughing has stopped, and he takes a deep breath. "What do you think?"

I run my eyes over the canvases. I've never seen anything like them before, and I doubt a pariah like me will be offered a chance like this ever again. I could learn from him.

I've begun painting again, fighting my way through, experiencing moments of joy, times when I see my visions take form, when the feelings that roil me are tamed in paint.

Six months ago, I wanted to be top in my class, Zoich winner, Krell's fawned-over protégée, but now that dream feels empty.

What feels right is to do all I can to be as good a painter as I can. And working with Willy Steam, helping him make his visions real . . . feels right on so many levels.

"I don't want any secrets or confusion," I say. "If I work on your painting, I want your dealer to know. And if someone buys it, I want them to know, too."

"Complete transparency." Steam glances at a half glass of water on the sawed-off tree trunk by his chair. "Agreed." His hand closes around the orange plastic glass, and the water inside sloshes back and forth as he goes to drink from the straw.

I'm tempted to jump up and help, but I don't because I know it would kill any chance I have to work for him.

I want this job, but I don't want him to regret hiring me. "You should check my references. My boss at Artsy says he'd be happy to answer any questions."

"Nope. I don't need other references. I have Collin Krell's."

My head spins, and nausea rises from my gut.

"You can't believe it," Steam says.

I shake my head no.

"I didn't either . . . at first. Collin was my student. I asked him for a name, and he suggested you."

Now I'm the one struggling to speak. "Did he say why?"

"He said he failed you."

"Not true. He taught me so much. He changed the way I look at painting."

"Yes, he said you progressed, but he was not the teacher you needed."

I'd love to ask Steam how Krell's doing. Taysha told me she heard he's in therapy. But I sense Steam's told me all he intends to about Krell. "When would you need me to start?" I ask.

"Is next week too soon?" he says. "I have a vision of a new painting and it's holding me captive." He smiles as if he knows I know what it feels like to be the prisoner of art.

I smile back. "I think I can make it happen."

We sit and talk through how he likes to work: a few hours in the morning, a break for lunch and a nap, and a few hours in the afternoon. I'd be free to stay and work on my own paintings during the break. Five days a week, no nights, weekends off to rest.

When I get to my car, I'm so high I toss my portfolio in the back and throw my arms in the air. "Yes!"

"Yes, yes, yes," I cry as I steer the car up the drive. My heart is swallow-swooping, and I have to share this unbelievable turn of fortune. I can't even make it back to Pasadena before I pull over.

I take out my phone and message Taysha to call me as soon as she gets out of class. I hit send, and my thumbs hover over the keys. There's one more person I long to share this with, but it's been over a month since we last talked, and I'm not the one who decided we were done.

I stow my phone in my purse and pull back onto the road. A hawk glides down the canyon and rises over my car. He circles in front of me, riding the currents like he weighs absolutely nothing.

CHAPTER 77

Saturday morning, I slip on my oldest, softest shirt and ease it over the tattoo on my wrist. The skin is still tender as I rest my finger on the word inked in cadmium green: CLARITY.

When I walk into the kitchen, a donut is waiting on a plate by the coffeemaker, and because Mrs. Mednikov had breakfast hours ago, I know the donut is for me. I break off a small piece and it crumbles on my tongue, tasting of cinnamon and apple cider.

The thaw between us began two nights ago when I came back from working with Willy Steam. "There is soup," she said as I walked in the door. My heart skipped a beat because it had been weeks since we last ate together, but I tried to sound nonchalant. "I'd love some. I'll set out the bowls."

Our conversation over dinner was tentative, as if she didn't want to promise and I didn't want to disappoint. We passed each other questions like fragile china plates. She pretended she was only mildly interested in my enigmatic boss, but I saw right through her.

I pour some coffee and carry the donut to the porch, ready to tackle my new work in progress. Since I delivered Iona's portrait, I've been free to paint what I want.

It's only been a couple of weeks since I began assisting Willy Steam, but the give-and-take between us as we break down a face and reinterpret it in color and shape feeds my painting in a way CALINVA never did.

The morning sun bathes my canvas in golden light, highlighting the areas that still need work. The composition of my newest self-portrait isn't the problem. I stand in the gray-black ashes of a house, gazing at the viewer, my left hand stroking a bluebird nestled in the hair on my shoulder.

Tired but not broken is what I want the eyes to convey, but I haven't nailed them yet.

I prep my palette and am deep into painting when a movement in the garden catches my eye. I glance over, expecting Mrs. Mednikov, but it's not her, it's Kevin.

What the hell?

I draw in a breath, and push back the tears that would fill my eyes if I let them. CALINVA students are back from break and Taysha told me she'd seen Kev around campus, but I didn't expect to hear from him, not after his monthlong silence. And to show up like this?

The screen door squeals as I push it open. I stand on the top step, my hand locked on the handle. "Why are you here?" It comes out harsher than I mean it to, but so what.

Kevin sways a little and takes a half step back. "I guess I should have called, but I thought . . ."

You thought I'd hang up.

"Stephania told me you were out on the porch so I . . ." He raises his hands in surrender.

My heart is still bruised, and it would be easier if I hated him, but I don't. Kev's got something to say, and maybe I'm being weak, but I want to hear it. "You can come in."

Kevin's careful not to touch or even brush against me as he comes up the steps, but when he sees my canvas, he walks right up to it. I close the screen and hang back by the door.

He shoves his hands deep in his jeans and leans in until his nose almost touches the surface. "This is—what you're doing with color and shape, it's—really different."

His mouth hangs open and I don't fight the pride I feel at how the painting affects him. "Thanks. I don't know if you heard, but I got a job as Willy Steam's assistant. I'm learning a lot about technique."

Kevin continues to study my painting, his eyes tracing the lines of the figure until they focus on the face. "It's not just the technique that's different. You seem like you're in a better place."

"Getting there."

He shifts from foot to foot, and I sense he wants me to help him out and make this easier, but he's just going to have to suck it up and say what he came here to say.

After a long moment, Kev finally meets my eyes. "I had a lot of time to think over the break, and I realized I owe you an apology. You didn't go looking for a way to screw Krell, and you'd never have painted that copy if that guy hadn't set you up. I refused to see that, and I'm sorry."

I nod, not sure how to answer.

Kevin's apology doesn't erase the hurt I felt when he abandoned me, but at this moment I feel as if he sees me—not the me I pretended to be for him or the me he believed I was, but the real me.

He takes a step toward the screen door. "Okay, well, I guess I should go."

Something pulls in my chest, and I press down with my fingers to quiet it. He reaches for the handle, and as his hand closes around it, I realize what I want.

"There are apple cider donuts," I say. "Mrs. Mednikov made them fresh."

His eyes relax, and his lips curve into a tentative smile, and I offer him one back. We turn and he follows me into the sunlit kitchen.

I don't know where this will take us. Maybe we can recover, and maybe we can't, but wherever we go from here, I intend to show Kevin the me that is real, the one that is flawed and sometimes ugly, light and dark, honest and true.

Author's Note

When we picture people who are homeless, we usually don't think of college students. They don't match stereotypes we have in our heads or stand out on campus, but are often invisible, hoping to appear normal and fit in.

Today, an estimated sixty thousand college students in the US struggle with housing and food insecurity. Lacking the financial resources to pay for a dorm room or apartment, they are forced to couch-surf or sleep in a library or car, or to decide whether to pay their rent or their utility bills. They may skip meals and go hungry. Some cannot afford to buy textbooks because what little money they have must go to food.

These students can be found at top state universities as well as local community colleges. Many work and receive student aid, but it is not enough to cover all their expenses, especially if they are young parents or help support other members of their families.

But students like you are making a difference at their schools right now. Here are a few examples of what is happening on campuses today.

Food pantries where students can come to get free food and toiletries have been created at 350 colleges across the country, and more are under way.

At a number of campuses, students donate the unused portions of their meal plans to support the campus food bank.

Inventive students around the US have created social media apps so a student can invite a peer for a meal in a campus dining hall, or alert hungry students to leftover food from a catered event, or connect food banks with local restaurants so unused food can go to those who need it.

A growing number of schools are helping students find temporary housing when they have been displaced. In 2016, a UCLA graduate student opened the first of two shelters in Los Angeles for homeless college students.

Staff and volunteers at campus resource centers are helping students sign up for government programs that assist with food, child care, rent, utilities, and medical expenses.

How can you get involved?

In November, take part in your local Hunger & Homelessness Awareness Week activities such as a food and clothing drive. See HHweek.org for more information.

Check out what programs are available on your campus already and volunteer, donate, or increase awareness.

To learn how to set up a food bank on your campus, download a free Toolkit for Campus Food Pantries from the Student Government Resource Center at studentgovresources.org.

To raise donations for your campus food bank, download a free toolkit from CUFBA, the College and University Food Bank Alliance.

You can make a difference!

Acknowledgments

What I Want You to See is about perception: how we view the world, how we want to be viewed, how we succeed or fail to perceive what is right in front of us.

And because it's nearly impossible for writers to see clearly what we've written, we depend on our editors and fellow writers to tell us if we haven't yet gotten what's swirling around our brains down on the page.

I was truly fortunate to be paired with a great editor who saw my novel's potential. If there's a master artist among agents, it's Sarah Davies, who matched *What I Want You to See* with Laura Schreiber.

Laura pushed me to go deeper and refine what I'd only sketched. She challenged me to paint my characters more subtly and saved me from my worst creative impulses. Thank you, Laura. This book is ten times better because of you.

Thank you to the Freeform team. Mary Mudd offered knowledgeable insights and penetrating questions. Jamie Alloy brilliantly translated the spirit of my book into a cover that makes people say, "Wow!" Dina Sherman connected *What I Want You to See* with librarians, the connoisseurs of YA art.

Many thanks to Leda Siskind and Nina Kidd, who soldiered through the first semi-opaque drafts. Thanks also to

Victoria Van Vleet, Karen Sampson, Kendra Kurosawa, and Bill Povletich, who helped define the early pages. The story benefited from the invaluable perspectives of Rebecca Maizel, Lynn Becker, Kris Vreeland, Eric Talkin, Larissa Theule, Nicole Maggi, and Julie Berry. But of all my writer friends, Tami Lewis Brown deserves a crown of laurels for reading the full manuscript three separate times.

Thank you to art experts Will Brown, Raissa Choi, Inez Litas (Liparini Restoration Studio), and Barbara Santucci, and to my legal eagle, Sue Wright. Sabine would not be as well-drawn if it were not for Joseph Wiederhold and Angela Sanchez, who illuminated the emotional life of a homeless teen by generously sharing their experiences.

Very special thanks to Kayla Cagan, Kim Purcell, Carrie Arcos, Mary McCoy, and Elle Cosimano for their support.

Since songs can illuminate character, I'm overjoyed that Mandolin Orange gave me permission to use a line from "One More Down," written by Andrew Marlin. Thank you, Andrew and Jimmy Rhine, for your kindness.

This book is dedicated to my brothers and sisters. You've always made me feel loved, but the depth of your support has both surprised and touched me.

And to Bob, thank you for giving me the time and space to write, and for always saying, "You should do that." I couldn't have done any of this without you.